LATITUDE REVENGE

Other novels by Karl C. Klontz

Stand at Bay

Mirrors

The Leopard's Lines

LATITUDE REVENGE

KARL C. KLONTZ

ISBN 978-1-7291598-1-1

Design by Sensical Design & Communication

Dedicated to those who view justice as a river
and righteousness as a never-failing stream.

The eye is the first circle;
the horizon which it forms is the second;
and throughout nature this primary figure
is repeated without end.
—Ralph Waldo Emerson

Justice without force is powerless;
force without justice is tyrannical.
—Blaise Pascal

Even the seasons form a great circle
in their changing, and always come
back again to where they were.
—Chief Black Elk

Prologue

ABOVE THE DESERT of Sudan, sweltering heat rises to form towering clouds. After traveling thousands of miles in prevailing easterlies over a blistering Sahara, the clouds descend toward the Atlantic where they draw on Earth's rotation to take on a spin of their own. By sucking moisture from the ocean, they become swirling tempests, some of which ignite into hurricanes which torment lands beyond.

I

SEPTEMBER . . .

Jones Bridge Road in Bethesda, Maryland is a street in search of an identity. At its western terminus, the four-lane road ferries scientists to the National Institutes of Health, commuters with IQs so high the road becomes a neuron in its own right. A block away, the pavement forms the southern rim of Walter Reed National Military Medical Center where courageous soldiers receive treatment for injuries sustained in the line of duty. A short distance later, a golf course belonging to a posh country club parallels the road as does a woodsy park across the street. Interspersing these zones are neighborhoods whose residents see the writing on the wall: little Bethesda is growing in a way that will leave it little no more.

And then, during afternoon rush on a fall day, little Bethesda went to war.

From the sky, bullets rained upon drivers as they turned onto Jones Bridge Road after leaving Gate Number 5 of Walter Reed Hospital. After a day of caring for the ill, military caretakers became the traumatized. If there was a time the road needed a bridge to match its name, it was then as bullets spewed enough blood to turn the road into a river.

ON A TREE-LINED street which intersected Jones Bridge Road, a storm raged in a townhouse condo where bed sheets pulled and creased.

"You're *so* hot," Beverly purred.

Sweet nothings revved Cal Hartley's engine. The Army Private First Class (PFC) pinned his fiancé to beige sheets with ripped muscles, primal strength, and drenched skin. For Hartley, love making didn't warm; it went straight to boil, and after a cataclysmic groan, he collapsed.

Beverly glided a hand over her partner. It brought her a racy pleasure to grope his pecs and abs. Resting a palm over his pounding heart, she smiled but only momentarily. "What's *that*?" she cried.

Hartley lifted his head and looked south. With a gentle grasp of an organ on the retreat, he examined his scrotum. "Are you having your period?" he asked.

"That's not blood! It's a rash!"

Hartley stood and slipped into jeans.

"Where are you going?" Beverly asked.

"To the emergency department! My balls feel like hot coals."

A short bicycle ride brought the soldier to Jones Bridge Road, but because the afternoon rush kept him from entering traffic, he balanced on the pedals to wait for an opening. When one came, he darted between cars to the left lane and turned into Walter Reed's Gate Number 3, the nearest entry to his fiancé's home. Eerily, both westbound lanes of Jones Bridge Road were abandoned while gridlock mired the eastbound ones.

A flash of his pass allowed Hartley to enter Walter Reed where he whisked by a Wendy's and the commissary. Because he worked in the base's security unit, he knew the most direct route to the emergency department, but as he cycled, the blare of sirens along Jones Bridge Road unnerved him. Amplifying his distress was a fear that Zika virus had caused his testicular pain. A month earlier, the virus was detected in the county, leading public health authorities to launch a massive spraying campaign. Only a day ago, Hartley saw sprayers near his fiancé's house. With the full spectrum of Zika's disease-causing abilities yet to be defined, he fretted his testes had become a new front for the virus to display its wrath. Worse, he feared he might've transmitted Zika sexually to his fiancé just as she was trying to get pregnant.

At the emergency department, Hartley registered but refrained from sitting because of his scrotal pain. After a short wait, he was summoned by a medic to an examining stall where he'd begun stripping when he heard a speaker blare, "Base lockdown, active shooter, Gate 5; base lockdown, active shooter, Gate 5." Bare-chested, he bolted to the lobby where he called his supervisor. "What's happening? I just heard about the lockdown!"

Hartley listened to the dismaying news: A sniper was picking off pedestrians, bicyclists, and vehicular occupants leaving the base through Gate 5 onto Jones Bridge Road. Although police had staked out the area, emergency vehicles couldn't access the injured because of active fire.

"Where are you?" his supervisor asked. "This is your day-off."

"I'm in the emergency department with fever and balls that feel like they're about to explode! I'm worried about Zika virus!"

"Forget Zika," his supervisor shot back. "I'm worried you caught something from that fricking drone!"

Two days earlier, a drone had been spotted swooping down repeatedly from puffy white clouds over Walter Reed with a fine mist spewing from it. On one descent, a sharp shooter from Hartley's unit felled it.

"What have the forensic folks learned from the drone?" Hartley asked.

"Very little, other than its motor was made in Saudi Arabia."

"What about the mist it released?"

"No results yet."

Hartley brooded over a new worry: the drone had released Zika. "What about the one in Annapolis?" On the same day, a second drone had appeared over the U.S. Naval Academy that also released a fine mist.

"They couldn't shoot it down before it disappeared over the Severn River."

"PFC!" the medic called.

Hartley waved him off through more blaring from the speaker. "Should I pick up a rifle and report to Jones Bridge Road?"

"No, we're covered," his supervisor replied. "Find out what the hell's wrong with you!"

Hartley's attention turned to a television in the lobby which aired a live view of Walter Reed's Gate 5 along Jones Bridge Road with stalled vehicles backed into the base because of fender-benders plugging the intersection. The scene recalled views of multi-car crashes on wintry freeways where vehicles pointed helter-skelter with fronts of some jimmied onto rears of others. To his horror, he saw an SUV flipped on a sidewalk while, beyond it, a fallen bicycle with its helmeted figure lay motionless on the asphalt. Sickeningly, the camera shifted to six bodies in military fatigues littering a bus stop while nonstop gunfire pelted vehicle occupants who slumped behind shattered windshields. At one point, a driver fled his car only to be shot steps from his door.

And then, strangely, everything fell silent.

Hartley watched the camera shift to a wooded area beside Gate 5 where armed guards emerged from the trees. He recognized some as his colleagues, one of whom pointed across Jones Bridge Road to the sky. The camera followed his outstretched arm to a towering pine tree located just inside the golf course as a voice hollered, "Up there, in the tree!"

The camera lifted Hartley's eyes through boughs, but before reaching the top, it stopped at a branch where a mechanical assembly came into view. Through the blur of pine needles, Hartley made out a machine gun with a camera secured to its barrel, both of which sat atop a swivel device affixed to the bough.

"Move down!" Hartley shouted at the television. "See if the shooter's fleeing!"

As if on cue, the camera dropped to the fairway, but no one was there. A return to the war zone showed flashing lights of emergency vehicles advancing toward the carnage, and when the camera zeroed in on the bus stop where Hartley had seen the six figures earlier, the faces of the fallen came into view. The sight ravaged Hartley as he recognized a friend among them, a young man with an unmistakable neck tattoo.

2

REAR ADMIRAL GARRETT Fitzgerald regarded the two stars of his flag officer's rank as a set of extra eyes. Whether he wore them as pins on U.S. Navy khakis or on shoulder boards with whites, he believed they helped him command a task force of three hundred health specialists across the globe. His unit, the *Strategic Team for the Reconnaissance of Emergent Medical Events*, or STREME, managed unforeseen health occurrences affecting U.S. military personnel worldwide. As an infectious disease specialist, he began his career at a county hospital in Atlanta before moving across town to the Centers for Disease Control and Prevention where he braved assignments in West Africa battling Ebola virus. His intrepid work there as a Commissioned Corps officer in the U.S. Public Health Service led the Armed Forces to recruit him as the director of their newly-formed STREME.

Fitzgerald took a catalog of professional contacts with him to his new job, one being a urologist named Wilbur Dunn he went to medical school with at Brown University. Despite their different backgrounds, the two grew close at Brown. While Fitzgerald was a product of private New England schools, Dunn matriculated from public schools in Nevada before attending a state college in Montana. At the beginning of medical school, they learned they shared a bond in having earned a scholarship from the National Health Service Corps that paid tuition and a monthly stipend to cover the costs of school. In exchange, each promised to work in primary care in medically-underserved areas for a required period following residency training.

It astounded Dunn that Fitzgerald had qualified for the scholarship given his family wealth, but then Dunn discovered Fitzgerald's independent roots. In addition to having paid his way through Dartmouth College by working part-time and taking out student loans, Fitzgerald volunteered regularly at soup kitchens on weekends.

Being recipients of federal scholarships wasn't all that bound them. Each decided during third year of medical school to pursue specialty training rather than become primary care doctors, and that meant persuading the National Health Service Corp to drop its primary care requirement. After protracted negotiations, each prevailed, Dunn gaining permission to become a urologist and Fitzgerald an infectious diseases expert, but each signed an agreement committing to work at least four years in an underserved area after completing residency training.

Even before the two learned about their common scholarship, Fitzgerald singled out Dunn as a kindred spirit. While dissecting cadavers during the first week of school, they worked on adjacent teams during anatomy class, and one day Fitzgerald was captivated by Dunn's response to a classmate who'd asked him why he decided to become a physician.

"I'd never seen eyes as sad as those of a mother who lost her baby at birth," Dunn told his dissection partners. "That's when I decided to become a doctor."

Asked to elaborate, Dunn did so, and as he spoke, Fitzgerald left his team to listen.

"My mother worked as a midwife at the Indian reservation where I grew up," Dunn began. "One night, a woman in her ninth month of pregnancy called our home in desperation because she'd gone into labor and couldn't deliver at the Indian Health Service hospital where she'd received prenatal care because their obstetrics unit had closed due to underfunding. She'd been advised to apply for financial aid to deliver elsewhere, but she found the paperwork too confusing to complete. When my mother told the woman to call 9-1-1, she refused because she feared it would cost too much to pay for an ambulance."

By now, Fitzgerald had inserted himself into Dunn's circle around their cadaver. He was transfixed not only by Dunn's six-four frame, jet black hair, and bronze complexion, but by his curved nose, high cheekbones, and chiseled jaws.

"I was fifteen," Dunn continued, "and I rode with my mother to the woman's house. It was located in a remote section of the reservation which normally would've taken forty minutes to reach, but because it was pouring that night, it took an hour."

Acknowledging Fitzgerald with a nod, Dunn continued. "When we reached the woman's house, we found a teen in labor.

My mother examined her, and after assessing the status of the cervix and timing and intensity of the contractions, she concluded the girl was transitioning to the second stage of labor, the hardest and most painful part for most women. Overwhelmed by contractions, the girl writhed and screamed for help as she clenched her grandmother's hand. While my mother took the girl's vitals, I arranged a portable ultrasound my mom had taught me to set up, and it showed the girl had a large blood clot between the placenta and womb which prevented the baby from getting oxygen." Dunn's shoulders sagged. "And then the baby's heart stopped beating."

Dunn glanced at the ceiling. "With labor continuing, I held the girl down while my mother inserted a large-bore intravenous line into one of her veins through which we ran saline as fast as possible. Probing the birth canal, my mom found it free of blood, and with the girl's blood pressure and pulse stable, she guided a dead baby into the world."

By now, classmates from other tables had stopped dissecting to face Dunn. Aware of the attention, the twenty-two-year old of Paiute ancestry spoke softly: "I'll never forget my mom's expression at that moment because she faced two hurdles: performing CPR on a newborn and trying to stop blood from gushing out of the birth canal. After handing me the baby, my mom injected oxytocin into the IV line and began massaging the girl's uterus to stem the flow, all the while telling me how to resuscitate the newborn. With shaking hands, I laid the infant on its back, suctioned its mouth, and then tilted its head to open the airway, but the baby didn't breathe. I then sealed my lips over its mouth and nose and delivered two rescue breaths which made the baby's chest rise, but still, no respirations occurred. In the meantime, the rate of blood flow from the baby's mother accelerated, worrying my mother greatly. 'We need to get her to the hospital!' she warned. 'What about the baby?' I asked. 'Give her thirty chest compressions using two fingers below the nipples, and then check again for breathing.' "

Dunn clutched his hands before his lips.

Having inched closer to Dunn as he'd spoken, Fitzgerald was nestled beside him now. "So, what happened, Wilbur?"

The tall young man with red flecks in his lava-black irises inhaled deeply. "I couldn't resuscitate the baby, and with the girl bleeding profusely, we wheeled her to our car and laid her across the back seat. As my mom drove to the hospital, I held the baby in my lap in the front seat and felt its cold skin through a gap in a towel. When we reached the emergency department, doctors rushed the teen to the intensive care unit for severe blood loss."

With dozens of eyes on him and the dissection room silent, Dunn walked to a windowsill. Looking down, he stood with shoulders slumped while, thirty feet to his rear, Fitzgerald remained at the dissecting table but knew exactly what Dunn was looking at: a tree-lined walkway below with bricks arranged diagonally. A day earlier, he, too, had gone there to settle his nerves from the stress of dissections.

3

ON THE WALL of Garrett Fitzgerald's Pentagon office, a clock hummed from the minute hand making its rounds. Shocked still by the news of a sniper attack at Walter Reed, he stared at the moving hand. Two days earlier, he'd crossed the Potomac to speak at Walter Reed, and after completing his presentation, he met Wilbur Dunn at NIH a block away. Dunn had driven there from his job at Johns Hopkins Hospital in Baltimore to meet Fitzgerald to discuss findings from an NIH-sponsored clinical trial both were involved in.

Following medical school, their friendship deepened as both moved to California for residency training, Dunn to the University of California, San Francisco, and Fitzgerald to Stanford. And while each left New England for different reasons—Fitzgerald to experience California living and Dunn to return closer to his Nevada roots—they remained in close touch. As Bay Area neighbors, they met regularly for six years, but upon completing their programs, they separated, Dunn moving to Baltimore to join Johns Hopkins while Fitzgerald moved to Atlanta.

Despite living in different states, they kept in close touch and because their wives had become good friends during their Bay Area years, the four met at least once every year. After nearly a decade of long-distance interactions, however, the couples celebrated when the Fitzgeralds moved to Virginia so Garrett could begin working at the Pentagon, a job that put him only forty miles away from Dunn's position at Hopkins.

Inconsolable after the Walter Reed shootings, Fitzgerald called his friend. "Wilbur, did you hear the news?"

"What news? I just got out of the operating room."

Fitzgerald relayed the details.

"Son of a *bitch*!" Dunn snapped. "I hope they killed the sniper!"

During their years of friendship, Fitzgerald had witnessed Dunn's temper repeatedly, but in recent months the outbursts had escalated to rage on occasion. A recent incident involved a urology resident at Hopkins who'd assisted Dunn in the operating room to remove a temporary stent from a patient whose ureter had ruptured in a car crash. Before the ureter could be sewn together, however, they used scalpels to pick away at scar tissue that had formed around the stent. Starting at opposite ends of the dissection field, they removed adhesions until their hands approached one another's.

"Okay, I'll finish the job," Dunn barked.

Rather than extract his hand from the surgical field, the resident rested the back of it against Dunn's.

"I said, move!" Dunn repeated.

The resident did nothing.

"Dammit! Are you deaf?" Dunn shouted.

The resident jerked his hand, severing the external iliac artery below the ureter. Instantly, blood flooded the pelvis.

"Look what you've done!" Dunn shouted. He clamped the severed ends of the artery before pushing the resident from the table. "Get a vascular surgeon!" Enraged by the resident's blank stare and slow response, he elbowed the man in the gut, spun him about, and kicked him toward the exit.

With the resident stumbling from the operating room, Dunn bellowed, "I'll never operate with you again!" Later that day, the Chair of the department ordered Dunn to his office where he reprimanded him for his behavior and ordered him to see a therapist and enroll in anger management training.

Mindful of Dunn's temper yet anguished by the Walter Reed shootings, Fitzgerald addressed him with care. "Wilbur, there was no sniper at Walter Reed. A rifle was mounted in a tree and fired remotely."

"*Remotely*?"

"Yes, it sat on a motorized swivel that was controlled online with the aid of a hotspot."

"Bastards!" Dunn shouted. "I'd go after them if I could!"

"But, that's not why I called, Wilbur. There's another matter we need to discuss."

"Fire away," Dunn said, realizing instantly his poor choice of words.

"I just received reports that service members at both Walter Reed and the U.S. Naval Academy in Annapolis are coming down with fever and swollen, painful testicles. Well over a dozen are sick so far. Not only that, but two days ago, drones were seen flying over each military base, and witnesses reported a fine mist came from the drones."

"What was in the mist?" Dunn asked. Receiving no response, he repeated the question only to hear a faint voice far from the receiver.

"Wilbur!" Fitzgerald shrieked. "Gotta go…check the news… there's been a second attack!"

ON 9/11 OF 2001, it was Wilbur Dunn who uttered the same words —*…check the news…there's been a second attack!* He spoke them to Garrett Fitzgerald after rushing to his friend in a lecture hall at medical school. With the lecture about to begin, he handed Fitzgerald an Ericsson T66 mobile phone displaying a text from a friend who'd announced a second plane had struck the World Trade Center.

Now seventeen years later, Dunn changed into street clothes at the Johns Hopkins Hospital as he reeled from the news Fitzgerald had conveyed about the shootings at Walter Reed. A quick scan of his phone after he'd hung up with Fitzgerald revealed breaking news of a second sniper attack at a major military base, this one at the U.S. Naval Academy in Annapolis, Maryland. To get a better grasp of the situation, he hurried to a conference room holding a television where others were already huddled. Across the screen a crawl read, *U.S. Naval Academy attacked following assault on Walter Reed.* Above the ticker, an aerial view showed sailboats in disarray across a body of water while a voice projected above the whir of helicopter rotors: "That's the Severn River emptying into the Chesapeake Bay. On the right is the U.S. Naval Academy with Annapolis Harbor around the bend. Those boats belong to the Naval Academy's intercollegiate sailing team, and almost every crew member has been killed or injured by sniper fire."

Dunn's eyes riveted on the distressed vessels. Never before had he seen a fleet in such disarray.

"We've got Lasers on their sides and one turtled," the reporter continued. Silence fell as the camera panned waters shimmering in late afternoon sunlight. "Oh, my God, and over there are Collegiate Style 420s and Flying Juniors with sails flapping aimlessly." The reporter's familiarity with sailboats impressed Dunn, a man attuned more to mountains and deserts than to the sea. He watched the camera shift again. "And that's an N26 that normally carries a crew of four, but it holds only three bloodied bodies as its fourth member floats in the water."

A zooming-out brought to view a sole racing dinghy under control with its headsail and mainsail taught from tropical winds. From equatorial Africa to the Gulf of Mexico, the Atlantic churned with storms that pursued a course over the Leeward and Windward Islands, into the Gulf of Mexico, and then over the U.S. Mid-Atlantic before they cut across the Atlantic toward Bermuda and the British Isles. Forecasters called for the trend to continue as high-pressure systems over the North Atlantic and Yucatan acted like pinball machine pop bumpers channeling storms over a well-worn path. Left in their wake were floodwaters and wind damage that had set records for economic destruction in a hurricane season with two months still to go.

On the monitor, Dunn watched the two crew members of the dinghy that was still in control hike off a side to keep the vessel speeding ahead. With rapt attention, he listened to the reporter.

"That's a Vanguard 15," the voice announced, "and it's heading straight toward Santee Basin along the eastern perimeter of the academy."

Suddenly, one crew member fell into the water.

"He's been shot!" the reporter wailed.

With the Vanguard's rudder and mainsail unattended, the vessel wavered. Peering at the scene, Dunn sensed the predicament the sole survivor faced: attempt a rescue of his partner or sprint ahead. It became a moot point, however, as a shower of bullets riddled the sailor's back to leave the vessel floating aimlessly in a watery cemetery.

"Who's killing them?" Dunn shouted. Bewildered faces about him offered no response, but in his pocket his mobile vibrated. A glance at it showed it was Garrett Fitzgerald calling again. "Are you seeing what I'm seeing?" Dunn cried. "Midshipmen being gunned down on the Severn River!"

"Yes, but you can help!" Fitzgerald said.

"*How*?"

"You remember I told you about those service men ill with fever and swollen testicles at Walter Reed and the Naval Academy? Well, I've just learned of more cases, and I need your help to find out what's making them ill!"

"Can you believe that?" Dunn blurted, his eyes locked to the television. "The sniper's firing circles into the sails of the boats!" He watched sunlight stream through the holes.

"I see it," Fitzgerald replied. "The same thing happened at Walter Reed. They shot a circle into the hood of an SUV."

"*Why*?"

"I don't know, but that's not why I called. I need your help with the illnesses!"

"What do you want me to do?"

"While trauma teams deal with the shooting victims at the bases, I'm forming another team to look into what's causing our service members to come down with fever and scrotal swelling. I need you on that team."

Dunn grasped his forehead to keep a flashback from tormenting him. Each time he felt stressed, the memories of an event that took place eight months earlier forced him to relive it — a massive truck rushing toward him with its grill taller than the SUV he drove; a jerking of the steering wheel; a desperate attempt to avoid striking the truck; a yellow banner in black lettering reading *Long Load* on the truck's bumper crashing through the windshield; and then the SUV slicing in half.

"Wilbur, are you there?" Fitzgerald beckoned.

"I… I…"

"What's wrong, Wilbur?"

"Dr. Dunn," another voice called through Dunn's phone. Calm and collected, it continued: "It's not just your friend, Garrett Fitzgerald, who needs your help. Your nation needs you at this pivotal moment."

Steeling himself, Dunn tasted gastric acid at the back of his throat. "Who's speaking?" he asked even though he was certain he knew who it was. The southern drawl, undulating cadence, and pronunciation of "nation" as "nay-ya-shun" came from only one man he knew.

"Wilbur," Garrett Fitzgerald interjected, "I should've told you I'm in a conference room at the Pentagon with a group of colleagues, one being the Vice President of the United States, Atticus Quincy Thornbridge. That's who just addressed you. With me as well are the Secretary of Defense and several Senators from the Armed Services Committee. They were down the hall when the shootings began, and we assembled for an impromptu meeting."

The Vice President spoke again, languid as usual: "Dr. Dunn, we've good reason to believe the drones that flew over the bases released a biological warfare agent, so let me be more direct than Dr. Fitzgerald. You *will* help us figure out what the agent is that's sickening our service members or you'll go to jail! Those are your only two options. The court was lenient with you given the Federal offense you committed in Idaho eight months ago, but leniency has its limits. If you refuse to help your nation, it'll be jail."

Mouth bitter from bile, Dunn approached a receptacle and spat into it.

"So, what's your decision?" the Vice President demanded. "The clock's ticking."

4

THE ROUTE WILBUR Dunn took from Johns Hopkins Hospital to his therapist's office on Baltimore's Federal Hill traversed different worlds. After passing tenements, it skirted Little Italy, the Inner Harbor, and the financial district before reaching Otterbein, a condo haven close to Oriole Park at Camden Yards. As he rode the remaining way, he studied the cracks, lines, and stains on the streets with a goal of registering exactly 2.23 miles on the high-precision tachometer his 1966 BSA Hornet motorcycle sported. Since his first trip from the hospital to the therapist's office the week before had registered that distance, he set out to replicate it.

It was an excursion that brought Dunn angst, one he undertook at the behest of his boss who demanded he see a therapist after assaulting the resident in the operating room. Rather than consult a shrink at Hopkins, Dunn chose one elsewhere to preserve his privacy, and to leave as faint a trail as possible, he vowed to pay cash for each session.

Along the summit of Federal Hill, he parked in a driveway before an elegant home across from a park overlooking the Inner Harbor with its piers, restaurants, and aquarium. A push of a button triggered a buzzer that opened a gate leading to a walkway lined by flowers that ended at a door with a brass plaque reading, *Harold S. Toddmeyer, M.D.* The front door opened as Dunn reached for its handle.

"Wilbur, it's great to see you again," a bespectacled man in a brown tweed suit said.

The familiarity of a second visit to Toddmeyer's office allayed only some of Dunn's discomfort. As a surgeon, he'd referred patients to psychiatrists but had never consulted one himself. He followed Toddmeyer to a well-lit room overlooking the harbor, and while some of the blinds were lowered to block the setting sun, others remained up to allow a view of ships in the distance.

Mandatory niceties followed before the psychiatrist bore in. "Last week, we discussed anger in your life and, in particular, factors which led you to accost the resident in the operating room.

Today, I'd like to expand that discussion, but first I want you to tell me how long you've been angry."

"Since childhood," Dunn replied. "Anger seeped into my bones from bare shelves, tattered clothes, and limited choices, and it remained since then. For the most part, I've managed it reasonably well until two weeks ago when I lost control in the operating room." Dunn bowed his head. "I've apologized to the resident."

"What sorts of things make you angry?"

Dunn assessed the man before him, wondering how much to divulge. "Revelations, mostly."

"What kind of revelations?"

The skin around Dunn's eyes tightened. "I'll give you an example: As a boy, I became enraged to learn my father committed suicide because of me."

Not a flinch from the therapist. "How old were you when you learned that?"

"Seven."

"Who told you?"

"My mother."

"That must've been difficult for her and for you. Why did she tell you?"

"Because I'd asked her repeatedly who my father was."

"And like that, she said he'd committed suicide?"

"She didn't beat around the bush; poverty didn't afford that luxury."

"How did your father kill himself?"

"He drove off a cliff."

"And how old were you when he took his life?"

"Less than a day old. After taking one look at me, he left our house in his pickup, and when he reached the Sierras, he traveled along an abandoned gravel road where he steered the pickup over a slope. The truck hurtled five hundred feet into a gorge where it was consumed by a river raging with melted snow. It wasn't until late summer when a hiker discovered a rusting chassis along the shore. The license plate and vehicle identification number identified the pickup as my father's."

"Did they find his body?"

"No, they think it got stuck under a ledge in the river."

"How do you know his death was intentional?"

"My father was an excellent driver even though he was eighteen at the time. He drove a pickup as if it was an extension of his body."

"He was just eighteen?"

"Yup, and my mother was sixteen."

"Perhaps he rode into the mountains to process his thoughts."

Dunn shook his head. "He'd already processed them; he left a suicide note on my mom's dresser."

Toddmeyer rubbed his hands. "Who helped your mom rear you?"

"My aunt. Before I was born, the two moved out of their father's house because he was an alcoholic who abused them. They rented the cottage I grew up in."

"How'd they afford it?"

"My aunt worked at a library outside the reservation." Dunn's lips cracked but not wide enough to smile. "Every evening, she brought books home that she and my mother read to me. As a result, I learned to read early, but I paid a price for it: Classmates called me a nerd, bullied me, and taunted me for being different. I was an alien, even among my own." Dunn winced. "Have you seen photos of terraced rice paddies in foreign countries where green strips of fertile land wrap around hills?"

"Yes," Toddmeyer replied, "but why do you ask?"

"Because, those terraces mirror my life. With every rejection, mock, and taunt I received as a kid, I scaled what I felt was another terrace. I climbed them because my mother inspired me to do so. She told me I didn't have to conform to the world as it appeared; that unemployment, substance abuse, violence, and poverty weren't de facto properties of human life; and that no one could keep an Original American from soaring in the way of eagles."

"Your mother was an inspired woman."

"When I was six, I sat in the front row at her high school graduation. Later, as I did homework each night, she sat beside me doing hers as she climbed her own terraces that took her from being a nursing assistant to a registered nurse and finally to a nurse practitioner. It was she who inspired me to become a physician."

Dunn blushed. "And I held her as a model for choosing a wife."

Toddmeyer glanced at Dunn's wedding band. "Last week, I asked about your wife, but you chose not to talk about her. Are you ready to talk now?"

The room fell silent. Slowly, Dunn stood, walked to the window, and wept.

5

PRIVATE FIRST CLASS Calvin Hartley was not pleased. In the past twenty-four hours, his private parts had been examined by a medic, an emergency medicine doctor, a surgeon, and an infectious disease expert, and because none knew what afflicted the soldier's scrotum, they admitted him to the hospital.

One of the first tests done was to check a blood specimen for newly formed—or so-called IgM—antibodies against mumps virus; the presence of such antibodies would mean Hartley had recently contracted mumps. A contagious disease readily spread by respiratory droplets released through coughing, sneezing, saliva, and by contaminated towels, sheets, and similar items, mumps was once a common childhood disease in the U.S. before a vaccine introduced in 1967 all but eliminated it. But a rise of anti-vaccine activists touting the specter of autism and other ailments linked to routine immunizations caused vaccination rates to swoon in pockets of the country. As a result, the number of reported mumps cases began spiking from outbreaks in crowded places like universities where mumps spreads readily. Although the military scrupulously ensures personnel remain fully immunized, protective antibody levels in some vaccinated persons can fall over time, placing them at risk for mumps. In addition to causing fever, chills, body aches, and swollen salivary glands, mumps produces painful swelling of one or both testicles in about a fifth of post-pubertal males. Referred to as "orchitis," this complication resolves but not without permanently decreasing sperm production in some men.

Most worrisome to Hartley's doctors were results of an ultrasound of the soldier's scrotum which mirrored those from other men stricken by the same ailment at Walter Reed and the Naval Academy. When the results found their way to Garrett Fitzgerald at the Pentagon, he called Wilbur Dunn just as his friend had reached home after seeing the therapist. "I'm sorry I didn't warn you the Vice President would be on the call earlier today," Fitzgerald lamented.

"What can I say? Atticus Quincy Thornbridge knows I'm behind the eight ball."

"There's no eight ball here, Wilbur, but if you insist there is, you can remove it by helping us."

"I don't know, Garrett, my schedule's tight and—"

"I've taken care of your schedule. I spoke to your boss at Hopkins, and he cleared the way for you to help me."

"I won't do it—not if Vice President Thornbridge is involved! He's still trying to punish me because of that accident I had with the logging truck in Idaho." Dunn removed from his wallet a business card for the attorney who'd defended him in court following the accident. It was in the attorney's office before the trial he learned the Vice President was going to testify against him for the plaintiff. He also learned Thornbridge was pushing for Dunn to be monitored by a court-ordered surveillance program for years should the jury convict him. Dunn's attorney was outraged by what he thought was inappropriate meddling by a political figure.

"Look, I'll keep a leash on Thornbridge," Fitzgerald promised. "In the meantime, just know he respects your expertise."

"The guy hates me, Garrett! He told my attorney after the trial he abhorred illegal immigrants. That was a clear reference to Consuela." Twelve years earlier during residency training in San Francisco, Dunn married a woman who confided that she was living in the U.S. as an undocumented immigrant.

"I know," Fitzgerald parried, "and I detest Thornbridge's politics on immigration, but all I'm asking is that you go to Annapolis and Bethesda tomorrow to examine our men with swollen testicles. Then call me after you've seen them. I'm sending you a list of their names and locations now."

Moments later, Dunn received the list. The next morning, he drove to Annapolis where he examined eight ill men at the Naval Academy's sick bay before driving to a nearby hospital where four others had been admitted with more severe manifestations. At both sites, the ill were isolated to prevent spread of a potentially transmissible agent. He went to Walter Reed next where he split his time in like fashion between outpatients and those hospitalized, bringing to a total twenty-two patients examined that day. By sunset, only one remained, a soldier named Calvin Hartley.

Fatigued, Dunn donned a gown, gloves, mask, and shoe covers before opening a door labeled, *Isolation Precautions In Effect.* Inside, he found a young man watching a televised update of the shootings from the previous day. "Mr. Hartley?"

The soldier sat upright. "Yes, sir."

"I'm Dr. Wilbur Dunn from Johns Hopkins. Your doctors asked me to see you."

Hartley muted the television. "Thank you for coming, sir. I hope you can tell me what's wrong with me."

Dunn rounded the bed to Hartley's side. "I'll do my best, but first I need to ask some questions and examine you."

After taking histories all day, Dunn listened to yet another account of an illness that began the preceding day with fever and a feeling of heaviness in the groin that quickly worsened to painful swelling and reddening of the scrotum.

"My doctors said I might have mumps even though my salivary glands aren't swollen," Hartley volunteered. "Do you agree?"

Dunn slid his fingers across and under Hartley's jaws before doing the same with his neck. "Everything's normal; no enlargements."

"So, what do you think about mumps?"

"You don't have it."

"Why do you say that?"

"Because, if mumps had sickened you and the others I saw today, *some* of you'd have shown the classic swollen salivary glands of mumps, but no one did. In addition, I'd expect to have heard about a bunch of others on the bases with what I call "garden variety" mumps—folks with fever and swollen glands but without testicular swelling." Dunn broadened his shoulders. "And there've been no reports of women with mumps-like illness; mumps doesn't discriminate between genders."

"What about my blood test for mumps? They haven't told me the results yet."

"Funny you should ask. The lab called me while I was coming here to report that blood samples taken so far from *all* of you with this illness are negative for mumps IgM antibody, an antibody we'd expect to see present in your blood if you truly had mumps." Dunn shook his head. "Like I said, this isn't mumps."

Turning to the window, Hartley looked into the darkness. "So, what is it?"

Dunn reached for the curtain and pulled it around Hartley's bed. Motioning to the soldier's groin, he said, "Let's take a look."

Dunn found a scene familiar to one he'd seen throughout the day, a swollen red scrotum, only in this instance the sac was angrier than any others he'd seen. Dilated blood vessels bulged from the scrotum which looked like it might explode at any time while, above it, Hartley's member was completely normal.

Gently, Dunn slid three fingers under the scrotum and, lifting it, placed a penlight behind its skin folds. Frowning, he asked, "Do you have pain when you urinate?"

"More discomfort than pain."

"When's the last time you had sex?"

The soldier stirred. "Yesterday morning."

"Did you notice anything unusual?"

"Yeah, heaviness in my balls with burning when I came."

Dunn replaced the gown, opened the curtain, and took a seat with relief that he'd examined his last patient for the day. "Let's discuss things that cause testicles to swell. The first is called 'testicular torsion.' It results from a testicle twisting and, in doing so, entrapping the spermatic cord from which it hangs." Dunn cupped a hand. "Think about a pear hanging from a tree. Twisting it causes torque on the stem, and if you twist enough, the stem breaks. A similar torque on the spermatic cord cuts off blood flow to the testicle which causes testicular swelling and pain." He paused. "But it's exceedingly rare for both testicles to twist at the same time to produce swollen testicles as you're showing."

"Wouldn't it be highly unlikely, too, sir for testicular torsion to occur in a bunch of other men at the same time?"

"Exactly, and that holds true for the other causes of testicular swelling we'll discuss, so much so we can exclude them as causes of your illness." One by one, Dunn reviewed the conditions—cancer, trauma, inflammatory diseases, hernias, and arcane entities such as fluid-filled sacs within the testes. "Something else is at play here," he concluded.

"Any guesses what it is?"

"Something I've never seen before."

Hartley tensed. "Damn *drones*! They caused this, didn't they?"

"Too early to say; let's see what the forensics experts find." Dunn leaned forward. "In the meantime, there's a special test I'd like to do on you, Mr. Hartley, and I'm hoping you'll consent to have it done."

"What's the test?"

"A testicular biopsy."

"I don't like the sound of that."

"I understand, but I'd numb the area first before inserting a needle to collect tissue. It's a test that would provide a definitive view of what's going on inside your testicles."

The soldier looked at the television which showed photos of the shooting victims from earlier times in their lives. Pressing the off button, he said, "Get me better, Doc! I wanna find the bastards who did this, and if that means having a needle stuck into my balls, go for it!"

THE HONEY-YELLOW WOOD of the condo door Dunn opened was unlike any in his building. It came from a cottonwood tree that grew in a meadow along the eastern slopes of the Sierras near his boyhood home on the Walker River Indian Reservation in western Nevada. On a trip to the reservation three years earlier, Dunn noticed the tree had toppled in a recent storm, and because he'd spent hours as a boy playing under its boughs, he hired a craftsman from the reservation to remove a section of its vast trunk and carve a door from it. After shipping it to Baltimore, he had it installed at his condo. Carved into both surfaces were depictions of Walker River and its surrounding desert and mountains, scenes which brought Dunn solace each time he entered or left.

After opening the door, he traversed a hallway holding baskets and bowls woven by Paiute women. Among them was a fan-shaped winnowing basket, a beaded bowl with animal figures, a conical burden basket, and a seed basket in the shape of a bottle. For Dunn, the collection was more than a display; it was a bond to the past, an ancestral link that infused him with energy each time he passed the vessels.

Dropping his satchel in the living room, he started for the liquor cabinet but refrained from pouring himself a drink because of a voice within that admonished him for having consumed too much in recent weeks. During high school, he promised his mother repeatedly he'd imbibe responsibly to avoid the ravages of alcohol that marred many on the reservation, and now, even though his mother's spirit was all that remained, he intended to honor his promise.

As an alternative to liquor, he went to the kitchen where he extracted a bag from the refrigerator which contained sections of a knobby brown root. After removing a piece, he set it into a pot of water which he brought to a boil before reducing it to a simmer. Stirring the root, he lowered his head to inhale an aroma of parsley, carrot, and parsnip which unfailingly relaxed him.

It was his mother who introduced him to the versatility of fernleaf biscuitroot, an herb which grew along the dry, rocky slopes near the reservation. While growing up, Dunn accompanied her into the mountains to collect the plant. As a member of the carrot family, it rose from a woody taproot and sent out green shoots after snow melt which could be cooked and eaten as greens. By summer's end, the plants stood as tall as five feet with feathery leaves and yellow flower heads arranged in umbrella form. No part went wasted as the seeds and leaves flavored cooked dishes while the roots went into tinctures, oils, and poultices.

A tonic prepared by boiling the roots, however, was what Dunn resorted to most often. When consumed hot, it lessened the severity and duration of headaches that began to torment him during adolescence. Preceding each headache were bizarre symptoms that presaged a throbbing pain in his orbits and forehead, and in medical school he learned the names for these migraine forerunners—"paresthesias" for numbness and tingling; "scotomas" for blind spots; "scintilla" for flashing lights; and "aphasia" for difficulty in finding words or speaking.

To his surprise, the tonic conferred an additional benefit: it eased his mind. At first, he thought the calming effect arose from an abating migraine, but when he drank the herbal extract in the absence of a headache, he noticed a profound stilling of the sort practitioners of meditation or yoga described. During his residency years, he consumed a cup of tonic daily to cope with the rigors of training, and later, after becoming an attending physician at Hopkins, he relied on it to weather the demands of surgery.

With midnight passed, he carried a mug of steaming tonic to the study and sat in a recliner. Sipping from the mug with his legs raised on a foot rest, he settled his eyes on a canvas across the room. Painted by a Paiute artist, it depicted a young man in rawhides feeding a fire along the wind-protected side of a boulder while tethered nearby a horse shielded itself from a withering snowstorm that whitened the prairie save for the tips of windswept grass. For years, the scene had instilled in Dunn a deep sense of peace and consolation because he identified with a Native American who seemed to find comfort in drawing apart from the world to seek communion with nature. But then, recently, a facet of the work began to distress him: the blowing snow and pitch-black skies of the horizon portending an intensifying storm.

It was the snow that anguished him especially because it reminded him of a night eight months earlier when, driving a rental SUV, he ascended a mountainous gravel road that was reserved for timber trucks and off limits to the public in Idaho's Sawtooth National Forest. He'd taken the road as a shortcut to get back to the airport in Boise to catch a flight back home with his wife, Consuela. With side-swiping snow reducing visibility to almost nil, he listened to a weather report on the radio explain a term unfamiliar to him: "bombogenesis." It referred to a low-pressure area exploding into a blistering storm. From the Northwest, the storm had unexpectedly changed course to aim for the Rockies, and as it moved it intensified from moisture, heat, and wind. Because a mass of Arctic cold preceding it had left temperatures in the mountains near zero, the blizzard that followed pummeled the slopes of the remote region Dunn and Consuela traveled.

Through snow-caked headlights, Dunn never saw the fallen tree across the road. When he struck it, the steering wheel jerked from his hands and sent the SUV skidding across the road just as a massive truck rounded a bend. In the second before impact, Dunn saw snow streak across the truck's headlights before the beams lit up his wife in ghostly silver. And then it came, a crushing blow followed by a stomach-twisting spin during which Dunn felt the wind and snow pelt his face. Dazed but conscious, he fumbled about before finding the seatbelt release.

Because his door had jammed, he rolled sideways to escape through the passenger side which he presumed Consuela had done because she was nowhere to be found. When he suddenly fell to the road, he looked up to discover the SUV had been sliced in half from front to back. To his horror, above him only feet away, a bulldozer was chained to the top of a truck trailer which had jackknifed to leave the cab squeezed between a pair of trees over an embankment.

He shrieked for Consuela, but his cries went unanswered. After stumbling around the rear of the trailer, he made his way forward along the heavy equipment transporter, stepping over bumper sections, seat fragments, and engine parts as he advanced. Devastated by Consuela's absence, he continued to call for her only to confront waist-high drifts at the front of the truck where he encountered a scene more gruesome than any he'd seen as a surgeon—metal grates of a gargantuan grill holding an entwisted leg with a shoeless foot dangling from it. Beneath the grill, dripping blood formed red holes in the snow which the wind quickly covered.

Overcome, Dunn dropped to his knees to look under the truck for what remained of Consuela but found only snow. He pounded the grill as if beating it might reverse what had happened, only then noticing the truck's engine still idled as its headlights glowed. Trudging to the driver's side of the cab, he banged on the door, but because it remained closed, he grasped a bar and pulled himself up a three-step ladder to peer through the window. Inside, he saw a six-inch diameter branch had pierced the windshield to impale the driver's head. In skewer-style, it penetrated the mouth to pin the head back such that the eyes bulged to the point of exploding.

A press on the handle allowed Dunn to open the door. After ascending a final step, he tried to enter the cab but was prevented from doing so because of the branch and lifeless body before him. When he released the seatbelt, he jiggled the corpse but not enough to dislodge it, and for a moment, he considered moving to the opposite door but rejected the plan when he saw a tree blocking it from outside.

Pinning himself between door and driver's seat to shield himself from the wind, he reached for his phone. With fingers numbed by the cold, he dialed 9-1-1, but the call failed from lack of service. Using the phone's flashlight, he directed the beam at the dashboard where he saw a spiral cord dangling from a CB radio. By gripping the steering wheel, he pulled himself in enough to lie on the driver's lap limbo-style beneath the branch which he used to wiggle in further. Stretching his arm, he grasped the mike and, cupping it in his palm, selected a channel labeled *Emergencies*.

A distress call yielded a clear response which allowed Dunn to convey to a dispatcher the dire situation he was in. In short order, the trucking company identified the location using a GPS tracker, but with the blizzard battering the area, he was warned a day might pass before rescuers could reach the site. "Stay in the cab, keep the engine running for heat, and make sure the exhaust pipes remain clear to prevent carbon monoxide poisoning," he was told.

With the passing of hours, a rescue team arrived but for Dunn yet another storm was brewing, one that would unleash its fury in a federal courthouse.

6

FROM HIS BED, Dunn listened to the whistle outside. Over time, he'd grown accustomed to its three notes depending on wind speed: a *do* with gentle breezes, *re* from leaf-rustling gusts, or *mi* from steady, forceful winds. On days with varying wind speeds, he was treated to *do-re-mi*, but on that morning *re* carried the song from easterlies spawned by a hurricane named Stanley whirling off the coast of South Carolina. Although forecasters called for the storm to graze the Outer Banks before veering out to sea, its rain bands were expected to lash Baltimore late that afternoon.

Weather issues were the last thing Dunn wanted to deal with. Although the herbal tonic he'd consumed the preceding night had relaxed him after an intense day of examining military personnel, his time before the painting in the study led to nightmares in which he envisioned crashing into moving objects of one type or another. In each sequence, gory scenes of body parts spewing about caused him to awaken startled.

Abandoning bed at sunrise, he heard his phone chime. A glance at it tempted him to dismiss the call, but he knew that wasn't an option. "Yes, Alex," he groaned.

"Did I miss your call yesterday?" Alex Granfeld asked.

In no mood to confront a sardonic probation officer, Dunn answered, "I didn't call because I was busy seeing patients."

"Oh," Granfeld replied, "I'll let the judge know that."

Dunn knew better than to spar with Granfeld; doing so only complicated matters. In the past eight months, he'd already been arraigned, hired an attorney, and traveled to Boise, Idaho for court appearances which culminated in a jury conviction for trespassing in a national forest and for involuntary manslaughter. His productivity as a surgeon at Hopkins had taken a hit, as had his research in the lab. Adding to his anguish was a memorial service he'd arranged for Consuela which left him beyond drained.

"You know the terms of your probation," Granfeld warned. "They include calling me once a week."

It was the first time Dunn had skipped the required call, and he found the preceding ones worthless because all they entailed was a review of his community service hours. He confronted Granfeld: "I'm sure you've seen the headlines about the base shootings, and I've been tasked by the Defense Department to investigate a bizarre illness which has accompanied them. Yesterday, I examined twenty-three ill men."

"You could've texted me to let me know that."

"You're right, I should have, and it won't happen again." Dunn was aware of the risks of dissing a probation officer. Despite his conviction, he dodged prison time because the judge looked favorably upon Dunn's reason for traveling to Idaho in the first place: to offer medical services pro bono to police battling protesters at a site proposed for an oil pipeline. Although the protests were organized by Native Americans with whom Dunn commiserated, he rejected violence, even when perpetrated by those who rightfully believed the land was sacred.

"That's good," Granfeld said, "because, as you know, your case is high-profile. The VP calls me often to make sure you're abiding by your probation terms."

Dunn huffed. He thought it was a strike of cruel fate that in a nation of more than three hundred million people the driver of the heavy transport truck he'd struck during the blizzard in Idaho's Sawtooth National Forest happened to be the godson of the Vice President of the United States.

Granfeld, whispering now, said: "Be careful, Wilbur. I don't need to remind you that the VP can make your life hell."

DURING MEDICAL SCHOOL and residency, no topic fascinated Dunn more than the anatomy and physiology of the male reproductive tract. So simple yet complex; elegant, too, even if its components hung like a hammock.

He found it miraculous that the testes should reside in a cul-de-sac with all their connections and wrappings intact after making a long journey during fetal development from the abdomen through canals on both sides of the pelvis. And then, beginning at puberty, to produce some 1,500 sperm per second—over a hundred million cells each day—was stupefying.

But something terribly wrong had happened to swell and redden the scrota of twenty-three warriors at two military bases, and Dunn was determined to find the cause. Haunting him especially were results of ultrasound exams on the patients. Each showed a shredding of the thick fibrous capsule called the tunica albuginea which surrounded the testes and divided the sperm producing areas into lobules. When describing the fibrous capsule to patients, Dunn suggested they think of a pomegranate's membranous pith which separates the juicy, sweet fruit into compartments. Never before had he seen the tunica albuginea chewed up as in these men. Worse, the sperm-producing areas were left in tatters, a finding that compelled him to request PFC Hartley to undergo a testicular biopsy.

After performing the procedure, Dunn delivered half of the sample to the lab at Walter Reed and the other half to Johns Hopkins. The next morning after speaking to his probation officer, he called a colleague at Hopkins named Krishna Bhatia to ensure the sample was being analyzed. Eight years earlier, Dunn convinced Bhatia to leave a research position in Stockholm, Sweden to join Dunn's lab at Hopkins. It was a coup to recruit Bhatia because he was a world-renown researcher with an MD, a PhD, and a star-studded career researching the male reproductive tract. Particularly appealing to Dunn were his dual credentials as pathologist and molecular biologist, a duo that allowed him to straddle clinical medicine and lab work.

"Krish, a favor to ask," he said after placing the call.

"Good *morning*, Wilbur," Bhatia replied, his Indian accent tamed but present.

"Good morning," Dunn voiced, remorseful for neglecting to greet a man who took greetings to heart.

"What can I do for you?" Bhatia asked.

"I want to make sure the specimen I dropped off last night is in your hands."

"It is. Are we running the standard tests on it?"

"No, we need to go the extra mile on this one." Dunn laid out his requests.

"What makes this one special?" Bhatia asked.

"It came from one of the soldiers at Walter Reed involved in the outbreak of testicular swelling."

Bhatia lowered his voice. "Yeah, I heard an update on that on the news this morning! Why are you seeing the men?"

"The Defense Department asked me to."

Whispering now, Bhatia said, "There's speculation a biological warfare agent may be involved here."

"That's one of the reasons I called. I'm relying on you to determine if that's true."

AFTER HIS CRASH in Idaho's Sawtooth National Forest, Dunn avoided driving cars. Instead, he bought the 1966 BSA Hornet motorcycle which he steered now through the rain to Johns Hopkins Hospital. His choice of motorcycle was influenced by age—the older the model, the better, but ultimately, he settled on a BSA because it was vintage and because its English manufacturer developed the cycle for racing in deserts, open spaces which brought solace for Dunn.

Before leaving his condo, he was relieved to hear another update on Hurricane Stanley which called for the storm to veer more abruptly to sea than anticipated, yet even with the change, bands from Stanley were still expected to strike Baltimore. For that reason, Dunn wore an orange rain suit similar in color to the Mandarin Red of his motorcycle. After reaching Hopkins, he entered the hospital, changed into surgical garb, and went to the operating suites where he discovered his surgeries had been cancelled.

"What's going on?" he called out.

A stout woman with the presence of a drill sergeant approached him. As chief scheduler for operating rooms, she bore her eyes into Dunn's. "Your department Chair told me to cancel your surgeries because you've taken on a new project."

"That's news to me!" Dunn replied, storming to a stairwell where he sprinted six flights up to his boss's office. "Why'd you cancel my operations?" he demanded.

A gray-haired man raised his eyes above a pair of half-rim glasses. "Ah, Wilbur, I'm glad you stopped by," Francis Bateman said. "I'm disappointed you hung up on me this morning before we finished our discussion." An hour earlier, Bateman had called Dunn to confirm he'd given Garrett Fitzgerald permission to recruit Dunn to assist with the Pentagon investigation of illnesses at the military bases.

"I hung up because I felt we should discuss the matter in person," Dunn replied.

"Okay, you're here, so let's discuss." Bateman stood, pointed to a seat, and shut the door. "I'm concerned about you and your patients, Wilbur," he said before sitting. "I've received some complaints from the operating room regarding patient safety."

"What sort of complaints?"

Bateman leaned forward. "Your operating times have grown in the past few months, and that concerns the anesthesiologists."

"I've had some tough cases which couldn't be rushed."

"No one's asking you to rush. What worries me is you're second-guessing yourself, and that costs time. You know darn well that delays under anesthesia lead to complications."

" 'Second-guessing'? Is that what you call careful surgery?"

"I checked the records myself, Wilbur. You're taking about forty percent more time now to complete surgeries of similar difficulty as before. That's one thing..."

"Is there something else?"

"Yes, your behavior in the operating room."

"Look, I pushed a resident, okay? I'm seeing a shrink and attending an anger management course as you told me to."

Bateman shook his head. "It's more than the pushing incident." He glanced out a window at Baltimore's skyline. "Our neurologists confirmed a diagnosis of absence seizure in the resident you assaulted. He's had several more seizures since you pushed him." Bateman's eyes saddened. "He's dropping out of our program to find a non-surgical residency."

Familiar with the disorder, Dunn lowered his head in shame. While the condition usually presented in children, it could also manifest in adults, and based on what the scrub nurse and anesthesiologist had told him after the event, the resident exhibited a classic blanking-out episode before Dunn pushed him.

"And another thing," Bateman continued. "Our scrub nurses have told me you're exhibiting compulsive behaviors while operating, and that's worrisome. Those behaviors could explain the longer operating times."

"Compulsive behaviors?"

"Yes, like demanding particular manufacturing brands of retractors, scalpels, or other instruments and insisting on specific colors of sutures. In some instances, they've had to retrieve additional equipment intraoperatively when they didn't think it was necessary. That's unacceptable."

Staring at the floor, Dunn remained silent. Since losing Consuela, he'd adopted routines which added considerable time to his daily life. Among them were pre-bed checks to verify each dial on the stove was turned off, the refrigerator door fully closed, and the front door locked. The final act was the most arduous because it entailed placing his thumb and forefinger on the key to the deadbolt, turning it to the locked position, and then making sure it was in place by stooping to confirm the bolt crossed the void. For good measure, he maintained steady pressure on the key to convince himself the bolt remained affixed, and when he was sure it had, he'd start for the bedroom only to reverse course to repeat the routine.

"Look, Wilbur, I know it's been difficult," Bateman said. "Losing Consuela, battling in court, being on probation, and seeing a psychiatrist. Believe me, no one wants healing from you more than I. There aren't words to describe how much I respect you ... value you ... *praise* you for what you've done for our program. It's nothing short of a miracle how you've advanced our research program in male infertility. Colleagues tell me regularly they're in awe of your accomplishments, but right now you're an impaired physician, and I want you to take a break from your duties to heal. Helping the Pentagon with its investigation sounds like just the right medicine."

Dunn rose but remained in place.

Bateman stood as well. "Wilbur, you know darn well the struggle we face as urologists. We've got one of the highest burnout rates among physicians. The latest survey reported that something like sixty percent of urologists nationally met the criteria for professional burnout. Those are horrible numbers which reflect the tremendous stress we're under. So, take some time off; work with the Pentagon. We'll cover your clinic and operating schedules while you do, and in the meantime, I want to see you weekly to keep in touch. We'll figure out the right time for you to resume your duties."

"I've run out of leave," Dunn replied. "I used it all to deal with legal issues and to plan for Consuela's memorial service."

"You've got sick leave. I've authorized it."

"But my research…"

"The folks in your lab are extremely capable."

"But I'll need their assistance for certain tasks with the Pentagon investigation."

"We'll do our part for the nation," Bateman assured him.

Dunn turned. "One more thing…

"What is it?"

"I'm not burned out."

Bateman walked around Dunn to face him. "Fine, let's just say you're under tremendous stress."

The two stared at each other before Bateman broke the silence. "What is it, Wilbur? There's something you want to say."

Dunn's lips quivered. "I never told you that my mother died four months ago just after my trial began in Idaho. I've been in denial about it ever since. Her death was totally unexpected as she was in her fifties and was as vibrant as a teen, yet she died of a broken heart."

EARLY IN HIS career, Dunn cast aspersions on the medical construct of a "broken heart," deeming it more relevant to sappy poems and weepy love songs than to human physiology—until his mother died of heart failure. Then it became personal.

Well before his mother passed, he heard colleagues speak of patients who "died of a broken heart" and saw the term in publications, although physicians often referred to the condition by its scientific designation, "stress cardiomyopathy." In Japan where the ailment was first described in 1990, doctors called it "takotsubo" heart failure after the earthenware urn used to catch octopuses because of the heart's tendency in the condition to balloon at its apex before death. Curiously, the problem wasn't a plugging of arteries with cholesterol but, rather, a dysfunctional firing of heart muscles, and most who experienced the condition were postmenopausal women, a demographic which applied to his mother when she died.

What pained Dunn most was he felt responsible for her death. Intense physical or emotional stress triggered broken hearts, and he was sure the stress he'd inflicted on her by crashing into a truck in the mountains of Idaho had set her heart off kilter. Several months after the accident, she developed fatigue, shortness of breath, and a vague discomfort in her chest, shoulders, and belly. When Dunn encouraged her to see a physician, she insisted her symptoms weren't troublesome enough to pursue. Unconvinced, Dunn scheduled a trip to Nevada to evaluate her, but his trip came too late: A week before he was due to depart, she died suddenly. A neighbor discovered her in bed after she failed to show up for a walk.

Beside himself, Dunn insisted that an autopsy be done which revealed a ballooned heart with no arterial blockages. In the span of four months, he lost two women he loved, and his grief was compounded by guilt for having taken from his mother a relationship with Consuela that she cherished. The two women met not long after Dunn first met Consuela at a clinic for the homeless in San Francisco's Tenderloin district where she worked as a nurse and where Dunn volunteered one afternoon as a urology resident. He traveled with Consuela to Nevada to introduce her to his mother, and the two women bonded immediately. It wasn't just Consuela's survival of a harrowing crossing of the Mexico-U.S. border as a toddler with her father that made Dunn's mother respect her; she also admired Consuela for excelling in school while living with an aunt in the Salinas Valley and for graduating from college before she became a nurse.

Two months after his mother died, Dunn returned to the Walker River Indian Reservation to spread her ashes across Lake Walker where she often strolled. Before returning to Baltimore, however, he was approached by one of his mother's neighbors who told him three men dressed in dark suits had showed up one day at his mother's door a month before she died. Who the men were and why they appeared was a mystery to the neighbor, and despite repeated attempts to pry details from Dunn's mother, she failed. From that time forward, Dunn's mother declined in health until she died from a broken heart.

7

SHORTLY AFTER MEETING with his boss and learning that his clinical duties had been suspended, Dunn started for his lab to inform his staff about the upcoming changes, but before he could get there he received a call from Garrett Fitzgerald.

"Thanks for seeing the men at the bases yesterday," his friend said. "The report you sent me last night was sobering."

"It's an exceptionally unusual disease, Garrett. I've never seen anything like it."

"Which worries me because you've seen just about everything that can go wrong with the male reproductive tract." Urgency filled Fitzgerald's voice: "Can you come to the Pentagon this morning for our first meeting of the team I've assembled to investigate the illnesses? We're due to start in an hour."

"Impossible!" Dunn said, glancing at his watch. "It's eight-thirty and with the weather as it is, traffic between Baltimore and the Pentagon will be horrible."

"You won't need to drive," Fitzgerald assured him.

Twenty minutes later, after swapping blues for street clothes, Dunn boarded a Black Hawk helicopter on the hospital's helipad. Part of the Army's 12th Aviation Battalion stationed in Fort Belvoir, the copter made a detour while flying from Camp David to the Pentagon to pick Dunn up. In the craft were members of the Joint Chiefs of Staff who were returning to headquarters after meeting with the President in the Catoctin Mountains. Dunn took a seat in the rear where he kept his stomach in-check during the bumpy flight by shutting his eyes and holding his head as still as possible. The only time he looked out the window was when the helicopter touched down, and when he glanced at his watch he was astonished to see that it had taken only thirty minutes to reach his destination.

Finding the assigned conference room in the Pentagon was another matter. Even with an escort, he lost his bearings within the seventeen miles of hallways that course one of the world's largest buildings. As with previous trips to Fitzgerald's office, he was bedazzled by the spectrum of uniforms he passed in the corridors—greens and khakis, whites and blues, and camouflage battledress, among others. Upon reaching the conference room, he found a similar array on display, although some of the assembled wore civilian attire.

"Dr. Wilbur Dunn!" Fitzgerald announced, rushing to meet his friend at the doorway.

Dunn joined a group seated around a table where introductions were made. Among the sixteen attendees, he recognized two in addition to Fitzgerald, one being the director of infectious diseases at NIH, a man Dunn likened to a czar given his status and power, and the other a garrulous man who chaired the pathology department at a medical school in Washington, D.C.

"Folks," Fitzgerald began, "I called this meeting because we'll be working to determine what's sickened our men at Walter Reed and the Naval Academy. I'm confident we'll find the cause because you're some of the smartest people I know. If need be, we'll add to the group, but for now we have experts in many fields of medicine and science, and our resources come from the military, NIH, medical schools, and CDC. However, monumental tasks lie before of us as we seek the cause of illness and a means to prevent its spread, if necessary. An additional challenge will be keeping the public informed of our findings. Each task is fraught with difficulty, and time is of the essence."

Fitzgerald reviewed the group's marching orders: Communications would take place electronically and by teleconference with Fitzgerald and the NIH czar co-leading the group; team members would have broad latitude to perform functions as needed; and the public would be informed through news releases issued by the Defense Department after clearing a chain of command. "In that vein," Fitzgerald continued, "we have Major Roger Able here from our DoD Public Affairs office who will keep abreast of what we learn and convey our findings in layman's language to others outside the team."

Turning to Dunn, Fitzgerald said, "And now, Wilbur, may I ask you to summarize what you learned yesterday while interviewing and examining the patients? Although I forwarded the report you sent me last night to those present, we'd appreciate having a quick synopsis."

Dunn leaned forward. "I evaluated twenty-three men yesterday at Walter Reed and the Naval Academy who displayed an illness characterized by fever and painful swelling of the testes. They ranged in age from nineteen to fifty-six, and while four were civilians, the rest were military personnel."

A slender woman raised an arm: "Your report stated all were white. That's unusual, isn't it?" Earlier, during introductions, the woman had identified herself as a CDC epidemiologist.

"It *may* be unusual, but I caution against drawing conclusions on race as more cases may come to our attention."

"Nonetheless," she persevered, "the military is a diverse place, and I find it striking that no African Americans, Asians, or Pacific Islanders have reported being ill yet."

"That's not the only oddity," a microbiologist noted, a pale man with thick glasses who looked like he'd spent his career hovering over petri dishes. "So, far, this disease appears to affect only men, and that's astounding."

"I agree," the pathologist echoed, a perma-smile on his face.

It intrigued Dunn that a man who worked with corpses and tissues should be the happiest-looking person in the room. "It's an interesting observation which I can't explain," Dunn said, "unless the agent responsible for causing the illness is something that exclusively targets the male reproductive tract without damaging other tissues in common to men and women." He raised a hand. "But, again, I remind you we've just learned about these individuals who've fallen ill, and there may be other sick people out there, including women."

"True," a toxicologist agreed. "I found it notable, too, that before becoming ill, all of the men were current on vaccinations, healthy, and reported no urologic or sexual issues."

"Right," an internist added, "and each indicated being outdoors on the bases at the time the drones were spotted."

"Are you suggesting the drones played a role in causing the illnesses?" an immunologist piped.

Fitzgerald raised a hand. "Folks, we'll hear more about the drones and shootings at a briefing following our meeting, so let's hold off on that discussion for now." He motioned for Dunn to continue but was stymied when the microbiologist, pen-in-hand now, spoke again.

"Just for the record, what day were the drones seen?"

"Four days ago, on Monday," Dunn replied.

"And you said in your report that the men's symptoms began about thirty-six hours after that, right?"

"Yes."

NIH czar: "Thirty-six hours is an incubation period that falls within the realm of many infectious diseases—*if* it's an infectious disease, which I suspect it is given the men had fever."

"But, microbes aren't the only agents that cause fever," the toxicologist noted. "Severe chemical poisonings can produce fever, as from pesticides, for example."

Dunn was impressed by the participatory nature of Fitzgerald's team, and because the topics raised were central to the outbreak, he made no effort to curtail the discussion.

"Yes, chemical poisonings can cause fever," the czar acknowledged, "but my point was this: the passing of two days between the spotting of drones and onset of illnesses provides an interval with which to evaluate possible causative agents. From that perspective, I agree with Dr. Dunn's assertion that release of mumps virus from the drones cannot explain the illnesses because mumps typically has a two-to-three-week incubation period, far longer than the two days that elapsed between drone spotting and illness onsets." The czar leaned back in his chair. "Not only that, but with mumps, scrotal swelling isn't an early manifestation of infection but, rather, one seen a week or two after the parotid glands in front of the ears become swollen."

"Very true," the microbiologist said, his eyes boiling with thought behind his lenses. "Too many things are going against mumps here: absence of salivary gland pain, tenderness, or swelling; the fact that the men were current with their mumps vaccine; and negative blood test results for mumps." He stroked his goatee and turned to Fitzgerald. "But, just to be complete, let me ask this: Was there a recent mumps vaccine campaign at the two bases?"

"I'm not aware of any," Fitzgerald replied. "We keep our service members current on vaccinations, but we haven't had a blitz, so to speak, of mumps vaccination recently." He frowned. "What makes you ask?"

The microbiologist creased his forehead. "Because, as you know, the current mumps vaccine incorporates a weakened, but still living, mumps virus—a so-called live, attenuated virus. That makes me wonder whether selected lots of vaccine were produced inappropriately to yield mumps virus with enough of its original virulence factors to cause the illnesses we're seeing."

"Unlikely!" the czar exclaimed. "Vaccine manufacturers are exceedingly careful with production practices, and besides, if that had happened we'd be seeing mumps cases among female vaccine recipients." He bulged his cheek with his tongue. "But I'll take it upon myself to investigate the matter."

The microbiologist wasn't done: "Dr. Dunn, I saw no mention in your report of PCR test results for mumps virus. Can you address that?"

"Excuse me, doctor," Major Roger Able interceded. "I'm not familiar the term you used, 'PCR.' "

Another stroke of the goatee. "It stands for 'polymerase chain reaction.' It's a test that amplifies a specific segment of RNA or DNA present in a sample of blood, tissue, or other clinical specimen. With mumps, for example, clinicians often rub a cotton- or foam-tipped swab along the inside lining of the mouth—taking a buccal swab, so to speak—before running a PCR test on it to look for mumps virus RNA." Turning to Dunn: "So, were any specimens submitted for PCR testing to look for mumps virus?"

"Yes, some were," Dunn replied. "They were buccal swabs, and all came back negative for mumps RNA. I'm having the lab at Hopkins run the test on a testicular biopsy I performed last night at Walter Reed on one of the patients. I'm certain it'll come back negative, too, but we need to run the test to be complete."

Fitzgerald tapped his watch. "We need to bring this to a close, but before doing so, I believe you have some late-breaking news from your lab, Wilbur. Please share that news now."

Dunn nodded. "As I arrived here, a member of my staff at Hopkins called to report that the testicular tissue I just referred to showed massive destruction of the sperm-producing compartments by inflammatory cells. Based on those results, I can say authoritatively we're dealing with something that's novel and extremely worrisome." He wiped his forehead. "Let's just hope it's not transmissible from person-to-person."

8

THE FIRST TIME Wilbur Dunn considered becoming a urologist was in his first year of medical school as he listened to a lecture on the cells comprising the testes. A professor introduced a colorful slide, and the aha moment occurred.

The slide was a three-dimensional cartoon that showed four cells side-by-side shaded in light green that looked like Christmas trees on a holiday lot, only the trees had their tops cropped to leave their plump bottoms resting on a thin layer labeled "basal lamina." Pointing to the trees, the professor announced, "These are Sertoli cells in the testes. They nurse sperm to life."

Cradled in the boughs of the Sertoli cells were spherical red ornaments that ran from bottom to top where they transitioned into miniature bullet-shaped cells with wiggly tails. "And these are sperm," the professor continued. "They're created by successive divisions of cells we call 'spermatocytes' which come, in turn, from progenitor cells known as 'spermatogonia' which lie along the bottom of Sertoli cells." He turned to the audience. "Imagine an elevator ride going up each Sertoli cell with progenitor cells boarding at the base and sperm getting off at the top."

The next slide showed the same scene only in cross-section. It revealed nuclei in the Sertoli cells and in the spermatogonia and spermatocytes, but it was the borders between Sertolis and sperm-forming cells the professor pointed to. "These are 'tight junctions' that allow very selective passage of nutritional components from Sertoli cells to sperm-producing cells."

"Check out those Christmas presents at the top of the trees!" Dunn whispered to Fitzgerald at the time, referring to mature sperm that pooled along the top of the Sertolis. "I'll take those presents any day."

The professor moved on to discuss another cell type in the testes called "Leydig" cells located just beneath the basal lamina that, when commanded to do so by the pituitary gland, squirted out testosterone which seduced Sertoli cells to rev up sperm production.

Enthralled by the cells and molecular biology of human reproduction, Dunn entertained the idea of a career in obstetrics/gynecology but rejected the notion because of memories of the dead baby he'd held as a teen. Instead, he settled on urology because it owned the domain of Christmas tree-shaped Sertoli cells, maturing wiggly sperm, and reproductive physiology that fascinated him.

During his final year of medical school, he spent a month working in a lab at Brown University to study interactions between testosterone and receptors on Sertoli cell membranes. The work piqued his interest so much that, after finishing his residency in urology in California, he remained in San Francisco an extra year to complete a fellowship in reproductive surgery. The skills he acquired and research he conducted during his six years in San Francisco caught the eye of Francis Bateman, the Chair of urology at Johns Hopkins University, who offered him a faculty position at Hopkins. Initially, Dunn didn't think he could accept the offer because of his obligation to work in an underserved area as payoff for his medical school scholarship, but Bateman convinced the National Health Service Corp to allow Dunn to take the job in exchange for providing pro bono urological care to uninsured residents of east Baltimore who lived near the hospital. As a bonus, Bateman provided Dunn with a lab and initial funding to research abnormalities of spermatogenesis.

It was his admiration for the orderliness of sperm production within Sertoli cells, then, that alarmed Dunn as he studied a photo Krishna Bhatia had sent him while Dunn met with Garrett Fitzgerald's investigative team. While Bhatia had warned him in a phone call before the meeting that the sperm-producing regions of PFC Hartley's testicles had been destroyed, Dunn was shocked to see the damage pictorially.

Examining the photo in a Pentagon hallway after Fitzgerald's meeting had ended, Dunn told Fitzgerald he needed a minute to examine the findings in more detail.

"You have sixty seconds before the next briefing starts," Fitzgerald warned. "Don't be late because there'll be admirals and generals in attendance who don't tolerate tardiness."

Dunn nodded and honed his eyes on the photo. The tissue destruction was so severe he wondered whether Bhatia had damaged the specimen while preparing the slides, but he quickly discarded the notion given Bhatia's skills. "I can't believe it!" he whispered to himself. He gasped at the sea of white blood cells invading the sperm-producing areas and at the now shredded basal lamina which no longer separated Sertolis and their sperm cells from underlying Leydig cells and blood vessels. He realized now that Bhatia's earlier reference to the chaos as the "Battle of Cajamarca" was apropos even though he was in no mood at the time to hear another history lesson from his colleague.

"Hear me out!" Bhatia had pleaded. "In 1532, when Spanish forces led by Francisco Pizarro ambushed Inca ruler Atahualpa, the Spaniards killed thousands of unarmed Incans in the grand plaza of Cajamarca. And thus began the conquest of the Incan civilization of Peru." After a brief pause, he continued: "PFC Hartley's testes look like the aftermath of the Battle of Cajamarca."

THE BRIEFING ROOM Dunn entered held a conference table unlike any he'd seen before, one made from two slabs of black walnut that ran side-by-side some thirty feet with a joint line polished by time. For a moment, he felt he'd entered a hunting lodge, but the sight of photos on the walls depicting military aircraft, vehicles, and battle formations disabused him of the notion.

With the briefing about to start, he hurried to a chair beside Fitzgerald's. Glancing about, he discovered a group far larger than the one Fitzgerald had assembled and was comprised primarily by active duty military personnel. Being in the civilian minority, he thought about the question he'd posed to Fitzgerald the day before, namely: How could he assist in the investigation of an outbreak at two military bases when he lacked a security clearance?

Fitzgerald's response unsettled him: "You're forgetting the government knows everything about you from the court trial in Idaho."

Dunn looked more closely at the attendees, and when his eyes met those of a man glowering at him from a seat at the distant end of the table, he cringed. Although Vice President Atticus Quincy Thornbridge had testified against him briefly on behalf of the widow of the truck driver he'd killed in Idaho, the two had never sat at the same table. Dunn diverted his eyes to pretend the encounter meant little to him, turning instead to the general who began the meeting.

"Ladies and gentlemen, I mean no disrespect by skipping introductions, but that's what we'll do to delve straight into our presentations. I've asked several people to update us on the shootings at Walter Reed and the Naval Academy and what we've learned about the drones that flew over each site. As such, each speaker will introduce him or herself, and if anyone has a question, I request you introduce yourself first. That way we'll get through our agenda." His face lengthened. "So, without delay, let's have law enforcement officials from the Army and Navy present their findings."

With the lights dimmed, a projector illuminated a screen. Dunn used the opportunity to steal a glance at the Vice President, but their eyes locked. Had they been alone, he would've confronted the VP for the phone call he'd placed to Dunn's attorney after the trial to express his disdain for Dunn's deceased wife, a woman he'd referred to as "a little dark girl in ragged clothes who'd crossed the border with her vagrant father." Equally distressing to Dunn were Thornbridge's assertions that by attending nursing school in California, Consuela had usurped a position from a legal citizen; that her job following nursing school at a clinic in the Tenderloin district of San Francisco placed her with people of her worth—losers; and that she'd never deserved to earn a green card after marrying Dunn because she'd lied about entering the country legally. "Damn good thing such people can't become full citizens of our nay-ya-shun," he'd asserted.

Calming himself enough to focus on the briefing, Dunn listened to details of the shootings. Eerily, nineteen victims had been picked off at each site to bring the total to thirty-eight—twenty-five dead and thirteen hospitalized with many in critical condition. From those about the table came the same question repeatedly: What meaning resided in the number thirty-eight, the exact amount of time which lapsed between the firing of the final bullet at Walter Reed and the initial one in Annapolis.

"I presume *everything* has meaning," the presenter replied. "Our challenge is to decipher that meaning."

While Dunn shared the distress expressed for what appeared to be a carefully calculated toll, he couldn't suppress a morbid fascination as details revealed a North African connection to the shootings. At both attack sites, a Sudanese-manufactured "Khawad" machine gun had been mounted on a swivel and fired by remote control using a high-resolution webcam manufactured in Libya. Khawads, the presenter added, had a history of being fastened to Land Cruisers in Sudan by government armed forces who pillaged residents of Darfur. As for the bullets, they came from a factory Sudanese arms merchants had established in the desert of neighboring Chad.

A Navy commander near Dunn who'd circled his thumbs incessantly since the meeting began couldn't contain his question any longer: "How could someone haul a fifty-pound remote weapon station up an evergreen tree in a golf course across from Gate 5 without being seen?"

"It was done at night, sir," the speaker replied. "There are no sentries at the gate after dark. That's probably why the site was chosen for the attack—that and because of the heavy flow of traffic that passes through the gate each afternoon."

A different weapon setting had been used in Annapolis, one in which the Khawad had been hidden inside a hillside bush pruned to allow the swiveling gun to pick off targets in the Severn River. MPs found the weapon at a promontory just upriver and across from the Academy after rushing there when witnesses reported hearing gunfire from the area. The attack site offered an unobstructed view of dinghies rounding the bend from Annapolis Harbor.

"At both sites," the speaker continued, "the weapons had been installed with exceeding care." Stooping, he produced a bag from which he extracted a tangle of nylon and metal which he unraveled to form a ring whose bottom half consisted of chain links while an arched metal band formed the top. Branching from each side of the ring were nylon bands that presumably ran to reins of some sort.

"That's a halter," a woman said from Dunn's side of the table. She spoke with a soft voice, one barely audible over the projector's hum.

"Indeed, it is," said the presenter. "We found it neatly arranged atop a shemagh under the Khawad at the Annapolis shooting site."

"Atop a *what*?" a voice asked.

This time the presenter lifted from the bag a scarf of the kind Dunn had seen in photos of Middle Easterners who wore similar red and white checkered headdresses, only this one had elaborate tassels along its edges. "A shemagh," the presenter continued. "It's a—"

"—headcloth," the woman with the soft voice interjected. "It's basically a scarf or shawl, also called a ghutra, hattah, or keffiyeh. It's designed to protect one from sand and heat in the desert."

"Ah, that's Colonel Linda Abrams speaking for those who don't know her," the general said.

"I'm sorry, sir, I should've introduced myself."

"Not a problem, please continue."

"I know shemaghs well," she volunteered. "I wore one in the Sahara often." The Colonel stood, rounded the table, and collected the halter from the presenter. Holding it up, she explained, "This is a steel camel bosal, or noseband. It's used as a bridle without a bit to steer a camel by controlling its nose." Moving into the projector's beam, she tilted the halter's metal band. "There's often an inscription here," she added, craning her neck. "And here it is. It's in Arabic and says, 'Made in Chad.' "

Dunn shuddered as a recurring theme struck him. Two days earlier, while watching live coverage of the shootings in Annapolis, he'd seen bullets riddle a sail of a dinghy to allow sunlight to stream through it. Following that, when Garrett Fitzgerald had phoned to ask for assistance, he'd learned about sniper fire at Walter Reed leaving bullet holes in the shape of a circle in an SUV's hood. Now, standing before him, a Colonel held a camel's bridle which projected a circular image on the screen, one which reminded Dunn of Hurricane Stanley's resilient eye.

ENGROSSED BY DISCUSSIONS that had turned from shootings to the fallen drone over Walter Reed, Dunn ignored the taps on his forearm. Only when they became more forceful did he divert his gaze.

"Meet me outside," Fitzgerald told him, motioning to the door.

Dunn returned his eyes to a slide showing an aerial view of a factory in Saudi Arabia where the drone's motor was manufactured.

"Now!" Fitzgerald said, tapping his mobile against Dunn's arm. "I'll let the general know why we're stepping out."

The two men united shortly in the hallway. "What is it?" Dunn asked. "I wanted to hear about the drone."

"You have more pressing issues. There's a story about to break claiming the government is covering up the cause of what's sickened the twenty-three men at the bases."

"How can there be a cover up of what's not known?"

"Irrational things happen when people are afraid."

"Who's claiming there's a cover up?"

"The wife of one of the civilians you examined yesterday in Annapolis."

"Which one?"

"A guy in his thirties who works at the Naval Academy's heating and cooling plant. His wife freaked out when she had to put on protective gear before entering her husband's hospital room."

Dunn recalled the man well. "Yeah, he told me he'd spent hours on a rooftop dealing with air vents the day the drone flew over the Academy."

"Well, his wife's so concerned about his health that she contacted a reporter who, in turn, called our DoD press office this morning for specifics. The reporter told us the wife believes we're hiding the fact that a biological warfare agent made her husband ill. We need to dispel that notion immediately."

"Do we know it's wrong?"

"There's no evidence it's right!"

Dunn's eyes sank in deepening sockets. "I'm worried these men will become infertile."

"The question is, from what? I've asked our pathologists at Walter Reed to send a portion of PFC Harley's biopsy to Ft. Detrick so they can examine it for biological warfare agents. In the meantime, you can help, too."

"How?"

"Our press office has organized a briefing for reporters this afternoon on the illnesses. I want you to take the lead in addressing them since you're an expert in the male reproductive tract and because you examined the men."

"You know I'm not the man for that."

Fitzgerald was prepared for the protest. During their final year of medical school, seniors elected a classmate they believed exemplified the finest qualities of a physician, and Dunn was one of three placed on a ballot for a final vote. Before the vote occurred, Dunn lobbied classmates to vote for the other two candidates, but when graduation took place, he won the award.

"Look, I know you're a private man," Fitzgerald said, "but people need to hear an expert speak to the facts, and you're that man." He glanced at his watch. "C'mon, let's go; the briefing starts shortly."

9

AT DAY'S END, Dunn sat with a mug of steaming tonic before the painting of the winter scene in his study. More than ever, he sought to rekindle the peace that had eluded him in recent months while visiting the painting. He lifted a hand toward the oil colors with palm forward as a minister does when giving a benediction, hoping that a blessing might flow from the canvas to his weary soul. It was not to come, however. Instead, he felt a growing gap between himself and the young man in rawhides who fed the fire along the wind-protected side of the boulder as blowing snow and a dark sky drew the two apart.

He sipped his fernleaf biscuitroot tonic to calm nerves frayed by the day. Following the morning meetings, he stood before cameras and the press to describe the illnesses, discuss what the government was doing to investigate their cause, and inform the nation that no new cases had been detected in the past twenty-four hours. Speaking assuredly, he insisted no evidence suggested illnesses had passed from person-to-person or that a biological warfare agent had been released. He concluded by presenting guidelines the government had issued to help physicians diagnose and report additional illnesses should they arise.

Following the briefing, he flew by helicopter to Annapolis and then to Bethesda to revisit his patients. He was dismayed to see testicular swelling had increased in some of the men compared to his initial exams, but he was relieved that none exhibited complications involving other organs. At the Naval Academy, he performed an additional testicular biopsy and asked several men to submit serial sperm samples for testing.

But now, at one o'clock in the morning with his neck stiff and head throbbing, he abandoned the painting to begin his rituals of checking the security of his condo. He addressed the task with renewed urgency because upon coming home he'd discovered fresh grooves carved into his door around the lock. Despite the late hour, he called the building manager to ask if other tenants had heard or seen anything suspicious that day. Hearing none had, he concluded the attempted break-in was connected somehow to a phone call he'd taken while examining patients earlier in the afternoon at Walter Reed Hospital. It came from an *Unknown caller*, and he debated whether to answer it but did so thinking it might be someone calling about the press briefing he'd given.

"I just saw you on television," a female said to him. "You spoke well."

"Who is this?"

"I will be leaving a phone for you in a blue plastic bag under a holly bush in the park beside your condo. Look for it as soon as you get home, and make sure you keep the phone close so we remain connected."

Dunn broke out in a sweat. In the past, he'd evaluated patients with mental illnesses who'd presented to emergency departments with urological disorders, and in instances when the patients presented with florid psychosis, he sometimes felt a blurring of personal borders. On such occasions, he fortified his defenses to keep from being drawn into the murky world of unstable thoughts and emotions. "What's your name?" he asked.

"I will tell you when we meet."

"Who says we'll meet?"

"I do because you need me."

Dunn struggled to place the accent, one he attributed to a person fluent in both a Romance language and Arabic as the speech was mellifluous at times yet staccato at others. "Why would I need someone I don't know?"

"Because, I can explain the events of the last few days."

"Which events?"

The cluck of her tongue was sharp. "Come now! Too many people have been killed, injured, and sickened at the military bases, and worse may come unless we meet."

"Where are you?"

"Close."

"Give me an address."

"Twenty-three Infertile Street, Barren, U.S.A."

"That's it!" Dunn lashed out. "Don't mock our soldiers!"

"I am not mocking them. The men *will* become barren."

Dunn squeezed the phone to his ear. During the press briefing, he'd divulged the number of men with testicular illness but refrained from discussing a prognosis—a calculated omission he, Fitzgerald, and DoD brass had justified given the early stage of illness. "How do you know the men will become infertile?"

"Do not underestimate me. I know much about the killings and illnesses, and this I can say with certainty: They have a good deal to do with who you are as a person, so stay close, monitor the phone I will leave for you, and pack a bag. We depart soon." She cleared her throat. "And know this above all: You and I travel the same circle of life."

When the caller hung up, Dunn froze in the hospital ward where he stood at the time. Hours later, after seeing his patients, he returned to his condo, but before entering the building, he went to the small park the caller had referred to, a green space with a circular brick walkway lined by benches where dog walkers sat as their canines frolicked in the grassy center. Late that night, however, he found himself alone there, and he surveyed the area for a holly bush. Spotting it at the end of the park, he approached it warily, noticing then a small plastic bag tucked near the base of the bush. He looked about to see if anyone was watching before he lifted the bag gingerly and opened it. Inside, he found a smartphone of a brand he didn't recognize, one thicker and heavier than his iPhone and equipped with an antenna. Present also was a sheet folded in quarters with hand-written instructions on how to use a satellite phone.

It was then he went to his condo and discovered the fresh grooves etched into the wood of his door. After opening it, he proceeded cautiously, leaving the door open in case he needed to exit abruptly. Making his way past the baskets and bowls displayed in the cabinet, he went to the kitchen where he collected a butcher's knife which he wielded as he checked the premises. He left no space unexamined and paid special attention for hidden microphones or cameras. Finding none, he stripped into pajamas, but before slipping between the sheets he took a long, hard look under his bed.

10

THE STREETS OF Baltimore were deserted at four a.m. when Dunn left the city. Even I-95 was abandoned save for lumbering semis steered by drivers impervious to fatigue. After leaving the interstate, he traveled a short distance to the airport where he left his motorcycle in a short-term lot.

Those who boarded the pre-dawn flight with him did so groggily. Having slept fitfully, he plopped into a window seat with an empty space beside him. Headset in place, he drifted off for the four-hour flight to Denver before connecting to a second flight to Billings, Montana. After landing, he staved off hunger long enough to pick up a rental car which he drove to a grocery store to purchase breakfast and rations for the journey ahead.

Familiar with Billings from previous visits, he stopped short of I-90 and reached for the satellite phone he'd retrieved the previous night. Its manufacturer, Vestel Trade Company, was one he didn't recognize, and when he looked it up using his iPhone, he discovered it was headquartered in Manisa, Turkey almost due east of Athens across the Aegean Sea. Among the instructions left with the phone were a contact number and a statement claiming that while the mobile's GPS was traceable, its communications were not.

He turned it on and acquainted himself with its screen before composing a text…

Going into mountains; out of touch for now.

Having debated whether to use the device, he regretted doing so now because it violated a tacit oath he took to work in confidence with Garrett Fitzgerald and DoD officials on a matter of intense national security. While texting on a device a stranger had left him was perhaps not as hazardous as picking up an abandoned suitcase outside an airport only to claim it as personal luggage, he knew it was ill-advised to leave a digital footprint on a satellite phone, yet he did so because he thought sending the text might allow him to pry important information from a woman who'd displayed insight into the illnesses at the bases. Compelling him further was her statement, *You and I travel the same circle of life,* one that addressed a matter very much on his mind, namely, circles.

From Billings, Dunn had a choice of two routes to take. One headed west before looping southeast, and the other east before circling southwest. He chose the latter because it cut through the Crow Indian Reservation. Years earlier as a college student, he'd presented a poster at a conference in Arizona for Chicanos/Hispanics and Native Americans who aspired to become scientists. One of the judges was a Crow Indian who Dunn lunched with following the competition. Dunn was interested to learn the man was a physician assistant who blended Native American and Western healing traditions in his practice on the Crow Indian Reservation, and when the man offered Dunn an internship at his clinic the following summer, Dunn accepted it. The experience solidified Dunn's decision to go into medicine.

He cruised through the reservation now, eager to reach his destination beyond it. Shortly after entering Wyoming, he left I-90 for U.S. Highway 14 heading toward Bighorn National Forest. With the end of September nearing, he knew it was a gamble to drive into the mountains because snow storms could arise rapidly and close roads abruptly. He moved on, nonetheless, committed to walking his circle.

The Bighorn Mountains were familiar to him because he'd visited them almost every year for the past two decades for treks akin to those pilgrims take from France over the Pyrenees to a cathedral in Spain's Santiago de Compostela. In Dunn's case, the trail he often hiked was one etched into the earth in past centuries by Native Americans that was so deep its course was discernible even in drifting snow.

With a series of peaks in view, Dunn glanced at his pocket altimeter which registered just over four thousand feet. The device also served as a barometer which he checked often for sudden drops which could presage the arrival of foul weather. For a moment, it brought him angst to enter a national forest after having been convicted for involuntary manslaughter the last time he visited one, and with courtroom memories still vivid, he proceeded with vigilance, slowing before curves and abiding by speed limits. At one point, when a logging truck rounded a bend with a full load, he hugged the mountainside to give the truck extra space. It took minutes for his heart to settle even as a pit remained in his belly when he glanced at the empty seat beside him.

To keep fresh, he lowered his window. In the incoming wind, he detected an aroma from the Yarrow plant, or *Achillea millefolium*, a plant that bloomed from May through September and grew in the valleys of Bighorn all the way up to and beyond the timberline. Its flat-topped tiny white flowers clustered in umbrella style not unlike fernleaf biscuitroot, and when its feathery fern-like leaves were trampled by bear and antelope, they released a pleasant spicy aroma which resembled a blend of oregano, rosemary, and other herbs.

A hundred forty miles into the trip, Dunn reached Burgess Junction, a fork in the road 8,040 feet high where route Alt 40 branched off U.S. Highway 40. Pursuing the alternate route, he passed a lodge and a shuttered snowmobile outlet before crossing meadowlands rimmed by conifers. As he drove, he kept an eye out for eagles, falcons, and mountain bluebirds, and when he reached the North Tongue River which ran along his left, he pulled over and walked to the river to splash cold water across his face. The snow melt sent shivers down his spine, prompting him to look warily at what appeared to be fresh snow capping the mountains in the distance, a stark reminder to move on.

After passing a sign for *Bald Mountain Campground*, he sharpened his eyes for the next turn, one that came when he reached Forest Development Road 12. The needle of the altimeter registered steadily higher elevations as he climbed the gravel road to an empty parking lot where he stopped. Donning his coat, he prepared to depart the vehicle but paused when he saw a flashing light on the satphone.

A response awaited…

I told you to stay close, yet the GPS tells me you have strayed.
I am ordering you to return immediately. We need to leave!
Irina

WHETHER HE APPROACHED it by foot or car, Dunn felt as if he walked on air when he reached the outskirts of Medicine Mountain National Historical Landmark. Perhaps it was the racing clouds which lifted him, or the breathtaking summit views, or the spirits of ancestors which remained from hundreds if not thousands of years of visits. Whatever the gravity-defying force was, it allowed him to glide along the mile-and-a-half path from parking lot to sacred site.

"Medicine Wheel" was what most people called the skyward sanctuary. Dunn called it his inner circle. The place grounded him, connected him to Earth.

He was eighteen when he first set foot there. His mother had loaned him a car and instructed him to drive a thousand miles from their home at Walker River Reservation to Medicine Wheel in Wyoming. The trip served two ends: a present for graduating from high school, and a visit to adulthood's door. Medicine Wheel was one of hundreds of stone circles built by Native Americans long ago on hills and mountaintops throughout the northern plains of the U.S. and in Alberta and Saskatchewan. The wheels, or "sacred hoops" as some called them, likely served as places for worship, ceremonies, and rituals. Dunn's mother chose Medicine Wheel in Bighorn for her son to visit because of its importance and well-preserved status. He drove the distance alone and camped along the way, but when he reached the base of the mountains beneath Medicine Wheel, he backpacked an ancient trail toward the venerated site. It was dusk when he pitched camp below the summit, and with the weather clear that night, he forwent a tent and lay beside a fire as he peered at the stars.

Twenty years later, walking now from parking lot to Medicine Wheel, he hiked rocky terrain which hosted occasional conifers that defied the tree line. When the Wheel came into view, he paused to petition the sky and clouds for permission to visit the site. Only then did he advance, coming to a path which encircled limestone boulders and rocks arranged in the shape of a wagon wheel. It was a large wheel—some seventy-five feet in diameter—with twenty-eight spokes radiating from a central hub, or cairn, that was roughly ten feet across. Outside the wheel were six smaller cairns, also circular.

If there was a theme to Dunn's excursions to Medicine Wheel, it was to seek guidance. He looked to the circle with its alignment to sun, moon, and stars as a source of wisdom. During his first visit, he prayed for help to begin manhood without a father, and because the visit endowed him with fortitude, he returned to the Wheel regularly to re-connect to his inner being. During these visits, he sought stamina and direction to undertake other challenges, among them college, medical school and residency, and devotion, love, and fidelity in marriage.

With wind kicking up and clouds darkening the horizon, he walked the perimeter of the Wheel in clockwise direction. Rarely had he been alone as he was now as even the ranger who often greeted visitors at the parking lot or at the Wheel was nowhere to be found. Cherishing the solitude, he ran a hand over sections of rope that stretched between wood posts cordoning off the Wheel. From experience, he'd learned that by doing so he could clear his mind to be fully present in the moment. Along his fingers and palm he discerned the rope's strands and fibers, constituents which helped him attune to the elements of nature: earth, air, sun, and water. But then a predicament arose: Should he run his hand over a colorful scrap of cloth draped over a section of rope or leave it be? On previous visits, he refrained from touching prayer tokens left by others because he respected their sanctity. On this day, however, he yearned for connection as eight months of loneliness had taken a toll. Gently, he caressed the fabric, feeling its folds give way under the pressure of searching fingertips. For an instant, he was subsumed by a current of supplication between petitioner and higher power. Warmth infused his hand.

Recalling a verse of a song in Paiute his mother often sang while they collected fernleaf biscuitroot in the Sierras, he sang…

bagootsoo … padooa … ggwe'na'a … esa …

He repeated the verse with its undulating cadence as he circled the Wheel, his palm on the rope and eyes on the path.

bagootsoo ... padooa ... ggwe'na'a ... esa ...

After completing a full revolution, he began another one. With each step, he lowered his voice until the song became a whisper as his thoughts turned to the animals named in the song: buffalo, bear, eagle, wolf.

In his contemplative state, he wouldn't have noticed the falling snow had it not been for the numbing cold of his fingers. Like a thief, the frigid flakes stole from his digits their sensation of rope, fabric, and feathers, forcing him to depart the transcendental realm for a physical one.

With heavier snow falling by the minute, he started for the parking lot, but from the cloud bank which had descended upon the summit, a brief opening allowed him to glimpse golden hues of autumn meadows in the broad vistas below. And then the clearing vanished, and all became grey and white.

RED EYE FLIGHTS had no place in Dunn's life, or so he vowed years earlier, but then he broke the pledge after visiting Medicine Wheel. A restless segment from Billings to Denver followed by another to Baltimore landed him on the East Coast at sunrise where his first stop was at a coffee shop to purchase a double latte. Sitting at a table with caffeine infusing his mind, he read a series of texts and emails Fitzgerald had sent over the past twelve hours.

Urgency reined in Fitzgerald's demand to know why Dunn had missed the previous day's teleconference without notice. The group, Fitzgerald insisted, needed daily updates on the clinical status of the patients, and skipping calls without warning was unacceptable. *Either you're with us or you're not,* Fitzgerald texted. *I need to know your decision.*

Rattled, Dunn promised to update the group at its next meeting at eleven that morning after examining patients in Annapolis. Switching to the Turkish satphone, he opened a text awaiting him...

You've returned to Baltimore, I see. Today, you are to go to Henlopen Acres Marina in Rehoboth Beach, Delaware, and do not disobey me this time! You will stand on the pier at exactly three p.m. Be there alone or a plague of biblical proportions will follow. And remember, do not disclose anything I've told you!
Irina

Dunn was outraged. Not since childhood had anyone ordered him about in such a fashion, the last time coming when his mother scolded him as a boy after he'd misbehaved. With defiance, he began responding but because his trembling hands caused him to strike several wrong keys he soon relented, packed the phone, and strode off.

Forty minutes later, he pulled into the parking lot of Anne Arundel Medical Center in Annapolis where he rode an elevator to a ward where four men from the Naval Academy were held in rooms isolated from others on the floor. Before he could see the first patient, however, a nurse informed him that one of the men had been discharged the previous day.

Surprised, Dunn inquired who'd discharged the man. He learned the orders came from a urologist from Walter Reed who'd visited the hospital the previous evening. Given the patient's improvement, the urologist determined he could move to a home in the area that served as a quarantine station for outpatients afflicted by the disease.

Irate, he called Fitzgerald. "What the hell's going on? I'm at the hospital in Annapolis and just learned one of the patients was discharged yesterday without my knowledge!"

"You were AWOL!" Fitzgerald parried, "so I recruited another urologist." He swore under his breath. "Jeez, Wilbur, what's with you? You can't just disappear like that! Why didn't you answer my calls yesterday?"

Dunn leaned against a wall. "I needed some time, okay? Sorry I didn't get back to you."

"You can't do that! If you're going to work on my team, you gotta be committed."

"I am committed! There's nothing more I want than to find out what sickened our military personnel, and we just made a major breakthrough in that regard."

"What breakthrough are you referring to?"

"The pathologist on my staff, Krishna Bhatia, sent me an email moments ago saying that, while reviewing the tissues more closely, he discovered a virus."

"Which virus is it?"

"He doesn't know, but he says it's an unusual one given its exceptionally large size. He's working with virologists at Hopkins to identify it."

"It better not be mumps! We've told the world mumps isn't responsible for the illnesses."

"It's not; Bhatia said it's way too large to be mumps."

Fitzgerald moaned. "Still, this is bad. The last thing we need is a novel virus attacking our bases."

"I'll keep you posted," Dunn said, anxious to hang up.

"Please do, and in the meantime, I'll inform Ft. Detrick of what you told me. They have plenty of expertise in virology as well." Fitzgerald sighed. "Wilbur, if you can't make a call in the future, tell me in advance. Because of your absence yesterday, I'm going to keep the urologist from Walter Reed on the team. It won't hurt to have a backup given that we may be dealing with a new disease here."

TEN MINUTES BEFORE his eleven o'clock teleconference was to begin, Dunn slipped into an Irish pub in downtown Annapolis for a second dose of caffeine. Having examined the three hospitalized men along with nine others held in an outpatient quarantine house on the grounds of the Naval Academy, he was exhausted from lack of sleep. He drew comfort, however, from a text Fitzgerald had just sent stating no new cases of the testicular disease had been reported at either base or, for that matter, in the communities at-large. Reassuring as well was the discovery that three of the nine men in the quarantine house no longer had fever and reported less pain in their testicles. On the other hand, it concerned Dunn that the three hospitalized men continued to have scrotal swelling and redness, markers of ongoing testicular inflammation.

Nursing a cup of coffee, he huddled in a corner of the pub and dialed into the conference. Through ear plugs, he listened to the roll call, bristling when Vice President Atticus Quincy Thornbridge announced himself. It baffled him that the politician would join the call when he had no medical expertise to offer, an issue Fitzgerald addressed promptly by informing the group that the VP had requested to listen-in to keep the President abreast of developments.

Efficiently, team members shared their updates. Most notable were ones provided by the toxicologist and microbiologist. Each discussed laboratory assessments of remnants recovered from the reservoir of the drone felled over Walter Reed, results they'd learned just minutes before the call. The toxicologist reported that no chemicals, drugs, pesticides, or toxins had been detected, but the microbiologist declared an unusual organism had been identified in the drone's liquid remnants.

Heart pounding, Dunn asked: "What do you mean by 'unusual organism?' "

"My staff reported that amoebas were present in sediment in the drone's reservoir."

"*Amoebas*?" Dunn echoed.

"Yes, given their size, the microbes were recognized readily."

"What about other organisms?"

"Some bacteria as well," the microbiologist replied, "but initial tests indicate they aren't pathogens."

Fitzgerald: "Wilbur, this seems like the right time for you to share what you learned this morning."

"I was informed by a pathologist at Hopkins that he discovered a virus in the sperm-producing regions of the testicular tissue obtained from a Walter Reed soldier. They're trying to identify the virus as we speak."

"A pathologist found a virus?" the microbiologist asked. "How did he discover it?"

"He saw it under a light microscope."

"Impossible! Viruses are too small to be seen by light microscopy."

"Not this one; it's gigantic."

"Back up a moment," the NIH czar said. "At our first meeting, you said the men showed elevations in white blood counts, right?"

"Correct," Dunn replied.

"Did they display a lymphocytosis?"

"Hold on," Roger Able, the DoD press officer, interjected. "Define that term."

"Lymphocytes are a type of white blood cell," Dunn explained. "When the proportion they constitute of all white blood cells is abnormally high, we use the term 'lymphocytosis.' Viral infections often cause a lymphocytosis." He paused. "And, yes, the men did display elevated levels of lymphocytes."

Czar: "Very interesting; that's certainly consistent with a viral illness."

Next discussed was a report from the epidemiologist who confirmed the absence of new cases on the bases and elsewhere. "Specifically, we've seen no instances where ill men transmitted infection to others either before or after they sought medical attention, and that's reassuring. Nonetheless, we're following all individuals who had contact with the ill men to monitor their health, and we've begun drawing blood from these contacts and others—both men and women—who were outdoors on the bases at the time the drones were spotted. Given Dr. Dunn's report of a virus being identified in testicular tissue from one of the ill men, we need to evaluate very carefully whether the virus may have infected others without producing symptoms, and this applies to women, too. I'm not aware of any infectious disease that restricts itself to just one gender."

"So, what you're saying," a drawling voice interjected, "is we really don't know yet what the full picture is regarding transmissibility of this illness, yet Americans rightfully want to know whether they need to be concerned."

Fitzgerald responded to the Vice President. "Sir, we can cautiously reassure Americans that no transmission has been observed thus far from person-to-person. At the same time, we're taking precautions by keeping the ill men isolated until we know the true cause of the illness."

Dunn gritted his teeth. It wasn't just the Vice President's voice that unnerved him, but his need to leave for Rehoboth Beach, Delaware and the warning Irina had issued with her command that he get there by 3 p.m....

Be there alone or a plague of biblical proportions will follow.

FROM ANNE ARUNDEL Medical Center in Annapolis, it was a short jaunt to Route 50 east. Dunn knew the freeway well from previous trips he'd taken with Consuela each summer to a beach rental on Fenwick Island in Delaware. He preferred the spot over nearby Ocean City or Rehoboth Beach because of its relative tranquility, although given a choice, he'd spend vacations in the Rockies, Sierras, or Cascades. Consuela, on the other hand, enjoyed the sand, surf, and soft-serves of summertime because they reminded her of growing up in California.

Shortly after leaving Annapolis, Dunn crossed the Severn River. On his motorcycle, he caught glimpses of the water and its sylvan shoreline from the bridge, yet the sight of the Naval Academy downstream recalled the distressing scenes he'd seen on television of sniper fire picking off midshipmen as they tried to race for safety. After crossing the river, he considered taking the next exit to visit the promontory where the Khawad machine gun had been discovered, but a glance at his watch told him he needed to move on.

At the toll booth before the Chesapeake Bay Bridge, he was relieved to see no lines. Mounted along the approach, however, were electronic warnings of sustained winds of thirty miles per hour blowing across sections of the bridge, remnant winds from a recalcitrant hurricane which, while moving out to sea, still whipped the coast with residual fury. Dunn payed his toll and set off cautiously along the four-mile span but allowed himself occasional peeks of ships below.

Although the beach wasn't Dunn's thing, he was amazed by how crossing the Bay Bridge made him feel as if he were traveling between countries. From the urbanized, buzzing life on the west side, the ribbon of asphalt over the Bay carried one to a bucolic, slower-paced life of farmlands and small towns with antique shops and Kiwanis clubs which hosted chicken barbecues on weekends. Without Consuela at his side, however, he navigated lonely roads with a lump in his throat along fields of corn and soybeans, a lump which grew when he passed a favorite dairy of Consuela's that ran an ice cream stand they frequented each trip. Leaving it behind, he sped ahead as he inhaled aromas of manure and chicken coops before the air turned salty.

Each time Dunn approached the shore, he was thrown off by the strip malls which appeared. They lined the coastal thoroughfare outside beach hamlets with those of Rehoboth Beach sporting especially trendy brand name outlets. As always, he passed them with scorn, a man who, while too young to have experienced the days of old when family businesses reigned, longed for simpler times with more personal touch and less corporate veneer.

Although he'd visited Rehoboth Beach on occasion to walk its boardwalk and play the arcades, he had to consult his GPS to determine where the marina was located. After crossing a canal at the outskirts of town, he left the main artery for a side road that took him past a cemetery into surprisingly woodsy neighborhoods. Another turn led him into what felt like a gated community, only there was no gate but, instead, a stone sign reading, *Henlopen Acres.* Entering the area, he found himself surrounded by affluence as he passed multi-million dollar homes where Mercedes, Jaguars, and other expensive cars lined the driveways. This was old money, the kind passed through generations which respected tradition; here there were no roughshod condos or makeshift rentals, no sloppy convenience stores or nickel-and-dime trinket shops. Rather, holding sway were elegance, suavity, and unpretentious grandeur, a place where a passing motorcycle's engine might stir an "ahem" from residents inside mini-palaces.

Dunn knew he was close to his destination when he passed a landmark labeled *Henlopen Art League* on his right. Just beyond it, on the opposite side, he found the object of his search, a cozy, rustic marina with cabin cruisers, yachts, and motorboats. It was nestled in wetlands amongst cattails through which a canal meandered to the sea, although from where Dunn stopped, he couldn't see the ocean itself. Rimming the wetlands were mammoth homes which stood on stilts with balconies overlooking saltmarshes above which pelicans flew.

The parking area was a small gravel lot with spaces for roughly two dozen vehicles, although not a single car was present. Here, Dunn presumed, one walked or bicycled from home to vessel. Sitting along the entrance to the pier was a quaint cabin which functioned as an office, so Dunn left his motorcycle to see if it was attended. He found the place shuttered in line with the rest of the marina where mainsails were covered and flybridges sealed. With a hurricane having knocked on the coast's door, boat owners had battened down the hatches, and it appeared no one was ready to emerge.

Since he'd arrived eight minutes before the appointed time, he walked along the pier to search for signs of human activity but found none. In its place, he listened to cattails rustle, water lap, and hulls creak. If a marina could be a desert, he thought, this was one, which led him to wonder if he'd been duped by a deranged woman who'd seen him on television, discovered where he lived, and delivered a mobile to a park near his condo as a means of keeping him tethered. But why she'd want to do so was a mystery, especially given her choice of leaving a satellite phone. With his watch now registering 3:02 p.m., two minutes beyond the deadline, he concluded he'd been deceived and vowed to remain only three more minutes.

Standing near the pier's end overlooking the canal, he heard the hum of a motor. It came from an area where the canal turned through the marsh on its way to the sea. With time, the hum grew louder before a dinghy appeared. It was steered by a solo operator sitting before a motor. With the craft some seventy yards away, all Dunn could see was a torso and head, the two seemingly fused by what appeared to be a neck cape cap whose flaps blew in the wind. As the dinghy approached, more details emerged, including the presence of a scarf of some kind beneath the skipper's cap yet visible above the top of a life jacket. It wasn't until the vessel was in shouting range that Dunn was sure it was a woman who steered the craft. He watched her glide in a smooth curve to the pier's end where she halted with a reverse thrust.

As the tide was low, the woman sat some four feet beneath the pier, her attention focused on the shore. "You are Wilbur Dunn," she said. "I know it is so."

Dunn recognized the voice from the call he'd received two days earlier, but it wasn't the words which lured him so much as the scarf beneath the woman's cap. Its red and white checkers were identical to those on the headdress the presenter had displayed at the Pentagon briefing—a "shemagh" as it was called. In the wind, its tassels gyrated, but not nearly as much as Dunn's wits.

II

"SIT," THE WOMAN said. "We must talk."

Lowering himself to the pier, Dunn dangled his legs over the dinghy. It allowed him to look more closely at the woman who remained seated, and only then did he note her blue eyes and olive skin. "Who *are* you?" he asked.

"You saw my name in the texts."

"I did, yes... Irina, but you provided no last name."

She raised herself to scan the marina and parking lot. "Are you alone?"

"Yes, and you?"

"Does it look otherwise?"

Dunn eyed the canal. "How do I know you haven't left others around the bend?"

"No one is there," she insisted, glancing at the sky. "I am always alone."

"Do you live here?"

"No, I come from afar."

"Where's 'afar'?"

She became agitated. "It is not safe to talk here!" She gripped a post to steady the dinghy and ordered Dunn into it.

"Not a chance!" he volleyed. "It's *you* who needs to come with me because if you have details about the shootings and illnesses as you claim, you must share them with my colleagues."

The woman scoffed and removed her cap and shemagh to unleash a torrent of dark brown hair. "They are not your 'colleagues'! They are not even your people!"

Dunn stood and glared at her. "Who are you to tell me who my 'people' are? You know nothing about me!"

"Do not shout!" the woman said, looking about anxiously. She folded the shemagh and slipped it beneath the seat before replacing her cap. While doing so, the dinghy inched away from the pier. "I have given you the opportunity to learn from me," she said, "but it is your choice whether to accept it or to remain in the dark."

"We won't remain in the dark," Dunn countered. "We'll capture those who attacked us."

She lowered her eyes. "I hope you do, but that will be difficult."

"Less so if you help us. When you called me, you said you could explain the events of the last few days." Dunn pointed to the shemagh beneath the seat. "Since you dress like the people who attacked us, I'll take you for your word."

"How do you know what your attackers wore?"

"We found a shemagh just like yours along with a Khawad machine gun at the attack site in Annapolis."

"*We*?" she jeered. "There you go, again! You have been brainwashed."

From his pocket, Dunn removed the Turkish mobile and waved it at her. "You were foolish to give me this. We'll mine it to reveal your identity."

"Do it, then! Abandon your roots."

"What's that supposed to mean?"

"Come and I will show you."

Incensed, Dunn weighed the pros and cons of accepting her offer. To his dismay, the pros came readily, as in his desire to learn how she knew the soldiers would become infertile and what she'd meant when she spoke of a "plague of biblical proportions."

"I'm not going with you," he declared.

Lifting her eyes to the sky, Irina said nothing as her hair blew across her face. "I will leave, then, but first I must give you something." She reached under the seat for a small cardboard box which she offered Dunn.

"What's in it?" he asked.

"Something that belongs to you."

Warily, Dunn stooped and, leaning over the pier, took the box. It was small enough to cup in a palm yet large enough for Dunn to see Arabic print along it sides. Gently, he removed the lid, unfolded the wrapping paper, and flinched at its contents. "Where did you get this?" he asked, face ashen.

"Come and you shall learn."

Dunn grazed a fingertip along a child's moccasin, one whose tongue had tiny beads sewn into it in the shape of a flower with blue petals and a red pistil while, along the toe cap, its creator had dyed the hide to depict a series of black crests above turquoise and orange slopes resembling mountains. A lace, broken at one point but now tied in a knot, ran through three eyelets along each side of the vamp. "I wore the partner to this moccasin as a child," he volunteered, voice cracking. "I always wondered where the other one went."

"Well, now you have the partner to keep."

"But, where did you get it?"

Irina tapped the seat beside her. "Come, we travel the same circle of life."

Haltingly, Dunn lifted the moccasin's tongue and, craning his neck, studied its undersurface. "Oh, Lord!" he moaned. "It *is* the missing one; the lettering proves it." In his hand, the moccasin felt so small yet carried a weight which tugged at his soul. After peering at it again, he gently returned it to the box, replaced the lid, and lowered himself into the dinghy.

THE WIND FROM the west was brisk enough to whip the cattails sideways, forcing the woman Dunn knew only as Irina to concentrate to keep the dinghy in the center of the canal. To do so, she steered the bow at an angle into the wind to prevent the inflatable from blowing into the reeds.

Although the gusts on the Bay Bridge had tested Dunn's patience as a motorcyclist, they hadn't unnerved him as they did now. Feeling the dinghy might flip at any time, he tightened his life jacket. "Where are we going?" he called.

"To the tri," Irina replied.

" 'Tri?' "

"Trimaran."

"Where is it?"

"At sea."

"How far out?"

"A bit."

Even though he acknowledged her need to concentrate, Dunn found her curtness annoying. "And once we reach the tri, then what?"

"We set sail."

"For where?"

"Afar."

Afar…a bit… He wanted to clutch her answers and stretch them as one pulled taffy. Castigating himself for permitting his emotions to lead him into the dinghy, he resented succumbing to a tiny moccasin simply because it held three letters that, when combined with four more embroidered into the moccasin he'd worn as a child, formed a meaningful Paiute word. He worried that a reference he'd made long ago in a blog post about his lost child's moccasin had made him vulnerable, and the prospect of becoming a hostage became more real as he glanced at the shemagh along the dinghy floor.

"That word, 'afar,'" he said, "you used it before to describe where you came from."

"True."

Yet another four-letter word. "Look, I want to know where we're going!" he demanded. "And, yes, I'm shouting because I won't be taken hostage!"

Even with a visor angled over her brows, Irina's frown was visible. "You are not a hostage!"

It brought Dunn comfort to leave the reeds and approach the town of Lewes just north of Rehoboth Beach. Although he'd never been there before, he knew it was home to a ferry that crossed the Delaware Bay to Cape May in New Jersey. Peering at an approaching bridge, he saw a sign for motorists to turn right to access the terminal's loading bay. Shortly later, they came to private homes and then commercial developments—Fisherman's Wharf, Irish Eyes Pub & Restaurant, and Lewes Dairy. The comfort of civilization was fleeting, however, because after motoring beyond a yacht club they reached an opening to the Delaware Bay which for boat enthusiasts was a gateway to the Atlantic but for Dunn a point of no return.

"Where's the trimaran?" he asked.

Irina's arm went up. "Beyond the bay."

For the elaborate response, Dunn was grateful, but amongst the towering swells they encountered his fear of flipping intensified.

While the ride along the canal had been bumpy, the heaves and drops he faced now in open waters churned his innards.

"Cape Henlopen State Park," Irina announced, pointing across the bay. "You will see the tri after we round the point."

A sandy spit formed the cape's point, one Irina skirted to avoid its treacherous currents. With the Atlantic appearing like a stage behind an opening curtain, Dunn peered longingly around the passing point to an uninterrupted line of sand stretching toward Rehoboth Beach. He longed for the power to walk on water so he could sink his feet in the sand, but as it was, the beach faded from view. Forlorn, he turned toward the sea where a three-hulled vessel came to view. "The trimaran!" he exclaimed.

It was a vessel unlike any he'd seen, not only because of its third hull but also because of its spacey, futuristic design. "It looks fast," he observed.

"Very fast; it will take us to the Azores in just over three days."

Dunn pivoted. "Did you say 'Azores'?"

"Yes."

"But, they're across the Atlantic!"

"Some two thousand miles away."

"Why would we go there?"

"I was instructed to take you there."

"By whom?"

"My brothers."

Exasperated, Dunn raised his arms to protest but quickly grabbed the dinghy's side with a passing swell.

"Be careful!" Irina cried. "You have already cost us time by traveling to Wyoming. Do not make me rescue you from the sea!"

Dunn vented his anger by squeezing the edge of the seat, but as they approached the trimaran, his attention turned to a name inscribed along its stern. "Am I seeing correctly?" he asked. "It reads *Ba'wă*."

"Yes," she replied. "Do you know the word?"

"Of course! It means *circle maker* in Paiute."

Irina nodded. "Yes, very apt for the journey you're about to begin."

TO APPROACH THE trimaran, Irina steered the dinghy toward the stern with exceeding care to keep from being overturned by swells. After providing Dunn with an exit strategy, she inched toward an aluminum ladder at the end of the center hull. Timing the ups and downs, she then juiced the throttle just enough to allow Dunn to grasp the ladder rungs and pull himself onto it.

From there, he crawled to a gunwale along the stern and scaled it to reach the main deck. The cockpit he stood on was elliptical and roughly twenty feet across. Along its fore section were two ship's wheels, one port and another starboard while capstans, controls, and instruments occupied the area between them under a streamlined cover that shielded the helm from the sun. Looking ahead, he saw a towering mast in the middle of the center hull which was bordered on each side by crossbeams that stretched to outrigger hulls with netting between them. In all, he estimated the tri to be a hundred feet long by seventy wide, by far the largest sailboat he'd been on.

Moving to port, he caught a rope which Irina threw to him from the dinghy. While tying it to a cleat, he watched her slip out of the inflatable onto the center hull which she traversed to retrieve the aluminum ladder.

"Go inside," she told him when she reached the cockpit.

As he descended a ladder into the interior of the center hull, he stole a glimpse of Irina working a winch to raise the dinghy. At the ladder's base, he opened a sliding door to enter an austere saloon holding a carbon fiber table and six Spartan seats.

Looking about, his eyes settled on two framed photos on a wall. Both were large by most standards, or perhaps it was their contents which enlarged them. One showed the trimaran sitting on a transporter inside an immense hangar. Dunn presumed the photo had been taken the day the trimaran began its journey overland for a christening at sea, but in its terrestrial pose, the vessel's central hull and winged outriggers made it look like a beastly creature from dinosaur days about to take flight. A placard below the photo read, *Baʻwă—circle maker.*

Shifting to the second photo, Dunn's stomach twisted. It depicted a hooded man lying face-up on a metal bench bare-chested with arms and feet shackled. From above, water flowed from a bucket onto a face covered by a towel while beneath the photo another placard cried out, *No justice in lines, only in circles.*

While Dunn studied the photos, he felt a sense of motion, but he attributed it to queasiness engendered by the second photo. Turning, he looked through a porthole and noticed an outrigger hull cutting through the ocean with a ribbon of whitewater behind it. He realized then there was a heel to the tri, one that required him to climb a gradient to the opposite side where he peered through another porthole which showed the second outrigger suspended some eight feet over the water like an airborne missile while, behind it in the distance, the coast faded.

Feeling trapped, he extracted his iPhone, but when he dialed 9-1-1, the call failed. "*No!*" he cried. A similar failure occurred when he repeated the maneuver with the Turkish satphone. Enraged, he threw the device to the floor where it shattered. "Get me out of here!" he shrieked, stomping his boot on the satphone remnants.

In short order Irina appeared wearing a helmet and vest with buckles for holding life lines. "What are you doing?" she screeched.

Dunn stormed across the saloon, clasped her by the arms, and threw her to the floor. Pointing to the photo, he wailed, "You plan to have me waterboarded, don't you?"

Although the helmet had dampened the force with which Irina struck her head, she managed to stand and stumble to the galley where she brandished a knife. "Touch me again, and I will kill you!" This time, it was she who pointed to the photo, holding the knife toward it. "Do you know who he is?" she blurted.

"How could I? A towel blocks the face!" The prospect of being tortured in similar fashion buckled Dunn's knees, dropping him to the deck.

In the galley, Irina set the knife on the counter and stepped forward. "Get up and have courage."

"Courage? You're not the one held hostage!"

"I told you before, you are not a hostage. You chose to come with me."

Dunn reached into his pocket and extracted the moccasin. "How did you get this?"

"My father asked me to give it to you."

"Who's your father?"

She pointed to the wall. "The man being waterboarded. God willing, you will meet him soon."

Dunn glared at the photo. "*That's* your father?"

"Yes."

"Why was he tortured?"

"He will explain the reason to you. In the meantime, you must determine what caused the men at the military bases to become ill."

"Don't play with me! You said earlier you could explain the events of the past few days."

"Only in general terms," she rejoined. "*You* need to figure out the details."

Dunn glowered. "You said the men would become infertile. How did you know that?"

"My oldest brother, the radicalized one, told me. He flew the drones over the bases to release a mist that contained an agent he claimed would cause men to become infertile."

"What was the agent?"

"I do not know."

"Was he responsible for the shootings, too?"

"Yes. He used remote control technology to fire Khawad machine guns."

"Where was he when he did that?"

She stirred. "Here on the trimaran."

Welling with anger, Dunn erupted: "That makes you an accomplice!"

Tears welled in her eyes. "I know I may go to hell for allowing him to launch the attacks from here, but I had no choice because he threatened to kill you if I banished him from the tri."

Dunn approached her. "He threatened to kill *me*?"

She nodded.

"But, I don't know him!"

"He knows of you, however, because my father told him you are one of a few people with sufficient knowledge to prevent a more serious attack with the agent he released from the drones. And then after learning you had been recruited to investigate the illnesses, he doubled his efforts to find you. That's why I rushed to contact you."

Agitated, Dunn looked about the saloon. "Where is he now?"

"Most likely in Baltimore looking for you; that is why I called you. I did not want him to succeed."

Dunn's face whitened. "So, *he* was the one who tried to break into my condo."

Irina stepped forward and cupped Dunn's elbow. "You are safe here. We have left him behind."

"Does he know we're together?"

"No! I said nothing about contacting you because he would be enraged if he knew I had come for you."

Dunn narrowed his eyes. "Did you bring him to the U.S.?"

"Against my will, yes." Her shoulders sagged. "He extracts a large toll from those who do not cooperate with him."

"Where did you sail from?"

"North Africa."

"With Khawads, drones, and an agent to sicken the men?"

"Yes," she whimpered, turning to go.

Dunn seized her arm. "Wait, you mentioned your father knew who I was. How can that be?"

"Do not be naïve! You have a large presence online."

Dunn shuffled. "If you're referring to my blog, I stopped posting seven months ago."

"I know. I read your final post and was moved to tears by the grief you expressed for Consuela's death." She watched Dunn lower his eyes. "I also read many of your earlier posts regarding your views on political and scientific matters pertaining to Native Americans. You are well known for your stands."

Dunn looked up. "Why did you read my posts?"

"My father cares for the topic of justice which you discussed at length. He told me about your blog, and from your posts I discovered what you did and where you lived." She pointed to the photo as a tear rolled down her cheek. "I am very close to my father because he taught me how to sail. I am training now to break the single-handed round-the-globe sailing record." She glanced at the ceiling. "And with all the hurricanes about, the winds are phenomenal."

"When did you get to the U.S.?"

"Eight days ago."

"Where did you moor?"

"All about, but mostly at sea to keep from being seen. When my brother disembarked, he did so at night with his supplies."

"Did you help him set up the drones and machine guns?"

"Of course not! I would rather have died than do so!"

"But he couldn't have managed alone. Who helped him?"

"A young man who recently became radicalized in the U.S."

"And after setting up his supplies, your brother returned to the tri to launch the attacks?"

"Yes, and after doing so, he set out to find you before we were to sail back to North Africa."

Dunn rippled his forehead. "Earlier, while riding in the dinghy, you spoke of your *brothers*. How many do you have, and whose side are they on—yours or your oldest brother?"

"I have two brothers in addition to my oldest one, and they side with me. They deplore what my oldest brother did in your country!"

"Where are the younger brothers?"

"In North Africa."

Dunn shuddered anew at the connection to North Africa. From the Pentagon briefing came news that the Khawads had originated from Sudan, the bullets from Chad, a webcam from Libya, and the drone's motor from Saudi Arabia. Now a family from North Africa was drawing him closer to the continent. "Are you being honest about your younger brothers disapproving of what your oldest one did?"

"Completely honest! You must believe me; they are good men."

"So, why do they want me to go to the Azores?"

"Because, we have a plan for how you can prevent my radicalized brother from causing further harm."

"What harm are you speaking of?"

Her face hardened. "One involving damage of biblical proportions."

"There you go again! You've said that several times. What do you mean by it?"

Irina walked to a porthole and looked through it. "The winds from Hurricane Stanley are strengthening, and I must tend to the tri."

12

THE TRI'S NAVIGATION cabin was wedged deep within the central hull between the galley and sleeping quarters. Dunn sat in its cramped confines before a desk which held a laptop pushed to one side by a heap of logbooks and magazines with pages curled from humidity. On a world map tacked to the wall above the desk, red ink spanned the globe along its oceans as bold letters proclaimed, *Irina Mostafa—proposed solo circumnavigation route.*

Dunn drilled his eyes into the laptop which only moments earlier he'd discovered allowed Internet satellite access without the need for a password. Having destroyed the Turkish satphone Irina gave him, he considered the find a treasure trove.

Checking his email, he encountered a lengthy queue awaiting him. Among the emails was one from Krishna Bhatia with a subject line, *Bigfoot…*

> *Wilbur,*
>
> *Initial results indicate the large virus in the soldier's testicles belongs to a family of viruses called* Megaviridae, *or megavirus. While researchers have reported megavirus causing pneumonia, there are no reports of human testicular infection. I call the virus Bigfoot because on electron microscopy it looks like a fat footprint…*

Chest pounding, Dunn searched the Internet for details about a virus he'd never heard of. He had no difficulty finding information about it, including a report stating the virus was discovered in 1992 in water extracted from an air conditioning system in England during an outbreak of pneumonia caused by the virus. At the time, investigators concluded the organism was a bacterium because it mimicked one on Gram stain, but eleven years later the microbe was revealed to be a giant virus that exceeded the size of some bacteria and possessed a genome larger than any other known virus. Over time, additional megaviruses were recovered from water and marine zooplankton which shared architectural features, the presence of roughly 50 ancestral genes coding for key functions, and an ability to reproduce within hosts without hijacking the latter's cellular equipment.

"*What*?" Dunn said after reading a statement that set him on edge. He re-read it to make sure his eyes hadn't deceived him…

Megaviruses often reside and multiply in amoebas, and for that reason, researchers use amoebas to cultivate the viruses.

"*Amoebas!*" he muttered. The word taunted him as he recalled the microbiologist on Fitzgerald's team announcing amoebas had been found in sediment from the drone's reservoir. He fired off an email to the team to report Bhatia's identification of the virus and to implore the microbiologist to look for giant viruses in the amoebas.

Leaning back, he glanced at the map above the desk only to notice a shaded gray bar he hadn't seen before. It ran across the globe exactly along the thirty-seventh and thirty-eighth parallels north, a bar which transected the U.S., the Mediterranean and tip of North Africa, sections of Greece and Turkey, and parts of Pakistan, China, and South Korea. Of concern were two red pins placed side-by-side within the bar to demark Bethesda and Annapolis in Maryland. He cursed loudly.

After a few moments, Irina appeared at the doorway with her helmet on. "I hear everything you say, you realize."

Dunn looked about the cabin. "Have you bugged the place?"

She pointed to a black dot on the ceiling. "There are microphones throughout the tri which transmit to speakers in my helmet. The system allows crew members to communicate."

"Then remove your helmet if you don't want to hear me."

She glowered. "It would not be safe to remove my helmet while I am on deck."

Dunn studied the woman. She wasn't tall—five feet five, he guessed—but she had a commanding presence. Had she worn a fire suit rather than waterproof gear, she would've resembled a NASCAR racer. "Let me ask you something," he said, pointing to the map. "Why are the 37th and 38th parallels north shaded across the globe?"

"To symbolize lines of injustice," she replied.

"I don't understand."

She leaned over the desk and ran a finger along the shading. "Justice systems which permit torture provide no justice at all."

Still unclear as to how latitudes pertained to justice, Dunn switched gears: "What about the pins? Why are they placed over the military bases your brother attacked?"

"Because they fall on a line my oldest brother calls a 'latitude of revenge.' "

Dunn examined the pins more closely to confirm their position along the 38th parallel north. "That's it!" he blurted. "Your brother shot a total of thirty-eight people at the two bases and allowed thirty-eight minutes to elapse between firing the last bullet in Bethesda and the first in Annapolis to symbolize the 38th parallel, didn't he?"

"Yes, it was a key element of his latitude revenge." She furled her brows. "What does the Bible say—*Eye for eye, tooth for tooth, hand for hand, foot for foot,* ...?" She paused. "Is the world a better place because of those words?"

"I'm not a prophet," Dunn replied.

"Then, become one because the question of justice will confront you as you travel the circle of life."

WITH THE OCEAN glowing from a setting sun, two streaks trailed the trimaran like ribbons on fire, one from an outrigger and a second, more subdued one from a keel which lifted the center hull above the sea. Standing at the helm, Irina Mostafa conveyed a commanding presence over the vessel. Like a trim jockey atop a thoroughbred, she left no doubt as to who controlled every facet of the race.

She afforded only a glance at Dunn when he joined her on the cockpit. "Tether yourself with the rope," she told him. "I'm not turning back for man-overboard."

Dunn secured a line to the vest Irina gave him earlier. Looking over the gunwale, he said, "We're literally flying over the water."

The sight of the ocean passing so quickly made him retreat to the vessel's center.

"With the right timing, you can harness a hurricane's winds," Irina said.

Dunn tugged his line to ensure it was tight. "Do you make it a habit to ride hurricane coattails?"

"I harness the winds as they come."

Dunn looked at the sails. Each stretched over a hundred feet and was aligned to capture the wind with precision. Had it not been for the ocean, he would've thought he was on an airplane because the sails looked like wings. While working in the navigation room, he'd noticed a manual which described the sails as grids of carbon yarns laminated between layers of film of a type used to toughen plastic, all of that coated by a lustrous synthetic fabric to yield a turbo-charged sail. "I assume these are Hurricane Stanley winds," he said.

"Yes, wrap-around winds."

"I've never seen a season with so many hurricanes."

"With more to come, and that worries me."

"Why? You harness them for speed."

"But every storm is a blade with two edges: power and destruction." She pointed to the ladder which dropped to the cabins. "So, go back to work because you may see the destructive side of a storm to come."

"No," Dunn replied, "I'm not going until you explain yourself!" He stepped closer to her. "You refer to ominous things like a 'plague of biblical proportions' and now to an impending storm, but you provide no specifics."

Irina shifted her hands to the top of the wheel, pulled her shoulders in, and dropped her head like a turtle retracting into a shell.

Dunn glared at her in silence before retreating. Upon reaching the navigation cabin, he found an email from Garrett Fitzgerald…

Wilbur,

What in God's name have you done? Vice President Atticus Quincy Thornbridge just called to say he'd heard from national security folks that a motorcycle belonging to you was found at a marina in Rehoboth Beach, Delaware. While that alone makes me wonder where you are, it's what the VP told me next that blows my mind: He said the email you just sent to our investigative team about the need to look for a virus in the amoebas came from the very same computer the sniper used to fire Khawads and fly drones. Tell me that's not so!

Dunn pounded the desk and berated himself for being so careless as to use a laptop on the tri after learning from Irina that her brother had launched the attacks from the vessel. He grasped it to throw it against the wall but refrained from doing so since the damage had already been done: He was sure IT experts who'd identified the IP address using data gleaned from webcams at the shooting sites or from communication equipment in the felled drone had everything they needed to frame him as an accomplice.

Defiantly, he set the laptop down and remained online to read more about megaviruses, learning of their resistance to heat, ultraviolet light, and environmental extremes, all of this convincing him that megavirus released from a drone could have survived to infect humans on the ground below to yield a testicular infection unlike any he'd seen before.

He composed a response to Fitzgerald…

For the moment, forget about my motorcycle and laptop. Just tell me one thing: Were giant viruses present in the drone reservoir?

IF THE ADAGE, *You are what you eat*, held true, Dunn believed Irina Mostafa was a woman of simplicity. Among the plastic bins she stocked in the galley were fresh fruits and vegetables, whole grains, and dried beans of various types. That wasn't to say her cuisine was boring: An expansive rack running from one end of the galley to the other held an array of spices and herbs, each labeled neatly, and it piqued Dunn's curiosity to find that many labels were printed in foreign languages, some with lettering he didn't recognize.

But one bin complicated the profile of simplicity. It held dehydrated ingredients packed in aluminum pouches which resembled meal rations used by astronauts and soldiers, only here, they contained not meals but single ingredients—yucca, plantain, cassava, ground maize, and other items which Dunn associated with diets in less affluent nations.

With his stomach grumbling, he selected three constituents for a make-shift dinner: corn, squash, and lentils. To his delight, the corn was on the cob although its husks suggested it had been picked days earlier from a harvest site across the Atlantic. Nonetheless, he shucked two ears and began steaming them while he prepared a dish from dehydrated squash and lentils. When everything was ready, he served a plate for Irina and started for the helm, but with only one hand free, it was a challenge to scale the ladder.

Because he saw no sign of his partner on the cockpit, he moved to a gunwale and looked fore prior to moving to the opposite side to continue his search. In the falling darkness, he noticed a bright light appear on netting that stretched between crossbeams connecting the center hull to an elevated outrigger. A closer inspection revealed the light came from an LED mounted to Irina's helmet, and he watched it move along the netting toward the outrigger. In a moment, a glow fell over the tri as the moon burst forth from a cloud, allowing Dunn to watch his skipper maneuver in silvery outlines.

Unsettled by the juxtaposition of night and ocean, he slipped the dinner plate into a slot beside a cup holder and locked it into place with a swiveling brace. He then retreated to the galley where he dished himself what remained of dinner and ate it rapidly in order to return to work.

Sitting before the laptop again, he went online to search for insight into the workings of a vindictive mind. It was one thing, he thought, for Vice President Atticus Quincy Thornbridge to feel aggrieved for losing a beloved godson in a freak accident in Idaho, yet another to use his political rank to interfere in legal proceedings stemming from the accident. Of particular concern to Dunn was Thornbridge's pressuring of the court to subject him to a multi-year surveillance program overseen by a probation officer. Although the judge instituted a far shorter monitoring requirement due to expire shortly, Dunn was convinced the Vice President had taken matters into his own hands by implementing a surveillance program of his own, one that entailed meddling in the investigation of illnesses at the bases and relaying to Fitzgerald discoveries by others that Dunn had abandoned a motorcycle in Delaware and used a terrorist's laptop to send personal emails.

Thus, only one option remained as far as Dunn was concerned: Launch a counteroffensive against the Vice President even if it required running it on a killer's laptop.

13

DAWN ARRIVED IN the form of a lightening of the porthole beside Dunn's head. Through the night, he'd glanced at it repeatedly with each awakening only to find it dark, but now with a new day beginning, he looked about for Irina but saw no sign of her. Shortly after retiring the previous night, he'd heard her enter the galley to brew a pot of coffee, but as to whether she'd slept at all he hadn't a clue.

Sitting up, he bumped his head against the bunk above his, one of a dozen in the sleeping quarters beyond the navigation cabin. It was a short commute to the laptop he'd abandoned the night before, but before setting out to work, he noticed the map on the wall held three additional pins—a blue one with a tag reading *Present location* some five hundred miles off the U.S. coast; a yellow one far to the east over western Turkey; and, to his chagrin, a green one piercing western Nevada to demark the Walker River Reservation. Eerily, all of the pins occupied locations within the 37th and 38th parallels north.

Turning his attention to the laptop, he found an email from Krishna Bhatia urging him to phone immediately, but lacking the means to do so, he emailed his colleague: *Are you online?*

A response followed…

Why aren't you answering your phone? I called several times last night and again this morning! We need to talk!

Dunn sensed the presence of national security moles in the U.S. watching every stroke he made, but he continued nonetheless…

Phone not working… use email for now.

Bhatia:

Based on early results of testing PFC Hartley's megavirus, we've determined it's a strain of virus that hasn't been described before. We're growing more viruses in amoebas to examine the viral proteins and genes in detail.

In his readings, Dunn had learned that over the millennia megaviruses were thought to have worked like miniature vacuum cleaners, usurping genetic material from other microbes. While such genetic robberies were common among bacteria, viruses, and parasites, megaviruses set themselves apart by the magnitude of their thievery. Simplistically, he viewed their fat bodies as byproducts of gluttonous genetic hoarding.

His response…

What have you learned so far about the virus?

Bhatia:

Something most interesting: At least two proteins in its outer membrane are remarkably similar, but not identical, to ones in paramyxoviruses.

Dunn shuddered because paramyxoviruses comprised an entirely distinct group of viruses that had bedeviled humans for centuries. Among them were measles virus and mumps virus, the latter a nemesis to human testes. He took to the keyboard…

Be more specific! What paramyxovirus proteins?

Bhatia:

Attachment and fusion proteins.

Dunn was familiar with the proteins from previous research. Paramyxoviruses used them to initiate infections by attaching to and then fusing with cells that lined the human respiratory tract, and from there they entered the bloodstream to spread through the body. He was about to reply but didn't because Bhatia sent a new email…

Of more concern is that a closer examination of the pathology slides from PFC Hartley indicates megavirus invaded his Sertoli cells.

Dunn bolted backwards, knocking over his chair. Pacing the cabin, he repeated the word, *invaded...invaded...invaded.* The concept of his beloved Christmas tree-shaped Sertoli cells in the human testis being penetrated by a microbe astounded him because he knew of no pathogen that did that, not even mumps virus. For sure, mumps virus raided the testes where it disrupted sperm-producing areas, but it didn't invade Sertoli cells which remained intact through the infectious and recovery stages of mumps infections.

A glance at the screen showed another missive from Bhatia...

Gotta run. Trying to figure out how megavirus invades Sertolis.

THE HEAD ACROSS the hall from the navigation cabin was a cramped space that held a toilet, sink, and shower, and as he peed, Dunn peeked out a porthole at swells racing by like sine waves beneath an airborne outrigger. To direct his stream, he gripped the edge of the sink to keep his balance.

After retrieving a cup of freshly brewed coffee from the galley, he returned to the navigation cabin to resume the counteroffensive against Atticus Quincy Thornbridge. It was a two-pronged offensive he planned to undertake, one that called first to learn what he could about the Vice President's upbringing and years as a young adult, and a second to focus on Thornbridge's political career.

Of special interest to Dunn were hints of discrimination Thornbridge had shown against others of differing race, creed, or religion. Because the VP had professed abhorrence for illegal immigrants, Dunn suspected his hatred extended to Native Americans, and that pained him because while growing up his mother had taught him that people were equal regardless of background and that skin color, religion, or heritage didn't define a person so much as heart and soul. Moreover, she insisted that Spirit which ran through each of us endowed the land with amber waves of grain, purple mountain majesties, and plains—like those about the reservation—with rocks of brown, beige, and rust.

It was from his mother that Dunn acquired a passion for fairness, so much so he began blogging in college about justice in the context of current events. His views sparked heated debate, such as when he implored protestors to use nonviolent means to express opposition to a bronze statue of William McKinley in a coastal northern California town. To those who viewed the former President of the United States as an oppressor of Native peoples, Dunn's call for nonviolence was an abdication of his Native American heritage. In contrast, he was applauded after being arrested for demonstrating peacefully against the dismantling of a revered monument in South Dakota.

Following his conviction for involuntary manslaughter and trespassing in Idaho eight months earlier, Dunn ceased blogging because he felt he'd committed the mother of all injustices: taking the life of two people—his wife's and that of a truck driver—by selfishly pursuing a shortcut through a national forest.

But now, culling the Internet, he resumed what he viewed was a renewed quest for justice. He learned Atticus Quincy Thornbridge was the oldest of five children born to a Mississippi cotton farmer, that he was reared with privilege and discipline, attended parochial schools, earned Eagle rank as a Boy Scout, and attended church each Sunday. Yet from the surrounding cotton fields came blemishes akin to rusts and smuts, especially during Thornbridge's college years: a broken jaw from a brawl at a football game; allegations of cheating on exams; and charges, eventually dropped, of date-rape alleging Thornbridge had placed a hand over his victim's mouth to keep her from screaming only to have half his pinkie bitten off. Overall, however, Thornbridge's digital footprint was positive, particularly with respect to what one writer called his "reformation after college." With an eye on entering politics, he became a police officer, an alderman, and then a state legislator before serving in Washington as a Congressman, but after being defeated following his fourth term, he left politics to work at the CIA.

Not surprisingly, Dunn found little about Thornbridge's CIA career, but whatever he did during his six years of duty there, it provided him with sufficient heft to regain a spot in Congress. As a junior Senator from Mississippi, he rose quickly through the ranks of the Senate Intelligence Committee with a reputation for being a hawk, unlike any, when it came to hunting down perpetrators of 9/11/2001.

Of most interest to Dunn was Thornbridge's leadership in establishing the Guantánamo detention camp at the U.S. naval base in Cuba, or *Gitmo* as it was known. With a U.S. President unwilling to blemish 1700 Pennsylvania Avenue with unsavory details of a military prison built to incarcerate terrorists, Thornbridge assumed the role of Proponent-in-Chief. Among his top priorities was to stock the prison with enemies of America, and he did so by aggressively rounding up suspected terrorists flown to secret interrogation prisons outside the U.S., or "black sites," where they were tortured. Years later, when a real estate magnate ran for President, Thornbridge accepted the tycoon's offer to join the ticket. The pair swept into office with what they claimed was a mandate for law, order, and immigration reform.

Yet, from all Dunn learned about the Vice President, two items struck him in particular. One was a cryptic, single-paragraph clip about a hospitalization Thornbridge had undergone as a Senator. According to the story, Thornbridge experienced a life-threatening allergic reaction to an ingredient of a barbecue sauce he'd eaten at a Texas-style rib feast thrown for military brass in Merced, California. Despite canvassing the Web for more details, Dunn found none, but that didn't surprise him given the nature of the soirée and the Senator's penchant for secrecy. Nonetheless, the hospitalization intrigued Dunn because it occurred at a medical center where he'd spent a month as a urology resident while training in urology in California. Dunn traveled to Merced from San Francisco as part of an exchange program for residents, and while he was in Merced, he became good friends with the hospital's director of urology, a man he kept in touch with as years passed.

The second item which struck Dunn was more personal. It related to the VP's passion for visiting Idaho where he went fly fishing with a beloved godson. Although the godson wasn't identified, Dunn knew it was the truck driver he'd killed in Sawtooth National Forest because during the court trial the man's weeping widow had described her deceased mate's love for fly fishing with his godfather, the Vice President of the United States. During trips to Snake River, the two reportedly spent their days fishing before grilling trout for dinner.

On a whim, Dunn whisked an email to the urology director at the hospital in Merced. It was largely a greeting but one that also contained a request: Would his friend check a medical record generated years earlier from a visit by a U.S. Senator named Atticus Quincy Thornbridge? Specifically, did the medical record specify which ingredient in the barbecue sauce caused the near-fatal reaction? It was just curiosity that led him to ask, Dunn explained, one based on recent interactions he'd had with the nation's VP.

FROM THE GALLEY, a pleasant aroma wafted into the navigation cabin, one that reminded Dunn of a scent emitted when his mother mixed flour, water, salt, oil, and baking powder into a dough that she allowed to rise before rolling and frying it in oil. He'd eat his mother's frybread for breakfast with honey or jam, although a variation he savored was one which substituted sour milk or yogurt for baking powder to yield a delicious sourdough.

Stepping into the galley, he saw a disc-shaped flatbread lying on a tray with brown crests surrounding a depressed beige center. Missing from the disc was a wedge which he presumed Irina had eaten. After breaking off a section, he dipped it into rhubarb sauce in a bowl beside a note reading, *Thanks for dinner last night. Breakfast is on me.*

Eager to see Irina, he started through the saloon but stopped short when he noticed a pair of legs descending the ladder.

"Wilbur, we need to talk!" she called.

In moments, she appeared with windswept hair, furled brows, and lips parted as she breathed heavily enough to cause her tee shirt to rise and fall with each breath. "I just spoke with my middle brother, Pablo, and he asked why you haven't been using the satphone I left near your condo."

"How would he know I haven't used it?"

"He monitored its communications."

"You told me that wouldn't be possible!"

"I misled you," she replied, lowering her shoulders. "But, if it is any consolation, Pablo would have been the only person to know how you used the mobile."

"Where did he pick up skills to monitor cell phone communications?"

"He learned them as a boy while helping my father run a business selling and repairing mobiles." She offered Dunn her phone, one identical to the Turkish model she'd left near his condo. "Use this one for your work."

Dunn refused it. "I'm using the laptop in the navigation cabin."

"That one is not safe!"

It was Dunn who drooped his shoulders now. "So I learned; a colleague from the Pentagon told me your brother launched his attacks from the laptop." He told her about the email he'd received from Garrett Fitzgerald notifying him that intelligence sources in the U.S. had discovered his use of the device.

She grimaced. "It is my fault. I should have thrown that laptop out before you boarded the tri. I covered it with logbooks on the desk intending to do so but forgot."

"I share the blame," Dunn replied. "I was foolish to have used it."

"So, use the satphone!" she insisted, offering it again. "We can share it."

This time, Dunn took the device and, sitting in the saloon, opened his email to discover one from Garrett Fitzgerald…

Wilbur,

I'm begging you to return to the U.S.! We used the IP address from the laptop along with tracking technology to locate exactly where you are in the Atlantic. Satellite photos show you're on a trimaran traveling due east along the 37th parallel. What I don't know is why you've been connecting to so many

URLs dealing with the Vice President. Don't go there, Wilbur. Just turn yourself in!
Garrett

Oh, and yes, we found giant viruses in the drone reservoir. Ft. Detrich is identifying them now.

DUNN VIEWED SAILING on a racing tri akin to visiting a foreign nation. He felt like a waif on the vessel, and just as one senses estrangement for not knowing the language of a distant land, he fumbled for words when speaking about his surroundings. At times, he had to ask Irina to translate when she used nautical terms, as when she referred to a rotating or canting wing mast, curved foils in the floats, or a daggerboard to convert forward motion into a windward lift.

It was different when it came to mechanics. As a surgeon, he was comfortable assisting Irina repair a hydraulic motor used to trim the sails. Crouching beside her on the cockpit, he held a flashlight and handed her tools as needed, tasks he viewed as appropriate for a second mate charged with contributing to the safety of the vessel.

With repairs completed and sun setting, he went to the galley to put the finishing touches on dinner. When the job was done, he returned to the cockpit to invite Irina to the table, but before summoning her, he stood at the top of the ladder to watch her at the helm. As always, she was tethered by a lifeline, but because she wore no helmet, the wind parted her hair in back to send its locks billowing forward. The part reminded him of a girl he had a crush on in high school, a Paiute Indian from the reservation who rode the bus with him to high school seventeen miles away in Yerington, Nevada. Returning home on warm days, she'd lower a window, and because she'd swivel in her seat to talk to girls behind her, the wind parted her hair along the back of her head. From his seat across the aisle, Dunn pretended to look about innocently, but what he really did was steal glances of her blowing hair, smooth brown skin, and shoulders undulating in laughter. He never mustered the courage to ask her out because his self-perception as a lanky nerd kept him from doing so.

Securing himself to a lifeline, he moved to a capstan close to Irina but not so close to invade her space. Rather than invite her to dinner, he asked, "How is it a Portuguese woman would come to be named Irina Mostafa?"

"Who said I'm Portuguese?"

"Why would we go to the Azores to see your father otherwise? The Azores belong to Portugal."

She said nothing.

"I suppose you could be from Brazil or Angola where the national language is Portuguese, a language I know you speak because I found a novel written in Portuguese in the galley. I slipped it into a plastic bag to protect it while I cooked."

Irina stepped aside to a control panel where she brought a screen alive before entering several commands. "Shall we eat? I've set the autopilot."

Dunn led her below where he served sunflower seed cakes and quinoa before sitting across the table from her.

"Impressive," she said.

"One of my mother's favorites. I couldn't have made it without the wonderful ingredients in your galley."

"I stock it that way because I want to remain connected to people I respect."

Dunn took the first bite to encourage her to eat. "What people are you referring to?"

She raised a fork but held it still. "Indigenous peoples of the world, groups like the Aymara of Brazil, Masai of Kenya, and Hmong, Tibetans, and Adivasi in Asia, people who lost their lands by assimilating into nation states. I completed a Master's in anthropology because I wanted to learn more about them and their present challenges."

Silence fell as the two ate before Irina spoke again. "Does it make you uncomfortable to discuss indigenous people?"

"Why should it? I'm one of them."

"I know, and has it been a challenge for you?"

In earlier years, being a minority member of society brought Dunn pain at times, not from overt discrimination but from difficulty blending. As he grew older, however, he realized it was he who lived on terrain which his ancestors hunted, fished, and harvested while most around him were transplants from distant lands. Whereas he walked the soil countless generations before him had trod, others molded footsteps on earth foreign to their ancestors, and from that angle, he considered indigenousness an honor.

Still, although he was comfortable discussing his experiences as an original American of Paiute origin, it made him uneasy when questioners broached the subject pedantically, and with Irina, he sensed an element of that. "Life is a challenge for everyone," he said. "Do you know anyone who escapes it?"

Irina pondered the response. "Not really."

"Do you have what you call 'indigenous' blood in your family?"

"None I am aware of."

"Then, why are you so private about your background?"

She set her fork down and looked away. "My mother is Portuguese and my father Egyptian. The two met in Egypt where my father owned a cell phone business." She lowered her eyes to her plate and resumed eating. "I am enjoying your mother's recipe."

It was Dunn now who set his fork down. "Thanks, it was she who insisted I learn how to cook as an important life skill and, besides, I enjoy it." He looked at Irina more closely. "May I ask how you learned English so well?"

"I went to an international school in Alexandria along the Mediterranean."

Dunn noticed a subtle change in the shade of her irises, one that turned her eyes a deeper blue. As it was night and neither the sun nor sea could have produced the change, he concluded it was her reference to school or the Mediterranean that did so. "Did you like your school?"

"I liked that it overlooked the sea. While my classmates focused on schoolwork, I dreamed of sailing."

"Which I assume you began at a young age."

"Yes, my father introduced me to a sailboat when I was four."

"What about your brothers—do they sail?"

"Not with passion."

"And did I hear correctly that your three brothers are older than you?"

"Yes, I am the youngest."

"The baby."

She smiled. "In a sense."

"Did all of you go to the same school?"

"No, my oldest brother went to madrassas because he wanted to follow the footsteps of my father by studying the teachings of Islam."

"Why didn't all of you attend madrassas?"

"My mother wanted us to get a secular education at a multilingual school."

Dunn glanced at the photo on the wall. "Was it your father's education that put him in harm's way?"

Irina ejected from her seat. Glaring at Dunn with elbows flared, she said, "There was nothing about my father's education that put him in harm's way! He was a caring man who loved his family deeply just as he does today." She removed her plate and carried it to the galley. "When you have finished your dinner, you may join me in the navigation cabin where I have something to give you."

Appetite stymied, Dunn met her at the desk where she moved the pin which marked their location. "If the winds cooperate, we will reach the Azores in two days from now," she said.

Dunn watched her draw a series of spirals across the Atlantic to the Caribbean. Using the flank of graphite on her pencil, she then added blotches over Africa from Mauritania in the west to Sudan in the east. "You're drawing storms, aren't you?" he asked.

"Yes, one of which may be especially destructive."

While waiting for Irina on the pier the day before, Dunn had checked the news and saw a story entitled, *Hurricanes to continue battering U.S. in historic season*. "Why do you say a storm will be especially destructive when we've had some bad ones already?"

She swept her hand over the horn of Africa. "The sands of the eastern Sahara are especially hot these days, and that provides the fuel for storms." She set her pencil down and lifted a small box. "Open it. It is for you."

Surprised previously by the contents of a box she'd given him, Dunn lifted the lid to find a rock with delicate fanning blades. "What is this?"

"A desert rose, or in French what is called a *rose des sables.* It is formed in the desert by the evaporation of water from shallow salt basins which leaves mineral crystals in the form of rose petals."

Dunn ran a finger over the thin circular plates. "Why are you giving this to me?"

"My youngest brother, an agronomist, wants you to have it. He told me it offers clues as to how a plague of biblical proportions may overcome the world."

DUNN FOUND IT coincidental that the individual units which formed cell membranes, one of life's most important molecular building blocks, consisted of wiggly chains resembling sperm. Packed side-by-side to form a bilayer around cells, the stringy units inside cell membranes oriented their bulbous phosphate heads out and their fatty chains in. Sprinkled within the bilayer were proteins which served as gatekeepers to control the entry and exit of key constituents into and out of cells.

A key focus to Dunn's research was to characterize the proteins present within Sertoli cell membranes. He viewed the proteins as miniature docking stations for hormones which directed Sertoli cells to carry out specific functions in their sperm-nurturing tasks. By understanding the nature of the proteins, he hoped to develop drugs to combat male infertility. His research partner, Krishna Bhatia, played a vital role in the quest, yet sitting in the navigation cabin with Irina's satphone checking email, he felt betrayed by one Bhatia had just sent…

Wilbur, they're saying you're a traitor! What's going on?

Factoring in a two-hour time zone difference between his present position and Baltimore, Dunn figured it was a good time to call Bhatia who he suspected would be tucking his kids into bed.

"Hello," a voice answered warily.

"Krishna, it's me! I'm calling from a satellite phone. I'm not a traitor!"

Bhatia's voice was little more than a whisper: "Then why did they come to the lab today to claim you were?"

"*Who* came?"

"Five men from national security agencies."

"Give me names!"

"I got only one: 'Garrett Fitzgerald.' "

"*Fitzgerald* said I was a traitor?"

"Yes." Bhatia sighed. "Jeez, Wilbur, I couldn't believe what he told me. Did you leave the U.S. yesterday with terrorists who attacked our bases?"

"I left yesterday, but not with terrorists! I'm sailing across the Atlantic with a woman who insists I can stop a 'plague of biblical proportions' from striking our nation, but to do so, I have to meet her father in the Azores. I know nothing about him other than that he was tortured in the past."

Bhatia groaned. "Tortured? By whom?"

"I don't know."

"What does this woman mean by 'plague of biblical proportions'?"

"She doesn't have details because it's a radicalized brother of hers who plans to unleash the plague, the same guy who attacked the two bases."

"If it's her brother, she's gotta know!"

"No, the two don't get along. The woman denounces what her brother did."

"A *plague*—like the bubonic plague that swept the world in the fourteenth century and killed over fifty million people in Europe alone?"

"She doesn't know, but a guy who's evil enough to pull off attacks like those at the bases could have something horrendous up his sleeve."

"Well, at least we don't have to worry about megavirus because the virus hasn't spread beyond those currently ill. Garrett Fitzgerald confirmed this while he was here."

"It's too early to know that for sure," Dunn cautioned.

"Perhaps, but it's comforting to see no new cases coming forward as the hours pass. That's good evidence to suggest person-to-person spread isn't occurring. Fitzgerald also said researchers at Ft. Dietrich are developing a test to detect antibodies against megavirus which will be used to test blood from people who were in close touch with the ill men as well as from those who were outdoors when the drones flew over the bases. That should tell us much more about the transmissibility of megavirus."

"That's good," Dunn said, "but it won't stop a deranged man from releasing an agent worse than megavirus if he's determined to do so."

SATISFIED WITH DUNN'S assistant abilities, Irina recruited him for another repair job as their second night at sea wore on. A flickering light outside the sleeping quarters posed a sparking hazard, and after starting at a bank of batteries buried within the tri, she followed the circuit forward until she discovered the problem: a faulty wire leading to a junction box. Because the box was beyond her reach in a recess, she approached Dunn in the navigation cabin. "I'm sorry I left dinner abruptly," she said. "It was rude of me to do so after you prepared such a wonderful meal."

"No worries," Dunn replied. "I was wrong to raise the topic of your father's waterboarding."

She pointed to the flickering light beside her in the passage. "Will you help me fix this?"

Dunn joined her beside the recess which held the faulty wire. Following a flashlight beam she pointed into the void, he received his marching orders. "I can do that," he chuckled. "I'm used to tight spaces while operating."

Reaching into the abyss, he severed a damaged wire before crimping a new section to it. Upon leaning back to gesture for a screw he needed to replace, he met Irina's eyes inches from his. Her closeness caught him off guard, and when he raised his hand to take the screw, he felt her hand caress his. Pulse quickening, he asked, "What is it?"

"I like the connection you're making."

"The one in there or out here?" he asked.

She smiled. "That is for you to answer. Either way, I hope the connection lasts."

THE MIDNIGHT HOUR approached, yet Dunn struggled to keep his eyes from wandering to the sleeping quarters where Irina lay fast asleep on a bunk only six feet from where he sat in the navigation cabin. Craning his neck, he watched her chest rise and fall with each breath, the first time he'd seen her sleep since they'd set sail. Because she lay on a side facing him, he ran his eyes along her hair which flowed across her temple before separating over an ear. It struck him again as it had upon meeting her that she was a woman of curves and angles more pronounced than many. From the arcs and grooves of her ear, he moved to her cheekbones which tilted slightly up to frame her eyes in a fashion that reminded him of an Abyssinian cat that used to wander into his apartment in San Francisco during his residency training years. He wanted to stroke Irina's hair as he'd done with the cat and glide his fingers along her skin, but because that was out of the question, he held her with his eyes as he moved them across her lips and chin. After reaching the base of her neck, he longed to explore the shadows of her breasts but refrained from doing so, returning his eyes to the satphone.

It was one thing to have feelings, he admonished himself, another to succumb to them.

14

UPON AWAKENING ON his third day at sea, Dunn rolled in his bunk to look for Irina but found her mattress empty. That didn't surprise him, however, because while sleeping he thought he'd heard her get up in the middle of the night. For diligence, discipline, and steadfastness as a skipper, he gave her superior marks.

Turning his thoughts to an email exchange with Krishna Bhatia the day before, he remained flummoxed by two revelations his partner made: first, that the giant virus in PFC Hartley's testes possessed two proteins that were similar to ones in a group of viruses distinct from megavirus, namely, paramyxoviruses; and second, that the giant virus had invaded what Dunn had always considered was an impenetrable bastion within the male gonad— the Sertoli cell. He composed an email to lay out a research plan even though he knew Bhatia would have his own...

> *Krishna,*
>
> *Here's my theory: After infecting humans, megavirus uses its version of attachment protein, A, and/or fusion protein, F, to invade Sertoli cells.*
>
> *To test this theory, I suggest we create an antibody against megavirus attachment protein, A. Then connect that antibody to attachment protein A to effectively block it from working as it normally does. Then expose megavirus with the blocking antibody attached to A protein to healthy Sertoli cells to see if the virus still infects Sertolis.*
>
> *Next, repeat the process with fresh megavirus which have their F protein blocked by antibody to see if the virus infects Sertoli cells.*
>
> *Finally, use antibodies to block both A and F on megavirus before exposing Sertoli cells to the virus.*
>
> *My guess is that by blocking either A or F or, possibly, by blocking both A and F, we'll prevent megavirus from invading Sertolis. If this is true, we can conclude that A and/or F*

proteins on megavirus's outer membrane allows the virus to infect Sertoli cells.

What do you think?

EAGER TO CHECK in with Irina, Dunn stood to go but froze with the arrival of an email on the satphone from his former mentor in Merced, California, the director of urology he'd written the day before to inquire about a hospitalization by Atticus Quincy Thornbridge…

Dear Wilbur,

What a surprise to hear from you! An honor, too, what with all you've accomplished in the twelve years since you were here. I've followed your progress in the literature, reading every paper you've published. Let there be no doubt: You're an accomplished expert on spermatogenesis.

Now, as to your question about a U.S. Senator hospitalized here four years ago, it was a big deal because, at the time, Atticus Quincy Thornbridge had just become a candidate to run for Vice President. His symptoms upon arrival by ambulance at our emergency department suggested he was having a severe allergic reaction, and our first theory was he'd become allergic to a medication he was taking for rheumatoid arthritis. Turns out we were wrong: his allergic reaction was due to a protein present in a barbecue sauce he ate at a conference here in Merced.

We cut no corners to figure out what triggered his reaction. It proved to be a fish protein in the barbecue sauce. Unbeknownst to the Senator, he developed the allergy before visiting Merced, and when he consumed the barbecue sauce that contained anchovies, his lungs and circulatory system collapsed. He was rushed here under CPR and survived thanks to our emergency department.

So, that's the story. This is all hush-hush, of course, because it relates to a sitting Vice President who's planning to run for President in four years. For that reason, I trust you'll keep this quiet.

As for the job I offered you here years ago, it remains open any time you want it.

Dunn waited for his pounding heart to settle, only then turning to a question that tormented him: Was it correct to assume that a fish-allergic person who reacted severely to protein in anchovies could also be expected to react to protein in a completely different fish—trout?

Reading about fish allergy online, he soon learned his answer: The principal allergen in fish was a protein called parvalbumin, and it was present in fish across a wide range of species. Moreover, he learned that fish allergy was one of the most common types of food allergies, that about forty percent of people with fish allergy experienced their first reactions as adults, and that in addition to eating fish, touching fish or breathing its vapors while it was being fried or baked could trigger severe allergic reactions.

With the additional information, he composed an email to his attorney…

Jim,

I just learned from a trusted source that Atticus Quincy Thornbridge experienced a life-threatening allergy to fish four years ago in California. Given this, I'm stunned that at the trial in Idaho the widow of the guy I killed testified Thornbridge had traveled to Idaho repeatedly in recent years to fly fish with his godson. Can you find a way to verify whether that's true?

AS DUNN STOOD to go to the helm, he noticed the seas were rougher than at any time since departing. The deeper troughs between swells added a lunging element to their forward drive, one that forced him to splay his arms and stand with a broad-based gait to keep from falling. He hoped the roughness wasn't slowing their pace as his sights were set on reaching the Azores late the following day.

He examined the map before him in the navigation cabin. When Irina had first announced they'd reach the Azores in just over three days, he didn't believe her, but then he witnessed the tri's speed and understood how others had sailed in a similar vessel from Nova Scotia to Spain in three and a half days, a journey of almost three thousand miles. He also learned of a French sailor who'd circumnavigated the globe solo in forty-nine days and three hours by sailing at an average speed of twenty-eight miles per hour. Even faster times had been set by crews of ten to fourteen people, but that was a different scenario from the one faced by solo sailors who experienced sleep deprivation and fatigue.

Dunn made his way through the saloon to the ladder which he scaled with extra care given the roiling ocean. Even before he reached the deck, he heard Irina call to him from above.

"Get down! They're circling us!"

Halting three rungs below the cockpit, Dunn asked: "Who's circling?"

"Just go down! Look through a porthole at the sky."

When Dunn reached the saloon, he collected a pair of binoculars and, scanning the halcyon sky, saw a silver fuselage reflecting sunlight from an altitude of less than ten thousand feet. The airplane made a wide arc that continued in a circumference with the trimaran marking its center.

"Listen to me!" Irina called from the saloon entry. "We must have a plan in case they send a ship to intercept us."

"Who are they?"

"I do not know, but we must prepare for intruders!"

Irina rushed past him to the navigation room and returned shortly with the laptop which she tossed through a porthole into the ocean. "There, if they want it, they can dive for it!"

"Why'd you do that?" Dunn protested. "It held sensitive information our authorities could have used."

"I will not help the oppressors!"

"What oppressors are you referring to?"

Irina went to the waterboarding photo. "You can ask my father. He will tell you who they are."

"I may not even see him if they seize us and we don't cooperate."

"You *will* see my father! I will push the tri to its limits to ensure you do!" She grasped Dunn's arm. "Now, come with me!"

Dunn followed her into the sleeping quarters where she stooped at its far end. Craning her neck, she pointed a flashlight under a bunk. "Kneel," she ordered. "Do you see anything unusual under there?"

Dunn looked about the space. "Not really."

After handing Dunn the flashlight, she slid under the bunk on her back with her head just clearing a metal sheet above her. "Hand me the wrench," she called. With the tool in hand, she slid to the far wall where she removed four bolts along the hull which allowed her to detach a panel. "Your turn!" she said after sliding out. "See if you can fit into the hull."

At six-four, Dunn had an onerous time sliding under the bunk to the cavity Irina exposed. "What's in there?" he asked.

"Nothing currently, but if the oppressors board, you must hide inside the hull."

"I'll suffocate!"

"No, there is sufficient air."

Lying beside the cavity, Dunn lifted himself over a short ledge into a recess which was dark and noisy from the sound of water striking the hull outside. "I'm in, but I don't like it!" he hollered.

"Now come back out!"

Reversing course, he wasted no time to stand once free. "I can deal with tight places," he said as he massaged a kink in his neck, "but that's a nasty one."

"At least it is not a jail." She nodded over her shoulder in the direction of the photo in the saloon.

"Have *you* been in that cavity?" he asked, pointing to the bunk.

"Yes," she replied. "My oldest brother sent me there to pack the Khawad machine guns, web cams, and drone parts he forced me to sail with from North Africa to America. He insisted the items go there to ensure they would not be seen."

Dunn cringed at the prospect of hiding in a space which once held the weapons used to attack his nation.

"You must not go up to the deck again," Irina cautioned. "Otherwise, the satellites will see you."

SEQUESTERED WITHIN THE tri, Dunn felt like an asylum seeker confined to an embassy. Portholes afforded his only views of the world which at that point consisted of an outrigger cruising over the water on one side while its partner sliced through swells on the other. To bide time, he used Irina's satphone to search online medical journals for the latest publications on male infertility. Because the settings of his search identified articles in multiple languages, he was confronted with a lengthy list with the most recently published papers cited first.

As the world of male infertility research was a small one, he recognized many of the authors on the list. A benefit of his search program was that, even if an article was published in a foreign language, an English abstract accompanied the citation. For papers with compelling titles, he read the abstracts to gauge the soundness of the findings, and if he thought the research was solid, he made a mental note to read the papers in full later. Midway through his search, he came to a citation which astounded him, one for an article published in Arabic whose authors were affiliated with an agricultural research station in the Sahara and a medical school in Cairo, Egypt. The paper had just appeared in an Egyptian journal and was entitled, *An Outbreak of Testicular Swelling Involving Tourists in the Republic of South Sudan.*

He raked his eyes across the abstract…

> *We report an outbreak of testicular swelling and subsequent infertility involving four men traveling by camel through the Imatong Mountains of South Sudan. Examination of testicular biopsies revealed invasion by a giant virus.*

Mind reeling, Dunn clicked a link to access the full text but found the download to be unnervingly long. After the article finally appeared, he minimized it to pull up a map of South Sudan to learn where the Imatong Mountains were. He found them in the southeast part of the country just north of Uganda.

"Irina!" he called.

Through a speaker on the wall, a voice replied, "What is it?"

"Can you come here? I need you to translate something!" While he waited, he did another search, this one for the agricultural research station where one of the authors worked. When several entries appeared in Arabic, he summoned Irina again.

"Wilbur, hide!" she shrieked. "A ship is coming!"

Dunn rushed to a porthole, but all he saw was a tempestuous ocean. Crossing the cabin, he peered out the opposite side and froze at the sight of a destroyer cutting through the water directly at them. Retrieving the binoculars, he focused on the ship and made out the number *126* on its bow and a U.S. flag streaming from a mast.

"I told you to hide!" Irina barked from the saloon entry. "They will board any moment, so go to your spot! I will be right there to bolt you in."

NECESSITY KEPT DUNN from rebelling against his confining quarters. In the dark, he lay in a fiberglass tomb rolling back and forth as his ankles, hips, and elbows struck the hull with every roll. The restricted space reminded him of boyhood games of hide and seek when he'd slip into a rusting petroleum tank near his home on the reservation, a spot which remained secret because no one thought he'd be foolish enough to resort to a hole-ridden container frequented by snakes. As a precaution, he drummed the exterior before swishing a stick within it to scare away creatures; only then did he enter the tank.

In his newfound coop, he drew relief from the trimaran's deceleration because it tempered the force of his knocks against the floor, but he knew the vessel's slowing meant intruders could board at any time. Having slowed from a sprint to a crawl in the span of ten minutes, the tri left him sweating in its bobbing hull.

As he listened for clues to what was happening about him, he heard a ship's horn and then a voice over a loudspeaker command crew members of the trimaran to assemble at the helm. Moments later, an engine's groan became audible, one he presumed belonged to a motor boat approaching the tri. His suspicion bore out as a heated exchange erupted on the cockpit. A male voice demanded Irina to show her passport and declare the purpose of her voyage, to which she replied, "I am training for a circum-globe solo race." Testy words ensued, followed by a torrent of footsteps which reverberated on the hull above Dunn.

Before long, confrontational voices moved to the saloon, and because of the intensity of the discussions, Dunn heard every word, most conferring technical details from treaties of the seas.

"I am familiar with the United Nations Convention on the Law of the Sea," Irina declared, "but UNCLOS does not give you the right to board a private vessel in international waters! Read Article 89. It affirms that no State may subject any part of the high seas to its sovereignty."

"What about Article 111?" a booming voice volleyed. "It declares a warship may pursue a foreign vessel when authorities of a coastal State have reason to believe the vessel violated the laws and regulations of the State."

"What laws and regulations did my vessel violate?"

"A trimaran with these exact features was seen in the Chesapeake Bay ten days ago near the U.S. Naval Academy and then again off the coast of Lewes, Delaware three days ago."

"And that violates the rules and regulations of your nation?"

"It does if the vessel ferried terrorists who attacked our nation."

"You have no proof this vessel carried terrorists!"

A momentary lull, then: "If you're innocent, why did you erase the GPS history on your cockpit navigation module?"

"It malfunctioned, forcing me to wipe it clean."

Another pause as footsteps entered the galley. "Ma'am, we're going to search every inch of your vessel, but you can make our job easier by giving us the laptop."

"What laptop?"

"You know the one—the laptop used to discharge the Khawads and fly the drones over the bases. We know it's here."

The sound of boots striking the floors about Dunn frayed his nerves. From the navigation cabin, he heard a voice ask, "What was on the wall here?"

A moment later, Irina replied, "Nothing."

"Then why the peeling tape? It held something."

Dunn heard a hastily stowed map beside his chest crinkle each time he inhaled. Louder still was the sound of a drawer opening, one he recognized as belonging to the desk in the navigation cabin.

"Is this your satellite phone?" a man asked.

"Yes, but it's broken," Irina replied.

Dunn admonished himself for not removing the device he'd destroyed shortly after boarding the tri.

"Don't worry, we'll fix it."

"Leave it!" Irina demanded.

"Why? Does it contain something you'd prefer to hide?"

Irina said nothing.

Sweating profusely, Dunn worried IT specialists would recover every keystroke he'd made on the device, but his worries turned to the sounds of bunk beds being dismantled.

"Cut every mattress open!" a voice ordered.

Hammers battered metal as wrenches loosened bolts, and from his confinement, Dunn prepared himself to be found. He squeezed his arms to his sides and clenched his legs to make himself as small as possible.

"Nothing here, sir!" a voice announced. "We've stripped everything."

Dunn grazed a finger along the metal panel beside him which served as his sole barrier.

"Move out!" came an order.

Footsteps shuffled away, and with the bangs, tings, and clings silenced, Dunn heard a renewed confrontation in the saloon. "Do not touch that!" Irina shouted.

"We're taking it, ma'am," a commanding voice bellowed.

"It belongs to me!"

"Where did you get the photo?"

"It was given to me!"

"By whom?"

Silence.

"I asked you a question, ma'am!"

"What do you say in your nation?" Irina replied. "Something about 'taking the fifth'? Well, I do that now."

"This photo doesn't belong here, ma'am. I'm removing it."

"Why, because it reveals a CIA black site?"

"We do what we have to do to keep our nation safe, ma'am."

"Torture endangers a nation."

"I'm no judge, ma'am, and neither are you. We need to leave legal matters to the courts."

"And therein lies the problem! Your justice system is flawed. It is constructed in linear fashion, much as a latitude, and with such rigidity comes flagrant injustice!"

"Moving out!" the voice called.

In minutes, the groan of an engine reversed course and faded. In his catacomb, Dunn was bewildered that he should sweat and shiver at the same time, a physiologic malfunction, he concluded, that stemmed from hot air and cold fear combining to short circuit his system.

IN A FINAL show of force, the destroyer flanked the trimaran before veering away. From the cockpit, Irina growled at its sailors as she resumed a due-east course. Only when the naval vessel disappeared did she retrieve Dunn.

"What did I tell you?" she lashed out as Dunn inched his way to freedom. "The oppressors came!"

"I heard just about everything," Dunn replied, surveying the dismantled bunks and shredded mattresses. He followed Irina to the saloon. "And I see they took the photo of your father."

She broadened her shoulders. "They cannot hide their torturous ways!"

From his pocket, Dunn removed a vibrating satphone.

"Who is it?" Irina asked.

"My attorney."

"Why did you contact him?"

"I need a legal opinion."

"About what?"

Dunn said nothing as he read...

Wilbur,

Very disturbing news you shared about the Vice President's diagnosis of severe fish allergy four years ago. It's clearly at odds with the widow's assertion that her husband fly fished with the VP in recent years. Yet it mystifies me that you should raise the topic as you assist federal authorities investigate illnesses at two military bases. I advise you to drop the matter and keep a low profile while you remain under court-ordered surveillance.

Jim Edwards

Disappointed by his attorney's refusal to inquire into the VP's claim of fly fishing with his godson, Dunn was baffled by what Edwards left beneath his name—a phone number with an Idaho area code he didn't recognize.

A quick calculation revealed it was eight a.m. Idaho time, late enough to explore who the mysterious number belonged to.

EVEN BEFORE DUNN left the U.S., Idaho was in the news because of forest fires scorching the state. With a high-pressure system locked over the Midwest, hot air streamed north from Mexico to leave the Rockies sweltering. From Arizona to Alberta, fires raged but none more so than in Idaho and western Wyoming where Sawtooth, Caribou-Targhee, and Bridger-Teton National Forests blazed. Large swaths of Grand Teton and Yellowstone were shuttered to visitors as photos depicted animals hobbling on burned legs.

With such turmoil abounding in the state, it was with apprehension that Dunn called the number Jim Edwards left him.

"Hello?" a woman answered.

"Good morning, this is Dr. Wilbur Dunn. May I ask whom I'm speaking with?"

"Your name again?"

"Wilbur Dunn."

"That's what I thought I heard! You killed my husband!"

The venom in her voice stung Dunn and made him recall the testimony she'd given about the emotional devastation and financial hardship that resulted from her husband's death at Dunn's hands. He blamed himself anew for what he did and regretted calling the number without first consulting Edwards. "Hear me out," he pleaded. "All I want to know is whether your husband truly fly fished with the Vice President of the United States as you stated in court."

"You called to ask me *that*?"

"Yes, it's critical I know the truth."

"Are you calling me a liar, because if you are, I'll haul you back to court for libel!"

The line went dead.

SATPHONE IN HAND, Dunn felt the weight of the world in his palm. Shaken by the widow's anger, he went to the galley to seek refuge with a cup of coffee. As with the other ingredients stocked there, the coffee beans were exotic and labeled with care: *Arabica bean, Yirgacheffe brand, Ethiopia.*

After brewing a pot, he poured a cup, sipped from it, and then placed it in a holder in the saloon where he engaged the satphone. He found it curious that, unlike many in the digital age, Irina showed little interest in her mobile as she requested to use it infrequently. Instead, she focused exclusively on her sailing chores, interspersing them with communions with sea, sky, and wind. It recalled for Dunn the words she'd uttered at the pier in Delaware before they'd left: "I am always alone." Solitude, he concluded, was her beloved partner.

Addressing his own needs, he retrieved the article he'd downloaded earlier which described scrotal swelling and subsequent infertility in four tourists traveling by camel through South Sudan. "Irina," he called with a measured voice, "can you come here when you're free?"

She appeared shortly and placed a palm on his shoulder as if she, like he, needed a human touch after the morning's intrusions. "You are no longer shouting, and I appreciate that," she said.

"Old dogs can learn new tricks."

"You are not old, but wise from experience."

He looked at her affectionately. "May I ask your age?"

She removed her hand, rounded the table, and sat across from him. "Twenty-five."

A *child*, Dunn thought. He rebuked himself for allowing inklings of attraction to fester in the past day, inklings which raised troubling questions like, How soon is too soon to have feelings after losing one's wife? Is fourteen years too large a age gap to span? What happens after we reach our destination?

He slid the satphone across the table. "Can you translate this?"

She lifted the device and began reading, first in Arabic before translating into English. "Four French males traveled to South Sudan to view wildlife in Bandingilo National Park. They followed wildebeests and other migrating animals return to the highlands after rains subsided in the valleys." She set the phone down. "I know Bandingilo National Park because I visited it with my youngest brother, the scientist. The park hosts the second largest migration of wildlife after the Serengeti, only tourists do not know of Bandingilo because of the civil war that ravaged South Sudan for twenty-two years. Fortunately, the animals remained safe during that time."

Dunn eyed the phone to prompt her to continue reading.

"Because of the difficult terrain, the four white males traveled on camels with two African guides. Midway through the month-long journey, the camels became ill with testicular swelling. Two days later, the four tourists developed a sensation of heaviness in the groin which progressed to painful swelling and reddening of the scrotum. Because the men were too uncomfortable to travel, the guides sheltered them in an unmanned military outpost in the mountains where they were evaluated by one of us, a physician, who flew from Egypt at the request of the South Sudan government." Irina lifted her eyes. "A set of initials, *OMF*, is provided in parentheses in the text."

Dunn took the phone and scrolled to the author line where he found the senior author was named *Omar Mohammad Fakhoury*. His affiliation was listed as a faculty member at the school of medicine at

Cairo University in Egypt. Relinquishing the phone, he beckoned her to continue.

"At the end of the second day at the outpost, as he was preparing to depart for Cairo with clinical samples, OMF fell ill with symptoms identical to those of the four men. Recognizing the transmissibility of the illness, OMF remained at the outpost to keep from passing the disease to others while traveling to Egypt. In the meantime, the four tourists recovered sufficiently to depart for Uganda from where they continued traveling to reach their homes."

"Wait, re-read that section."

Irina did.

"Are you sure you've translated correctly?" Dunn asked.

She double-checked the text and nodded. "Yes, why?"

Dunn's face turned ashen. "I'll tell you in a moment, but keep going. I want to hear about the 'giant virus' they spoke of in the abstract."

Irina: "After recovering at the outpost, OMF returned to Cairo with clinical specimens, including testicular tissue from one patient…" After scrolling repeatedly, Irina looked at Dunn. "The text ends there."

Dunn took the phone and worked it without success. "I don't understand, there's clearly more to the article, but it's missing. Was my download faulty?"

"Repeat it," Irina advised.

Dunn did so only to produce the same results. "No! I *really* want to hear about the virus." He set the phone down and, closing his eyes, envisioned the swirls Irina had drawn on the map to depict storms moving across the Atlantic. "We're in for big trouble," he moaned.

"Why do you say that?"

"Because, the storms that cross the Atlantic carry tons of Sahara sand in their winds."

IN BIRDS, THE fusion of clavicles at the base of the neck forms the furcula, or wishbone, which strengthens the skeleton for flight.

As a child, Dunn often vied with his mother to see whose wish would come true while pulling wishbones. Secretly, he longed for even breaks because he wanted the wishes of his mother and his to prevail, but more often than not, he came out on the short end.

He thought about those days of wishbone pulling as he examined a map of hurricanes dotting the Atlantic. So far that season, their trajectory remained one with a wishbone shape with its junction over the Gulf of Mexico. For two straight months, one hurricane after another had shifted course in the Gulf to bend north toward the mid-Atlantic or along the eastern seaboard thanks to stationary high-pressure systems over the Yucatan and central U.S. And it wasn't just the U.S. that paid a toll; Ireland, England, and Scotland had experienced devastating floods, too. The photos were wrenching—cars carried in raging waters, trees felled like toothpicks, and neighborhoods turned into muddy graveyards.

15

DARKNESS ON THE third night at sea brought renewed obsessions and compulsions, ones as intense as those Dunn experienced at home. When he boarded the tri three days earlier, he hoped he'd left them behind and that his new surroundings would dampen the mental duress that came with darkness, but it wasn't to be as a drooping sun rekindled his anxiety.

He hid his compulsions from Irina. Only when she was at the helm or tending to duties elsewhere did he act them out—ensuring knives were stowed in the galley; bins tightly secured; and the door to the head latched to keep from swinging. With the sleeping quarters in disarray, he could no longer inspect the spaces beneath the bunks, but that didn't prevent him from raking his eyes across the mattresses, poles, and frames which he feared might hold a stowaway from the naval vessel.

In the saloon, he tackled a new task: gauging the degree of heel to the tri. By now, he knew that maintaining a consistent heel was key to achieving speed, so he paced from one side to the other to convince himself the tilt remained steady. Satisfied, he stood before a porthole on the windward side to watch the missile-shaped outrigger jet over the moonlit sea. It reminded him of flights when he'd gaze through a window at the tip of an engine under a wing and marvel at how it propelled the airplane at blazing speeds.

Obsessions tempered, he turned to an email from Krishna Bhatia…

Wilbur,

We're working full-time on how Bigfoot invades Sertoli cells.

Your theory about blocking attachment and fusion proteins on Bigfoot's outer membrane didn't prevent the virus from penetrating Sertolis, so some other mechanism allows the virus to invade the cells.

As you know, though, we've made progress over the years identifying roughly a hundred proteins on Sertoli cell membranes. It's possible one of these proteins serves as a docking port for Bigfoot. To test that possibility, we're blocking each protein one-by-one to see whether by doing so we can prevent Bigfoot from invading Sertolis. Stay tuned.

Dunn raced his fingers across the mobile…

Krishna:

Take exceeding precautions with megavirus! I discovered an article in Arabic which described a giant virus that caused testicular swelling and infertility in four travelers in South Sudan. Ominously, one of the authors, a physician, became ill after evaluating the patients, which suggests person-to-person transmission occurred. While we haven't seen such transmission in the U.S., we can't allow any of our staff to become infected. As for me, no symptoms yet, but be careful with this virus!

Dunn provided Bhatia the citation of the article in Arabic and asked him to get it translated into English. He continued…

I know what you're thinking: If the strain of megavirus in South Sudan is the same one we're dealing with in the U.S., why did it transmit from the four ill men to a physician who examined them while we're seeing no secondary spread in our country? I can only speculate that the South Sudan strain differs just enough from our strain to allow it to spread, Otherwise, the clinical features of illnesses in both places are identical.

STIR CRAZY, DUNN slipped into the night to find Irina at the helm.

"What are you doing here?" she asked, pointing to the ladder. "I told you to remain inside for the rest of the journey. Otherwise, the satellites may spot you."

"Let them spot me! I'm done hiding." Having raised his eyes to the sky, Dunn found it difficult to lower them as the star-studded canopy reminded him of nights on the reservation.

"You are drawn by the stars, aren't you?" Irina asked, her voice soft now. "You spoke of them often in your blog posts."

"I did," Dunn replied. He lowered his eyes and moved closer to her. "What led you to my posts to begin with?"

"My youngest brother, Yuri, introduced me to them."

"The agronomist?"

"Yes."

"Why did he read them?"

"He was intrigued by your references to Native American beliefs on the timing of plantings with respect to the moon's phases."

A year earlier, in a series of posts about civil disobedience, Dunn beseeched protesters and law enforcement officials to draw upon the moon to mediate conflicts. If the lunar cycle swayed oceans, induced fertility, and boosted harvests, its forces could resolve disagreements, he contended. Critics were quick to ridicule the notion, to which Dunn responded: If the moon lacked the influences ascribed to it, why would generations of Native Americans have tracked the passage of time with names for full moons, as in "wolf moon" for January when canines howled in hunger, or "flower moon" when blossoms appeared and corn was planted? "Moons and stars," he said presently, "they have much to teach us."

"As does the wind, the breath of stars," Irina replied, her hair whipping about but not enough to hide her frown. "And by tomorrow this time, the wind will have delivered us to the outskirts of the Azores where we must separate." She tightened her grip on the wheel.

"Who will meet us there?"

"My middle brother, Pablo. He will take you closer to the stars."

DUNN HAD HOPED to remain on deck longer with Irina, but her steely silence turned him away. Returning to the saloon, he mourned the loss of women in his life. When she was alive, Consuela had both consoled and lifted him by her presence and words. He drew comfort from listening to her voice and her laugh as she elevated words to merriment. To fill the void after she died, he tuned into other women's voices hoping they'd lift him the way Consuela's had, but it didn't happen—not until he met Irina, that is. In her voice he discovered freshness, resoluteness, and a dogged matter-of-factness that infused vibrancy and strength.

The chime of the satphone instilled hope he might be able to deliver the device to her, but a glance at it showed a caller from Idaho was on the line. Cautiously, he picked up, saying, "Wilbur Dunn."

"Thank you for answering!" a woman said frantically.

Dunn recognized the voice. "I thought you'd never speak to me again."

"I've been at wits' end," the truck driver's widow exclaimed. "I'm sorry for lashing out at you earlier."

"Why did you call?" Dunn glanced about the cabin as if he might find her there given the clarity of her voice.

"I need to tell you something!"

"Are you alright? You're breathing heavily."

"Because I just ran up a hill from my house to a friend's so I could call you from her phone. Mine's being monitored; I'm sure of it."

"Monitored by whom?"

"The feds. They're listening to everything I say."

"Why?"

"Because, I'm not willing to be bought off anymore."

"Bought off for what?"

"For propagating a lie."

"What lie?"

"That Atticus Quincy Thornbridge was my husband's godfather."

"*What*?"

"You heard me! It's a lie." The woman sobbed.

"Please," Dunn implored, "tell me why you say it's a lie." While he waited for the widow to compose herself, he moved to the navigation cabin where he readied a pen and paper. When she spoke again, he paraphrased her words…

…Vice President never was her husband's godfather…
…all a hoax created after accident in Sawtooth National Forest…
…Vice President offered her money after her husband died…
…she needed money to raise an autistic son…
…in return, she did whatever the VP told her to do…
…now her conscience troubled her; she wanted out of the deal…
…VP threatening her if she pulls out…

"What sort of threats?" Dunn asked.

Composed now, she replied, "To take my life and yours, too."

WITH A PROJECTED arrival in the Azores less than twenty-four hours away, Irina used the satphone more now, conducting her business in Portuguese and Arabic. When Dunn asked her what the flurry of calls and texts was about, she replied, "logistics." Between her calls, he kept a close eye for missives directed his way, and when he received one from Krishna Bhatia urging him to call, he did.

"I have the article in full," Bhatia told him.

"In English?"

"Yes."

"Read it to me!"

As Bhatia did so, Dunn was relieved to hear details dovetail with Irina's translation, but when Bhatia came to the part about the physician-coauthor with the initials *OMF* traveling from Egypt to South Sudan to evaluate the four ill Frenchmen, he interrupted his colleague: "There was no mention of the physician having contact with camels, right?"

"None," Bhatia confirmed. "Why do you ask?"

"Because, if there was no contact, it's reasonable to conclude he became infected from his patients."

"Unless he picked up the virus from a doorknob, clothing, or something else contaminated with camel excretions."

"That's possible, but the fact that he feared transmitting the disease to others while traveling makes me think he suspected the illness was transmissible from person-to-person."

"True."

"Keep reading."

As Bhatia approached the point where Dunn's version had truncated, Dunn closed his eyes to concentrate...

After recovering at the outpost, OMF returned to Cairo with clinical specimens collected from his patients. Among the specimens was testicular tissue which revealed a giant virus within the sperm producing areas. On close examination, the virus was found to have invaded Sertoli cells which were destroyed as a result. The surrounding cellular elements were left in disarray in a flood of white blood cells. Correspondence with physicians who evaluated the four tourists following their return home indicated all had become infertile with subsequent testicular biopsies showing widespread scarring. Similar results were obtained from a convalescent biopsy obtained from one of us, OMF, who experienced an illness identical to that of the patients.

We conclude a giant virus acquired from ill camels by airborne or hand-to-mouth transmission of camel excretions caused four French tourists to become ill with testicular swelling and subsequent infertility. Moreover, one of us, OMF, was infected secondarily by person-to-person transmission after examining the ill patients. Importantly, OMF had no direct contact with camels and wore gloves and washed hands regularly while evaluating the patients. For this reason, we believe the giant virus passed from patients to physician by airborne transmission. Although we cannot explain why the two African guides remained well, we encourage vigorous surveillance for this yet-to-be-named giant virus that renders males infertile.

"That's it," Bhatia said. "Sounds like the illness we're seeing here except for the lack of person-to-person transmission in the U.S."

"I'm not so sure," Dunn countered.

"What are you doubting?"

"Without person-to-person spread in the U.S., it's hard to argue it's the same virus."

"It'd be highly unusual for two *different* megaviruses to cause testicular swelling within a couple of years of each other—one in the U.S. and another in Africa!"

"Unusual but not impossible. We need to determine the race of the two African guides. It's a critical factor that could explain why only the tourists became ill initially."

"How do you propose to do that?"

"Leave it to me," Dunn replied. "I have a plan."

16

ON WHAT IRINA had promised would be their last day at sea, Dunn awoke to a fiery scintillation along the ceiling of the sleeping quarters. In his groggy state, he imagined being in a discotheque looking at a brilliant mirror ball, but then he saw the light's true source: reflections from the water streaming through a porthole. From a mattress on the floor, he raised a hand with thumb flexed to mark his fourth day at sea.

"Are you greeting someone?" Irina asked.

Dunn found her lying on her side on an adjacent mattress behind him which he'd cleared the night before from the rubble of the sleeping quarters. She lay in a pair of sweats with her hair matted and eyes adjusting to the light. "So, you *do* sleep," he observed.

"As I need to." She sat up and crossed her legs yoga style before tapping her mattress. "Join me," she said.

Mindful of his boxers, Dunn straightened them as he moved to Irina's side. Through a porthole he saw a flaming orange ball just above the horizon as a blue carpet stretched before it.

"We should reach the Azores before dark today," Irina said.

Dunn was struck by the glow upon her face, a dappling of red and orange produced by sunrise shining through the porthole. The colors evoked memories of a trip to the Oregon coast he'd made during college to visit a friend who'd lost his mother to cancer, a Native American woman who'd married a man from Thailand. Dunn was intrigued by the marriage which blended Native American and Buddhist beliefs, and as he and his friend had walked the beach after the funeral, they collected red and orange agates and jasper which had washed ashore following a storm. They used the stones to create a mandala in the sand, and with sunlight piercing spray thrown off by thunderous waves, the stones glowed in mottling orange and red as he saw now on Irina's face. "You're especially beautiful in the light," he told her.

She took his hand, squeezed it, and peered at him. "I was so sorry to read that you lost your baby."

Dunn retracted his lips as he did when he felt hurt. On only two occasions had he addressed in his blog the prospect of having a family with Consuela, the first coming in a post he wrote shortly after marrying her in which he conveyed how loving a mother he thought she'd be, and the second a month before she died when he expressed excitement about her pregnancy. "It wasn't meant to be," he whispered.

Dunn felt the mattress shift before a fingertip gently grazed his cheek to wipe a tear away. He watched Irina place the finger to her lips before she wiped a tear of her own only to touch Dunn's lips with it.

"I must go," she said. "We are approaching a shipping lane that calls for me to pay close attention."

As he sat alone in the blazing light, Dunn thought about a summer he'd spent before medical school on the Crow Indian Reservation interning for the physician assistant he'd met at a scientific conference in Arizona during college. On weekends, he'd drive ninety miles east to the Northern Cheyenne Indian Reservation where wild horses roamed the hills. While camping on a ridge overlooking a gorge to another ridge, he'd see a mare appear on the second ridge at sunrise and look his way. In the blowing wind, her mane whipped about as she pawed the ground, and having spent a good deal of time with horses, he knew pawing could be a gesture for boredom, curiosity, thirst, or other feelings. With this horse, however, he was convinced the mare was asking, "Do you dare to know me?" For that reason, he hiked repeatedly to the opposite ridge to look for the horse, but each time he went there she was gone. It was she who commanded their encounters, not he, and he learned to accept that.

He glanced through the doorway to the galley and saloon which Irina had traversed after leaving him. She was much like the elusive horse, he concluded, a woman who was able to strike a chord deep within by cutting through fat to bone and bypass acquaintance to intimacy, a woman who had no qualms about addressing the loss of what was to be Dunn's first child.

He shifted his gaze to the porthole brimming with jasper light.

ALTHOUGH IT WAS six hours earlier in Boise, Idaho, Dunn felt compelled to call Jim Edwards even though he knew the call would awaken his lawyer. A tangle of concerns troubled Dunn, none greater than what he perceived to be stalking by the Vice President. How lawyers would label the charge Dunn didn't know, but he believed the widow's assertion that Atticus Quincy Thornbridge had paid her off to falsify a claim that he was her husband's godfather constituted perjury or obstruction of justice of some sort, and he looked to Jim Edwards for guidance as to what the next legal maneuver should be.

He dialed the firm's 24/7 number and waited for a response which came shortly. "I need to speak to Jim Edwards," he told the receptionist, a woman whose voice seemed unnaturally pert for the hour.

"It's the middle of the night, sir," she reminded Dunn.

"I know, but this is urgent!"

"It can't wait until morning?"

"No, I need to speak to Mr. Edwards immediately."

"Your name?"

"Wilbur Dunn."

"Please hold."

Dunn heard a click, then: "Jim, is that you?"

"Wilbur," a sleepy voice replied. "I trust you received my email and that's why you're calling at this hour."

"I spoke to the widow yesterday."

"I hope you were careful! I violated protocol by sharing that number."

"I'm glad you did." Dunn summarized what he'd learned.

"You're saying both she and Thornbridge perjured themselves in court?"

"That's what she claims. She admitted taking a payoff from Thornbridge in exchange for asserting the VP was her husband's godfather."

"Why would Thornbridge do that?"

"I'm hoping you'll help me answer that."

"Wilbur, let me remind you: We're talking about the Vice President here."

"Yes, and I'm on a racing trimaran two-thirds of the way across the ocean approaching the Azores with a woman named Irina who contacted me to say she could explain the events at Walter Reed and the Naval Academy. I need your help!"

"You're sailing to the *Azores*! Why?"

"Because, Irina insists that if I meet her father I might be able to stop a plague of biblical proportions from being unleashed."

"Lunacy, Wilbur! None of this has anything to do with Thornbridge! What you need to do is to connect this woman, Irina, with our national security folks."

"I tried, but she refused to cooperate, so I'm going to meet her father. In the meantime, I need to find out why Thornbridge has me in his crosshairs. The widow claimed he's threatened to kill me."

"That's madness!"

"Look, he's stalked me since the accident in Sawtooth National Forest, and as you know, he's called my probation officer to check on me routinely. Now he's attending meetings of a team I joined at the Pentagon to investigate the illnesses at the two bases even though he has no medical expertise, so my guess is he joined to snoop on me."

Edwards sighed. "What do you want *me* to do?"

"Go over everything from the trial to see if anything stands out as unusual given what the widow just told me. Nothing can be taken at face value anymore, including the VP's story about fly fishing with his godson; no fish-allergic guy in his right mind would ever do such a thing!"

Edwards remained silent for a moment. "Actually, there's an affidavit I could re-read more closely."

"What does it pertain to?"

"The company from which you rented the SUV that you crashed into the logging truck. It details the damage sustained by the SUV."

"What does that have to do with Thornbridge?"

"I'll review it again, okay?" Edwards said testily. "I'm going on instincts. In the meantime, keep our national security folks abreast of your whereabouts in the Atlantic."

"We're in close touch," Dunn replied, saying nothing about the commandos who raided the tri the day before.

SIPPING COFFEE IN the saloon, Dunn felt exiled as each pitch and roll underscored how far he'd traveled from home, and to preserve what connection remained, he checked the satphone frequently even though the early morning hours of the Atlantic meant darkness still gripped the U.S. When a text arrived, as one did now from Krishna Bhatia, he seized the phone with anticipation...

Call me!

Dunn did so instantly. "You're up early," he told Bhatia.

"Because I wanted to tell you how Bigfoot invades Sertolis. The virus has a third protein in its outer membrane which we believe it also acquired from a paramyxovirus."

"What protein are you referring to?"

"SH protein."

"SH?" Dunn exclaimed. "No one knows what that protein does for paramyxoviruses! Are you sure it's SH?" Years earlier, Dunn had worked with mumps virus to study whether its SH protein, also called *small hydrophobic protein*, helped the virus invade the human testis. It didn't.

"It's not *identical* to SH protein from mumps virus, but very similar, and for that reason we believe megavirus acquired the gene to produce the protein from a paramyxovirus. The reason we know Bigfoot's SH protein allows megavirus to infect Sertoli cells is because when we blocked SH protein with an antibody, Bigfoot no longer invaded Sertolis."

"But mumps virus has SH protein, too, yet it doesn't infect Sertolis!"

"And here's the reason: Bigfoot's SH differs from mumps' SH by two amino acids, and that's enough of a difference to allow the two proteins to act differently."

While working with mumps' SH, Dunn had a colleague create a crystal of the protein which he studied with x-ray diffraction to identify the location of each atom. The result was a gorgeous molecular model that portrayed the protein's 3-D configuration, yet Dunn was left to wonder why nature had created a protein without a known purpose. Now he had an answer albeit one for an SH protein which differed somewhat from the one he'd studied.

Bhatia continued: "I tell my students that when it comes to proteins, it's all about locks and keys. For megavirus, the function of SH protein is to be a key that fits perfectly into an enzyme that functions as a lock in Sertoli cell membranes."

"Phenomenal," Dunn said, "but two questions remain: Why does it appear that, so far at least, Bigfoot causes orchitis only in Caucasians, and why didn't the virus spread from person-to-person on the bases?"

The second question troubled Dunn the most. He worried that if the virus in South Sudan was closely related to the virus in the U.S. and had passed from the French travelers to the physician who evaluated them, transmissibility was a real concern. On the other hand, if transmission from person-to-person had occurred in South Sudan, why didn't it happen in the U.S.? It made him wonder again whether the physician in South Sudan had acquired the virus from camel urine or saliva unknowingly.

"We're looking into those questions," Bhatia replied.

Dunn's thoughts raced. "It'd help us greatly if we obtained the South Sudan virus to see how it compares to our strain."

"Do you know anyone in Cairo?"

"In Cairo, no, but in Istanbul, yes, a researcher who recently published a paper describing interaction between chronic stress and reduced sperm counts. I'll see if he'll reach out to the folks in Cairo."

After remaining silent for a moment, Bhatia said, "That's fine, Wilbur, but what I really want to know is when you're coming home."

WITH A PROJECTED arrival in the Azores less than eight hours away, Dunn peeked through the portholes for signs of land. He longed to see something other than rising and falling swells and the drab interior of a racing tri, but finding nothing, he checked the satphone to discover an email whose username made his pulse bound.

DudleyHumpback was a moniker his anatomy team had respectfully applied to their cadaver during the first month of medical school. Out of deference, the quartet whispered the name while huddled over the corpse, but because Dunn was sure fewer than a dozen classmates had heard it, he was astounded to see it reappear as a username…

You're being eavesdropped! Find somewhere safe and call me at 202-402-2202.

The number was as mysterious as the emailer, and keeping both fresh on the screen, Dunn rushed from the saloon to the ladder which he scaled just enough of to catch Irina's eye on deck.

"Get down!" she growled, motioning toward satellites unseen.

Dunn placed a finger to his lips and beckoned her to take the satphone he held out for her.

Leaving the helm, she took it, and after reading its screen, she drew back and combed the cockpit before signaling Dunn to join her on deck. Assisting him with his vest and lifeline, she then led him to a hold beyond the mast where he'd seen her retrieve a bucket the day before. It was a dark recess which barely accommodated a broom and assorted cleaning supplies, but Irina's outstretched arm signaled Dunn to enter it.

Lowering himself, he watched the door close above his head. With only a sliver of light entering the void, he dialed the number *DudleyHumpback* had provided. A response came immediately… "Are you in a safe place to speak, Wilbur?"

Dunn recognized the voice as Garrett Fitzgerald's because he'd never heard anyone else accent the second syllable of his first name the way Fitzgerald did. "Define 'safe,' " he parried.

"I guess nowhere's safe now because they know exactly where you are and have placed microphones about the trimaran. They've listened to everything you've said since the raid."

"Who's on the line besides the two of us, Garrett?"

"No one, I promise!" He sighed. "It's a prepaid mobile I got just to call you."

"Why'd you take the risk?"

"Because, I don't want you captured, and that could happen any time!" His pitch rose: "How'd you evade the commandos?"

"That'll remain a secret."

"Wil... *bur*, the next time they intercept you, they'll seize the tri and haul it to drydock to find you! They're furious you called your attorney about the Vice President. They have Jim Edwards under surveillance, too."

Dunn shuddered at the prospect of losing Edwards as a confidant. "Look, I've got dirt on Thornbridge! He paid the widow to create a false front of being a godfather to the man I killed in Sawtooth, yet he was no such thing. I'm going to find out why he did that!"

"Don't mess with Thornbridge, Wilbur. He'll get the better of you concerning a delusional widow."

"She didn't sound delusional to me yesterday. She insisted Thornbridge paid her to arrange the godfather scheme, but she wants out of the deal now."

"She *is* out! Far out."

"What do you mean?"

"I just learned a coroner in Idaho determined she committed suicide last night. She left a stack of oxycodone by her bed."

From Dunn's hand, the satphone fell to the deck where it remained beneath a broom while he struggled to compose himself.

UPON RETURNING TO the helm, Dunn found Irina holding an open notebook across which she'd scrolled, *What did you learn?*

He penned a response...

> *That was a friend from the Pentagon. He confirmed the commandos planted microphones all over the tri.*

Irina scoured the control panel again for implants before whispering in Dunn's ear: "They have more than listened; they have followed us, too." She handed Dunn a pair of binoculars and pointed toward the stern.

Although the sun was well into its ascent, an orange blush remained on the water. Above it, Dunn saw three vessels trailing them. "When did you notice them?" he whispered.

"At daybreak."

"Are they gaining ground?"

"No, they are traveling our speed." With a sudden tilt of the tri, Irina lunged into his chest but without delay extracted herself and reached for the notebook as if embarrassed for losing balance. In the notebook, she wrote, *Come with me. We have much to plan.*

At the saloon table, she sat beside Dunn and whispered, "How well do you swim?"

Dunn stiffened. "What does it matter?"

"We need to change our drop-off plans for you." She leaned back and ran her eyes over his body. "You are tall and thin, so I must ask you to wade a hundred meters after you leave the tri in the Azores. Can you do that?"

Dunn demurred. "If the currents aren't strong, yes, but why would I have to?"

"So they will not see you depart the tri."

Dunn listened to her plans which called for slipping into open waters and then swimming through a patch of ocean pricked by rocky projections. Upon reaching one, he'd find a cave to wait in for her middle brother, Pablo, to rescue him. His hiding place inside would be an excavated pocket she called a "hypogeum" where ancient Azoreans entombed their dead.

"Are there bones there?" he asked.

"In some hypogea, yes, so you must choose a resting spot accordingly."

17

THREE CLUSTERS OF islands stretching hundreds of miles in a northwest-southeast swath comprise the Azores archipelago nine hundred miles west of continental Portugal. Because the islands overlie a junction of three of the world's principal tectonic plates—the North American, Eurasian, and African—the archipelago is active seismically with volcanoes dotting its faults. One volcano, Mount Pico on Pico Island, rises over seven thousand feet and is Portugal's tallest mountain.

Dunn's first view of the archipelago came at sunset as he stood with Irina on the cockpit. In the distance, golden rays splashed across a rocky projection erupting from the sea. With binoculars, he examined the geologic formation which reminded him of Yosemite's Half Dome or the second-tallest peak overlooking the harbor of Rio de Janeiro, a granite summit known as Pão de Açúcar, or "sugarloaf," but what impressed him especially was the forest of smaller rocky spikes which pricked the sea like whiskers needing a shave.

"Our gateway to the Azores," Irina whispered.

"It looks hostile," Dunn murmured.

"Which is why I picked the area to drop you off."

Dunn assessed the most massive projection of the forest. "You said I'd have to swim a hundred yards to reach a cave in that tower, but it looks to be much farther than that from where the spikes begin."

"We will motor through the spikes."

"Is that possible?"

"If you know them as I do, yes." She looked at Dunn solemnly. "I come here to be alone because no ships dare approach the area."

For good reason, Dunn thought. The closer they came to the projections the more they looked like knife blades. "How did such a place come to be?"

"Volcanic eruptions." Irina left a hand on the wheel while placing the other on Dunn's shoulder which she used to pull herself close to his ear. "If we were here in broad daylight, you would see different hues of blue from varying depths of a submerged caldera ahead. The grand projection was formed by successive eruptions from the volcano's center while the smaller spikes around it arose from lava spitting from smaller vents."

Turning with the binoculars, Dunn focused on the ships with their lights aglow in the growing dark. "They're gaining on us."

Defiantly, Irina kept her gaze ahead. "Take the wheel," she commanded.

Beneath his feet, Dunn felt the deck vibrate as the motor came to life with a soft purr that mixed with the lapping of waves against the hulls. He watched Irina move swiftly to lower the massive sails before returning to resume control of the vessel. After taking another glance at the ships, he stooped to whisper but grazed her ear with his lips. "Will I see you again?"

She turned and with her large blue eyes searched his. In her gaze were questions more than answers as she lifted a hand and gently rubbed a fingertip over the center of his upper lip. Wrapping her arms around him, she pulled him close and kissed him tenderly.

"What was *that*?" Dunn whispered as he held her to his chest.

Impossibly, her eyes grew larger. "You know the answer." It was she who glanced at the ships this time, prompting her to point to the ladder and whisper, "Now go below and prepare to leave."

DUNN DISCOVERED THERE was no "slipping into" a wetsuit as Irina had described but, rather, a tug-of-war that progressed in inches as he heaved on the thick neoprene. Bit by bit, he yanked it over his calves and thighs before pushing his arms through the sleeves. After pulling a strap attached to a zipper along his back, he felt like a tube of toothpaste compressed from the outside.

Meanwhile, about him, everything was in transition: evening turning to night, tri slowing to a crawl, and heart and lungs accelerating as his departure neared.

Do not forget your boots and gloves and to pull up your hood.

Dunn eyed the notebook Irina held before him. He took her stingy nod as an approval of his wetsuit and then watched her rip the sheet on which she'd written the words before burning it in the galley sink. It surprised him that she'd left the cockpit at all given the advancing ships, yet he was grateful she had because his heart throbbed to see her after they'd kissed. His pulse raced faster yet when she took his arm and pulled him close.

"The ships are carrying a helicopter, armed motorboats, and a submersible, so you must do exactly what I told you."

Her proclamation left Dunn feeling woefully inadequate. He worried that armed motorboats loaded with Navy SEALS would spot him as he swam or, worse, that a submersible might emerge from the depths to snag him with a robotic arm.

"I need to tend the helm," Irina said, "but I will return to tell you when to leave."

Dunn went to a porthole where he saw moonlight draping the first rocky spike they'd passed. It was a strategic landmark because Irina had told him that Portugal's territorial waters of the Azores officially began several hundred meters beyond the spike, and if the U.S. Navy planned to raid the tri again, they'd have to do so before entering Portugal waters; to do otherwise without permission would constitute invasion of a sovereign nation.

Sweat pooled beneath Dunn's wetsuit, yet he felt a hand grasp his arm, and when he turned, he found Irina peering at him with an unmistakable expression suggesting it was time for him to depart. Cupping her shoulders, he whispered, "You've left me swirling by that kiss. What's going on?"

Her peer deepened. "Look into your heart; the answer is there."

"You can't *do* this, Irina—bring me aboard a tri with the lure of a child's moccasin and a vague claim that a man in a photo being tortured will explain how he got it." He reached for the notebook in Irina's hand and opened it. "I'm not a blank sheet you can scroll your lips across willy-nilly."

She drew back. "Is that how you perceived my kiss—'willy-nilly'? Did it lack meaning? Yesterday, while we fixed the light together, I saw feelings in your eyes. Was I wrong?"

"I don't know."

"Very well, it is time for you to go! They may board at any time!" She strutted to the ladder and began climbing to the helm.

Dunn raced after her. "Wait!" he whispered, rushing to catch her. Midway up the rungs, he saw her look down at him with a finger across her lips. With her other arm, she pointed to the sea to command him to go.

Upon reaching the deck, Dunn crept to the stern where he donned his fins, mask, and snorkel. He found a waterproof bag there, too, which contained a flashlight, power bar, drinking water, and assorted sundries Irina had packed for him. With everything secure, he mounted the gunwale and crawled along the center hull to its end where he glanced across the water to find two motorboats racing toward him from a ship under a moonlit sky. The sight sent a chill down his spine yet swelled his courage to drop into the water.

A few seconds passed before a cold shock gripped him through the neoprene, but the layer of water that formed between his skin and suit soon warmed as he began swimming in the direction Irina instructed. To his relief, buoyancy wasn't an issue because of the wetsuit, and because he'd snorkeled before, he knew how to clear his mask which allowed him to keep track of a moonlit dome a hundred yards away where he was to take refuge.

After swimming freestyle until his arms burned, he flipped onto his back and kicked his fins. At the top of a swell, he caught a glimpse of the tri only to see it come alight a moment later in strobes pointing at it from behind. On a subsequent rise, he saw two motorboats chasing the tri with its sails taught, but then a current pulled him around a rocky outcrop and he turned his attention to the approaching dome.

Looming in his mind was Irina's warning he had only one chance to land the dome, and to do so, he needed to take exquisite care to align the approach. Any misjudgment would sweep him past an opening to a cave where he was to hide and leave him flotsam in an expansive ocean.

Even in moonlight, the water turned into a collage of hues as the sunken caldera revealed itself in a web of varying depths that portrayed as lighter-colored areas followed by darker ones. From the shallower depths came menacing spikes which forced Dunn to adjust his course repeatedly to keep from striking them.

With the dome in clear sight, he stopped swimming to gauge the strength and direction of the current. To his relief, he realized he was being pulled toward his target, introducing the next challenge: to negotiate a current which Irina said would bifurcate before the dome. If he got caught in the wrong direction, he'd miss the cave with no chance to swim back.

Kicking his fins with fine-tuned precision, he watched the dome's mighty walls approach. And then the current separated to send him in the direction he sought, but the rapidity with which it flowed made him worry he'd fly by the cave's mouth. With just yards separating him from the wall, he kicked his fins to reach the rock surface which he glided along with one hand on it at all times.

Everything came down to feel then, and in moments he sensed his arms lunge through a gap. Kicking with every muscle fiber available, he propelled himself toward the cave's opening, but the current proved too strong to conquer. With a desperate lunge, he grasped a ledge on the downstream end of the cave's mouth and clung to it with one hand as he prepared to become flotsam in a desolate ocean.

DUNN FOUND IT ironic that his survival depended on finding a way into a mausoleum. Fearing cramps if he kicked or pulled against the current any longer, his thoughts turned to the horse in the painting in his study. While its master stooped over a fire in the blowing snow, the animal pressed against a boulder to shelter from the wind, a position much like the one Dunn assumed now.

Drawing strength from the horse, he angled his fins in a fashion that caused the current to push his body against the rock and in doing so, found it easier to hold the ledge. Using the strength that remained, he pulled himself forward to get a second hold on the rock which allowed him to advance upstream. With a series of kicks, he propelled himself into the cave's entrance where he noticed a sudden freedom from the current. In the darkness, he extracted the flashlight from his bag and, turning it on, discovered a passageway that made him think he'd entered an abandoned mining tunnel only here the tunnel was watery with no floor in sight.

He pressed ahead to an oval chamber shaped like a spaceship he'd ridden as a boy at an amusement park where an enclosed capsule spun at dizzying speeds to send his back against a wall. He waited for the spinning to begin only to realize this was no joy ride about to start.

Resting for a moment, he mulled how the chamber had come to be, concluding volcanic gas from a lava spurt had somehow remained in place as the lava cooled. Shining the light about, he noticed primitive paintings along the walls that depicted boats, fish, and a sea monster part-squid, octopus, and dragon. It comforted him that the ceiling was far higher than the passageway and that the high-tide mark left ample room for dryness. Although the prospect of running out of oxygen if high-tide sealed the opening crossed his mind, he worried more about losing battery power in his flashlight. And then fear gripped him: Had Irina sent him here to die? If so, his bones would join those of others in the watery graveyard.

COMING TO HIS senses, Dunn surveyed the chamber for a place to exit the water and unload his bag. He began swimming around the perimeter to examine its sloping walls which rose some twenty feet to form the domed ceiling. Pocking the walls were indentations of varying sizes, and when he came to one of ample width, he placed his palms on it and kicked his fins to plop atop it. To his surprise, he found a pool beside him holding urchins and starfish but no bones.

After removing his fins, he scaled a slope toward another indentation higher up, pausing along the way to inspect cavities which held decaying bones in depressions Irina referred to as hypogea. Looking down at one point, he noticed a large fish race by.

Upon reaching his target indentation, he summoned the courage to peek over the ledge into what turned out to be a large hypogeum. Its contents stunned him: a rock placed above a laminated sheet of paper which read…

Dr. Dunn,

Connect the cable Irina gave you to your satphone and then extend the cable to the cave entrance. I will come for you when I can.

Pablo

Dunn's confidence in Irina surged. When she told him earlier of the need to change drop-off plans in the Azores to evade U.S Navy commandos following them, he worried her choice of a cave located among hostile rocky projections bore too much risk of failure. His doubts peaked when she told him that his satphone would serve as a locating device for Pablo to find him if he successfully ran a cable from the cave center to the ocean where an inflatable balloon would transmit a GPS signal to Pablo.

Unpacking his bag, he connected the satphone to the end of a cable and then secured the mobile on the hypogeum floor with a small rock atop it. A descent of the slope returned him to the water which he swam through to the cave entrance where he inflated a small balloon at the cable's end before releasing it to a current that whisked it away as far as the cable would allow.

Job done, he started for the interior only to notice a narrowing of the passage from a rising tide. Feeling imprisoned, he swam into the chamber and directed his flashlight to his resting spot to make sure it surpassed the high-tide mark, only then making the ascent to begin his wait.

From his perch, he kept a close eye on the rising water while he prepared mentally to make a dash for the exit should a freak tide inundate the chamber. Unlikely as it was, the prospect of a rogue wave or tsunami flooding the cave also crossed his mind, and when he reached for his canteen and felt it jiggle, he discovered he'd placed it atop a mound of bones.

THE SOUND OF dripping water jarred Dunn from a dream of being waterboarded in a marine torture chamber. Sitting up, he wiped his sweaty forehead and, with heart racing, fumbled for the flashlight but found no need to use it as a silver sheen stretched across the water. Following the light's course, he saw it came from a dipping moon aligned with the passage which had reopened from a receding tide.

A check of the satphone invigorated him with the discovery of an email from Krishna Bhatia…

You asked earlier why we're seeing Bigfoot cause testicular swelling only in Caucasians. We believe we have the answer: a difference among races in the structure of the protein receptor on Sertoli cells Bigfoot uses to attach to them. After testing five hundred samples of testicular tissues from our freezer, we found that, among Caucasians, the sugar chain on the protein receptor which serves as a docking port for Bigfoot's SH protein has an additional mannose sugar molecule compared to the sugar chain in African Americans and Asians. This almost certainly changes the 3-D configuration of the receptor on Sertoli cell membranes and makes it possible for megavirus to attach to Sertolis predominantly in Caucasians. Moreover, when we sequenced Sertoli cell DNA from members of different races, we found genetic code for the extra mannose sugar in Caucasians but not in African Americans or Asians.

Solving this matter allows us to turn our attention to your other question: Why hasn't the virus spread from person-to-person?

"Impossible!" Dunn shouted, his voice echoing through the chamber. While he knew genes encoded proteins to have short sugar terminals, the fact that human genetic content was 99.9 percent identical across races made it untenable that a protein located in the cell membrane of Sertoli cells should differ among them.

He wiggled to find a more comfortable position to respond to Bhatia, but with the start of the third word of his response, he saw a text arrive from a number he didn't recognize and, opening it, read its words with trepidation…

Remove the cable so the balloon floats away! They are coming for you!

DUNN HAD JUST returned to his hiding spot after retracting the satphone cable as instructed when he saw light beams crisscross the dome's ceiling as swimmers' fins struck the water. Voices speaking English with American accents ensued, the first stating, "Yes, sir, we'll go inside to see what's there," and then, "Make it fast; a Portuguese patrol boat's coming!"

Moments later, the first voice again, only now from inside the chamber: "Look at his place! The walls are riddled with recesses."

Splashing sounds, then: "Sir, I found some bones; it's a graveyard!"

"Whatever, inspect every recess."

"But what about the Portuguese Zodiac?"

"Work fast!"

More swimming sounds before and urgent command: "Go check that recess near the ceiling! It's bigger than the others."

"Okay, but I'll have to remove my fins to get there."

"Do it, and then we'll go!"

Dunn heard a grunt followed by the sound of a body plop onto a ledge. A light beam then struck the ceiling immediately above him and grew more intense as the sound of breathing intensified. Inside his hold, Dunn clenched a fist to defend himself.

"Call it off!" a cry came from below. "The Portuguese have ordered us to evacuate!"

A loud splash was followed by kicking sounds that filled the chamber. To Dunn's relief, they grew more faint by the moment before disappearing altogether, but even in the silence he remained motionless on his back to allow his pulse to slow, all the while fingering the remnant of a bone beside his half-empty canteen.

DAWN COULDN'T COME too soon. In the stillness of the chamber, Dunn watched moonlight fade from the water to leave the space so dark he recalled another oldie his mother used to play while mending clothes, one by The Mamas and The Papas called,

Dedicated to the One I Love. In it was a lyric, *And the darkest hour is just before dawn*. It was a theme he'd heard others sing about, too, as in Emmylou Harris's soulful rendition of *The Darkest Hour is Just Before Dawn*, and he'd experienced the darkness repeatedly while camping in the mountains, deserts, and plains of the U.S., a darkness that, like the present one, was accompanied by a bone-numbing cold.

As much as he longed for daybreak, he suspected Pablo would come under the cover of night, and since he had nothing to do but wait, he performed a ritual of gratitude for eluding the men who'd come looking for him earlier. It was a ritual he created by combining his ancestors' practice of burying the dead in caves and rock fissures with traditions of tribes from the southeast who exhumed corpses, cleaned the bones, and then returned them to the earth. Collecting bones from the floor of the hypogeum, he took them to the water and cleaned them gently before replacing them.

With the intruders gone, he repeated the task of extending the satphone cable to its former position outside the cave's entrance. He rewarded himself for the effort by rationing his protein bar and water for a pre-dawn snack, saving the remainder in case he had to wait out another day. With sweetness still in his mouth, he heard the satphone ring as an unfamiliar number flashed across the screen. He connected without saying anything.

"Wilbur? This is Jim Edwards."

"Jim, great to hear from you!"

"Am I imagining, or is there an echo?"

Dunn explained his situation. "What about you? Fitzgerald told me the Feds are surveilling you because of our discussion about the Vice President."

"Which is why I called from a clandestine phone."

"How'd you learn you were under surveillance?"

"A friend of mine from the Justice Department told me."

"How'd he know?"

"He's privy to all wiretaps in the U.S., and he became alarmed by the way mine was approved."

"Who approved it?"

"The White House, and they did so without a judge, court, or Justice Department review."

Sweating anew, Dunn unzipped his wetsuit.

Edwards: "Normally, wiretap applications of this kind go through the Foreign Intelligence Surveillance Court given the Feds currently view you as a possible abettor of terrorists. Yet, in my case, the application bypassed the Court and went to the White House instead."

"Who in the White House approved your wiretap?"

"I don't know; my friend is looking into that. In the meantime, I called to tell you the widow in Idaho is dead."

"I know, Garrett Fitzgerald told me yesterday."

"You shouldn't be talking to him! Refer him to me instead."

"I trust him, Jim. He called me from a prepaid mobile to talk in confidence."

"Wise up, Wilbur! Someone in the Pentagon is pressuring the coroner in Idaho to withhold critical findings from the widow's autopsy report."

"What sort of findings?"

"Toxicology results which indicate the woman didn't commit suicide."

"Are you saying it was a homicide?"

"Let's put it this way: She didn't die by accident or by self-inflicted means."

WITH A SEEMINGLY endless night over, Dunn immersed himself in his private saltwater pool. Having removed his wet suit, he rubbed his body to cleanse it of sweat that had soaked his skin since leaving the tri. Although the water was cold, he relished the freedom of nakedness without neoprene constricting each pore and tugging every hair. Until, that is, he heard a clank from the distant end of the passage, a noise distinct from the dripping water, lapping waves, and subtle yet audible hum of shifting currents he'd become accustomed to. He froze as the sound repeated itself—clank—and then again in series, each louder than the previous. Whatever it was that made the noise approached steadily.

Slipping out of the water, he scrambled to the hypogeum where he stooped behind its ledge. With eyes locked like a sentry's, he peered at the passage opening to await its entrant. It arrived shortly in the form of a scuba diver whose tank clanked against the passage ceiling a final time before the wetsuit-clad body moved to the bottom step beneath Dunn's refuge. Dunn's eyes sharpened as he watched the diver raise his mask to reveal a dark moustache above a set of well-cared for teeth.

"Dr. Dunn, I am Pablo," he announced. "Irina sent me for you." He nodded toward the passage as he lifted the satphone cable which he'd retrieved on his swim into the cave. "I am relieved the commandos did not find you. You must have removed this as I instructed. Thank you for doing that."

Reassured by Pablo's tender voice and mention of Irina, Dunn replied, "I appreciate the warning you gave me." He pointed to the wet suit he'd left along the slope. "If you don't mind, I'll get dressed."

"Dry clothes await you," Pablo volunteered, "so you will not have to wear the wetsuit much longer." Like Irina, he spoke with a staccato yet mellifluous fluency, chose his words with elegance, and avoided contractions. "I will leave you in privacy, so please meet me at the cave entry."

Dunn packed his bag and pushed his limbs into a soggy and now smelly wetsuit before entering the water. The morning light in the passage was bright enough to force him to squint as he swam toward the cave's entrance where he found Pablo waiting with a motor-propellered sea scooter.

"I wondered how you'd reached the cave," Dunn said, pointing to the vehicle.

"Without this, I could not have made it from the direction I came." With Pablo's mask resting on his forehead, his blue eyes and olive skin came to life, features uncannily similar to Irina's. "Going back is another matter; the current will assist us greatly."

Dunn left the cave behind Pablo who kept the scooter in front of them. Instantly, the current swept them forward through what remained of the forest of rocky spikes while, behind them, the massive projection faded from sight.

As with every forest, this one came to an end, and beyond it in the open sea a scene unfolded which Dunn found profoundly surreal: a seaplane tethered to the last of the forest's spikes. Lifting his mask, he called to Pablo: "Irina told me you'd be taking me closer to the stars, and now I know what she meant!"

"We have a long way to travel," Pablo replied, "so we must leave immediately."

DUNN APPROACHED THE craft with déjà vu, only now it wasn't a cutting-edge racing trimaran but a seaplane with equally futuristic vibes. Although he'd seen an airplane with pontoons land in Lake Walker near the reservation as a boy, the seaplane before him had a boat-like hull instead of pontoons. Above the hull was a fuselage topped by a sleek wing that held an engine with two propellers in tandem, one fore to pull the airplane and a second aft to push it.

Holding a rope which tethered the airplane, he watched Pablo load the sea scooter through a sliding door. He then allowed the current to pull him along the rope to the seaplane which he boarded, and once inside, he exchanged his wetsuit for dry clothes Pablo had set out for him. Moments later, he was joined in the cockpit by Pablo who started the engine.

Dunn noted the multiple screens which came alive. "Quite a panel," he observed.

"Amphibious aircraft are sophisticated," Pablo replied.

"Where are the wheels?"

"In the hull."

Although Pablo focused on the controls, Dunn pressed him further: "Do you fly for a living?"

"Yes."

"Who do you work for?"

"Various companies in North Africa. I fly their corporate officers around the world."

"Not in this airplane," Dunn quipped, looking about.

"No, in larger ones. I fly this one around the Mediterranean."

The force of acceleration pressed Dunn's back into his seat as the seaplane raced ahead. A series of thumps followed as the hull clipped the top of swells before finally lifting. It was a takeoff unlike any Dunn had experienced because the water's drag made him think they'd remain seaborne forever, but after lifting, the ride smoothened.

"I hope my sister treated you well," Pablo said, settling back.

"She did, and she's a remarkable skipper."

Pablo glanced at Dunn. "She said you were quite the gentleman."

"She's kind; I wasn't gentle when I boarded the tri."

Pablo's expression hardened. "That is understandable because we put you in a difficult position, but we did so because we do not want others to suffer."

"From what?"

"From the virus my older brother, Ibrahim, released at the military bases."

"Ibrahim?" Dunn repeated, intrigued that Irina had never mentioned her oldest brother's name.

Pablo's eyes narrowed. "I know what you are thinking: A man with such a name must be a radical, but that is not the case with my brother."

Dunn swiped a hand through the air as if to dissect two topics which confronted him: radicalization and the matter of megavirus. He addressed the latter which for him bore the most weight: "What do you know about the virus your brother released?"

"Very little other than he stole it from a laboratory in a town called Debdeb in Algeria along the border with Tunisia. After doing so, he threatened my sister with death if she did not sail him to America with the supplies he used to attack your country." He frowned. "And while sailing, he told Irina something quite odd—that the virus he carried on the tri lived in amoebas. Have you heard of such a thing?"

Dunn swiped his hand a second time to address the other topic. "I have, yes, but a moment ago you said Ibrahim wasn't a radical. Irina thinks otherwise."

"She is mistaken! Ibrahim has never been a radical. The problem is the two have never gotten along." He splayed his hands.

"What Ibrahim did in your country was reprehensible, and he must be brought to justice for that, but he is not a radical."

"Yet he converted to Islam and attended madrassas in Egypt."

"Does that make him a radical? In your country, millions attend religious schools but do not become militant Christians!"

"But, look what he did! It was ruthless!"

Pablo clenched his jaws. "I came not to argue but to help you get to my father. All I will say is there are many reasons I believe Ibrahim is not a radical, among them the commitment he displays to Muslim communities at-large; radicals lack such a commitment. For example, in the Bedouin communities of the desert, he pays for healthcare, food and clothing for children who have lost their fathers." The skin about his eyes relaxed. "Ibrahim is Muslim just as I and my younger brother, Yuri, are. Sadly, by doing what he did in America, he turned against the teachings of the great Prophet Muhammad."

"Is Irina Muslim?"

Pablo shook his head. "Her religion is the sea, sky, and wind, but do not get me wrong: She respects Islam greatly because of my father's devotion to it."

"Your father," Dunn said softly, "I saw his photo in the tri."

Furrows gripped Pablo's eyes. "Which is another reason I believe Ibrahim is not a radical: Radicals almost always rebel against their parents and relatives, but not Ibrahim. He adores his father."

FROM TEN THOUSAND feet, Dunn watched the Azores pass below. They looked like emeralds sprinkled across a carpet of blue whose hue brightened to azure along the coasts. Extracting the satphone, he felt the airplane suddenly bank. "Why the turn?" he asked.

"I want to catch the most favorable winds," Pablo explained.

Dunn renewed his focus on the satphone. "That's odd; I have no service." He pointed to the sky. "I thought satellites provided coverage everywhere for these devices."

"For the most part, yes, but satellites are not the controlling factor in this case; latitude is, and I just veered south of the 37th parallel."

"What does latitude have to do with service?"

"The satphones Ibrahim provided Irina for her trip to America were programmed to operate only within the 37th and 38th parallels north."

"Why?"

"He ascribes great importance to lines."

"I don't understand."

Pablo grimaced. "When a sphere is sliced along a plane, what geometric form results?"

"A circle."

"Yes, in other words, what appears as a line on a map becomes a circle."

"So?"

"Have you forgotten what you wrote in your blog about circles?"

"I wrote about them in several contexts."

"I am referring to when you wrote about circles as metaphors for justice."

"What does that have to do with satellite service?"

"To Ibrahim, justice is everything!" He pointed to a screen displaying a map showing their current position just south of the 37th parallel north. Scrolling out, he brought the entire Atlantic into view and ran two fingers along the 37th and 38th parallels. "These lines track your journey thus far. You started in Delaware along the 38th parallel and sailed due east to the Azores. While flying, we have taken a southeast course to enter the 37th parallel, but just moments ago when I saw you reach for the satphone I deviated south into the 36th parallel to show you the consequences of doing so." He pointed to an approaching island. "That is Santa Maria, latitude 36.98 degrees north."

Narrowing the map to display solely the 37th and 38th parallels, Pablo scrolled east over southern Portugal and Spain, northern Sicily, and southern Greece. When he reached Turkey, he homed in on a city named "Manisa". "That is where your satphone was manufactured, at a plant along latitude 38.61 degrees north."

"I still don't understand why Ibrahim fixates on lines," Dunn said.

"He believes many of the world's problems result from justice being meted out by systems that are linear and hierarchical rather than circular as he believes they should be."

Dunn nodded. "I made a similar point in one of my posts. He's probably referring to justice systems of the sort Native Americans believe in which allow for prominent input from families, friends, and elders—a community circle, so to speak." Dunn frowned. "Is Ibrahim a lawyer?"

"No, he is a mechanical engineer with extensive experience in the design of weapons systems."

"My Lord! That explains the remotely controlled machine guns he used at the bases."

"And the drones, too. He worked for years for the Saudi government to develop drone warfare technology they employed against Yemeni rebels."

"What led him into that work?"

Pablo advanced the map along the 37th and 38th parallels through the remainder of Turkey into Iran and Turkmenistan, but when an area appeared showing northern Afghanistan, he enlarged the map to bring into view a town called Yakkabog located along the 38th parallel just north of the Afghan border with Uzbekistan. Placing his finger on the town, he said, "That is what led Ibrahim into weapons research."

"What happened in Yakkabog?"

"Great injustice." With a tap of the screen, he reset the map to the Atlantic Ocean displaying their position over the Azores.

"What sort of injustice are you referring to?" Dunn asked.

"This is why we asked you to meet our father. He will explain everything."

ANOTHER BANK OF the seaplane, this time to the north, returned service to Dunn's satphone which displayed a missive from Jim Edwards…

Things are getting bizarre, Wilbur.

I mentioned in my last email that the widow hadn't died by natural causes or by her own actions. That was an understatement.

I just learned she was fatally poisoned by a chemical the U.S. Army created during the Cold War to use on Soviet spies. The agent was developed at a clandestine military research center called Edgewood located along Maryland's Chesapeake Bay. From the late 1950s into the 1970s, the program tested experimental chemicals on as many as 5,000 unsuspecting U.S. soldiers to see if any would function as truth sera. Exposure of the program led to Congressional hearings which revealed all records relating to the program had been destroyed. The only reason one of the program's chemicals was identified as the cause of the widow's death was because the coroner in Idaho ran extensive toxicology tests on her which detected a mysterious agent.

The test that revealed the agent was mass spectrometry, something you're familiar with, I'm sure, but which I knew nothing about. Apparently, it allows one to identify the chemical structures of molecules in specimens being tested. After running the test, the coroner showed the results to a professor he'd had years earlier in graduate school, an expert in mass spectrometry who worked for the Army at Edgewood two decades earlier while it ran its clandestine program.

So, here's the deal: The coroner just informed me the professor is certain results of testing of the widow's blood displayed the signature pattern for a chemical the Army developed in the early 1950s. How it surfaced to kill the woman is a complete mystery, but believe me, the matter is being investigated thoroughly.

On another note, I followed up on a court document I told you about earlier—one from the insurer of the rental agency you leased the SUV from before crashing into the logging truck. I was remiss for overlooking its fine print before the trial, but when I did so a few hours ago, I saw mention of a "possible non-stock deviation" in a component of the vehicle's suspension. On further inquiry with the insurer, I learned the "deviation" involved a part called a "control arm" that looks like a boomerang made from thick metal which holds the wheels to the chassis. Although the part was mangled by the impact, the inspector believed the control arm on the front left side may have been compromised previously. I tracked down the inspector to ask what he meant by "compromised" and learned he was almost positive the control arm had been damaged by what appeared to be a hacksaw before you drove the vehicle. When I asked him why he hadn't mentioned that possibility explicitly in the insurer's report, he told me his supervisor felt it was conjectural and instructed him to refer to the matter as a "possible non-stock deviation." What I conclude from this is that the SUV you rented likely had a damaged component that very well may have played a role in causing you to crash into the logging truck. I plan to interview every mechanic who worked on the SUV before you leased it to see if anyone can shed light on the matter.

THE DOUBLE WHAMMY from Edwards left Dunn puzzled and infuriated. On one hand was the ominous reference to a Cold War chemical which purportedly killed the widow, and on the other evidence that someone may have sabotaged the SUV he drove that killed his wife and an innocent man.

An arcane geometry principle haunted him. Called the transitive property, it stated that if a = b and b = c, then a = c. In this instance, he worried that if "a" was the Idaho widow who'd been poisoned, "b" was the poison, and "c" was him, it was entirely possible that he could be the next victim to be poisoned. For the first time since leaving the U.S., he was relieved to be abroad.

Troubling him, too, was Jim Edwards' oversight of fine print in a document pertaining to the damaged SUV. Attorneys were trained to read fine print; check that: attorneys were the *source* of fine print. It disappointed Dunn that a highly paid counsel would gloss over a finding of such importance, even if it presented itself as vaguely as a "possible non-stock deviation." He knew the finding wouldn't reverse the ill-fated choice he'd made to drive along a restricted forestry road, but he was convinced the jury and judge might have acted differently had they known about a possible defect in the SUV.

Sapped from his days of sailing, confinement in a cave, and discouraging news from Edwards, he looked out the seaplane and noticed a hazy line bookending what had been an endless horizon of blue. "Is that the mainland approaching?" he asked.

"Yes," Pablo replied, "the southwestern-most point of continental Europe. We will refuel there before moving on."

"Moving on?" Dunn snapped. "Where exactly is your father?"

"Be patient! You will meet him before long."

"Where, in Afghanistan?" Dunn asked, recalling Pablo swiping his finger across the map of the 38th latitude north.

Pablo scoffed. "We would *never* take you to the land of his abduction!"

Dunn swiveled. "Who abducted him?"

Pablo's lips quivered. "Ibrahim will tell you because he was the one who discovered our father had been imprisoned."

"Ibrahim! He's out to kill me! Irina told me so."

Pablo's eyes turned fiery. "Not true! He respects you for your views on justice."

"How could he? My views on justice condemn atrocities of the sort he committed!"

"You need to speak to him to understand his views."

"He's a murderer! I'd never see eye-to-eye with him on anything pertaining to justice."

"What if I told you it was law enforcement agencies in your country who imprisoned my father wrongly for sixteen years?"

"What agencies are you referring to?"

"The Central Intelligence Agency, among others."

"Why would the CIA imprison your father?"

"That is why Irina contacted you. She wanted you to see the evidence first-hand."

"She could've shown it to me in the U.S.!"

"No, she could not because the evidence remains in North Africa."

Wary of Pablo's vagaries, Dunn asked, "Are you an accomplice to Ibrahim?"

"Of course not! I detest what he did."

"Then, who helped him? He couldn't have pulled off what he did alone!"

"It depends what you mean by 'help.' He received assistance, but it did not come voluntarily. The virus he released over the bases came from a scientist in Algeria who runs a lab at an agricultural research station where my younger brother, Yuri, works. Ibrahim stole the virus from the scientist before releasing it in the U.S."

Breathless, Dunn asked, "Who's the scientist?"

"His name is Jacques Bedjaoui."

"How do you spell the name?"

"*B–e–d–j–a–o–u–i,* pronounced *Bed—gee—wee.*"

"I know the name! He was a coauthor on a scientific paper published recently which described megavirus infections in four men who'd traveled on safari in South Sudan."

"Yes, and the agricultural research station where Bedjaoui works is located in the town of Debdeb in Algeria."

"Why did he have megavirus in his lab?"

"That is a question you must ask my brother, Yuri, because he knows Bedjaoui well."

Beside himself, Dunn persevered: "Did Bedjaoui alter the virus which Ibrahim stole from him?"

"Why do you ask?"

"Because, the megavirus strain Ibrahim released over the military bases in the U.S. did not spread from person-to-person whereas it did in South Sudan."

Pablo put the plane into a descent. "Molecular biology is not my expertise. I must leave it to you to solve that mystery."

18

FROM THE AIR, the southwestern-most point of Portugal looked like a pudgy doughboy positioned upside down with its head pointed at an angle into the Atlantic. Along the doughboy's contours were cliffs with bases awash in white from crashing waves while plopped on its head was a handsome compound with terracotta-tiled roofs and a lighthouse.

"Cabo de São Vicente," Pablo noted, pointing to the cape. "The building was once a Franciscan convent erected in the sixteenth century."

Further east, a second cape had what appeared to be a town at its base with a fort visible to the naked eye. Glancing at the flight map, Dunn saw the name of the town and asked, "Are we going to land in Sagres?"

"No, we will touch down before that," Pablo replied, eying a desolate expanse of coast between São Vicente and Sagres.

With an eye on the water and a second on passing landmarks, Dunn felt his stomach drop as the angle of descent steepened. Along the cliffs of São Vicente he noticed deep grooves where birds landed to nest, and curious to see what kinds they were, he reached for the binoculars but was prevented from using them as the seaplane struck water. Why Pablo had picked that spot to touch down Dunn didn't know for it appeared to be totally devoid of human activity. "What's here?" he asked.

Pablo pointed to a cliff with a shadowy staircase descending to a cove nearly obscured by swells. "Follow the stairs up," he said. "What do you see?"

Dunn searched the cliff by starting at the bottom before moving higher. Three-quarters of the way up, his eyes settled on a structure carved into the rocks. "What is that?"

"My mother's house," Pablo replied. "She lives there part-year to escape the heat of Egypt and to be among the birds."

With the seaplane's air conditioning off, Dunn exited with Pablo, but despite the beauty of the cove and cliffs, his thoughts remained on Krishna Bhatia's contention that genetic differences among races accounted for Caucasians alone falling prey to megavirus-induced swollen testicles.

Pacing a pier which held a fuel depot from which Pablo filled the seaplane's tanks, he thought of instances where genetics explained different rates of disease among ethnic groups. One was phenylketonuria, a disease more common in persons of Irish, northern European, Turkish, or Native American descent in which levels of the amino acid phenylalanine rose to cause devastating effects unless proper treatment was instituted. Another was sickle cell anemia, a disease most prevalent in populations with sub-Saharan African ancestry and in those from Latin America, the Middle East, and southern Europe. Yet, for both examples, race alone didn't explain elevated incidence, leading him to question how a genetic difference allowed megavirus to invade Sertoli cells in Caucasians but not in men of other races.

Fingering a Paiute necklace he'd worn since visiting Medicine Wheel, he felt sweat stream down his forearm.

DUNN APPROACHED PABLO who'd just completed the refueling process. "Seems like an odd spot for a fuel depot," he noted.

"The company I fly for installed a tank here because I house-sit for my mother when she is in Egypt. It is actually well-suited for a depot because of its central location in the seaplane's routes." He pointed to the dark blue water. "And the depths permit small tankers to refill the reservoir."

Dunn shielded his eyes as he looked at the cliff. "Your mother's choice of real estate is unusual."

"Not if you're a bird-lover. She watches them through her windows, and as you can see, the guano-streaked rocks speak to the number of birds around." He cupped a hand over his forehead. "Ah, it looks like we have a visitor."

Dunn turned to find a woman with long, grey hair pulled into a ponytail complete her descent of the stairway. "Your mother?" he asked.

Pablo nodded. "She is bold today for normally she leaves me in privacy with my clients, but I told her you were coming."

Dunn was surprised his presence had drawn her attention given that he'd spent less than a day with her son, but then he wondered whether Irina had told her about their travels. He watched the woman emerge from the shadows wearing sandals beneath a long denim shirtdress with a wide belt. Sunlight gleamed from a pair of gold-plated earrings with hieroglyph inscriptions.

"Dr. Dunn, my mother, Alicia Da Costa," Pablo said, his demeanor deferential.

Recalling Irina telling him her mother was Portuguese, Dunn was struck by how the wrinkles of time had been subdued by sheer beauty and understood where Irina had acquired her looks. While the two differed in eye color—Irina's blue and Alicia's brown—they shared erect postures and an aura of strength and vitality despite diminutive statures.

"A pleasure to meet you, Mrs. Da Costa," Dunn said, offering his hand.

She declined it to take it and instead cupped hers around Dunn's cheeks. From her eyes came tears of anguish.

"Did I do something wrong?" Dunn asked, stooping to her level.

"Not at all," Pablo assured him. "My mother is emotional." In Arabic, he spoke sharply to her, causing her to drop her hands. Another address sent her back toward the steps which she climbed, her teary face finding Dunn's at each turn.

Confident she was out of hearing range, Dunn asked, "Why the emotions?"

Pablo raised an arm to direct Dunn to the seaplane. "Family is everything to her."

Perplexed by the response, Dunn stole a final glance at the woman climbing the steps while Pablo boarded the airplane.

TWO COCKPIT INSTRUMENTS drew Dunn's attention: the air speed indicator and the compass. While flying from the Azores to southern Portugal, they'd registered 165 knots along an easterly course, but now the air speed topped at 150 knots. "Why the slower pace?" he asked.

"The Sahara revolts," Pablo replied. "It sends its hot breath against us." He produced a map of the entire desert from Morocco to the Red Sea. "With climate change, evaporation packs more water and heat into the atmosphere and that, in turn, creates storms of greater intensity, some which whip their winds north into the Mediterranean." He tapped the air speed indicator. "We are fighting those winds now."

He altered the settings to produce a Doppler radar showing precipitation across the Sahara. "The greens, yellows, and reds are thunderstorms stretching from the Sudanese highlands to the Atlantic in an air pattern called the Africa Easterly Wave which carries the storms across the desert and launches them over the Atlantic. You may have heard recently about one of these storms causing mud slides in Sierra Leone that killed over a thousand people."

Dunn nodded, for throughout the summer, he'd followed climate stories closely, worrying that one in the unending series of hurricanes to strike the U.S. would make a direct hit on Baltimore.

"The storms that continue over the Atlantic are referred to as Cape Verde hurricanes," Pablo continued. "Their name comes from the islands off West Africa where the storms intensify." He winced. "The storms are like those in Ibrahim's soul, ones which led him to unleash his fury on your country."

"How long has he been an angry man?"

"For seventeen years, ever since he traveled to Pakistan."

"Why did he go there?"

"To look for our father who disappeared in that country in late 2001."

Dunn raised his eyebrows. "Your father traveled to Pakistan after the 9/11 attacks in the U.S.?"

"Yes, three months after the Twin Towers fell."

"Why did your father go to Pakistan?"

"He owned a mobile phone business which he ran from our home in Alexandria, Egypt. He went to Pakistan to check on his accounts there, only he didn't return." Pablo's face lengthened. "So Ibrahim went looking for him."

"How old was Ibrahim at the time?"

"Twenty-two."

"And you?"

"Nineteen." He shut his eyes for a moment. "I recall the madness of the time vividly. It was mid-December of 2001 when Ibrahim and I drove to the airport in Alexandria to meet our father who was due to return from Karachi which had been the last stop in Pakistan, but he was not on the flight. When we tried to reach him by phone, he did not answer, and that was very unusual because my father was wedded to his mobile." He wiped his brow. "So, exactly a week later, on the twenty-second of December, Ibrahim left for Pakistan to look for him."

"Pakistan's a big place. Where did he start his search?"

"In Karachi because it was there my father began and was to end his trip. Ibrahim set out to retrace my father's exact itinerary even though it upset my mother tremendously."

"Understandably." Dunn's thoughts raced back to post 9/11 when the U.S. and its allies began bombing Taliban strongholds in Afghanistan across the border from Pakistan in an effort to force Osama bin Laden from his hiding spot in the mountains. "What did Ibrahim learn in Karachi?"

"That my father had showed up at the stores which sold his phones, but no one knew about his disappearance."

"So, what did Ibrahim do next?"

"He traveled to the second stop on my father's itinerary, Hyderabad, where he discovered that, as in Karachi, all had unfolded as planned without signs of trouble."

"How many cities did he visit?"

"Seven in all, the very ones my father had gone to, and in the same order."

"Was it fruitful?"

"Yes and no. While visiting the capital of Islamabad, a store manager informed Ibrahim that my father had learned of a lucrative opportunity to sell mobile phones in the Afghan capital of Kabul, but to fulfil the deal, he would have to travel to Afghanistan as soon as possible."

Dunn's heart accelerated. "That'd be dangerous!"

"My father was a cut-throat competitor; he allowed no opportunities to slip away."

Dunn placed a hand on Pablo's forearm. "We've spoken much about your father without using his name. What is it?"

Pablo's eyes glistened. "Nasir." He rubbed his fingers tenderly along the throttles. "He shares my mother's passion for birds, especially birds of prey. He loves to watch them soar in the wind. In fact, it was his love for birds that led me to become a pilot." His gaze into the skies deepened. "When I fly, I feel like an eagle, which is what 'Nasir' means."

Dunn folded his arms around his heaving chest. For the moment, he'd heard enough and needed to process his thoughts.

19

ON THE DASHBOARD, a flight map displayed the 37th and 38th parallels north transecting the southern Iberian Peninsula with a symbol demarking the seaplane's position. The rectangle ran a hundred forty miles in a north-south direction with its corners formed by Cabo de São Vicente and a town called Ericeira just north of Lisbon in the west, and the cities of Mojácar and Santa Pola along Spain's Mediterranean coast to the east. Within the swath were names Dunn recognized—Seville, Córdoba, and Granada—while to the south were the coasts of Morocco and Algeria.

Despite probing Pablo repeatedly, Dunn remained in the dark as to their final destination. All Pablo would say was that another transition would come late that afternoon, one which would begin the final leg of Dunn's journey. To relieve his frustration, Dunn monitored his satphone closely and attended to messages as they arrived as one did now from his attorney…

More on that experimental chemical which killed the widow two days ago: It's called 'Duck's Nightmare' or DN. It was a gas that Army scientists at the Edgewood research center in Maryland administered to soldiers in the 1950s and '60s as a truth serum. The chemical's reputed advantage was its short life in the body: within an hour of administration, it was metabolized by the liver without leaving a trace. The only reason the chemical showed up in the widow by mass spectrometry was because she died of an abnormal heart rhythm which halted her blood flow, and that preserved remnants of DN in her blood before it reached the liver.

And remember that mass spec guru I mentioned earlier, the coroner's former professor who worked at Edgewood? Well, he told the coroner that while he was stationed at Edgewood he heard DN had two severe side effects associated with it. One was damage to nerves of the lower legs which left some soldiers walking with feet that flapped like a duck's, and the other was a heart rhythm abnormality called Torsade de Pointes. When it occurred, the heart problem began immediately after soldiers inhaled DN and caused their hearts to fibrillate wildly; several soldiers died as a result. The guru believes the widow succumbed to Torsade de Pointes induced by DN, but the question remains: How and why was she exposed to DN?

In that vein, the professor said he was going to talk to some former co-workers from Edgewood to see if any had ideas as to how DN resurfaced sixty years after it was supposedly destroyed. He'll be in touch if he learns anything.

AHEAD, A BLUE apron stretched as far as the eye could see. Along its border immediately below, a whitewashed town the map identified as Mojácar spilled down a hill to the Mediterranean, and with only the sea beyond it, Dunn engaged his pilot. "Earlier, you said that while visiting Pakistan after 9/11, Ibrahim learned your father, Nasir, had received a lucrative opportunity to sell mobiles in Kabul that required him to travel to Afghanistan. Based on what you said about your father being a competitive businessman, I presume he pursued the offer."

"He did, although he did not tell us at the time he was doing so because he did not want to frighten us."

"So, how did Ibrahim learn he went to Kabul?"

"The manager at the store in Islamabad who told Ibrahim about the offer said my father decided to go there."

"Despite the U.S. bombing in Afghanistan?"

"Fear had no place in my father's being! Everything was risk-reward, and in this case reward trumped risk."

"So, what happened to him in Afghanistan?"

"Ibrahim couldn't find out because the trail went cold at that point. The manager denied knowing anything further about Nasir even though Ibrahim was convinced he knew more."

"What kept the manager from coming forth?"

"Politics."

"In what regard?"

"The lucrative offer my father pursued involved working with an armed faction in Afghanistan that had splintered from a much larger group called the Northern Alliance. Are you familiar with that name?"

"'Northern Alliance,'" Dunn repeated. "It's familiar, but no details come to mind."

"The group was also called the United Islamic Front for the Salvation of Afghanistan, and they formed in 1996 to fight the Taliban who controlled Kabul. Following 9/11, troops from the Northern Alliance received support from the U.S. during its invasion of Afghanistan, and it was during that time that a faction within the Northern Alliance splintered from the larger group because of its opposition to the U.S. invasion. The splinter group was the one that offered the lucrative deal for cell phones which my father pursued."

Dunn nodded. "Yes, politics were at play."

"Which is why Ibrahim believed the manager at the store in Islamabad knew more about what had happened to Nasir but refused to divulge it fearing retribution for doing so."

"Tell me more about the splinter group that wanted cell phones."

"Its leaders were former mujahideen who had fought against Soviet forces during the Soviet-Afghan war from 1979 to 1989. Having seen more than two million civilians die during that war, they believed Afghans should settle their problems without intervention."

"Was the group ever affiliated with the Taliban or al-Qaida?"

"No, they opposed terrorist practices, suicide bombings, and harsh punishments such as whippings, death by stoning, or cutting off hands, none of which they believed were justified by Islamic theology or law."

"If that's true, I'd expect your father would have been safe with them. What happened?"

"Like I said, the manager in Islamabad divulged nothing, leaving the trail cold. For that reason, Ibrahim returned to Egypt."

"But, clearly you learned what happened to your father because you're taking me to see him!"

Pablo scowled. "You have allowed yourself to become sullied by the same impatience that stains your nation—instant gratification for everything. Many of us do not have that luxury, so you must learn to wait."

SULKING, DUNN STARED out the window at the sea. From eight thousand feet, he thought the swells looked like streamers waving in parallel as far as the eye could see. He longed to spot an island, a ship, or even a lonely rock, *anything* besides water which made him feel detached and alone.

With Pablo withdrawn into a world of his own, Dunn examined the flight map which showed them just north of the 37th parallel on a seemingly endless easterly track. Fingering the screen, he scrolled forward along the parallel to find a wide-open Mediterranean. Because he'd learned earlier the plane's range was nine hundred nautical miles, he knew another stop would come, but he didn't know when or where.

His spirits lifted, however, with the arrival of an email from Jim Edwards...

> *I've learned that two mechanics worked on the SUV before you rented it in Idaho. The first changed the oil and ran a series of checks when the SUV registered five thousand miles, and then a week later, a second mechanic inspected the differential, which, in case you don't know, is a chunky metal box at the rear which allows the back wheels to spin at different speeds while turning. He did the inspection because the customer who rented the SUV before you reported hearing a grinding sound from the area.*
>
> *I set out to interview each mechanic separately to corroborate their work reports. Problem is, according to the first mechanic, the second one didn't check the differential at all. Since the two worked at adjacent bays, each could see what the other did. The first mechanic told me he found it strange that his colleague had taken a hacksaw under the front of the SUV*

two days before you rented the vehicle without working on the differential at the rear.

After hearing this, I confronted the second mechanic, but he refused to talk. In fact, he quit his job right after I approached him. And here's the hooker: I obtained a court order to review his bank account and discovered the guy made a ten-thousand-dollar cash deposit the day after you rented the SUV. And that wasn't an employer's paycheck, by the way. It came from a source I'm trying to identify.

Bottom line: Someone almost certainly paid the second mechanic to sabotage the SUV you rented. By hacksawing part way through a control arm, he essentially disabled the vehicle before you drove it.

From the time he'd been sentenced in Idaho to undergo court surveillance for community service, Dunn felt he'd been under the watchful eye of the justice system, but with the revelation the rental SUV he'd driven through Sawtooth National Forest had likely been tampered with, he thought a far more intrusive Big Brother might have monitored him even before the accident. He wondered what he'd done to earn such a malignant intrusion, especially since he couldn't think of any patients who held a grudge against him to that degree or any friendships that had soured in a way that would explain such retribution.

That left two possibilities: first, he'd offended someone in a blog post, or second, the tampering was a random act of maliciousness by a deranged mechanic. Either way, he felt he had a noose around his neck, and one that was tightening with each passing hour.

PABLO EMERGED FROM his separate world and, seeing Dunn's distress, consoled him: "May I continue where I left off about Ibrahim's efforts to find my father in 2002?"

What Dunn wanted from Pablo was a turn of the seaplane and a landing where he could visit an American consulate to secure a replacement passport which would allow him to return to the U.S.

Once there, he'd pursue with zeal the matter of the alleged sabotage of the SUV. "Yes, I'd like you to continue," he said, "but I need a moment first to tend to something."

He typed *Atticus Quincy Thornbridge, Edgewood* into a search engine to see what resulted, but no connections followed. Changing tack, he searched *Atticus Quincy Thornbridge, Duck's Nightmare* only to produce distracting hits about floating plastic ducks, including one which described ducks losing air in a subterranean river of horrors. Deflated himself, he abandoned his efforts and told Pablo to begin.

The pilot was quick to speak. "Very well, I told you earlier that Ibrahim returned to Egypt after the manager at a store in Islamabad refused to divulge details about my father's pursuit of a business deal in Kabul. Well, a month after returning to Egypt, Ibrahim received a call from a clerk at the same store who claimed to have critical news about Nasir."

"What was the news?"

"He said he overheard discussions my father and the manager had about the Kabul deal and that because the clerk had relatives in Afghanistan, he took special interest in their conversation. A few days later, the clerk received a call from a nephew in Afghanistan who reported meeting my father as my father traveled toward Kabul."

"How did they meet?"

"The nephew worked at a roadside café in Jalalabad where my father had coffee during a bus stop."

Dunn raised a hand. "Remind me where Jalalabad is."

"Eastern Afghanistan along the road from Islamabad to Kabul; about four hundred thousand people live there."

With his memory refreshed, Dunn recalled news accounts after 9/11 reporting Taliban and al-Qaida activities near Jalalabad. "Go on," he said, "what came of the discussions between the two?"

"The nephew was amazed to learn my father sold mobiles at the store in Islamabad where his uncle worked. After expressing interest in cell phones, he said my father offered to hire him as an assistant if he succeeded in landing the Kabul deal." Pablo's voice cracked. "That is the kind of man Nasir is: He cares for others.

Before leaving the café, he gave the young man a business card." Pablo shifted in his seat before continuing. "A day after meeting my father, the young man called his uncle in Islamabad to report that the bus Nasir had ridden was stopped by al-Qaida fighters outside of Jalalabad. Passengers stated masked men had singled out Nasir, and after forcing him to disclose which suitcase was his, had fled with him." Pablo looked at Dunn with angst. "The suitcase was filled with cell phones."

"I'm not surprised: Your father was a salesman on his way to make a business deal in Kabul."

"You miss the point! Someone in Islamabad or Kabul must have informed al-Qaida that my father would be carrying cell phones while traveling to the capital, and cell phones at that time were a critical component in making improvised explosive devices, or IEDs."

"You're suggesting your father was framed?"

"Yes, and there is more: The nephew told his uncle in Islamabad that he'd heard that after my father was abducted, he was subsequently captured by foreign soldiers near the Khyber Pass in the mountains of Afghanistan near Pakistan."

"What foreign soldiers?"

"U.S. Special Operations forces."

"What was Nasir doing in the mountains?"

"No one knew at the time—not the nephew, not his policeman-father, and not the uncle in Islamabad."

"So, that was the news the clerk relayed?"

"Yes."

"What did Ibrahim do next?"

"He went to Afghanistan."

"Despite the war?"

"What would you have done if you learned your father had been abducted, not once, but twice in the same country?"

Dunn lowered his eyes. Fathers were something he had no experience with beyond the pain that came from not having one around, a pain eased yet not erased by the love of a devoted mother. Dodging the question, he said, "I'd like you to return to something you said earlier."

"What is it?"

"You said you were convinced that Nasir had been abducted from the bus because someone informed al-Qaida he'd be on it."

"Yes, what about it?"

"I'm wondering if there might be an alternate explanation: Is Nasir light-skinned?"

"Why would that matter?"

"If he was the only fair-skinned person on the bus, it could explain why he alone was abducted. After all, with the U.S. at war with Afghanistan at the time, one could understand why militants might force a light-skinned man from the bus."

A seeming eternity passed before Pablo replied: "My father has dark skin."

FROM AN ALTITUDE of ten thousand feet along the 37th parallel north, Dunn made out a mosaic of brown, beige, and green to the south. A glance at the seaplane's map showed North Africa had come into view—Algeria's northern coast, in particular, a ribbon which slanted northeast from its border with Morocco. He lifted the binoculars.

"Do you see the glistening white buildings of Algiers?" Pablo asked.

"Yes, and a tower before them."

"That is the twelve-sided lighthouse within a fort called Peñón."

With Africa beckoning, Dunn checked the trip meter and fuel gauge. From Cabo de São Vicente, they'd flown six hundred nautical miles which left the fuel tank a third full. "How much farther can we fly without refueling?"

"Far enough to reach our destination."

Just then a chime announced an email from Krishna Bhatia…

Wilbur,

Just got an express package from Dr. Omar Mohammad Fakhoury at the Cairo University Faculty of Medicine in Egypt. It contained live megavirus collected from the French patients in South Sudan as well as from himself (still can't believe he biopsied one of his own testicles!).

This is good because it will allow us to compare DNA from megavirus released over Bethesda and Annapolis (which we're calling MV-BA) with the virus which caused illness in South Sudan (MV-SS). While we're well into sequencing MV-BA's DNA, we've just started the process on MV-SS.

Dunn's response...

Outstanding! If we see any differences in genetic content between the viruses, it could explain why inter-person spread occurred with MV-SS but not with MV-BA.

PEN IN HAND, Dunn reviewed what he knew about megavirus by drawing an oval to which he added three proteins the giant virus was believed to have acquired from one or more paramyxoviruses. Chagrined still by Bhatia's declaration earlier that megavirus SH protein allowed the virus to infect Sertoli cells, he ascribed a name of his own to SH protein...

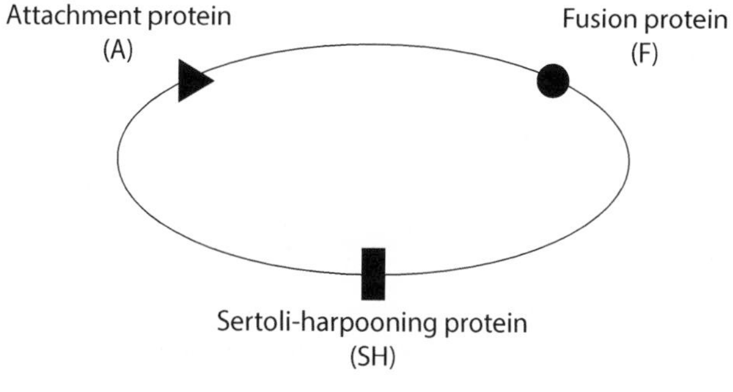

Each protein resided in the virus's outer membrane and performed separate functions. Proteins A and F initiated infection in victims by allowing the virus to attach to and fuse with cells lining the nose, mouth, and throat, actions that would explain how soldiers became infected by breathing or ingesting virus after it had been released from the drones. He assumed MV-SS had used the same portals of entry in South Sudan by spreading through the air or by hand-to-mouth-or-nose contact with virus present in camel saliva, urine, or hair.

A central question remained, however: Assuming MV-BA and MV-SS were closely related if not identical viruses, why did MV-SS spread from tourists to physician while MV-BA *didn't* beyond those who became ill? Surely, opportunities for inter-person transmission had occurred in the U.S. before ill service members were quarantined, yet no known transmission occurred. More than ever, Dunn was eager to learn results of blood tests Fitzgerald had spoken of designed to assess whether close contacts of ill persons had become infected silently—that is, had acquired the virus but showed no symptoms.

He folded the paper and tucked it away hoping Bhatia's genetic analysis of MV-SS would provide answers.

ALGERIA'S UNDULATING COAST became close enough for Dunn to identify the Gulf of Béjaïa followed by the towns of Jijel, Sidi Abdelaziz, and Annaba. With fuel levels lowering, he became dismayed when the seaplane dropped from eight thousand to four thousand feet only to hold there along the 37th parallel. He resumed his accounting of landmarks which became Tunisian in ownership, among them Sidi Mechreg, Cap Serrat, and a group of what appeared to be uninhabited islands along Pablo's side of the aircraft. "Is that where we'll put down?" he asked, pointing to the islands.

Pablo scoffed at the notion before barking in Arabic into his headset.

Resigned to fly until fuel ran out, Dunn sought consolation from an email from Jim Edwards with a subject line, *Duck's Nightmare*…

Wilbur,

Some news on how Duck's Nightmare resurfaced sixty years after it was supposedly destroyed…

The Idaho coroner's former professor consulted several aging buddies who'd also worked at Edgewood, one of whom revealed being contacted by the U.S. Army in 1999 after canisters containing toxic chemicals had been inadvertently pulled from the sea by a commercial trawler off New Jersey. Here's what happened…

While dredging, a fisherman on the trawler noticed some worn canisters within a hoisted net. After grasping one of the canisters, he felt a searing pain in his hand, arm, and neck after the canister discharged. In the meantime, another crew member noticed inscriptions on the remaining canisters which identified them as Mustard Gas *or* Duck's Nightmare.

After being rushed to port, the injured crew member was hospitalized for burns inflicted by mustard gas. Meanwhile, the vessel's skipper called police to report the discovery. In short order, military personnel from a naval weapons station nearby collected the canisters from the trawler.

When Army officials consulted the professor's colleague in 1999 about the event, they ordered him to remain silent on the matter. Now terminally ill with cancer, he defied his gag order for the first time by revealing the details to the professor. Of note is that while helping shutter Edgewood in the early 1970s, the professor's friend supervised the dumping of canisters of various toxic agents into the Atlantic off New Jersey.

I've contacted the professor to see if I can speak to his ill colleague directly.

UNCERTAIN WHETHER THE end to his flight would come by land or sea, Dunn surveyed his surroundings for touch down options. To his relief, the Mediterranean was calm while the coast held dunes and plains beyond them that were parched and flat. Both places, he concluded, offered opportunities to end the flight in privacy.

As the seaplane descended, Dunn scrolled out on the map to review the course they'd taken thus far, a twelve-hour journey over nearly 1,800 miles that, with one brief diversion, had remained along the 37th parallel. With evening falling, he longed to abandon the world of latitudes and simply plant his feet on the ground, one with palm trees whose fronds swayed toward the sea from an offshore wind that tempered the swells.

Touchdown came surprisingly quickly as the hull struck the sea. When Dunn looked to shore, he spotted a man on a dune towing an inflated dinghy. He wore an ankle-length, long-sleeved garment of the type Dunn had seen Arab men wear at mosques, one called a thobe whose loose fabric blew in the wind. "Who's that?" he asked.

"My younger brother, Yuri," Pablo replied.

Even from afar, Dunn could tell Yuri was taller and had a darker complexion than Pablo, but he couldn't see the man's hair because of the shemagh which covered his head. Adding to the challenge of discerning the man's features was a constant bobbing of the seaplane which made Dunn nauseous and eager to exit as soon as possible. The chance came shortly as Pablo opened the rear door, and in moments the groan of an outboard motor became audible before a greeting exchanged between brothers.

"Come, Dr. Dunn," Pablo beckoned.

Even with stirrings of seasickness, Dunn left his seat with mixed feelings. As he'd felt while leaving Irina and the trimaran, so too now he sensed a loss in departing a vessel that had become a safe haven in a seemingly endless foray into the unknown.

At the rear door, he looked down at a dinghy controlled by a lean man with a goatee and wire rim glasses whose demeanor suggested he'd come out of duty rather than desire.

"Get in," Yuri commanded. "Darkness falls."

Dunn lowered himself onto the seat beside the skipper. A glance at the man's legs showed them to be of similar length to his, and because their eyes occupied the same plane, Dunn concluded the two were equally tall, a finding which surprised him given the far shorter statures of Pablo and Irina.

After a brief exchange in Arabic between brothers, the dinghy accelerated toward the beach, but then, for an instant, the sound of sand scraping the bow competed with the roar of propellers whisking the seaplane into the sky, and in the falling darkness Dunn felt stranded between worlds.

"We carry the dinghy," Yuri barked. Like his sibs, he spoke English well, but in his case a Middle Eastern accent prevailed over a European counterpart.

Hoisting the bow over his head, Dunn bore the lighter weight of the dinghy as he trudged up a dune behind Yuri who carried the stern with its motor. At the summit, they paused among waving sea oats to look upon a dusty jeep below.

"It goes onto the roof," Yuri growled.

At the base of the dune, Dunn helped secure the inflatable and had barely taken his seat in the jeep when a rebellious motor whined before finally catching.

"Desert sands," Yuri seethed. "They plug the engine."

"It's hot," Dunn noted, "but this doesn't look like a desert to me." He pointed to palm groves in the distance.

"Put your head out the window and breathe," Yuri snapped as he accelerated.

Dunn did so only to inhale a cloud of invisible sand that choked his throat.

"You know nothing about deserts!" Yuri chided.

In the silence, Dunn watched a compass oscillate in a southerly course, and with the air conditioning gasping from a lack of coolant, he perspired profusely, but what bothered him more than heat was his driver's hostility.

"We set camp," Yuri grumbled after a short drive.

Although it was dark, Dunn was relieved to learn where they'd spend the night. It was a clearing among date palms which blocked the wind and afforded space to spread a tarp, and after they'd completed the task, Dunn assumed the duties of slicing tomatoes, onions, parsley, and mint while Yuri built a fire. In due time, the flames tamed to coals beneath a pot of water to which Yuri added a cup of bulgur and a pinch of salt. Before long, the ingredients combined to form tabouli to which Yuri added goat cheese which made for a tasty meal that the pair ate in silence. To Dunn's delight, Yuri then produced a pastry the size of a cinnamon roll with crispy twirls drizzled in syrup. "I'm enjoying this," he said. "What do you call it?"

"Deblah," Yuri responded, "a Tunisian favorite." He approached Dunn to collect his bowl. "Does it remind you of something you've seen recently?"

"Should it?"

"Very much so. I believe you were given a flower several days ago."

Dunn thought for a moment. "Not that I recall."

Yuri raised his eyebrows. "A *rose des sables!*"

"Oh, that—a stone flower."

"Yes, a 'desert rose.' I asked Irina to give it to you, and she told me she did."

"Why did you want me to have it?"

He stacked the bowls and set them into the back of the jeep. Facing away, he replied: "Because, I was told the *rose des sables* explains much about the virus which sickened your people."

Dunn stood from the fire and approached Yuri. "What do you mean by that?"

Yuri turned. "Did my sister tell you I am an agronomist?"

"Yes."

"And that I work at an agricultural research station in the Sahara?"

Dunn nodded. "But she didn't say what you do there."

"I am trying to increase grain yields among Bedouin farmers." He motioned to the fire. "Come, let us discuss the *rose des sables.*"

Before glowing coals, Dunn listened to Yuri describe how desert roses came to being, a process which involved flat crystals forming from sand and water as the latter evaporated from shallow salt basins in the desert. Over time, the crystals fanned into radiating clusters that hardened into shapes resembling rose petals, earning the name "desert roses."

"At the agricultural station where I work," Yuri continued, "there is a scientist who likens a protein on the surface of megavirus to a *rose des sables*. The protein has a distinct structure which allows it to fit like a hand into a glove or a key into a lock, in this case the glove or lock being another protein present in the testes of camels."

"My Lord!" Dunn cried. "You're speaking of the chemist Pablo told me about, the man from whom Ibrahim stole megavirus."

Yuri nodded. "Yes, and his name is Jacques Bedjaoui."

"Right, that's the name! How did Bedjaoui come to have megavirus in his lab?"

"He became sick from it."

"Where?"

"In South Sudan while traveling on safari almost two years ago with three friends from France."

Dunn threw up his arms. "Jacques Bedjaoui was one of the four travelers to fall ill?"

"Yes, and he feels very guilty now because it was he who invited his three friends to join him on safari. After recovering from his infection, he made megavirus a top research priority at the agricultural station where he has worked for the past decade. His first goal was to find where the virus resides in nature."

"Is it in camels?"

Yuri shook his head. "No, he talked with shepherds throughout the Sahara, and none had ever heard of camels developing swollen testicles as they'd done in South Sudan. As a result, he searched the desert for other niches and eventually discovered what he believes is a reservoir for the virus. He plans to publish a paper on his findings shortly."

Dunn jumped to his feet. "Where is this man, Bedjaoui?"

"In Algeria at the agricultural research station."

Dunn peered through a column of heat which contorted Yuri's face as a trick mirror might do, pulling a cheek one way and then another and turning Yuri's eyes into ghoulish spheres. "Where exactly in Algeria?"

"In a town called Debdeb near the borders of Tunisia and Libya."

Dunn shifted to the side of the fire to clear his view. "Take me there! I need to speak to Bedjaoui immediately!"

ACROSS THE TUNISIAN sky, stars shone with barely a twinkle. Only in one other place had Dunn seen stars so clearly, and that was at Medicine Wheel in Wyoming. During nights he slept there, he'd peer at thousands of lights dotting the sky and shift his gaze gradually toward horizons which still couldn't bend their light.

Sitting on opposite sides of embers, Dunn addressed Yuri who stood to go to bed. "When I arrived earlier today, why were you angry with me?"

"I was not angry with you but with Ibrahim. He has disrupted many lives, including yours, and I resent him for that."

Dunn watched Yuri arrange a blanket over the tarp, convinced a line divided the Mostafa clan with three sibs on one side and a lone wolf on the other. "Pablo told me Ibrahim set out to search for your father after he disappeared in late 2001."

"True."

"He didn't finish the account, however. Will you pick up where he left off?"

"What did he tell you?"

"He said that when Ibrahim traveled to Pakistan to trace your father's itinerary, he learned from a store manager in Islamabad that Nasir had traveled to Kabul to investigate a business deal, but that's where the trail went cold. Because the manager provided no further details, Ibrahim returned to Egypt."

"Anything else?"

"Yes, a month later, Ibrahim received a call from a clerk who worked for the manager in Islamabad who told Ibrahim about your father going to Kabul. The clerk said he'd overheard the conversation about your father and had learned from a nephew in Jalalabad that your father met the nephew at a café when Nasir's bus stopped there to allow passengers a coffee break."

Yuri nodded. "Go on…"

"Your father offered to hire the clerk's nephew if the deal in Kabul materialized, but things worsened when the bus your father rode was stopped outside Jalalabad by al-Qaida militants who abducted your father. Shortly later, the nephew learned from his policeman-father that Nasir was captured by U.S. Army Special Forces in Afghan mountains near the Pakistan border." Dunn paused to peer at Yuri. "And that's where Pablo stopped."

Yuri sat on the blanket with legs crossed. Gazing at the stars as if to sort his thoughts, he spoke following a considerable delay.

"After receiving the call from the clerk in Islamabad, Ibrahim traveled to Jalalabad in early 2002 to meet the clerk's nephew at the café where my father stopped for coffee. The young man's policeman-father was there as well."

"What came of the meeting?"

Yuri's expression soured. "Ibrahim learned from the policeman that the store manager in Islamabad had informed al-Qaida operatives in Afghanistan that Nasir would be traveling to Kabul with a suitcase full of cell phones, and because al-Qaida needed mobiles for building IEDs to battle U.S. forces, they abducted my father from the bus outside Jalalabad."

"Why didn't they just take his suitcase if cell phones were what they wanted?"

"They saw my father as a source for more phones, and for that reason they took him into the mountains southwest of Jalalabad where they beat him until he promised to provide a steady supply of mobiles." He winced. "Do you know the name 'Tora Bora'?"

"Sure," Dunn replied, culling his memories. "It's a complex of caves in Afghanistan."

"Yes, in mountains near Pakistan. In the 1980s, the Central Intelligence Agency financed the building of bunkers and tunnels at Tora Bora to support the mujahedeen in their battles against Soviet forces who occupied Afghanistan. Years later, following 9/11, the U.S. and Coalition partners bombed the area believing Osama bin Laden was hiding there. My father was inside a cave when the bombs struck. From a cell where he was being held, he watched al-Qaeda fighters battle U.S. Special Forces which besieged Tora Bora alongside Afghan militias who opposed al-Qaida." Yuri's shoulders drooped. "And then, on December 17th of 2001, my father was captured by Special Forces along with seventeen al-Qaida fighters. In the meantime, bin Laden escaped to Pakistan twenty miles to the south by horseback."

"How do you know your father was held captive at Tora Bora?"

"The nephew's policeman-father was a Pashtun tribal member whose older brother fought at Tora Bora with U.S. Special Forces in the December 2001 ground war. He was present when my father was captured at Tora Bora."

"What happened to Nasir after that?"

"He was taken away by U.S. Special Forces."

"To where?"

Yuri said nothing as his head sank to his chest.

DUNN WATCHED THE blanket over Yuri's sleeping body rise and fall with each breath. Sitting under the stars, he longed to stretch out as well on a surface that neither rolled with waves nor hovered over high tide marks inside caves.

Weary as he was, however, he remained awake to check his email using a new satphone Yuri had given him before retiring. It was the same model as the ones Irina had provided, but in this case, Yuri promised it had no latitude restrictions. Dunn was reassured to hear Yuri confirm that Ibrahim had provided Irina with satphones programmed to operate only within the 37th and 38th latitudes north to underscore his philosophical views regarding lines and injustice, but he also learned there was a practical reason for the programming: If U.S. authorities confiscated the phones, Ibrahim wanted them to puzzle over why latitude restrictions had been placed on them to begin with; psychology and mind games were an important component of his attacks.

Dunn stoked the fire before opening an email from Jim Edwards…

Wilbur,

I managed to reach the dying colleague of the professor I told you about earlier—the man who'd worked at Edgewood with the professor and who disclosed assisting the Army in the 1970s dispose toxic chemicals before Edgewood closed. He's in a hospice now dying from metastatic lung cancer, but I talked to him briefly on a three-way conference call the professor arranged.

Here's what I learned: After the fishing trawler dredged the canisters of mustard gas and Duck's Nightmare in 1999 off the coast of New Jersey, the military dispatched a submersible to see if any more canisters could be retrieved. Since all records at Edgewood had been destroyed in the '70s, no one knew how many canisters had been dumped on the ocean floor, so the only way to find out was to explore the site.

What they discovered was alarming: 98 canisters of Duck's Nightmare along with others containing mustard gas, nerve agents, and various toxic chemicals. Fearing the canisters might be dredged again or, worse, recovered by individuals with nefarious intentions, the military removed the canisters from the seabed.

But this is where things get bizarre: To ensure the recovered chemicals were destroyed, the military hired a contractor to undertake their destruction and recruited the professor's colleague to oversee the process. Of concern was that while 98 canisters of Duck's Nightmare were recovered, only 61 arrived at the contractor's detoxification plant. In other words, 37 canisters went missing somewhere between the ocean floor and the contractor's facility.

Our man, the professor's colleague, thinks he knows what happened to the missing canisters, but he grew too tired to speak any further. Since his hospice is in California, I'm boarding an airplane to visit him in person there.

My only hope is he doesn't die before I get there.

With eyelids sagging, Dunn placed a palm branch on the fire, removed the sandals Pablo had given him at the start of their flight, and walked to the unoccupied side of the tarp to get some sleep. Before laying his head on a folded burlap sack, however, he discovered another email, this one from Krishna Bhatia…

Hey Wilbur,

We finished sequencing the entire genome of megavirus recovered from the men in Bethesda and Annapolis (MV-BA) and found it contained just over 1.5 million base pairs. That's a whopping number compared to, say, poliovirus's 7,500 bases or mumps virus's 15,000 bases.

But in sequencing the DNA, we were not able to find genes for either attachment protein (A) or fusion protein (F) even though the two proteins were present in cell membranes of the virus recovered from PFC Hartley's testicular tissue. In contrast, we found the gene for SH protein, the one you call "Sertoli-harpooning protein," in all viruses tested.

This raises an ominous possibility: MV-BA may have been genetically engineered to preserve A and F proteins in its outer membrane which allowed virus released from the drone to infect people but had its genes for A and F knocked out to prevent the virus from spreading from person-to-person. (Remember, A and F proteins are essential for the virus to infect others after being released from someone already infected.) In the meantime, the SH gene was preserved to allow progeny virus to continue invading Sertoli cells in infected men.

We should have genetic sequencing results soon for MV-SS which Dr. Fakhoury sent us. Will let you know what we find.

Krishna

Dunn lifted his eyes to the sky and saw darkness deepen between the stars.

IF YURI HAD turned a corner the previous evening from irascibility to collegiality, he reverted at the break of dawn. "You have slept late," he admonished Dunn. "Drink your coffee so we may go."

Dunn glanced at his phone. "It's only five-thirty."

A snap against paper served as Dunn's rebuke. Turning a map toward Dunn, Yuri fanned a hand across Tunisia. "Five-thirty is late given the distance we need to travel today."

Dunn found it quaint that Yuri should consult paper in a digital age. "Are you suggesting we'll cross entire Tunisia today?"

"North to south, yes, and then some," he replied. "And you have altered the agenda I had for us today which troubles me greatly! If you want to meet my French chemist colleague, Jacques Bedjaoui, we must drive beyond the border to the Algerian town of Debdeb." He snapped the map again. "But, the distance is great."

Dunn retrieved a cup of coffee and stood over Yuri who bore his eyes into the map beside a rekindled fire. After locating the town of *Debdeb* just beyond Tunisia's southern border, Dunn saw that more than a thousand kilometers separated them from Debdeb.

"We will face difficult terrain along the way," Yuri warned.

"Why don't you call Jacques Bedjaoui so we can speak to him by phone?" Dunn suggested.

Yuri accepted the idea and stood to place the call. After a few moments, he spoke in French before hanging up. "He did not answer, so I left a voice mail."

Having taken Yuri's seat to examine the map, Dunn pointed to an inked-in circle just inside Tunisia's southern tip. "What's this?"

Yuri peered at him. "My father awaits you there." He lifted the map and folded it.

"You've asked a lot of me to come this far to meet him," Dunn carped. He dug his toes into the sand and flicked a dollop onto the fire. "And believe me, I'm going home as soon I've spoken with him."

Yuri stooped and grasped Dunn's wrist as a teacher wields a misbehaved student. Shaking it hard enough to spill Dunn's coffee, he kept his eyes on his phone. "Get into the jeep! He is back!"

"Who's back?"

"Ibrahim! He just texted to say he's coming for us!"

"How can that be? Irina left him in the U.S.!" Through his trip across the Atlantic, Dunn kept looking for news about Ibrahim's capture, but none came.

"Well, he is in North Africa now!"

Dunn extinguished the fire and donned his sandals while Yuri packed the jeep. Moments later, a press of the accelerator sent the vehicle lunging forward as sand spurted from its rear.

"I don't understand," Dunn called over the engine's roar, "how did Ibrahim escape from the U.S.?"

"He had help."

"From whom?"

"I do not know, but I suspect someone in the U.S. in the air freight sector assisted him."

"As in FedEx or UPS?"

"No, more likely someone at an airline that handles passengers and freight. He knows the aviation industry well."

"What gives him that knowledge?"

"He worked in aviation for years."

"Doing what?"

"Equipping drones with munitions."

"Oh, that's right; Pablo told me he equipped drones with machine guns that the Saudi military used to battle Yemeni rebels."

"Yes, and I suspect he relied on a contact from his work there to escape the U.S."

Dunn watched Yuri remove his shemagh to release a cascade of golden locks which flowed over his shoulders. Although the gold contrasted with the dark brown hair of Irina and Pablo, Dunn noticed a similar widow's peak common to all three.

Disbursing his hair with a shake of his head, Yuri asked, "Are you familiar with the Sahara fennec fox?"

"No."

"It resides in the desert. Those who know Ibrahim call him the *Fanak*, which means 'fox' in Arabic, because he lives in the Sahara like a fennec. He is nocturnal, as is the fox, and has large ears which he uses to listen for prey underground like the fennec does."

"Ibrahim lives in the Sahara?"

"He thrives there!"

"Doing what?"

"Being Ibrahim—what else?"

"How does he feed himself?"

"He hunts insects, birds, and small mammals." Yuri grimaced as if to dispel the notion of carrying on with such a life. "Do you read the Bible?"

"I'm familiar with parts of it."

"Then, perhaps you have heard descriptions of John the Baptist as a man who wore a leather belt and clothing made of camel's hair and who ate locusts and honey. Ibrahim is much the same." He shook his head. "But, let me be clear: Ibrahim is no prophet—far from it—yet some say he resembles John the Baptist physically."

"A wild sort."

"And elusive! He hides by day and prowls at night."

"Does he intend to harm us?" Dunn asked.

From a compartment between the two front seats, Yuri produced a revolver. "That remains to be seen."

TEXTING IN A jeep speeding over bumpy drylands tested Dunn. Despite his attorney's instructions not to communicate with Garrett Fitzgerald, he informed his friend at the Pentagon that the man who'd come to be known as the Navy Base attacker was now in North Africa. After sending the text, he was astonished Fitzgerald didn't reply immediately, and that made him think his friend had severed ties with him. Even so, he felt he'd done the right thing to send the text so Fitzgerald could alert others.

He set the phone down and looked at the terrain which was changing from flat, dusty drylands to verdant hills with shrubs that brushed the sides of the jeep.

"As you can see, Tunisia is not all desert," Yuri said, breaking the silence. "Nonetheless, the desert is expanding because of soil depletion from overgrazing and from climate change-induced erosion. Fifty years ago, the dry lands we just passed through were cattle pastures, but up here in the hills there is more rain to support plants like the one out there with the blue flower, *Rosmarinus officinalis*, more commonly known as the herb, rosemary."

Although he respected Yuri's knowledge of plants, Dunn wanted to discuss another topic he found far more compelling. "Earlier, you told me that in December 2001 your father was captured by Special Forces along with seventeen al-Qaeda fighters at Tora Bora in Afghanistan. What happened to him after that?"

Yuri cursed and lowered his window. "The air conditioning is worthless." He nodded toward Dunn's side. "Open yours, too."

Dunn released a pair of clips holding a plastic sheet across his glassless window. Folding his arms, he waited for Yuri's response.

"I mentioned it was the policeman-father of the café worker in Jalalabad who told Ibrahim about my father's capture at Tora Bora. He was doomed from that moment forward because his captors discovered a document in his possession which promised to supply al-Qaida with cell phones for assembling IEDs."

"But, the agreement was forced upon him."

"For sure, but why would U.S. Special Forces believe my father was anything but an enemy combatant with that document in his possession?"

"True, but earlier you mentioned the policeman's brother was among those who assisted U.S. Special Forces capture your father. How did he gain the confidence of those Forces?"

"He was friends with a militia leader who sided with the Americans during their invasion of Afghanistan in late 2001. Following the raid of Tora Bora, the militia leader and U.S. Special Forces were called upon to brief the newly appointed governor of the province where Jalalabad sits to inform him about what happened at Tora Bora. The policeman's brother attended the briefing as a security officer and heard the details about my father's capture."

"Did they discuss what plans they had for your father?"

Yuri's face tightened. "Yes, U.S. soldiers were to take him to a town in northern Afghanistan called Mazar-i-Sharif near the border of Uzbekistan."

"Why there?"

"That was Ibrahim's question, too."

"Did he get an answer?"

"Not in Jalalabad because the policeman did not have the answer, but he gave Ibrahim a contact in Mazar-i-Sharif who might know."

"Did Ibrahim go to Mazar-i-Sharif?"

"He had no choice!"

"That's crazy—traveling through a nation at war to ask about a U.S. detainee suspected of abetting al-Qaida!"

"You underestimate the *Fanak*," Yuri sneered. "He goes where he chooses." He craned his neck to inspect the sky. "And we may see him at any time."

RIDING ON ASPHALT brought mixed blessings for Dunn: While it provided more comfort than dirt, it sacrificed anonymity because of increased traffic. After encountering naval commandos at sea and hearing Yuri's warning that Ibrahim might appear at any time, he cringed each time a truck or car passed. His sole source of relief was a cool wind that rushed through his window, one which swept across the eastern margin of the Atlas Mountains stretching from Morocco to Tunisia.

To some degree, the sight of canyons between hills reminded Dunn of the western U.S. Instinctively, he searched the sky for eagles and bluebirds when, suddenly, a soaring falcon came to view. Lifting a pair of binoculars, he focused on the bird with its feet tucked along its body and wings spread in perfect symmetry. While it resembled a peregrine falcon, its smaller size convinced him it was a relative, one slimmer than a peregrine with a narrower head and shallower chest. He marveled at the blue-grey upperparts to its plumage, the brown cap of its head, and the dusky patches around the eyes.

"Barbary falcon," Yuri observed.

Dunn detected less vitality in Yuri's voice than when he pointed out floral landmarks, and he was about to confront Yuri on the difference in animation when his satphone chimed with an email from Jim Edwards…

Wilbur,

I write with a heavy heart because I just saw a man die. I shall not forget the quiet gasp of his final breath; may my ending be as calm.

I'm sitting in a hospice lounge in Eureka, California looking out at Indian Island with Arcata Bay surrounding it. Treetops sway as a rainstorm approaches.

I told you earlier that the man I'd come to see was a colleague of the professor the Idaho coroner had consulted, a man hired by the military in 1999 to oversee the destruction of toxic agents recovered from the seabed off New Jersey after a fishing trawler dredged canisters of mustard gas, Duck's Nightmare, and other toxic agents.

So, here's what the man told me before dying: While standing on a pier in 1999 watching naval officials unload the remaining canisters retrieved from the seabed, three men in black suits approached him. In hushed tones, they announced they worked for the CIA and had come to collect canisters for future research. With no one else around, the three agents transferred 37 canisters of Duck's Nightmare from a truck that held them to a sedan nearby. Their departing words to my informant were to say nothing about what happened.

You might wonder: After nearly two decades of keeping the secret as ordered, why did our man divulge the truth today? He gave me a reason: Knowing he was about to die, he felt compelled to reveal a truth that he could no longer hide, and because the professor had told him I could be trusted, he shared it.

So, now the tricky part—figuring out what happened to the 37 canisters of Duck's Nightmare after they fell into CIA hands. I think I know someone who can help me in that regard, a good friend of yours who appears to have fallen on hard times.

More to follow.

BORED FROM HIS confinement in a jeep, Dunn anthropomorphized it as a muscular biceps that yearned to flex its fibers off-road. This was no city-slicker he rode in but, rather, a dirt-roaming, dune-hopping, bush-sweeping four-wheel powerhouse. That's not to say it lacked accoutrements. A sound system of concert hall quality led him to tap his feet to the beat of North African music so soulful and energizing he almost missed the beat of a different kind: a vibrating satphone. He opened Krishna Bhatia's email…

Hey Wilbur,

Results regarding MV-SS's proteins and genes:

First, the proteins: Turns out MV-SS has A, F, and SH on its outer membrane, and the amino acid sequence of each protein is identical to its counterparts on MV-BA.

But things are different with genes. While MV-BA lacks genes which code for A and F proteins but has one for SH, MV-SS has genes for all three proteins—A, F, and SH. This convinces me that MV-BA was genetically engineered by starting with MV-SS and knocking out its genes for A and F. How else would one explain the similarities between the viruses?

Which leads to another question: If MV-BA was genetically engineered, who did it and why?

And on a completely different note, what's with your friend, Garrett Fitzgerald? He turned up at the lab today in civilian clothes to announce he'd been relieved of duties at the Pentagon. What gives?

Krishna

Troubled by the genetics Bhatia presented, Dunn found the news about Fitzgerald even more unsettling. He couldn't think of any possible justification for relieving such a qualified and competent man from his duties.

Eying an empty cigarette packet on the floor, he tore it along its seams and scribbled on its insides a summary of what he'd learned from Bhatia…

	MV-BA	*MV-SS*
Attachment protein (A)	*Present*	*Present*
Fusion protein (F)	*Present*	*Present*
SH protein (SH)	*Present*	*Present*
Attachment protein (A) gene	*Absent*	*Present*
Fusion protein (F) gene	*Absent*	*Present*
SH protein (SH) gene	*Present*	*Present*

The theme that emerged from the summary was that while both viruses possessed A and F proteins on their outer membranes which allowed them to infect humans, only MV-SS had the required genes—*A* and *F*—to equip progeny viruses with A and F proteins to facilitate person-to-person transmission. In the meantime, both MV-BA and MV-SS had SH protein and the gene to produce it in progeny to reap havoc in the testicles of those infected.

Dunn engaged Yuri with urgency: "Your protein chemist colleague, Jacques Bedjaoui, I *really* need to speak to him!"

"He has not responded to my voice mail."

"But *someone* knows where he is—a secretary, technician, supervisor!"

Yuri wrinkled his brows, pulled to the side of the road, and worked his mobile. After conversing with two parties, he said, "Something is strange: both people I spoke with told me Dr. Bedjaoui did not report to work today, and that never happens."

"Did you leave the voice mail on his personal or office phone?"

"He uses only a personal mobile."

"Does he have a wife we can call?"

"No, he is single."

"What about a roommate?"

"He lives in a guest house near the research center." Yuri's eyes lit up. "But, that gives me an idea: I will call the guest house owner. She is a responsible woman."

A conversation ensued in Arabic during which Yuri pressed the phone to his ear and slapped the steering wheel in angst. After hanging up, he said, "Bedjaoui is hiding because he fears for his life."

"Did the person you spoke with know where he went?"

"No."

"Who's he hiding from?"

Yuri surveyed the sky. "Ibrahim, and it is my fault because I introduced the two."

"When?"

"Several months ago. After telling Ibrahim about Bedjaoui's research with megavirus, my brother insisted on meeting him."

"What led to them falling out?"

"Ibrahim asked Bedjaoui for a vial of megavirus, but Bedjaoui refused to give it to him."

"So, Ibrahim stole the virus from Bedjaoui's lab?"

"Yes, but he did not get what he expected."

"In what regard?"

"The virus he stole was a tamer version of the one that lives in the wild. When Ibrahim discovered this was the case, he threatened to kill Bedjaoui!"

Dunn pounded his thigh. "I need to speak to Bedjaoui!"

Yuri's frown deepened. "I may be able to find him."

"Where?"

"At a place where he goes to be alone. I am the only person who knows that place."

"Take me there!"

"No, not now because my father is waiting to see you."

"Your father can wait just a little longer! I need to see Bedjaoui immediately to discuss the genetic components of megavirus."

Yuri sighed. "If he is where I believe he is, we will have to take a major detour, and I do not know if we can get there before dark."

WITH THE EXCEPTION of Jim Edwards' failure to read the fine print of a document referring to damage sustained by the SUV Dunn rented in Idaho before driving through Sawtooth National Forest, Dunn respected his attorney's skills and performance. For that reason, he felt uneasy violating Edwards' counsel to avoid speaking to Garrett Fitzgerald until further notice, yet he felt compelled to do so. After calling Fitzgerald's prepaid mobile, he waited anxiously. "Garrett, we need to talk!" he said when his friend answered.

"Wilbur, I'm surprised you called. Jim Edwards told me he didn't want us speaking without his permission."

"Why didn't you reply to my text about the Navy Base attacker being in Africa?"

"I passed the text to my superiors. They want to know your source."

"One of the attacker's brothers told me. I'm traveling with that brother now."

"Where are you exactly?"

"C'mon, Garrett, I can't tell you that, not after being raided by commandos at sea a few days ago!"

"Do you trust me or not?"

"I do, but I'm going to keep my location secret for now."

"I see you're calling from a new number, one Jim Edwards shared with me."

"Why would Edwards give you my number when he didn't want us talking directly?"

"Things have changed. He called me last night to ask for help."

"With what?"

"He's looking into a chemical called Duck's Nightmare. He believes it killed a woman in Idaho who testified against you in court."

"What do *you* know about Duck's Nightmare?"

"Only what Edwards told me, but he thinks I can help him investigate the matter."

"You've got your own issues! Krishna Bhatia told me you were canned at the Pentagon."

"Not 'canned,' just reassigned."

"Reassigned to where?"

"The Department of Veterans Affairs."

"To do what?"

"To shorten waiting times for our veterans at VA clinics and hospitals. I'm sure you've heard the news about excessive delays they're having."

"That sounds like a reassignment if not a reprimand! Who'd you offend?"

Silence, then "Top brass."

"What'd you do?"

"I opposed a proposal at the Pentagon to shut down the work your lab's doing at Hopkins with megavirus."

"They can't shut us! We're a civilian facility!"

"They've invoked the Homeland Security Act to argue your lab's not secure enough to prevent megavirus from falling into hostile hands."

"You could say that about *any* lab!"

"Not Ft. Dietrich. That's where the Pentagon wants the work done."

"I don't get it: Why would your opposition to closing my lab cost you your job?"

"I filed a complaint with the Inspector General of the U.S. Navy that outlined reasons for keeping your lab involved. That ticked off my superiors."

"This is a whistle blower case!"

"I'm pursuing that route."

"With a good lawyer, I trust."

"I've got help."

"From whom?"

"A U.S. Senator."

"Oh, Lord," Dunn moaned. "It's Craig Braniff, isn't it?"

"Yes."

Dunn was well-acquainted with Braniff. While in medical school in Providence, not a day passed without news about the revered Senator from Rhode Island who, in addition to winning hearts with his cranky, principled stands, held the record as the longest serving U.S. Senator, a tenure of forty-three years which surpassed the previous record set by a senator from West Virginia. Unlike the previous record holder, a man wedded to Senate precedent and parliamentary procedures, Braniff was a maverick, a legislator who drew on his experience as an infantryman in Vietnam to fight for causes he believed in even if it meant crossing party lines. With a plume of white hair jiggling like a rooster's comb, he strutted the Senate chamber to draw support from critics.

"You know damn well, Wilbur, I've never abused my friendship with Braniff. The reason I contacted him now was because something foul led to the death of the widow in Idaho, and Jim Edwards believes she was murdered by Duck's Nightmare."

"The widow's not your business!" Dunn shot back. "And who does Jim Edwards think he is—ordering me not to talk to you while he milks you for contacts!"

Forty-nine years earlier, when North Vietnam launched the Tet Offensive against more than a hundred cities and towns in South Vietnam, a U.S. Army platoon positioned beside a rice paddy outside a village came under assault. Outgunned, twenty-six American soldiers were killed before air support repelled the enemy. During the battle, the platoon's leader, a second lieutenant named Isaac Fitzgerald, threw himself atop a soldier just before a grenade exploded. The man the lieutenant saved was Craig Braniff, a native of Rhode Island who'd worked as an oysterman before he was drafted. Following the attack, the two became inseparable, not only because they hailed from the nation's smallest state and served in the same platoon, but because each left the war with shrapnel from the same grenade as a reminder of their bond. In Rhode Island every year, the Fitzgerald and Braniff families held reunions which only forged stronger bonds. When Garrett Fitzgerald's father, Isaac, passed away, Senator Craig Braniff delivered a eulogy that brought Garrett to tears. Dunn saw the tears because he sat beside his friend at the service.

"Jim Edwards isn't *milking* me for contacts," Fitzgerald replied. "He called for help, and I intend to comply."

"Geez, Garrett, I shouldn't have implied he's using you."

"Whatever, what I want to know is why you're in Africa!"

"I've got business here."

"What sort?"

"I'll be meeting a French chemist who's been working with megavirus, a guy who was one of four Frenchmen infected with megavirus while traveling in South Sudan on safari almost two years ago."

"I read the paper which described that event! It's making the rounds at the Pentagon."

"Well, I hope to meet the chemist today. He's hiding from the Navy Base attacker who, as I told you, just returned to North Africa."

"What did the chemist do to make him hide?"

"I think I know, but I need to speak to him to find out for sure." Taking a cue from Yuri, Dunn peered out the windshield at the sky as if an intruder might appear at any moment.

WHILE CROSSING THE Atlas Mountains, Dunn and Yuri traversed forests of fir, pine, and oak before coming to barren hills where palms clustered in ravines. Optically, Dunn felt he viewed the world through a kaleidoscope of greens which reverted to browns, reds, and yellows as the Sahara approached, but as fascinated as he was by the scenery, he couldn't stop thinking about Jacques Bedjaoui. "Drive faster!" he demanded.

"Be patient!" Yuri grumbled. "The road is narrow with many turns."

To divert his mind from Bedjaoui, Dunn took a different tack: "Tell me about Ibrahim's travels to Mazar-i-Sharif in northern Afghanistan in 2002. You said earlier U.S. forces sent your father there after capturing him at Tora Bora."

Yuri reduced the volume of the music. "It was a hazardous time to travel there," he noted. "While the U.S. and Coalition forces waged war, their partners in the Northern Alliance battled the Taliban for control of Afghan cities. Because of this, there were many roadside checks, and it took Ibrahim twenty-four hours to reach Mazar-i-Sharif from Jalalabad when normally it takes a third that time."

"How did he avoid being detained along the way?"

"He traveled at night when check points were less frequent, and he relied on his language skills."

"What did he speak?"

"Dari, one of two official languages in the country. Some refer to it as 'Farsi' or 'Persian,' and because he had a girlfriend in Egypt who was from Iran, he knew Farsi. That allowed him to come off as a native at check points."

"What did he do when he reached Mazar-i-Sharif?"

"He met a Pashtun relative of the policeman he'd spoken to in Jalalabad. Keep in mind, Pashtuns form the largest ethnic group in Afghanistan, and while they concentrate in the south and east of the nation, they form pockets in the north as well, including in Mazar-i-Sharif, the nation's third largest city."

"Did the policeman's relative know anything about your father's whereabouts?"

"He did because he worked as an airplane mechanic at the airport in Mazar-i-Sharif which American forces used after 9/11. Mazar-i-Sharif was the first Afghan city to fall to the U.S.-backed Northern Alliance in its battles against the Taliban. One day while servicing an airplane, the mechanic saw eighteen captives bound in chains escorted from a U.S. Air Force C-17 troop carrier that had just arrived from Jalalabad. The men were transferred to a Chinook helicopter which promptly took off toward the north. Because the

Pashtun mechanic was curious who the prisoners were and where they had gone, he asked an interpreter friend about them several weeks later."

"Why would the interpreter have known about them?"

"He boarded the Chinook with the prisoners."

"So, what did the mechanic learn?"

"He was told the eighteen men were seized by U.S. Special Forces and Afghan militia partners in caves at Tora Bora days earlier. All but one were Afghans or Pakistanis while the remaining one was an Egyptian charged with supplying Bin Laden with mobile phones for IEDs."

"The Egyptian being your father?"

"Yes, after speaking with the mechanic in Mazar-i-Sharif, Ibrahim was certain he was our father because while flying north with the detainees, the interpreter heard the Egyptian address a U.S. soldier in fluent English."

"Where was your father taken?"

"To a town called Yakkabog in Uzbekistan. Have you heard of it?"

"Yes, Pablo pointed it out to me on a map in the seaplane yesterday. He said a great injustice took place there, but he didn't amplify."

Yuri lifted a hand and squeezed his lips in a gesture Dunn interpreted as reticence to speak about the town as well. "It is a small place," he said after a moment, "but it weighs heavily on my family."

"I noticed on the map that it's located along the 38th parallel north just as are the two bases Ibrahim attacked in the U.S."

"That is why Ibrahim chose those sites—because they fall on the same line as one of your nation's black sites."

Five years after 9/11, Dunn heard the President of the U.S. acknowledge in a speech that the CIA ran a network of secret prisons called 'black sites' where enemy combatants from the War on Terror were harshly interrogated. It was a revelation prompted by reports from human rights groups and *The Washington Post* that such centers existed.

What Dunn never expected back then was that he'd intersect one of those sites, if only tangentially for the moment. Foreboding stirred within at the mention of the term.

THE KALEIDOSCOPE THROUGH which Dunn observed the world now displayed a collage of beige and russet. While he knew the Earth's largest desert lay ahead, its iconic dunes were yet to appear. For the present, hills hostile to life predominated, yet upon one summit he spotted the ruins of an ancient castle, or *ksar*, as Yuri called it, a Maghrebi Arabic word for "fortress." From the ruins, Dunn tried to resurrect an image of its former self, but that proved to be difficult given the crumbling walls and collapsed turrets which had surrendered to mother time and her insults of wind and sand.

The forlornness of the ruins turned Dunn's eyes to the satphone. Three hours had passed since he'd talked with Garrett Fitzgerald, and before hanging up, he'd received instructions from his friend to call for an update on how Senator Craig Braniff planned to address the issue of Duck's Nightmare. At the mercy of satellites, he placed the call which connected after a trying delay. "Any news, Garrett?"

"Yup, just got off the phone with Braniff who met with the Deputy Director of the CIA at headquarters in Langley, Virginia."

"Did he learn anything about Duck's Nightmare?"

"No, but he was introduced to the chief of the toxicology section at the CIA's lab, and that's where things turned weird."

"How?"

"He was told that just before 9/11 a small group of scientists splintered from the main lab to form their own research unit to renew the search for a truth serum."

"But, the concept of truth sera had already been debunked! There's no such thing as a drug that induces people to tell the truth who are otherwise unable or unwilling to reveal it. Didn't they know that from the Edgewood years?"

"Funny you mention 'Edgewood' because the name popped up in their discussions. The toxicologist said the scientists who splintered from the main lab were convinced Edgewood had produced promising leads for a truth serum. In fact, the catalyst for creating their new unit was the dredging of Duck's Nightmare by the fishing trawler in 1999."

"Is their unit still around?"

"No, it closed after a few years because of a lack of success, but they left their logbooks behind. Braniff gave them to me. I just began reading the first volume, and it confirms Duck's Nightmare spurred the creation of the group, but I've got over a thousand pages yet to read."

"The logbooks are in paper form?"

"Yes, because the group wanted to reduce the risk of being hacked."

"What did they call their unit?"

"*Triewð*."

"What does that mean?"

"It's a West Saxon Old English term for 'faith, veracity, or truth.'"

THE LATE AFTERNOON held a subtle haze across the western sky, one that, like a camera filter, allowed preferential passage of light of red wavelengths which set the horizon aflame. Having worn sunglasses through the day, Dunn removed them to watch an arcing sun leave the asphalt glittering.

"We need petrol and water before we enter a remote region of the desert," Yuri announced. Yet again he examined the sky. Lining the street about them leading into the city of Tozeur were palm trees, one of which a man scaled by cupping his arms around the backside as he neared a cluster of dates.

Just before the city center, they stopped at a service station beside the medina, a maze of narrow streets lined by shops selling rugs, shoes, spices, and other items. Leaving Yuri to attend the jeep, Dunn strolled to the market where he joined a throng whose footsteps trod the same paths countless others had followed since the 14th century when Sahara-crossing caravans entered Tozeur for respites. With limited time to look about, he stopped before an apparel store with an open façade. Among its items were jebbas worn by men which covered the body save for the forearms and calves, and patterned cotton fabric in the shape of towels called foutas which passersby wore over shoulders as evening set in.

A waving arm in his peripheral vision turned his attention to Yuri who beckoned him to return. In short order, they were on the road again where Yuri raised a paper sack holding dates.

Dunn accepted the offer and savored the sweet which followed.

"Deglet Nours," Yuri said, "which means 'finger of light.'" He extracted a date and gazed at it tenderly. "I love the translucent yellow, delicate touch, and honey flavor." Reaching for a second bag, he displayed a jar. "Try one."

After removing the lid, Dunn lifted a strip of meat from a pool of melted fat.

"In Libya, they call it 'gideed,'" Yuri explained. "This is beef, but gideed can also be lamb. It is used in many recipes, although my favorite way of eating it is with dates."

Dunn dangled a strip above the jar before ingesting it. He found the salt and spices a pleasant finish to the sweetness of dates. "Nice," he admitted, removing a second strip.

Yuri smiled. "Good, because that is dinner."

If it was, Dunn ate alone because Yuri paid full attention to navigating a dirt lane they'd turned onto just outside Tozeur, one which coursed southwest toward a flat expanse with a white veneer.

"Chott el Djérid," Yuri declared. "It means 'Lagoon of the Land of Palms' in Arabic."

"Is it a salt flat?"

"The largest in the Sahara, some five thousand square kilometers where less than a hundred millimeters of rain fall each year. During summer, it dries completely, but in winter a stream flows into its basin which lies fifteen meters beneath sea level."

The driving became arduous and required Yuri to lean forward to look for hidden ruts. Along one side they passed what appeared to be a shoreline, only in the throes of late summer when daytime temperatures exceeded a hundred ten degrees Fahrenheit, the water had evaporated to leave salt clumps with jagged edges. As they progressed, the clumps became larger which forced Yuri to maneuver around them, but because of their number, they struck some here and there to create a cacophony of crunching sounds.

"Is this the only way to go?" Dunn asked, frustrated by the pace.

"It is if you insist on seeing Dr. Bedjaoui. Even then, I cannot promise we will get there because if we drive over hidden mud it could suck us in like quicksand."

"*Mud*?" Dunn mocked. "There's no water here!"

Yuri shook his head disapprovingly. "Beneath the salt are mud pools, and if we sink into one, our journey is over."

Dejected, Dunn sat back in silence, although with only a rim of crimson lining the horizon, he asked, "No headlights?"

Just then, a shimmering silver object swooped from the sky only meters from the windshield.

"Did you see that?" Yuri shouted.

Leaning forward to scan the sky, Dunn said, "Yes, what was it, a vulture?"

"No, a drone!"

"Out here at dark?"

"Yes, I have feared this all day."

"Who'd fly a drone at this time?"

"Ibrahim! He found us!"

Dunn swiveled in a three-sixty to inspect the surroundings. Appreciating then why Yuri had scoured the sky all day, he asked, "Where's Ibrahim commanding the drone from?"

"Could be anywhere! As you saw in America, he flies drones remotely. For all I know, he could be in the Moroccan desert."

"But how did he find us?"

"The drone has infrared temperature sensors to detect the jeep's heat, and because we are alone here driving at night, he discovered us." He clucked his tongue. "He knows we are traveling to see my father, and for that reason, he would have surveilled this region carefully."

More than ever, Dunn regretted allowing a moccasin to lure him into a dinghy at Rehoboth Beach. "How close are we to Bedjaoui's hideout?"

No reply came as Yuri reached across the jeep and pushed Dunn's head down with commanding force.

"What are you doing?" Dunn cried.

"Stay down! The drone is out your window!"

Even with what felt like an anvil on his head, Dunn pivoted enough to peek through his window and what he saw terrified him: a platinum body with propellers on each of four arms flying feet from the jeep at the same speed. Extending from the drone's body like a mosquito's proboscis was a camera trained on his face.

"I said, stay down!" Yuri shouted.

Dunn heard a gun fire which left his ears ringing. A second shot followed, and when he turned his head to look up, he saw Yuri holding a pistol. "Did you get it?" he cried.

"I think so," Yuri replied, "but that will not deter the *Fanak*!"

THE OBJECT IN the distance changed forms eerily, at one moment compressing into a needle before stretching into a band only to repeat the process. Bathed in moonlight, it resembled an apparition which made Dunn think he was hallucinating. "What *is* that?" he asked.

"A Fata Morgana," Yuri replied. "Have you seen one before?"

"I've never heard the term. What does it mean?"

"It is a type of mirage."

"So, there's nothing actually there?"

"Oh, yes, there is a hill there, but its image is distorted by moonlight bending through a thermal inversion formed from a layer of cool air inserted beneath warm air. The arrangement distorts moonlight to produce the Fata Morgana, and if you run your eyes across the image you will see two zones with different properties."

"I do," Dunn said, noting a less translucent layer along the bottom.

With the bumpiness of Chott el Djérid behind them, Dunn released his hold on the door and settled into his seat, but he remained on edge from seeing the drone and hearing gunfire explode over his head. With one eye on the Fata Morgana, he kept the other peeled for more drones, ducking at one point when a shooting star streaked the sky.

"All is good now," Yuri assured him.

Familiar with the engine's groans, Dunn knew the jeep had taken on a subtle yet steady climb toward the distorted hill, one he saw now was rimmed with jagged edges. Beyond the hill were others of equal height and ruggedness, each with knobby projections which looked like they might collapse at any time. He wondered whether some had dislodged over eons to leave rocky mounds that littered the moonlit course.

When they reached the base of the first hill, Yuri stopped the jeep. "We walk now," he said.

Dunn followed him along steep walls with grooves and crags from which a large bird darted out. Distancing himself from the walls to prevent a second such encounter, Dunn remained in view of Yuri at all times. He found the hike to be more demanding than he'd expected because his feet sank into shifting sands, and for a moment he considered removing his sandals but thought better of it given Yuri's warnings about scorpions being present.

Upon reaching the distant side of the hill, the pair stopped before a clearing the size of an Olympic swimming pool surrounded by hillsides. In the breezeless night, drops of water could be heard falling from different heights into pools that occupied the clearing, acoustics so clear that when Yuri snapped his fingers the night itself seemed to crack.

"If we are to find Dr. Bedjaoui," Yuri whispered, "this is where he will be, but we must not surprise him as he will be armed. I snapped my fingers to announce my presence because he is accustomed to that from our work in the lab."

Dunn looked about the clearing to see if the snap had drawn the elusive man, but all he saw was dazzling moonlight, a scene so beautiful it reminded him of a nighttime trek he took in Puerto Rico once to a bay where phosphorescent plankton set the water on fire. "What's in the clearing?" he whispered.

"A garden of sorts," Yuri replied, taking Dunn's arm to lead him forward.

Dunn soon realized the clearing was really a depression, and seeing it was deep enough to fall into, he stopped before a sandy lip that surrounded the depression to discover that in places the sand gave way to vertical rock slabs which shimmered with watery films.

"Springs," Yuri whispered, pointing to the hillsides. "They flow into the garden."

Dunn understood why Yuri used the term "garden" because within the depression were countless structures that resembled flowers whose petals took the form of flattened circular crystals. Among the flowers were stubby growths interspersed with taller ones that stood like petal-encircled minarets to reach the level of Dunn's waist.

"*Roses des sables*," Yuri said.

"Fine, but where is Bedjaoui?"

"He may be in the chambers."

The men walked to a section of the depression where its rim permitted them to step from sand to pit without falling, and when they reached its floor, they stood in shallow water among *roses des sables* so dense they couldn't see across the garden. From there, they inched along a rocky slab which soon opened to a tunnel leading into a hillside, and it was there Yuri snapped again.

"Yuri?" a voice called from inside.

"Yes, Jacques, I'm bringing a visitor."

Just then, something flew out of the opening which caused Dunn to duck. "What was *that?*" he cried.

Yuri grasped his wrist. "Shhhh! They are only bats leaving the chamber."

"Bats!" Dunn protested, freeing his arm. "They can be rabid!" He was aware of spelunkers who'd contracted the fatal illness after exploring caves where rabid bats released the virus in their urine which the men inhaled in droplet form. "You go first," Dunn said.

Yuri produced a flashlight although it wasn't needed because enough light reflected from the garden to show them through the opening.

Following Yuri, Dunn squat-walked down a slope that sent his soles sliding forward along his sandals. Determined to keep pace with the man who equaled his height but was more limber, he exaggerated his waddle to move as quickly as possible, but in doing so, he grazed the ceiling every few paces which forced him to stoop even more into a back-breaking curl. "Your family has a thing for caves," he complained.

When the descent steepened after they made a turn, Dunn had to grasp the walls to keep from somersaulting as he struggled to follow the flashlight's beam. As he'd done the day before in the marine cave, he made a mental note of how to escape should a hasty retreat be required.

"Jacques?" Yuri called softly.

"Come forward," a voice answered.

Dunn felt a hand grasp his. "Stay close!" Yuri warned.

After rounding a second bend, they passed a trifurcation before reaching an alcove where a man stood with a candle. Although he appeared to be in his thirties, his thinness, disheveled hair, and sallow complexion made him look frail, and because the candle jiggled in his hand, he seemed overcome by fear.

"Dr. Dunn, this is Jacques Bedjaoui." Reverting to French, Yuri addressed his colleague who listened apprehensively.

In trying to stand to relieve his back, Dunn struck the ceiling which forced him to hunch once again. As he listened to the men converse, he took note of Bedjaoui's delicate hands, stick-like arms, and dainty nose and lips. When the two fell silent and he was met with an awkward stare from Bedjaoui, he offered his hand. "Please, call me Wilbur," he said. "I come as both friend and scientist seeking your expertise."

"I know your work," Bedjaoui replied in a thick accent. "You are well-known in the field of male infertility."

Dunn side-stepped to a section of floor with less guano, but the pungent aroma of ammonia arising from bat urine and feces remained strong. If fear had driven Bedjaoui into the cave for refuge, he was a terrified man, Dunn concluded. "May I get straight to the point?" he asked. "I have some questions for you."

"Go ahead," Bedjaoui replied.

"Twelve days ago, Yuri's brother, Ibrahim Mostafa, released megavirus over two military bases in the United States."

"I know," Bedjaoui replied. "I've followed the news."

"Then you may know that a day and a half after the drones released the virus, twenty-three men at the bases developed an illness identical to the one you experienced. I read the paper you published entitled, *An Outbreak of Testicular Swelling Involving Tourists in the Republic of South Sudan*. My lab has analyzed the virus which infected you as well as the one which caused the illnesses in the U.S."

With his free hand, Bedjaoui raised his mobile. "Yes, Omar Mohammad Fakhoury told me he sent the virus to your lab."

Dunn extracted the cigarette packet on which he'd scribbled the differences between the two viruses and tilted it into the candle so Bedjaoui could read its contents...

	MV-BA	*MV-SS*
Attachment protein (A)	*Present*	*Present*
Fusion protein (F)	*Present*	*Present*
SH protein (SH)	*Present*	*Present*
Attachment protein (A) gene	*Absent*	*Present*
Fusion protein (F) gene	*Absent*	*Present*
SH protein (SH) gene	*Present*	*Present*

"What do you make of the differences?" he asked.

"I *engineered* them!" Bedjaoui replied. "Ibrahim stole the modified version of the virus from me which he released in your country."

"Why did you modify the virus?"

"I needed a strain that would infect test animals but not spread beyond them."

"So, you removed the genes for attachment and fusion proteins which, when present, allow the virus to pass from animal-to-animal, genes which megavirus presumably acquired from one or more paramyxoviruses in the past."

"Or the other way around," Bedjaoui replied. "It's possible paramyxoviruses acquired *A*, *F*, and *SH* genes from megavirus."

"What animals did you infect with your modified strain?"

"Camels, mostly. I confirmed that after becoming infected, male camels developed swollen testicles and became infertile just as male humans do."

"Did you test female camels, too?"

"Yes, and while they showed signs of infection by producing antibodies against megavirus, their symptoms were mild and short-lasting."

Bedjaoui's response captivated Dunn because, earlier that afternoon, he'd received an email from Krishna Bhatia indicating that careful interviews conducted by military personnel of individuals who reported being outside at the time the drones flew over the military bases in Annapolis and Bethesda revealed that some women experienced a mild respiratory illness beginning thirty-six hours after the drones were spotted. Notably, blood tests developed by scientists at Ft. Dietrich to detect newly formed IgM antibodies against megavirus confirmed high levels in the women's blood, leading investigators to conclude megavirus had caused their short-lasting illnesses. It was no surprise that equally high levels of antibodies were detected in blood samples from ill males who developed swollen testicles. Bhatia concluded his email by noting that the antibodies against megavirus differed enough from antibodies against mumps virus to explain why vaccination against mumps hadn't conferred protection against megavirus.

"Yet, you saw no camel-to-camel spread?" Dunn asked.

"None, because transmission was impossible without genes to code for attachment and fusion proteins in progeny viruses."

"Right," Dunn said with scorn, "and Ibrahim confirmed your results in humans for you."

"*I* did not ask him to do that! He stole the virus from my lab."

"Nonetheless, had he taken the wild form of virus he could've triggered a pandemic!" Dunn composed himself. "What other animals did you expose the virus to?"

"Dogs, cats, and rodents, but none became infected."

"Why is it that only camels became ill?"

"Not *all* camels, but only certain ones."

"Which ones?"

"Bactrian camels," Bedjaoui replied. "Are you familiar with them?"

"Not really."

"There are two major species of camels, Dromedary and Bactrian. Single-humped Dromedaries are commonly known as Arabian camels and belong to the species, *Camelus dromedarius* whereas two-humped Bactrian camels belong to *Camelus bactrianus* and reside mostly in Central Asia. Three years ago, a safari business in South Sudan imported a herd of Bactrians from northwest China because they thought customers would ride more comfortably on two-humped camels than one-humped ones."

"Did your group ride Bactrians?"

"Yes, and as we stated in our publication, we are convinced we acquired megavirus infection from the camels."

"And you contend megavirus infects *only* Bactrians and not Dromedaries?"

"I know that for a fact."

Dunn shifted. "How can that be? I'd expect camels from the same genus to be equally susceptible to the virus."

"Come with me to the garden," Bedjaoui replied. "I shall explain why that is not the case."

"I TRUST YOU were familiar with *roses des sables* before you came to this garden," Bedjaoui said, pointing to a bed of desert roses rising from a slurry of sand, salt, and water cooling after a day of simmering equatorial sun.

"Yes, I know them," Dunn replied, "because Yuri's sister gave me one."

"Then you know that no two are identical as each creates a signature profile." He grazed a flower whose petals jutted in disparate directions from a central axis, some protruding at right angles from the sides of others. "Feel one. Does its graininess not speak to the roughness of life?"

Dunn slid a finger across a sandpapery surface, respecting Bedjaoui for relating an inanimate object to what Dunn presumed were personal tribulations.

"Even in moonlight," Bedjaoui continued, "you can see orange in the blossoms. It comes from iron oxide released from the hill above us." He swept his arm before him. "You notice the roses differ in color about the garden, and this is because the mineral content in the water beneath them varies depending on what leaches from the hills."

In docent fashion, he led his audience of two to another area, and while he paid close attention to the roses, he glanced at the hills every few steps. After making a flurry of head pivots, he settled his eyes on a rose like a monarch alights on milkweed. "Look at this. Is it not magnificent?"

Fanning from a stalk the height of Dunn's chest were creamy white petals unblemished by dust. Dunn slid his fingers along its intricate arcs, angles, and planes. "These petals are very smooth," he observed.

Bedjaoui beamed. "Like satin sheets." He fondled a petal's edge, adding, "Because the roses here are formed from gypsum, they are sharper and better defined than those made from other minerals. Camels shun their edges to avoid getting cut when they come to drink."

"Camels," Dunn repeated. "You brought us here to explain why megavirus causes testicular swelling in Bactrians but not in Dromedaries."

"I was getting to that," Bedjaoui said, compressing his mouth to register displeasure for Dunn's impatience. "Bactrians have receptors in their upper respiratory tracts for the attachment of megavirus whereas Dromedaries do not."

"That's implausible!" Dunn protested. "Two species of camels from the same genus shouldn't differ so profoundly."

Bedjaoui widened his stance. "Are you a camel expert?"

"Of course not, but—"

"Then, do not argue with me! I have spent my career trying to improve camel breeding, and for this reason, I have tested their blood and tissues extensively. From these tests, I discovered Dromedaries lack airway receptors for megavirus whereas Bactrians have them."

"Are you referring to megavirus's attachment and fusion proteins?"

"Yes."

"How do you explain such a large difference in susceptibility to a virus between two species of camels?"

"What you are overlooking," Bedjaoui contended, "is that the two species come from a diverse biological family that includes not only Dromedaries and Bactrians, but also wild Bactrian camels—a species of its own—as well as llamas, alpacas, vicuñas, and guanacos. While these members descended from a common ancestor in North America some forty million years ago, they went separate ways, some traveling across the Bering land bridge to populate

Eurasia two to three million years ago while others migrated to South America. Upon reaching Eurasia, the Dromedaries continued to the Middle East and Africa while the Bactrians resided in today's Afghanistan, Tajikistan, and Uzbekistan, a swath in ancient times called 'Bactria.'"

Unconvinced, Dunn said, "The parting of Dromedaries and Bactrians two to three million years ago isn't long in evolutionary terms. I find it hard to believe two species would diverge in such major fashion with respect to protein receptors in that short a period."

"They may have diverged before they left North America, and besides, once they settled, they faced starkly different terrains and climate which could have caused genetic divergence. Add to that stressors in the form of domestication, ones that could have impacted evolution significantly."

"But, evolution conveys benefits from favorable DNA alterations, so what gains came from the loss or acquisition of receptors for attachment and fusion proteins by one camel species?"

"For the sake of argument," Bedjaoui replied, "let us assume the common ancestor had respiratory tract receptors for attachment and fusion proteins, the two proteins that initiate megavirus infection. Now advance the evolutionary clock as descendants migrated to Arabia, Africa, and Bactria. It could be that at some point Dromedaries encountered in the African desert a megavirus equipped with attachment, fusion, and SH proteins. As a result, they experienced an illness that left them sterile, not in great numbers over short periods, but in low numbers over millennia."

Dunn wrinkled his brows. "Go on…"

"Sterility would be a powerful evolutionary incentive for Dromedaries to lose their receptors for attachment and fusion proteins because by doing so, they would no longer be susceptible to megavirus. At the same time, Bactrians preserved their airway receptors because they provided a benefit of some sort."

"You can't have it both ways!" Dunn railed. "If Bactrians were exposed to megavirus as well, why wouldn't they have evolved in similar fashion by shedding their receptors?"

"Bactrians were not exposed to megavirus."

"That's a convenient assumption!"

"It is a conclusion based on research."

"Whose research?"

"Mine. I searched their habitats exhaustively and was unable to find megavirus where Bactrians reside."

"Bactria is immense! You couldn't have conducted an exhaustive search of the region."

"I did, though! I traveled through the Kyzylkum, Registan, and Markansu deserts of Bactria to collect thousands of water samples that I screened for amoebas and viruses, and while I recovered various types of amoebas, none were colonized by megavirus."

"Did you run the same tests in North Africa?"

"Of course!" Bedjaoui moved several yards away to a shallow pool beneath a bed of roses the color of lapis lazuli. After kneeling, he dipped a hand into the pool and stood with it held out before him as water dripped through his fingers. "In the falling drops are amoebas laden with megavirus."

DUNN FELT A chill far cooler than one he could attribute to a breeze now blowing from the hills into the *roses des sables* garden. It was a chill that grew, in part, from the declaration Bedjaoui made about megavirus-laden amoebas being present in the garden's water. The assertion struck Dunn's ears like blowing snow, each syllable a frigid assault, and he distanced himself from the man who'd voiced them. Although he worried initially about becoming infected with megavirus back home, Dunn took precautions while examining patients, but now, standing only meters from a man who was likely immune from reinfection, he was angry with Bedjaoui for handling contaminated water so cavalierly. "You should've warned us immediately about the dangers of water here," he said.

"I did not tell you to drink it," Bedjaoui countered.

"Still, you dripped some through your hands which could've aerosolized virus to infect Yuri and me."

"I had a point to make: that the virus is present in certain salt basins in the Sahara."

"Including Chott el Djérid?" Dunn asked, concerned about his earlier travels along the dusty basin.

"No, not there because it does not have the right conditions."

"What conditions are you speaking of?"

"Copper at levels required to support the presence of megavirus in amoebas." He pointed to the outlines of a gully between adjacent hills. "With winter rains, copper leaches from the hills and drains into the garden, and thus the blue roses."

"Was copper present in other salt basins where you found amoebas with megavirus?"

"Without exception."

"Are you saying salt basins where Bactrian camels live lack sufficient copper to support amoebas with megavirus?"

"Some had the required copper levels, and some even had amoebas capable of hosting megavirus, but they lacked another critical factor—bats."

"*Bats*? What do they have to do with megavirus?"

"Think of a three-legged stool formed by bats, amoebas, and megavirus. If one leg is removed, the stool collapses. For megavirus to live in desert pools, it needs a host like an amoeba to withstand harsh environmental conditions, but it also needs a rare type of bat of the sort that lives here to sustain its lifecycle. After drinking water in pools like the one beneath us, the bats which reside here have an enzyme in their intestines that uses high levels of copper present in the water to alter the cell membranes of amoebas in a manner which allows them to ingest large numbers of megavirus. The bats then shed these megavirus-laden amoebas in their stools back into the pools where the cycle continues. For its part, megavirus confers benefit to both amoebas and bats by helping ward off other pathogens. It is a beneficial relationship among the three that I assume has sustained itself for eons. And because this species of bat lives only in a narrow swath along North Africa and nowhere else, only Dromedary camels evolved to resist infection with megavirus whereas Bactrian camels did not."

"But, why human disease now?" Dunn asked. "As you said earlier, both Dromedaries and Bactrians likely came to Eurasia over two million years ago, and with human trade having taken place between North Africa and Asia for thousands of years, I'd think *someone* must have trudged Bactrian camels to North Africa before the South Sudan safari outfit did several years ago. If that's the case, we should've seen human megavirus infections resulting from contact with Bactrian camels long ago!"

"It's a fair point," Bedjaoui admitted, "but I have an explanation. The date-eating bats that live here have come under extreme stress in the past century, and that stress has contributed to human infection."

"What stress are you referring to?"

"A northward expansion of the Sahara into the lands the bats occupy."

"Are you referring to the effects of climate change?"

"Yes, recent studies have shown the Sahara increased in size by roughly ten percent from the early 1900s to the present, in part because of greenhouse gases due to human activities. That expansion is shrinking the niche the bats occupy."

"How does that explain the recent occurrence of human megavirus infections?"

"Desertification of areas where the bats reside is leading to higher concentrations of copper in watery pools of the sort here, and those higher levels of copper are allowing bats to increase the efficiency with which megaviruses enter amoebas. If that is true, it is likely that the Bactrian camels introduced to the South Sudan by the safari outfit consumed water containing amoebas with very high numbers of megavirus and that, in turn, facilitated human infection."

As Dunn pondered what he'd heard, he lifted two desert roses from a patch of dry ground after toppling from their pedicles. Holding them up to examine their intricate structures, he brought the two together and turned each around on its axis to see if one might fit into the other as a key inserts into a lock.

"What are you doing?" Bedjaoui asked.

"I'm trying to fit one rose into the other."

"Why?"

"Because that's what megavirus SH protein does with its receptor on Sertoli cell membranes." He examined Bedjaoui's fair complexion. "You're Caucasian, aren't you?"

Bedjaoui nodded. "My parents are old-line French, but why do you ask?"

Dunn approached Bedjaoui and, after kneeling in the water beside the lapis lazuli roses, began chanting, "*bagootsoo…padooa…ggwe'na'a…esa.*" Repeating the verse with arms sweeping from side to side, he slowly lowered his voice to a whisper before he bowed and, placing his lips to the water's surface, drank from its salty contents.

20

IN THE DARK of night with only moonlight as a guide, Yuri steered the jeep over hills that crossed the desert like ribs, each separated from the next by a valley which turned increasingly sandy as they traveled deeper into the Sahara.

The shadows in the jeep steered Dunn's mind to dark matters. Bedjaoui's assertion that megavirus resided in certain salt basins of the Sahara made him think about another elusive microbe, Ebola virus, which hid in rainforests of equatorial Africa only to cause periodic outbreaks. Whether initial infections with Ebola resulted from hunting primates or bat bites, once human infections occurred, they could spread rapidly. During a two-year epidemic in Guinea, Liberia, and Sierra Leone which began in 2014, an estimated 27,000 cases of Ebola fever occurred along with 11,000 deaths before massive control efforts by international public health authorities ended the outbreak. For Dunn, that experience highlighted the potential for disastrous results to occur when humans crossed paths with deadly microbes. He worried about megavirus unleashing itself from the wild to cause irreversible damage.

"What you did was madness!" Bedjaoui carped from the back seat. "You seemed possessed before you drank from the *roses des sables* garden. By doing so, you exposed yourself to megavirus!"

Dunn listened to the sound of sand grains strike the windshield, ones that reminded him of a summer spent in Montana as a university student when he camped in the mountains of the Flathead Indian Reservation. In early fall before the snows arrived, he'd listen to sleet pelt his tent. "I wasn't possessed," he said. "I was communing."

"With *what*?"

"The Spirits."

"What were you telling them? I could not understand the words you chanted."

"I was calling upon the buffalo, bear, eagle, and wolf in the language of my ancestors."

"Why?"

Dunn kept his eyes on the tracks Yuri followed, subtle lanes formed over centuries by passing camel caravans. Beside him, the plastic sheet across the window slapped his shoulder to remind him of how cold the desert became at night, a cold which forced Bedjaoui to retreat under a blanket. "The buffalo, bear, eagle, and wolf are my guides in life."

Bedjaoui sneered. "And they told you to drink water from the garden?"

Immediately after Dunn had done so, the trio fled the garden because of a warning Yuri received from Ibrahim stating a fleet of weaponized drones was searching for them, a fleet prepared to retaliate for the drone Yuri had downed earlier.

"I drank the water to test a theory," Dunn said.

"What theory?"

"Have you asked yourself why the two African guides who accompanied you in South Sudan never became ill despite being around camels which infected your traveling group?"

"Who said they did not fall ill?"

"In your paper, you stated, *Although we cannot explain why the two African guides remained well, we encourage vigorous surveillance for this yet-to-be-named giant virus that displays a capacity to render some males permanently infertile.*"

"Your memory serves you well, but you misinterpreted our words. We did not say the guides 'never became ill.' We said we could not explain why they remained well."

"You're splitting hairs."

"No, we wanted to leave open the possibility the men were infected earlier in their lives with megavirus and were therefore immune to reinfection."

"But, they would've known if they'd been infected! This is not a subtle disease!"

"It is a dramatic illness, indeed, but cultural sensitivities may have prevented our guides from admitting they suffered from a disease which caused testicular swelling."

"Did you ask them directly whether that had happened?"

"Yes, but they only stared at us blankly, and I understand why:

As Maasai Mara tribal members, they were very private and sparse with their words."

"What about sign language? I know it has its limitations but—"

"We tried it! We pointed to the camels' testicles and asked whether their own organs had enlarged in similar fashion."

"How did they respond?"

"More blank stares." Bedjaoui extracted an arm from the blanket and pointed at Dunn. "But, back to the central question: Why did you drink water from the garden?"

Dunn inhaled deeply. "I have reason to believe megavirus causes testicular swelling only in Caucasians and not in members of other races. That may explain why your guides didn't become ill, so I decided to drink the water to test the hypothesis."

Bedjaoui's head emerged from the blanket. "You are Native American, right?"

"Yes."

"Do you have Caucasian ancestors?"

For Dunn, ancestry was a complex equation because of missing variables. On his mother's side, he had Native American blood tracing back to at least 1900, but details blurred beyond that. There were ancestors, for example, who'd attended segregated tribal schools and a great, great grandfather listed as Indian on a federal census, but that's all he knew. As for the paternal side, he knew only that his father was Navajo. "I wouldn't be surprised if I had some white or black blood in me," he answered Bedjaoui, "but I can't say for sure."

"And why do you believe megavirus causes testicular swelling only in Caucasians?"

"Because, in the U.S., illnesses have struck only Caucasians and not African Americans or Asians. We also discovered that a sugar chain present on the protein receptor of Sertoli cells that binds megavirus SH protein in Caucasians has a different composition from the one in African Americans and Asians. We believe this difference alters the three-dimensional configuration of the receptor to allow megavirus to invade Sertoli cells in Caucasians but not in other races." Dunn lifted the *rose des sables* Irina gave him on the trimaran. Fingering its petals, he said, "In thirty-six hours, I shall know whether our 3D configuration hypothesis is correct because that was the incubation period for our soldiers in America."

"You cannot prove a theory with results from only one subject!" Bedjaoui chided.

Dunn nestled into his seat. "We don't have the luxury of time. If the strain of megavirus which infected you ever gets released to the public, it could change the world as we know it."

THE PARCHED DESERT floor held hexagon grooves like those on soccer balls, and as the jeep traversed them, it jiggled in a manner Dunn found sonorous.

"Your mobile!" Yuri called. "It chimed."

After a night of straddling sleep and arousal, Dunn saw a faint lightening of the eastern sky that heralds dawn, a light far more pleasing than the glare of the satphone which announced a text from Garrett Fitzgerald...

> *Still reading Triewð unit's logbooks. They describe testing of truth sera on War on Terror prisoners at CIA black sites following 9/11. Nothing yet about Duck's Nightmare.*

"Who contacted you?" Yuri asked.

"Oh, just a work colleague," Dunn replied, setting the mobile down. "Are you ready to tell me what happened to your father in Yakkabog after he was taken there from Mazar-i-Sharif in early 2002? I've asked you repeatedly about that."

"Yakkabog," Bedjaoui mumbled from the back seat. "It was a torture site."

Dunn turned to address him. "What do *you* know about it?"

"Ibrahim traveled there."

"Quiet!" Yuri snapped. "I will speak!" He took a moment to regain his composure. "After learning my father was flown to Yakkabog, Ibrahim traveled there to meet a contact which the Pashtun airplane mechanic in Mazir-i-Sharif had told him about."

"Who was the contact?"

"An Uzbek linguist who worked at the black site in Yakkabog."

"I'm surprised the linguist was willing to talk to Ibrahim."

Yuri snarled. "Revulsion breeds dissension."

"How did Ibrahim get to Yakkabog?"

"He hid in the back of a lorry owned by the mechanic's father, a farmer who transported silage to Uzbekistan routinely."

"And what happened when he reached Yakkabog?"

"He met the linguist who confirmed that eighteen enemy combatants captured at Tora Bora had been detained at the black site and that one of them was an Egyptian national who asserted his innocence."

"I'd expect *all* of them to have professed innocence."

"Not in fluent English! My father even provided his interrogators with the names and addresses of family members to bolster his claim of innocence."

"Are you saying he gave CIA interrogators *your* name and address?"

"Mine and my siblings, too. The linguist was so stunned by this he remembered each of our names and recited them to Ibrahim. From that point on, we were certain our father was among the captives."

Dunn recalled the photo in the trimaran. "His claim of innocence obviously failed."

"Yes, and he was placed in a diaper and beaten, subjected to cold, and questioned for eighteen hours a day. He was then shackled to a bar over his head to keep him from sleeping in a pitch-black cell with blaring music." Yuri fell silent, and in the void, other sounds filled the gap: a grinding engine, humming tires, and snoring from the back seat. After tucking a tuft of hair behind his ear, he spoke again: "Ibrahim also learned that an American CIA agent who wore a ski mask and sunglasses oversaw the torturing in Yakkabog. When the man spoke to guards, he did so in whispers."

"Did the linguist know the agent's name?"

"No, but he said he brought an arsenal of drugs that he administered to the prisoners."

"What sorts of drugs?"

"Pills and liquids, but one which was a gas given by mask from a metal canister."

Dunn broke out in a sweat. "Were there any markings on the canister?"

"Not to my knowledge."

"What about the CIA agent—any tattoos, scars, or distinguishing features?"

"None I know of other than he was average height and build. Like I said, he wore a ski mask and sunglasses which hid his face." Yuri stroked the lock still tucked behind his ear. "Then again, he wore a ring."

"That's odd," Dunn said. "I'd think someone trying to conceal his identity would avoid rings."

"Unless he normally did not wear them."

"Perhaps, but what did the ring look like?"

"It was bulky, contained a red stone, and had engravings in its band."

"What kind of engravings?"

"A football on a tee and goal posts at each end of a lined field."

"Any lettering?"

Yuri straightened his back. "Did you not notice the ring yourself?"

"How could I have?"

"It was in the waterboarding photo you saw in the trimaran." He worked his mobile and passed it to Dunn. "Expand the photo over the hand."

Dunn blanched at the renewed sight of the hooded man lying face-up on a metal bench bare-chested with arms and feet shackled. Above the man's head was a bucket held by a gloved hand but because the glove was thin and semi-opaque, he discerned a ring through the glove. Expanding the area to bring the ring into closer view, he confirmed the presence of a football and a field with goal posts, but it was fuzzy lettering around the oval stone that drew his attention.

Angling the mobile to optimize his view, he struggled to visualize the letters. Assisting him in the task was a thinning of the glove over the ring which resulted from the finger being flexed. He made out a *C* in black followed by a gray-colored four-point star and then the letters *USA* in red. Between the *C* and *USA*, an elongated point from the star filled the gap.

"What are you examining?" Yuri asked.

Dunn ignored the question as his thoughts raced to his freshman year in medical school when he occasionally sat beside a classmate who'd graduated from Rice University in Houston. Tall and lithe, the young man was a decorated swimmer during college, and on cold days in Providence he often wore a sweatshirt emblazoned with the very same symbol he made out on the ring—a four-point star between a *C* and *USA*.

"This ring," Dunn said, "I'm assuming the man who water-boarded your father got it in college."

"Which college?"

"One in the southern U.S., I suspect." He returned the mobile to Yuri, adding, "How'd you get the photo?"

"The linguist gave it to Ibrahim after learning it was our father who was tortured. He said he believed my father was innocent and resented providing linguistic assistance to harm him."

"Didn't restrictions prevent taking photos in a torture chamber?"

"The CIA agent snapped it himself because he wanted to document the renditions for his superiors in the U.S."

"How'd the linguist get a copy of the photo?"

"He collected the camera just after the photo was taken when the CIA agent rushed to an adjacent room to see a prisoner who had just died. The agent departed immediately for the U.S. without retrieving the camera."

HAUNTED BY NIGHTMARES of the photo, Dunn awoke from a post-dawn catnap to the sound of tires spinning in sand.

"We are stuck!" Yuri exclaimed.

Through sleepy slits, Dunn eyed a world starkly different from the one he'd left at sundown the evening before beyond Chott el Djérid. Surrounding him now were magnificent dunes cast in brilliant red from a rising sun, their slopes manicured with tumbling ridges which resembled rippling fountains. "Where are we?" he asked.

"At the southern tip of Tunisia, not far from my father's home."

Dunn looked to the rear and saw blurry tracks stretching between dunes. If a road had existed, it was buried now beneath blowing sand. Meanwhile, a sound from the front caused him to look ahead where he saw Yuri tugging a metal plate connected to a cable away from the jeep. When the cable reached its full length, Yuri sank the plate into the sand until only its top showed with a ring attached to it. With a flip of a switch back at the jeep, he started a winch that inched the jeep forward. After an agonizing period of groaning, the process freed the jeep from its hold which allowed Yuri to dismantle the system.

"Oh, no!" Bedjaoui cried from the back seat. "He has it!"

"Has what?" Dunn asked.

"The wild form of megavirus."

"*Who* has it?"

"Ibrahim!" Bedjaoui waved his mobile before Dunn. "I just received a text from a colleague saying Ibrahim broke into the lab late last night and demanded at gunpoint all of the vials holding the wild strain of the virus!" His nostrils flared. "He plans to release it with the hope of sickening millions, and he may succeed with a virus holding a full complement of genes!"

"Why didn't they tell you this last night?"

"Because, after collecting the virus, the *Fanak* gagged my colleague and tied him to a chair where he was discovered this morning by a security guard."

"This can't be!" Dunn cried. "At a minimum, we need months to develop a vaccine against megavirus, and that assumes a vaccine can be created!"

With the jeep moving again, Bedjaoui scanned the horizon. Pointing to a set of dunes in the distance where the wind whipped sheets of sand into the air like frenzied manes, he said, "It was on one of those dunes I learned about how great the *Fanak*'s hunger for revenge is. I was with Yuri's father, Nasir Mostafa, after he'd been released from jail, and he told me about Ibrahim's rage for what authorities in your country did to him."

"Where was Nasir jailed?" Dunn asked.

"At—"

"Quiet, Jacques!" Yuri hollered. "My father will tell Dr. Dunn what happened to him when they meet!"

"And when will that be?" Dunn asked.

"Not long!"

"Prove it," Dunn said, lifting his satphone. "I want to see exactly where we are on a map and where your father lives."

"Show him, Jacques," Yuri replied, "but do not say anything more about my father's release from prison."

Using his own mobile, Bedjaoui produced a map which displayed their position relative to Nasir Mostafa's home. Pointing the phone at Dunn, he said, "As you can see, we're close." He then switched modes to a satellite view and handed Dunn the mobile.

"What is *that?*" Dunn asked, studying the map.

"What are you looking at?" Yuri asked.

"It's a shape in the earth that looks like the sole of a shoe or…" He examined the spot more closely. "…or a paramecium." He looked at Yuri. "Is it a crater?"

"No, it is an oasis."

"And your father lives there?"

Yuri nodded, stopped the jeep, and removed a pair of binoculars which he directed at the dunes ahead. He passed the binoculars to Dunn. "Take a look."

Dunn scanned the horizon and moved slowly from one dune to the next, his pulse bounding at the sight of something eerily distinct along one slope. After straining to make out what it was, he said, "I see something that looks like a circle, but I can't tell what's forming it."

"Camels," Yuri replied. "They await us."

Dunn peered through the binoculars again. "Someone's on one of them."

"Yes, Ibrahim." He eyed Dunn with concern. "Are you ready to begin the most difficult part of your journey?"

BEING A MOUNTAIN person, Dunn was familiar with scaling foothills to reach taller peaks, but the experience of motoring up successively taller dunes was a new one. Each ascent brought better views of the circular formation of camels waiting on the tallest dune, but the views were evanescent as descents followed each climb.

He was struck again by the recurrent theme of circles. After appearing in television coverage of the shootings as a circular array of bullet holes in an SUV and in sails of racing dinghies on the Severn River, they emerged repeatedly in Irina's claim that they traveled "the same circle of life," in the name of the trimaran—*Ba'wă*, or *circle maker*—and on a placard beneath the waterboarding photo which read, *No justice in lines, only in circles.*

Nor were the references to circles restricted to Irina. He recalled Pablo asking him to identify the geometric form that resulted from slicing a sphere by a plane and, later, reminding Dunn of his blog posts which discussed justice in the context of circles. And now came the camels on the dune and, while not strictly a circle, the paramecium-shaped form on satellite map where Yuri's father lived.

From the back seat, Bedjaoui popped his head forward as he glared through the windshield. "There he is, the *Fanak!* Go around him!" he exhorted.

Yuri mirrored his gaze before leaning back. "He will find us no matter which way we go."

"Then, let me out!" A rear door opened.

"Close it!" Yuri shouted. "We are three, and he is one." He produced the pistol from the compartment. "And we have this!"

Bedjaoui turned to Dunn. "Give me your satphone! I've just lost service."

After receiving the device, Bejaoui toiled with it. "Here, take a look." He handed Dunn the phone.

A satellite weather map of Africa showed a conglomeration of purples, reds, and yellows in a massive storm a good distance to their south, but shooting off the tempest were bands that had already turned the horizon black. When Dunn set the map into motion, he watched the storm begin over the highlands of Sudan before it moved west across the Sahara in a trajectory that suggested it would pass to their south, but its monolithic size and intensification concerned him. To his dismay, preceding and following the storm were others which formed a line across the continent with several over the Atlantic already developed into well-defined hurricanes.

Inside his blanket cocoon, Bedjaoui moaned. "That storm to our south is the biggest yet to form this season. If it continues to build over the Atlantic as expected, it will be a monster. God help those in its path!"

Yuri stopped the jeep on a summit to view the way that remained, but in the blowing sand it was difficult to see.

"Where's Ibrahim?" Dunn asked, peering through the windshield.

"He is near, I assure you."

With the next descent, the jeep careened before stalling, and no amount of revving of the engine could free it from the sand.

"What now?" Dunn asked.

"We run!" Bedjaoui cried. "The *Fanak* will catch us otherwise!"

"Stay put," Yuri growled. "I will work the winch again." Before he opened the door, however, a camel appeared as a man sprung from it onto the hood where he stood with legs apart before the windshield.

Dunn ran his eyes up a soiled thobe encircled by a red sash carrying a dagger, and before he could lean back in his seat, the dagger plunged through the glass.

"Get off, Ibrahim!" Yuri shrieked. He fumbled for the pistol but lost grip of it before finally firing a shot.

A thump from the rear led Dunn to find Bedjaoui hunkered along the floor behind Yuri's seat, but if he'd meant it to be a hiding place, it wasn't to be. From behind the curled form the back door opened to reveal a red and white-checkered shemagh protruding so high it grazed the door frame. Before Dunn could stop it, the butt of an AK-47 swung through the air to strike Yuri in the back of the head which sent the pistol flying to the floor.

"Leave it!" Ibrahim shouted as Dunn reached for it. "I'll kill you if you touch it." After freezing Dunn with his cold eyes, he yanked on the blanketed heap to expose Bedjaoui. "Coward!" he bellowed.

"Yuri, do something!" Bedjaoui wailed.

Slumped against the steering wheel, Yuri lifted his head slowly. Through his golden locks blood oozed from the back of his scalp.

"Get out!" Ibrahim shouted at Bedjaoui, his foul breath invading the jeep. Seeing no motion, he grasped the chemist forcibly.

Dunn seized Ibrahim's arm. "Leave him! He did nothing wrong!"

Keeping a grip on his prey, Ibrahim glowered at Dunn, yet his glare tamed as he examined Dunn's curved nose, high cheekbones, and chiseled jaws. It was Dunn's lips, however, he settled on, tilting his head to study their contours. "You, of all people, should be on my side," he said.

In the few words he'd heard Ibrahim speak, Dunn concluded his grasp of English was superior to that of his siblings. There was no mellifluousness of Romance languages or staccato of Arabic but, rather, an almost homegrown familiarity with the language. "Why would I side with a murderer?" he asked.

"Because we share views on justice." His lip rose to expose a gold-capped incisor. "I've read your blog posts, Wilbur."

It unnerved Dunn to be called by his first name by a foul-smelling man with leathery skin, moles sprouting wiggly black hair—including one at the tip of a bulbous nose—and a bushy, unkempt beard which held dried nasal secretions or crusted remnants from an earlier meal. A shower the man hadn't had in days for his body odor exceeded the wretchedness of his breath, unleashing itself in waves with the force of tsunamis. By comparison, John the Baptist was a natty model.

"We can't possibly share views on justice," Dunn retorted, "because I reject violence entirely." He pointed to the AK-47. "You, on the other hand, shot thirty-eight innocent people in my country because of your vile obsession with latitudes. Twenty-eight have died while ten remain hospitalized. That's anathema to justice."

"I'm not obsessed with latitudes," Ibrahim replied. "It's linearity I detest in the context of justice." Releasing his grip on Bedjaoui, he straddled the seat above the chemist and barked at his brother in Arabic.

After struggling to leave his seat, Yuri appeared behind Ibrahim with a steel bridle matching the hackamore displayed at the Pentagon briefing.

Ibrahim took it and held it up before Dunn. "Do you know what this is?"

"Yes, it's part of a camel's harness. You left one at your killing site in Annapolis."

Ibrahim ran a finger over its metal arch to a straight segment which connected to a rope halter. Lifting the bridle, he swung it gently. "I did what I did in America to show that injustice breeds more injustice."

"So, you admit your acts were heinous!"

He nodded. "Yes, my latitude revenge was as heinous as the acts which spawned it."

"This is all about your father, isn't it?"

He tilted his head. "What have you learned about him?"

"He was captured in Afghanistan in late 2001, taken to a black site in Uzbekistan, and tortured there by a CIA agent, but that doesn't justify inflicting revenge on an entire nation seventeen years later."

"Revenge has its timing," Ibrahim replied, looking at Dunn through the bridle's circular form. Lowering it, he said, "Come, my father awaits you."

Dunn remained in place as Ibrahim left his seat, while from the rear, he heard Bedjaoui whisper frantically: "Do not let the *Fanak* take me!"

Before Dunn could respond, Ibrahim appeared at the driver's seat which Yuri had left vacant. Stooping, he reached for the pistol and slid it behind the sash next to his knife. While doing so, Bedjaoui bolted from the back and began running across the sand, but his escape was short-lived as a blast dropped him to the dune with a bullet to the head.

THE BLOWING SAND pricked Dunn's hands and face like a million needles, and because he was still numb from seeing Bedjaoui dead on the desert floor, he felt as if he were in the throes of a stroke. He turned from the wind to shield himself only to sense a pressure against his head as a hand passed across his face with a flapping fabric. "Stop blindfolding me!" he shrieked, jerking his head.

"I'm putting a shemagh on you!" Ibrahim answered. "It'll protect you from the sand."

A series of coils entombed Dunn's scalp, ears, and neck, and after the wrap was secured, he watched Ibrahim reapply his own shemagh only to discover the reason it formed a mound: atop Ibrahim's head was a beehive of dirty-blonde dreadlocks.

"Come, Wilbur," he beckoned.

Dunn distanced himself from Ibrahim as he walked toward four Dromedary camels lying in the sand. When one began to stand, Dunn glanced at its private parts out of curiosity even though he didn't know what testicular swelling looked like on a camel.

The camels responded to the approach of the men with raucous sounds that resembled belching or bleating, and when one blared Dunn was reminded of the sound of a Tibetan horn. A series of guttural bah-bah-bahs followed in rapid succession which sounded like a protracted sneeze. Stopping close enough to examine the mouth of one, he understood why its vocal repertoire was so expansive: Its upper and lower lips were fat and malleable which permitted it to add finishing touches to air already jostled about in an oral cavern where sounds reverberated.

"It's best you wear socks to prevent chaffing," Ibrahim said, offering Dunn a pair. "Pull them over your trousers."

Dunn resented being ordered what to do by a man he viewed as a cold-blooded killer, but fearing for his life, he did as he was told even though he noticed Ibrahim ignored his own advice. After donning the socks, he edged closer to Yuri to see how he was faring after taking the blow to the head, noticing then a patch of shemagh oozing blood along the back of his head. "Let me check your scalp," he said. "I'm concerned about the bleeding."

"Leave it!" Ibrahim growled. "Instead, approach this camel slowly from the side." He held a set of reins connected to the animal's halter.

Although Dunn was proficient at riding horses, he'd never mounted one which sat on the ground as the camel did now.

"Okay," Ibrahim continued, "insert your left foot into the stirrup and throw the other leg over the saddle to mount."

Dunn followed the instructions, although he exaggerated the lift of his right leg to clear a post which jutted from the rear of a wood stool which served as a saddle.

"Now hold the front post and lean back," Ibrahim said.

The camel lunged forward to extend its rear legs before tilting back to straighten the front ones, a procedure which whiplashed Dunn. Holding the front post, he watched the brothers mount with ease before the camels formed a line with Ibrahim leading, Dunn next, an unmanned camel following, and Yuri at the end.

The proximity with which he rode behind Ibrahim made Dunn feel subservient, all the more so because his reins remained in Ibrahim's control. "You're a heartless killer!" he shouted in the howling wind. "Your God will condemn you forever."

"If you're referring to what I did to Bedjaoui, he got what he deserved."

"What did he do to deserve a bullet to his head?"

"He shouldn't have tried to keep the wild form of megavirus from me when I went to his lab the first time to get it."

"He did what every sane scientist would do: Lock up a dangerous virus to keep it under wraps."

"Whatever, it cost him his life."

"When did you learn you'd taken the genetically altered version?"

"While I was sailing to America with Irina. I saw a text she received from Bedjaoui informing her of that."

"Nonetheless, you still caused much suffering."

"I did what I had to."

"Yet you failed in one regard: You didn't break into my condo in Baltimore."

"I didn't try to break in. It must have been your enemies in America."

"I have none there."

"Oh, come on! What about your court-ordered monitors?"

Dunn shifted in his saddle, unnerved that a beastly man who lived in the Sahara should know of his court-related surveillance. "What do you know about my monitors?"

Ibrahim slowed his camel to allow Dunn to catch up. When Dunn was immediately behind him, he said, "The FISA Court wrapped you into its tentacles long ago."

"FISA?" Dunn echoed. "As in Foreign Intelligence Surveillance Court?"

"Yes."

"I have nothing to do with them! They handle requests for surveillance warrants to monitor foreign spies in the U.S."

"Which is what some believe you are."

"A *spy?*" Dunn jeered.

Ibrahim eyed Dunn through a slit in his shemagh. "That's right, and that's why they began monitoring you in early 2002."

"You're nuts! I've done nothing to merit being under FISA surveillance!"

"Others would disagree."

Dunn kicked the camel to keep it aside Ibrahim's, but the animal merely hissed. "*Who* disagrees?"

"Those who fear my father so greatly they turned to the FISA Court to keep tabs on everyone connected to him."

"I have nothing to do with your father! I didn't even know he existed until Irina told me about him last week." A chill shot through Dunn's spine as he realized then that intelligence officials had intercepted Irina's call in which she announced plans to leave a phone for him under a holly bush near his condo. Ten hours later, after collecting the satphone, he discovered the gouges under his door lock. Worse, if Ibrahim was right that he'd been placed under surveillance just months after 9/11, he suspected officials could've readily learned of his plans to rent an SUV in Idaho nine months earlier and have found a way to sabotage it before he drove through Sawtooth National Forest. But, why they'd do that, he hadn't a clue.

"Why is your father so feared?" he asked.

"He can ruin careers."

"Whose careers?"

"Those who inflicted injustice on my father. To protect themselves, they've maintained a tight surveillance over those who know my father, including his family members." He turned again to look at Dunn. "That's why I live in the desert: They can't monitor me here."

"When did they place your family under surveillance?"

"About the time they began surveilling you, which was not long after my father was captured at Tora Bora in late 2001." He kept his gaze on Dunn as he sat sideways on the saddle. "I understand Pablo and Yuri told you about his capture."

"They did, but if the FISA Court began surveilling your family shortly after 9/11, you and your sibs were just children then."

"That's right, but they were concerned about our connections with the U.S."

"What connections?"

"My brothers, Irina, and I visited America during school breaks while growing up."

"Where did you go?"

"To northeastern Arizona to see our uncle."

"Where in northeastern Arizona?"

"The Navajo Nation."

Dunn grasped the saddle post to keep from falling.

"Are you alright?" Ibrahim asked.

"No, get me down! I'm going to be sick!"

FROM THE OUTSET, Dunn found riding a camel to be uncomfortable. Unlike a horse, it moved in side-to-side motions with fitful starts and stops that defied any rhythm. Upon setting off on the trimaran, he feared getting seasick, but to his surprise he was spared the malady. Not so on a camel: Its herky-jerky, capricious steps turned his stomach inside-out and led him to upchuck what remained of the leftover Deblah Yuri had offered him earlier in the day.

"Do you feel better now?" Yuri called from the rear.

"Somewhat," Dunn replied, touched that a man who'd taken a blow to the head cared enough to ask how he was doing. Having removed his shemagh to vomit, Dunn replaced it now only to notice remnants of vomitus on his trousers. Below the soiled area, just above a sock that had failed to hold a trouser leg, he felt a burning from gastric acid contacting skin chaffed from rubbing the camel. Adding to his discomfort was the snail's pace with which they moved. He swung a leg over the front post to redistribute his weight in an effort to become more comfortable. In the meantime, it disheartened him to see more dunes ahead without an oasis in sight.

To his relief, Dunn's camel fell behind Ibrahim's which resulted from Ibrahim dropping the reins when Dunn vomited. In the privacy which resulted, Dunn read an email from Jim Edwards…

Wilbur,

Wanted to let you know I'm working with Garrett Fitzgerald, Senator Braniff, and the FBI on Duck's Nightmare. I learned a CIA official code-named "StorALown1#2683" directed three agents in 1999 to go to a dock in New Jersey to collect 37 canisters of Duck's Nightmare from a U.S. Navy vessel that retrieved the canisters from the seabed. As you know, those 37 canisters spurred the creation of a splinter group called Triewð at the CIA which evaluated various chemicals as truth sera. Braniff is trying to pin a name to "StorALown1#2683" so we can interview him. In the meantime, I found the mechanic who serviced the SUV just before you rented it in Idaho. He's been subpoenaed to appear in court.

Looking up, Dunn was struck by what he saw. "Another Fata Morgana?" he asked Yuri who'd pulled aside him.

"No, that is my father's oasis."

The green haven was several city blocks in size although, true to its form on satellite map, it was shaped like a paramecium with a rim of turquoise water around it. With heat waves distorting the image, Dunn was reminded of photos of artificial islands plopped onto the Persian Gulf along Dubai's shores, only this island was multi-faceted with a green perimeter and a central hill lined by massive boulders. "That's some spring down there!" he remarked.

"Yes, and it flows year-round to keep the plants green."

Dunn felt the satphone vibrate, this time from an email Garrett Fitzgerald had sent with cc:s to Edwards and Braniff…

Finished reading the logbooks and confirmed Triewð shuttered after four years because of a failure to identify an effective truth serum. One of the last entries came from a team member called "StorALown1#2683" who said he'd take responsibility for destroying all remaining stocks. That presumably included Duck's Nightmare, but we need to contact this person to confirm the destruction. Senator Braniff, any headway identifying "StorALown1#2683?"

IBRAHIM SEETHED AS Dunn approached. "Give me your mobile!" he demanded.

"My phone is *my* business!" Dunn insisted.

An AK-47 swung around Ibrahim's side. "Give it to me!"

Ashen-faced, Dunn complied.

After opening the battery compartment to inspect the mobile's interior, Ibrahim glared at Yuri who'd stopped beside Dunn. "Why'd you give this to him?"

"He needs to communicate with his colleagues in America!"

"But this one has no latitude restrictions!"

"It would not have served him here if it did."

Ibrahim brandished the rifle again. "Go away! I need to talk to Dunn alone."

"If you harm him," Yuri warned, "I will kill you!"

"How?" Ibrahim sneered, reaching behind his sash for Yuri's pistol. "I have this now, remember?" He put it away as his brother departed, and when he was sure Yuri was out of hearing range, he addressed Dunn: "Here, take your satphone back. I don't care if you report my whereabouts because I'll be gone soon. I came to see you only to discuss your views on justice."

Dunn took the phone. "Well, I hope you've learned revenge holds no place in my views."

Ibrahim's dreads fell across his shoulders as he removed his shemagh. In the ropelike braids were pieces of straw, displaced threads, and a dead beetle. "But, in your blog posts, you called for separate criminal justice systems for Native American reservations. That sounds like you're fighting the white man's laws."

"Far from it; I called for separate systems because they'd alleviate overrepresentation of American Indians in prisons and provide them with greater roles in administering justice. They'd also address differences in sentencing between Native Americans and non-natives which've resulted from a flaw in our justice system stemming from—"

"—an 1885 statute in your country known as the Major Crimes Act." Ibrahim grinned. "I've read your posts carefully."

"So I see."

"Yes," Ibrahim continued, "you claimed that because of the Act, Native Americans are tried in tribal courts for certain crimes but tried in federal courts for other more severe ones such as murder, rape, arson, or manslaughter committed on reservations. Not only that, but convictions in federal courts carry harsher mandatory minimums than equivalent state punishments, and for that reason, Native Americans receive longer sentences than white people who commit the same crimes."

"Longer sentences aren't the only problem," Dunn replied. "Higher *rates* of incarceration occur, too. Native American men are jailed at a rate four-times higher than white men and Native-American women six-times higher than white women." A look of anguish came over Dunn. "Then again, behavioral factors play a role here, including alcoholism and early school dropout."

Ibrahim moved his camel closer to Dunn's. "Nonetheless, you've called for tribes to have the power of independent nations to address complaints before the United Nations."

"Yes, because Native Americans occupied the land now called 'America' long before whites arrived, yet under federal law tribe members are considered American citizens and therefore bound by federal statutes. I believe our roots to the land give us the right to petition a court of international standing to resolve disputes with our white brethren."

Ibrahim glanced at the advancing black clouds along the horizon. After dismounting his camel, he sketched a circle in the sand and used his body to shield it from the wind. "You'd think Mother Earth would be our guide when it comes to justice."

"How so?"

Ibrahim retraced the circle. "Begin with Earth's shape. Just as ancients believed it was flat before more insightful people proved it to be spherical, thoughtful people will eventually prevail in viewing justice not in linear but circular terms." He looked at Dunn. "You've written that in western models of justice, judges occupy the highest rungs and accused the lowest, and that there's no place for family elders or community leaders to contribute to rehabilitation of offenders or healing of aggrieved."

Dunn nodded.

"And that the western model of justice is a linear one with one end for entry of accused and another for exit, and that it's an adversarial and argumentative system in which rules of admissibility prevail over dialogue." Ibrahim's expression softened. "Now let me share my views on what mother Earth teaches us about justice: It flows like air and water and is expansive and ceaseless. We *tap* into justice; we do not create or administer it. The Bible says as much: *But let justice roll on like a river, righteousness like a never-failing stream!*" He stood beside his camel. "What pains me most about western justice is the exclusion of spirituality and shunning of prayer."

Dunn grasped his saddle post and squeezed it. "*You* speaking of spirituality after what you did to my country?"

Ibrahim obliterated the circle and swiped a line in the sand with his foot. "I attacked your bases because they fall along a line of unfathomable injustice. Like a knife blade, your country's justice system eviscerated my father's rights."

WHAT APPEARED AS a lifeless crater on satellite map resonated now in a riot of chirping despite the wind. If there was a Garden of Eden still on earth, this was it, Dunn concluded, one that survived because of its isolation.

But isolation was relative, he knew, for satellites could snoop from far above as one did now to deliver an email from Senator Craig Braniff...

Still haven't unlocked the names of former Triewð members because the key to their identities was destroyed when the group disbanded fifteen years ago. As a result, knowing who "StorALown1#2683" was remains a mystery. However, a search of databanks at internet service providers, text messaging servers, and social media outlets conducted by the National Security Agency discovered a hit for "StorALown1#2683" just after Triewd̄ closed its doors. Turns out "StorALown1#2683" was a password a customer used after opening an account at a self-storage facility in Washington, D.C. at about the time Triewd̄ shuttered. We've contacted the firm to request the customer's name.

While Dunn was reading the email, he hadn't noticed his camel had taken him closer to the water's edge where Ibrahim and Yuri were waiting for him. The two stood at odds, each glaring at the other in silence.

"Hold the post," Ibrahim told Dunn. With a cluck of his tongue, he made the camel buckle its front legs which sent Dunn lunging forward. After stutter-stepping its hind legs, the animal dropped to the sand.

Dunn dismounted and followed the two men into a thicket of reeds whose stalks were browned by summer but still grew flowers encased in silky hairs. From ahead came the sound of snapping shafts as his guides forged a path through the maze, and after descending a slope which required him to brace his feet against knobby rhizomes, Dunn stopped before a canoe made from dried reeds.

"My father built it," Yuri volunteered.

The symmetry of the vessel impressed Dunn as did a decorative braiding of twine and reeds which rose from its stern like a cat's tail.

"Egyptians have a long tradition of building papyrus boats," Yuri continued, "and my father learned the art while living in Alexandria. He built the boat Irina learned to sail on."

"She's come a long way," Dunn observed.

"Not as far as she hopes. She is determined to win the circum-globe race on the trimaran she named in your honor."

"She named the tri *Ba'wă* in my honor?"

"Yes, 'circle maker' in Paiute."

"She said nothing about that to me!"

"She holds her feelings close."

"Enough!" Ibrahim grumbled. He ordered Dunn and Yuri into the canoe before hopping into the stern. With his rifle at the ready, he used a paddle to push off into open waters frenzied with whitecaps that sent spray into their faces.

Undaunted, Dunn glommed his eyes on another Craig Braniff email . . .

> *Identified "StorALown1#2683" as Peter Ashley, a CIA agent who retired a few years ago. Records from the self-storage facility confirmed he rented space in Washington, D.C. We contacted Ashley to ask what he'd stored in the space, but he denied knowing anything about it. Ominously, he hired a lawyer right after we talked to him and is refusing to speak to us further. In the meantime, we have a plan to get to the bottom of this.*

WITH THE CANOE rocking, Dunn longed for the stability of the tri. Despite towering seas, its three hulls, windswept sails, and exceedingly competent skipper had ferried him without ever threatening to flip, yet the same couldn't be said for the canoe which listed with every gust. Despite the tumult, Dunn revisited a matter which lingered from the day before, one involving the ring worn by the man who'd waterboarded Nasir Mostafa. Convinced the *C*, *USA*, and interposing star signified a collegiate athletic conference, he went online to identify the universities in the Division 1 group. His search revealed eleven schools, some with formidable athletic programs.

He zeroed in on one university to search for clips that described the team's historical performance, and when he found a story about a Cotton Bowl championship the school's football team had won four decades earlier, his heart pounded as he emailed Garrett Fitzgerald . . .

> *I recently emailed a urologist at a hospital in Merced, California to ask him a question about whether a patient hospitalized*

there years ago had arthritis affecting his hands. Since I need an answer as soon as possible, I'm asking you to call him to get the answer and pass it to me immediately.

Dunn provided the urologist's contact information just as a branch struck his face.

"I told you to watch your head, but you paid no attention!" Ibrahim clamored. "Put the satphone away!" He jumped from the canoe and pulled it through prickly reeds which forced Dunn to tuck his arms into the vessel to keep from being pierced. When the canoe could go no further, Ibrahim ordered him out. "Follow Yuri," he barked.

After dissecting the thicket, Dunn reached a sandy bank where he finally stood upright. From there, he set off with Yuri as the two passed oleander bushes with whorled flowers before reaching a grove of date palms where the air turned noticeably cooler. Despite the temperature drop, he began breathing harder as the path steepened.

"Pistachio trees," Yuri called when they reached an orchard in its infancy. "I planted the trees last month for my father."

Dunn examined the thin trunks and tender boughs with their green pinnate leaves, a calming pastoral scene he relished if only for a moment as his satphone delivered a third email from Senator Braniff…

CIA agents inspected the self-storage facility in Washington, D.C. where Peter Ashley rented space and found two canisters labeled 'Duck's Nightmare' there. The contents are being tested as are fingerprints. Results to follow.

"Come!" Yuri called. "The winds are gaining!"

Livid from what he'd read, Dunn caught up to Yuri along a path which continued to steepen as it transitioned from dirt to stones. With each step, his feet slid back against sandals whose straps threatened to snap under the pressure. On each side were boulders which he'd seen while viewing the oasis from the dunes, ones which had seemingly rained upon the earth to leave some piled atop others to form gigantic cairns.

At points, he had to squeeze his shoulders to keep from striking the boulders, all the while keeping an eye out for snakes in a precaution honed through years of exploring the U.S. West. Testing his concentration further were whistles created by wind rushing through gaps between boulders that turned the hillside into a colossal organ, yet accompanying the whistles was a percussion element whose origin he couldn't identify.

He soon discovered its source: canvas sheets snapping in the wind. While some were mounted as a roof over a series of boulders occupying the oasis peak, others dropped to create walls of a sort. To keep the sheets in place, ropes threaded through eyelets were tied to stakes along the ground.

"My father's home," Yuri announced.

Dunn's emotions welled. Eleven days had elapsed since Garrett Fitzgerald asked for help to investigate illnesses at the military bases, and in that interval, he'd traveled to Medicine Wheel, crossed the Atlantic, and driven deep into the Sahara. While backpacking as a younger man, he came to view each journey as a life chapter, and this one was no different. While he had no control over its destination, travel partners, or duration, he'd become stronger for making it.

"Leave your sandals here," Yuri said, pulling aside a canvas.

Dunn bared his feet and stepped into a space reminiscent of a mudroom, only here hanging blankets comprised the interior walls. It took him a moment to adjust his eyes before he noticed intricate carvings on a sandstone boulder in the room's center. Approaching it, he recognized the etchings as trail markings of the sort Native Americans used as navigation guides—stick figures, concentric circles, arches, and the like. But capturing his attention especially was a carving of a pair of moccasins whose tongues displayed a flower with blue petals and a red pistil, while along the toe caps were sawtooth crests outlined in black with turquoise and orange fillings. Astonished, he asked, "Who did this artwork?"

"My father," Yuri replied, taking Dunn's arm. "Come, it is time you meet him."

As the pair approached a blanket beyond the boulder, Dunn recalled a trip to Colorado's Mesa Verde National Park he'd taken as a boy to visit cliff dwellings occupied in earlier centuries by Ancestral Pueblo inhabitants. Although the present dwelling was amongst sandstone boulders rather than in a cliff, he sensed a similar communion with Earth. Wiggling his toes, he cherished the hard, cool dirt as his satphone vibrated a second time in the span of a minute. He lifted it to view its screen.

"Leave it!" Yuri admonished.

"No, it's important," Dunn insisted. He opened the first of two texts, the first from Garrett Fitzgerald...

Merced medical records confirm severe rheumatoid arthritis of hands.

"That explains it!" Dunn muttered. He opened the next text but was prevented from reading it by a hand which squeezed his forearm.

"Show respect!" Yuri whispered. "My father has waited patiently to meet you."

Dunn lowered the mobile as Yuri pulled on the blanket before calling softly into the next room. A faint response followed. In tandem, they advanced to the next room which was larger than the first and held Persian rugs laid between more boulders. After sitting on one of Yuri's designation, Dunn positioned a cushion for added comfort.

"One moment," Yuri said, retracting a blanket that bordered a third room.

Dunn used the opportunity to read the second text, one from Jim Edwards...

Mechanic admits to sabotaging SUV in Idaho.

Dunn pounded his fist into the rug. For eight months, he'd reproached himself for pursuing a shortcut along a restricted National Forest road and allowing the steering wheel of a rented SUV to slip from his grip which led to the death of his wife and an innocent man. Now, with the news that the SUV had been sabotaged, he believed the two deaths were preventable.

Just then, the canvas roof quieted from a lull in the wind, and Dunn heard a *flap-flap…flap-flap…* coming from a room beyond the one he sat in. When a hand showed itself along the blanket edge and pulled it aside, he saw Yuri appear as he beckoned someone out of view.

Stealing another glance at the satphone, Dunn eyed a third text which had just arrived, one from Braniff…

Fingerprints from storage space—

"Dr. Dunn," Yuri called softly, "I would like you to meet—"

Dunn looked up to see the blanket entangling the subject of interest, and he seized the moment to return to the text…

Fingerprints from storage space belong to—

"Dr. Dunn!" Yuri demanded, his tone more urgent.

Exasperated, Dunn raised his eyes to see Yuri gazing behind the blanket.

"Father, come see who is here," Yuri said.

The blanket lifted sufficiently to reveal a pair of bronze-colored feet make a painstakingly slow progression toward its opening. After one foot rose and flapped on the floor, the second followed in similar fashion, and into view after a series of such steps came a stick-and-bones figure whose bowed head revealed a crop of salt and pepper hair above a curved nose.

"Father, look up," Yuri implored.

Dunn waited for the man to acknowledge his presence, but seeing no effort to do so, he stole a final glance at the mobile…

Fingerprints from storage space belong to Atticus Quincy Thornbridge

"*No!*" Dunn gasped. He stood and crossed the room to approach the man Yuri steadied. Reaching out, he took one of the man's hands and held it gently, a wafer-thin collection of bones and flesh. "Mr. Mostafa, I'm Wilbur Dunn. It's an honor to meet you after traveling days to get here." With no effort from Yuri's father to retract his hand, Dunn laid his other palm atop it. "May I ask you to walk forward as I hold your hand?" he asked the man.

Head still bowed, Yuri's father lifted a foot before flapping it down. Another flap followed from the second foot.

"How long have your feet dropped this way?" Dunn asked.

"For seventeen years," a wispy voice replied.

"Did someone beat your legs?"

"No, but they began flapping shortly after I was detained."

"Detained where?"

"In Uzbekistan."

From the man's responses, Dunn was convinced his accent was one he'd heard among residents of the southwestern U.S., but for the moment, he focused on the man's continued head bowing, worried it resulted from damaged nerves in his neck. "You were given a chemical by mask in Yakkabog, weren't you?" he said.

"Yes."

"My guess is that chemical damaged nerves in your legs which led to your foot-drop."

"What chemical are you speaking of?" the man asked.

"One called Duck's Nightmare. It was developed as a truth serum by the U.S. Army during the Cold War, and while it was supposedly destroyed in the 1970s, a stockpile was discovered by fishermen off New Jersey at the turn of the century. I have reason to believe the CIA administered Duck's Nightmare to prisoners captured after 9/11 to see if you and others would change answers to their questions after they gave you the gas." He eyed the man closely. "From what I've heard, a CIA agent gave you the chemical in Yakkabog."

"How did you learn that?"

"Ibrahim told me that when he went to Yakkabog in 2002 looking for you, he met an Uzbek linguist at the CIA black site where you were tortured. The linguist told him a CIA agent had given you something by mask, and because Duck's Nightmare comes as a gas, I'm sure that's what you were given. As its name implies, the gas causes foot-drop as a side effect." Dunn paused. "Do you know who the CIA agent was who gave you the gas?"

"No, because he wore a ski mask and sunglasses."

"Then, let me tell you his name: Atticus Quincy Thornbridge, the Vice President of the United States. I'm absolutely sure of it. For starters, we know Thornbridge worked at the CIA between his years in Congress and before he was elected Vice President, and while crossing the Atlantic with Irina, I saw a photo of you being waterboarded in Yakkabog. When I examined the photo more closely later with Pablo, I noticed two features that convinced me beyond a doubt that the man holding the bucket over your head was Atticus Quincy Thornbridge."

"What did you see?" Yuri asked.

"Two things: First, the man holding the bucket over your father's head had a stub of a little finger on his right hand. While he was in college, Atticus Quincy Thornbridge allegedly raped a woman who bit off half his pinkie while he cupped a hand over her mouth. Not only that, but the photo shows him wearing a ring on another finger with markings distinct for the athletic conference his college belonged to where he played football as a quarterback. The reason he didn't remove the ring before waterboarding you was because his knuckles were too swollen from rheumatoid arthritis to do so. A colleague of mine in California checked the Vice President's medical records and confirmed that Thornbridge developed severe arthritis as a middle-age man."

Flustered that Yuri's father kept his head bowed as he'd spoken, Dunn asked him, "Are you listening to what I'm saying?"

"Yes," the man answered.

"Then, why don't you look at me?"

The man blanched. "Because, the past haunts me."

"Understandably so; torture is despicable."

"It's not torture I'm referring to, but something else."

Dunn stooped to the level of the man's face, noting his prominent orbits. "What is that haunts you?"

The man lifted a foot and dropped it but remained in place. "When my children spoke to you about my past, it must have raised some questions for you."

Dunn broke out in a sweat. "It did, and I'd like to ask you one now."

"Go ahead."

Dunn's voice cracked: "Are you the true biological father of Irina and the three men who call you their father?"

"Why do you ask?"

Dunn placed a hand under the man's chin and lifted it gently to peer into his eyes. "Because, none of them looks like you. They have olive skin and blue or green eyes whereas your skin is bronze and your eyes are brown."

"My children acquired their mother's traits."

"Not really. I met her briefly in Portugal when Pablo refueled the seaplane beneath her home. I noticed she had olive skin, but her eyes were brown like yours. Inheritance of eye color is complex, but the fact that Irina and her brothers have blue or green eyes while you and your wife have brown ones leads me to believe one of you is not their biological parent. I'm guessing that person is you."

"But, you're only guessing."

"No, there's more. The ages of your supposed 'children' convince me you didn't father at least one of them."

"Which one are you referring to?"

Dunn stiffened. "Ibrahim."

"Why do you say that?"

"Because, I learned he's thirty-nine years old."

"So?"

Dunn clenched his jaw. "I'm thirty-nine, too, which convinces me you didn't father two children in the same year."

"You're right, I fathered only one child thirty-nine years ago."

Dunn's eyes glistened as he swallowed over a lump in his throat. "As I thought, and that child was me."

THE MUSCLES OF the neck twitched but left the head of the man before Dunn bowed. "Are you going to respond to what I said?" Dunn asked him.

"There is nothing to say other than that I met and married my wife in Alexandria, Egypt and had my children there, including Ibrahim."

"Yet, I understand you're a naturalized Egyptian. Where were you born?"

"In Tunisia. That's why I live here now."

"With your wife?"

"She visits as she can but has difficulty with the heat."

"But your English," Dunn noted, "it's peculiar."

"In what way?"

"Your accent resembles one I've heard among Chicanos and Native Americans who live in the southwestern U.S."

"It is what it is; I learned English here in Tunisia."

"But if you were born and raised here, why did Ibrahim tell me that he and his siblings visited America regularly during school breaks while growing up?"

"Because, my wife and I wanted them to get to know their uncle who lives in Utah."

"*Utah* or Arizona? Ibrahim said they went to the Navajo Nation in northeastern Arizona."

"He misspoke. Their uncle lives in a small town called White Mesa in Utah. It's just north of the Navajo Nation."

Dunn turned to Yuri. "Did Ibrahim get the wrong state?"

Yuri remained silent.

"Alright," Dunn said, addressing the man before him, "on whose side of the family is this uncle?"

"My wife's."

"What does he do in White Mesa?"

"He sells trinkets to travelers who visit attractions in the area."

Dunn raised his eyebrows. "Including the Navajo Nation?"

"Yes, among other places."

From his pocket Dunn pulled a plastic bag in which he'd stored the moccasin Irina had given him at Rehoboth Beach. After removing it, he held it beneath the man's eyes for him to see. "Does he sell items like this?"

The man's head wobbled. "I can't say because I haven't seen his shop."

Dunn pointed to the room to his rear. "Yuri told me you etched the figure of the moccasins I saw on the boulder back there."

"Art is my therapy."

"Why did you portray a flower with blue petals and a red pistil on them identical to the one on this moccasin?"

"It's a flower which blooms on the oasis here."

"And in the deserts of the western U.S."

"I wouldn't be surprised because the climates are similar."

"And what about the black crests along the toe caps? There are no such mountains on the oasis."

"There are no mountains, but if one views the oasis from afar through the haze of heat, the boulders project as mountains."

Dunn lifted the moccasin closer to the man's face. "I wore a moccasin just like this one as a child, but it was left-footed. I never had its right-footed partner until Irina gave it to me at your request."

"Why do you say it's the partner?"

"Because of the letters engraved here," Dunn replied, everting the moccasin's tongue. He ran a finger along them as he voiced each one…

S…u…m

"Sum," the man vocalized. "I presume that was the maker's name."

"What if I told you that on the underside of the tongue of the moccasin I wore as a child there were the letters…*a*…*k*…*w*…*a*…? Would that be meaningful?"

"Should it be?"

"Yes, because together, the letters spell *Sumakwa*, a word with special meaning."

The man buried his head in his hands and wept.

UPON QUESTIONING HIS mother as a child where the sole moccasin he'd worn came from, Dunn learned a friend of hers had given her a pair at her baby shower, but one was lost shortly after he was born.

Standing now before a weeping man, Dunn said to him: "You must know what *Sumakwa* means because it has made you cry."

For the first time, Nasir Mostafa raised his head and looked at Dunn through tears. "Yes, *Sumakwa* means 'to forgive' in Paiute."

Dunn choked with emotion. "Is that why you brought me to North Africa: to ask for my forgiveness?"

Tears wettened Nasir's feet. "I've wanted your forgiveness since you were born."

"So, you were the 'friend' my mother spoke of who gave the moccasins to her at her baby shower, weren't you?"

"Yes, I made them for you knowing I'd run from you as soon as you were born."

Dunn placed a palm beneath Nasir's chin to keep him from lowering his head again. In the face before him, he saw himself: curved nose, dark skin, chiseled jaws. "So, you *are* my father."

"I am," Nasir sobbed.

Steeling himself, Dunn asked, "Why did you leave me?"

"Because, I was eighteen, stupid, and confused! Just months before you were conceived, I dropped out of high school and fled home in the Navajo Nation to move to Nevada where I met your mother. I couldn't imagine becoming a father, so I ran."

"Mother told me you were Navajo."

"Yes, that's true, but I lied to you earlier: The uncle I referred to in the U.S. wasn't my wife's brother. He was my brother, and he lived in the Navajo Nation."

"Is he still there?"

"No, he died several years ago."

"Why did you leave the Navajo Nation when you were eighteen?"

"My father beat me every time he drank."

"You were born Gabriel Eagle Sanford, weren't you? I saw your name on my birth certificate."

He nodded.

"And on the day I was born, you sent a pickup over a cliff near Walker River Reservation to make it look as if you'd died."

He pointed to the moccasin in Dunn's hand. "I did, but I kept that one because I knew one day I'd summon the courage to ask you for forgiveness."

"Where did you go after sending the pickup over the cliff?"

"I worked on a ranch in California before trying to join the military, but they rejected me because I'd injured my shoulder while taming wild horses." He cupped his upper right arm. "It dislocates easily."

"When did you leave the United States?"

"When I was twenty. I went to Lebanon to teach English at an international school in Beirut but fled the country a year later because of political instability there. I moved to Alexandria, Egypt."

"Why there?"

"Because, a parent of one of my students in Beirut was a telecom executive who moved his business to Alexandria and offered me a job. Mobile phone technology was taking off then, and I saw a huge potential in the field."

"And that's when you became a naturalized citizen of Egypt?"

"Yes, after learning Arabic and attending a madrassa. I eventually opened my own mobile phone business in Alexandria, too."

"Is that where you met your wife?"

"Yes, shortly after her Ukrainian husband left her and their four children for another woman. She was about to return to Portugal where the children were born, but we fell in love, married, and remained in Alexandria where the children grew up."

"So, you're a *stepfather* to Irina and her brothers," Dunn said, turning angrily to Yuri. "Why did you and your sibs lie to me by calling him your 'father' all the time? He's *not* your father!"

"We view him as our father!" Yuri shot back. "Every bit of one—caring, doting, and tender. That will never change!"

"I don't expect you to call me 'father' because I don't deserve it," Nasir said. "I was never there for you as you grew up, and my heart grieves for the role I played in your mother's death."

"What role? You had nothing to do with her death!" Dunn exhorted. "You were out of the picture entirely!"

"If only that were true." Nasir closed his eyes and exhaled with shoulders slumped. "She received news that led her to become seriously ill, and I was a central part of that news."

"What news are you referring to?"

"A month before she died, the U.S. government sent agents to her home at Walker River Reservation to see her. They told her the government had decided to release me from prison after seventeen years of incarceration, but she was warned not to tell anyone about what happened to me."

Dunn's thoughts raced to a trip he'd made to the reservation to spread his mother's ashes over Lake Walker. While there, a neighbor told him she'd seen three men in dark suits go into his mother's house a month before she died, but the neighbor could never get his mother to say who the men were. "Where were you imprisoned all those years?" Dunn asked.

"At Guantanamo."

Dunn's jaw dropped. "Gitmo?"

"Yes, the Guantanamo Bay Detention Camp on the island of Cuba. I was one of the first twenty prisoners taken there by military guards on January 11th, 2002 after political appointees in the Justice Department declared the camp fell outside U.S. legal jurisdiction."

Following 9/11, Dunn kept abreast of matters pertaining to Gitmo and used his blog posts to express opinions about the prison. In one of his final entries, he wrote about the nearly eight hundred detainees that had been imprisoned since the facility opened, and he reproduced a list of the roughly sixty countries that had accepted detainees after they were released over the years.

"I knew of only one detainee at Gitmo who was born in the U.S.," Dunn said. "His name was Yaser Esam Hamdi, and he was released to Saudi Arabia in 2004. No mention has ever been made of a second detainee born in the U.S., and certainly not one held there for seventeen years."

"I knew Yaser Hamdi when he was at Gitmo," Nasir said, "yet it was I who remained at the prison until three months ago."

"Why were you released?"

"Because I was told Gitmo might close and prisoners needed to be relocated."

Dunn was aware of the contentious public discussions taking place in the U.S. regarding Gitmo's possible closure, debates which led to splintering within both political parties. Leading the charge to keep the prison open was the Vice President of the United States, a man who argued that closing Gitmo was tantamount to surrendering to extremists. "Why did you end up here and not in Egypt where you'd become a naturalized citizen?"

"I was supposed to go to Egypt, but a public defender at Gitmo learned of plans in that country to subject me to harsh interrogations, so he argued for me come here."

Feeling the vibration of his mobile, Dunn slipped a hand into his trousers but refrained from extracting the device. "You haven't told me how all this relates to my mother's death."

"Before the government sent its agents to see your mother a month before she died, she knew nothing about my whereabouts. As far as I knew, she believed I'd taken my life as everyone else believed, and I made no attempt to contact her after I left you because of the guilt I felt for leaving. As for my family in Egypt, they remained in the dark about my imprisonment at Gitmo the entire time I was there because the U.S. government never told them about my capture in Afghanistan or, for that matter, about my eventual release. I was ordered to live in Tunisia secretly for the rest of my life. The only people in Tunisia informed about my presence here were military officials who were to supply me with food, water, and shelter."

"So, why'd the men go to my mother's house?"

"Because of something Irina did."

"Irina, your stepdaughter?"

He nodded and wiped his eyes. "She's a hero in this country because she's preparing to sail a Tunisia-owned trimaran around the world in an upcoming race."

"I know the tri well," Dunn said, "but she didn't tell me it was Tunisian."

"It belongs to a wealthy realtor from Tunis, a well-connected man who learned through the grapevine about my arrival in Tunisia. After being barred by U.S. officials from traveling to the U.S. because of criticism he voiced recently regarding U.S. foreign policy, he told Irina I'd been sent here after being imprisoned at Gitmo for seventeen years."

"Why would he have done that when he didn't know about your connection with Irina?"

Nasir looked about the room. "I need to sit; my legs are killing me." He lowered himself onto a rug. "Like I said, the owner of the tri is a well-connected man. A close friend of his, a high-ranking Tunisian military officer, told him about me and my family in Egypt, including my relationship with Irina. The owner of the tri wasted no time in telling Irina about my imprisonment and release. Shortly later, my entire family came here to see me." He looked at Yuri tenderly. "For each of them, it has been difficult to learn about what happened to me, but especially so for Irina because she was the youngest when I disappeared and…" He paused to keep his voice from cracking further. "…because it was I who built her first sailboat and taught her how to sail."

"But, you said it was something Irina did that led U.S. authorities to go to my mother's house. What did Irina do?"

"She went to the U.S. Embassy in Tunis and warned your Ambassador that if the U.S. government didn't inform your mother and you about my release from Gitmo, she'd see to it that the world learned the truth. That's why the government agents appeared at your mother's house, but they made it clear she wasn't to say a word to anyone about what happened to me."

"Didn't Irina say she wanted me to be informed, too?"

"Yes, but some in your country resisted her demand."

"Why?"

"Because of your blog. They feared you'd spread the word about my unjust imprisonment."

"So, it wasn't just Consuela's death that broke my mother's heart," Dunn muttered, "but news about what had happened to you, too."

"Come, my son, sit with me. I see your pain."

Dunn found a place beside his father. "When did you tell your stepchildren about me?"

"When they were young; I wanted them to know the truth. I told them the worst decision I'd made in my life was to abandon you, and to make up for the mistake, I vowed to be the best stepfather I could be to them." He took Dunn's hand. "Even though I was gone from you, I did my best to keep track of your life."

"How could you do that from a jail cell?"

"I pleaded with a defense lawyer who came to Gitmo twice a year to see me to inquire into your doings. He read your blog posts to me."

Dunn squeezed his father's hand. "It could've been so different had you stayed with mother and me."

Nasir placed a fingertip on Dunn's upper lip and stroked its seamless central groove. "I wish I *had* stayed, but I had so many doubts, one being whether I wanted to remain with your mother." His eyes sank in their sockets. "And then, on the day you were born, I saw your cleft lip and cleft palate and flipped out. The only thing I knew to do was run because I didn't think I could be a good father." He kissed the finger and returned it to Dunn's lip. "For years, I've felt the shame that came from leaving you."

EVEN AS HE held his father's hand, Dunn felt a void as wide and deep as those which divide the Grand Canyon. In geologic terms, thirty-nine years was meaningless, yet for Dunn it was a gap that could never be closed. "You left not only me, but your country," he said.

The crow's feet on his father's face deepened. "When you're a foreigner in your own land, you look elsewhere for home."

"You're not a foreigner. Our ancestors tether us to the land."

He shook his head. "Those tethers ruptured with the treaties they imposed on us. We're a scattered people now. They call our homes 'reservations,' but we don't control them; politicians and bureaucrats do."

"Is it any better living abroad?"

Every movement, it seemed, was a struggle for Nasir, even lifting his eyes, yet he looked up at the blowing canvas with concern. "There is no perfect place to dwell except in the heart and soul, yet we search beyond them fruitlessly. I am content to make them my home."

"Father?" a voice called from the entry room.

"Come!" Yuri beckoned. "We are here."

Pablo appeared with hair disheveled from the wind. "Father, we need to leave! Severe bands from the storm are approaching. I will fly you to a safer place for now."

"No, I'll shelter here among the boulders," Nasir replied.

"But, the blowing sand will bury you!"

"I've been through worse."

While Pablo argued his case, Dunn checked his satphone to find a text from Garrett Fitzgerald which had arrived earlier…

Atticus Quincy Thornbridge is not responding to our summons. When we find him, we'll confront him about his fingerprints on the canisters and at the storage site.

"*Wilbur!*" a voice roared, "you won't prevail!"

Dunn looked up to find Ibrahim towering over him. With his dreads in a beehive again, his shemagh grazed the canvas. "Prevail with what?"

Ibrahim waved his mobile about. "Some are calling for a vaccine to be developed against megavirus, but I'll release the wild strain before one's available."

"I forbid you from doing that," Nasir said. "You will remain here with me during the storm."

Ibrahim brooded. "No, I must go, father! *Someone* must avenge the injustice inflicted on you."

"Revenge is not the answer, my son!"

In Dunn's palm, another vibration…

Idaho widow left a letter for police with her neighbor because she knew Atticus Quincy Thornbridge was about to show up at her house. Just got a copy of letter. It says…

Dunn shook the mobile in a futile attempt to resurrect Jim Edwards' truncated email, but his attention turned to a shouting match between Ibrahim and Pablo. When Ibrahim raised a fist to strike his brother, Yuri held him back. Glaring at his brothers, Ibrahim said, "Both of you are slaves to injustice!"

Pablo pointed to the exit. "So, go, release your virus! See how far you get."

"I will," Ibrahim exclaimed, backing up to leave, "and the winds will be my angels." He addressed Dunn. "It's time Caucasian males pay a price for the suffering they've inflicted, not only on your father, but on countless others, including your people. Look what they've done: They invaded your lands, killed your ancestors, and rounded you onto reservations like cattle." His expression hardened. "So, let megavirus be their judge."

Mentally, Dunn resurrected the image Bedjaoui had displayed of storms racing across the Sahara. It recalled for him a study he'd read recently in which researchers showed that some 800 million viruses fall onto every square meter of Earth each day. After taking to the sky in sea spray, dust storms, or by other means, viruses were believed to circle the planet in streams above weather systems but below levels at which airplanes fly before falling in torrents to the ground. If Ibrahim released the wild form of megavirus to the winds as he suspected he would, Dunn feared Irina's warning of *a plague of biblical proportions* would bear out.

In the meantime, his mental clock ticked on: Over twelve hours had passed since he drank water from Bedjaoui's garden, yet he felt well. "You're forgetting one thing," he called to Ibrahim even though he'd left the room. "*You're* Caucasian! If you unleash a pandemic, it could strike you, too."

The beehive shemagh returned in a gap created by a blanket pulled back. "That has already happened because I fell ill after removing the modified virus from Bedjaoui's lab." Ibrahim's gold incisor gleamed in a sardonic smile. "I spent a week in the desert with horrible testicular swelling and pain, but my infertility is of no consequence as my children are the storms."

WITH IBRAHIM'S DEPARTURE, the room fell silent save for the gyrating canvas. In a corner, Pablo and Yuri conversed privately while Dunn sat beside his father who seemed shaken by the discord. Using the quiet for his own purposes, Dunn read an updated email from Jim Edwards…

> *Sorry about the abrupt end to my last message. Meant to tell you about the widow's letter…*
>
> *In it, she said Thornbridge admitted to placing you under intense surveillance shortly after 9/11 when he learned as a*

CIA agent that you were the son of an enemy combatant he tortured in Uzbekistan. Even though he knew your father was innocent, he sent him to Gitmo because he needed to fill cells in the new prison he'd championed. Over the years, he kept your father's innocence secret until a lawyer representing Gitmo inmates filed a report claiming it was widely known among prisoners that your father was innocent. The only reason your dad remained imprisoned was because Thornbridge feared taking a hit to his career if it became known he'd jailed an innocent Native American of U.S. birth without cause. With Congress on the brink of closing Gitmo, Thornbridge worried you'd learn about what he'd done to your father and publicize it through your blog, so he sent CIA agents to your mother's house to place a gag order on her a few months ago. But that wasn't enough: Fearing your mother would tell you the truth, he set out to kill you by paying a mechanic ten thousand dollars to sabotage the SUV you rented in Idaho. The rest is history…

Numbed, Dunn turned to a text from Fitzgerald which arrived just as he'd finished reading Edwards' words…

Wilbur, run! They're about to bomb the oasis. They know you're with the Navy Base attacker. You have minutes to escape!

"Get out!" Dunn shrieked. He stood and lifted his father into his arms. "We're about to be bombed!"

ROUGHLY TWO THOUSAND steps separated Nasir Mostafa's dwelling from the water, a number Dunn had counted while ascending the hill, but as he raced down the slope, he listened for the roar of approaching bombers. What he heard instead was a gale force wind which bowed bushes and bent palms.

At the water's edge, he joined Pablo in steering a canoe through the reeds as each waded through waist-deep water. When they reached the open channel, they boarded the vessel only to be slapped by waves which pushed them back toward the reeds.

"Row hard!" Pablo ordered.

Dunn pulled his oar mightily, concerned Yuri wouldn't be able to battle the wind in a second canoe which was also to carry Dunn's father. Before leaving the dwelling, Dunn relinquished his father to Yuri who insisted on carrying him down the hill in a carrier hitched to his back. It troubled Dunn when Yuri rejected his offer to help with the descent, even more so when Pablo remained behind with his brother while he was sent ahead to descend the hill.

"Where is my father?" Dunn asked after glancing to his rear.

"He and Yuri will come shortly," Pablo promised. "Just row!"

Crossing the channel proved to be a challenge as the canoe slid back between strokes. Grindingly, they made their way toward a tall dune on the opposite side which exerted a blocking effect on the wind.

"I still don't see them!" Dunn fretted.

Saying nothing, Pablo hopped out and began pushing the canoe through shallow water.

"Where *are* they?" Dunn asked, braking the canoe by staking his paddle into the sand.

"Remove your paddle and keep rowing!" Pablo pleaded.

"Not until you tell me where my father is!"

"He chose to remain on the oasis."

"*Why?* He'll die there!"

"That was his choice."

"What about Yuri?"

"He took the other canoe to return to his jeep."

Dunn understood now why Pablo, Yuri, and his father had remained behind in the dwelling after he'd begun his way down the hill: They had plans to resolve. "Why would my father choose to die after being released from prison?"

"He has leukemia unresponsive to treatment. His days are numbered."

"Oh, my Lord!" Dunn wailed. "Why didn't he tell me that?"

"Because, he didn't want you to know he was about to die."

"And your mother—why isn't she here to be with him?"

"She has a heart condition and suffers from the desert heat. Her health deteriorated the last time she came here."

Dunn slapped the paddle angrily against the water. "When did my father learn he had leukemia?"

"Shortly after he arrived in Tunisia. Upon learning of the illness, Irina insisted we bring you here so he could see you before he died."

"That was *Irina's* plan?"

"Yes, when she was a little girl and learned about you for the first time, she began asking my stepfather to bring you to North Africa."

"Why?"

"Because, he spoke of you often, and she wanted to reunite you."

Dunn left the canoe to help Pablo pull the canoe toward shore. "There's something I want to know: As the years passed after my father failed to return from Pakistan in late 2001, did you, Irina, or your brothers think about contacting me in the United States? After all, you knew I existed because my father told you about me when you were kids."

"Of course we thought about finding you, but my mother forbade us from doing so because Nasir insisted repeatedly before he disappeared that he alone was the one who would reach out to you when the right time came."

DUNN'S THROAT BURNED as he climbed the dune, and whether it was the wind howling or his mind protesting the exertion, he heard a whistling before a series of thunderous detonations pummeled him to the sand. Looking across the water, he saw the oasis enshrouded in smoke and dust, and fearing more explosions were to come, he scrambled the last few yards to the peak where he hunkered just over the other side to view what remained of the oasis.

"Cruise missiles!" Pablo shrieked from beside him. "I'm sure of it!"

The two looked at each other with a common realization: They'd lost a man who'd played starkly different roles as a father—for Pablo, one who'd bolstered his formative years with love and guidance, and for Dunn, one who'd made a fleeting appearance at birth before fleeing.

Dunn blanched at the destruction. Through smoke, dust, and sand, he deciphered the outlines of a caldera where his father's dwelling once stood. While the boulders had once clustered along the top of the oasis, they were now strewn about the remaining slopes all the way to the water.

"Come," Pablo said, grasping Dunn's arm. "We need to leave before more missiles strike!"

Collecting his wits, Dunn slid down the dune which turned from sand to rocks before dropping into a ravine. Beneath him some twenty feet was an airplane almost hidden in mid-afternoon shadows at the distant end of the ravine. "How'd *that* get there?" he asked.

"It belongs to me," Pablo replied.

"What sort of airplane is it?"

"A STOL, or 'short take-off and landing' aircraft. I have flown it here several times to visit my father."

The two eyed each other as brothers, if only because each referred to the same man as "father." In this instance, the younger brother now led the older one down a steep path to the airplane. "Get in," he told Dunn.

Just then, another explosion shook the ground and sent rocks falling into the ravine from the dune above. In the silence that followed, Dunn wondered what remained of the oasis.

"Help me clear the rocks!" Pablo demanded.

While Dunn worked the space about the airplane, Pablo freed a corridor for taking off, and when both had completed their tasks and boarded the STOL, Dunn was struck by its austerity. Unlike the amphibious aircraft he'd flown in earlier, here there were no cushioned seats, leather upholstering, or digital dashboard. The passenger seat he settled into was little more than a metal frame with a thin layer of fabric covering it. "How are we going to take off with the winds raging outside the ravine?" he asked.

Pablo eyed Dunn's waist. "Fasten your belt!"

In moments, a whirring propeller accelerated the airplane so quickly all Dunn saw out his window were blurry walls that disappeared as the Sahara came to view. His stomach twisted at the sight of the oasis reduced now to an urn which released a beige plume into storm clouds above it. As the airplane bobbed wildly, he grasped the armrests. "Is there a bag in here?"

"Use your shirt," Pablo replied.

For the moment, Dunn's focus turned from motion sickness to Pablo's expression. "What's the matter?"

After a series of head pirouettes, Pablo sat bolt upright. "There he is! Do you see him?"

Dunn followed his outstretched arm to find a figure harnessed before a motorized propeller suspended beneath a parachute that looked like it might rip apart at any time in the fierce winds. "Who is that?"

"Ibrahim!" Pablo replied, slapping his thigh. "And I am to blame. I helped him build the paraglider and learn to fly it." He shook his head. "*Before* he went mad, that is." He nodded toward the ground. "He took-off from the same ravine we used, but all he needed was the last few meters before the wing and motor lifted him into the sky."

Dunn watched Ibrahim's thobe flail as the paraglider rose toward the clouds. He recalled again the study of atmospheric viruses and feared that with the flip of a switch a madman could seed the winds with a destructive virus that would cross the Sahara and Atlantic. "Why didn't he use a drone to release his virus?"

"He views this as his last earthly act," Pablo replied. As if to blot out his brother, he sent the airplane into an arc which removed Ibrahim from view.

In the silence, Dunn did the math: Moving west at an average of twenty miles per hour, a desert storm that morphed into an Atlantic hurricane could carry megavirus from Tunisia to Miami in ten days. Add to that a two-day incubation period and the world could see a pandemic of Caucasian male infertility. In the sky behind him, he feared a genie was about to escape a bottle to alter a planet.

Or perhaps the genie was already out.

"TAKE YOUR SHIRT off!" Pablo commanded.

The bilious liquid Dunn had vomited into the fabric smelled like sour milk. He stripped the shirt and wadded it. Twenty hours had elapsed since he drank from the *rose des sables* garden, but because none of the ill soldiers back home had reported nausea or vomiting before their testicles swelled, he was convinced his distress resulted from air sickness, not megavirus infection.

"I will get you a fresh shirt when we reach Tunis," Pablo advised.

For the first time since leaving Delaware, Dunn realized he was heading home, yet loneliness stirred within as it did after snowstorms when expectancy gave way to the humdrum of clean up. Deepening his letdown was a growing remorse for the loss of a father he'd never come to know.

"Your satphone," Pablo grumbled. "It is ringing."

Dunn answered it languidly.

"Wilbur, is that you?" a voice beckoned.

"Yes, Garrett."

"You're alive!"

"How'd you know I'd be at the oasis?"

"Late last night, the Defense Department got a call from an Algerian scientist named Jacques Bedjaoui who'd authored the paper on megavirus. He gave us coordinates for a site where he was sure the Navy Base attacker would be at a specific time, but he warned us you'd be there, too, along with other members of the attacker's family. Our intel checked Bedjaoui's background and found him to be legitimate."

"How'd you learn this if you're no longer at the Pentagon?"

"I have informants."

"The Base attacker escaped, Garrett. He ditched the oasis before the cruise missiles struck."

"I'm not surprised; he's a crafty guy. Interpol informed us he's an Egyptian munitions expert who was fired a year ago by a Saudi drone manufacturer because he stole secret designs for remotely controlled assault rifles mounted to drones. You can understand why alarms sounded when you sent an email from the laptop he used to launch his attacks on the U.S."

"Those alarms should be sounding now for the Vice President. It was because of his actions all this happened."

"Thornbridge is dead, Wilbur. I just got the news from Senator Braniff. The VP left a suicide note at a parking lot overlooking the Potomac River. He drove off a cliff into the river across from Georgetown. Park Police found his note and gave it to the Secret Service."

"Thornbridge took his life?"

"Yup, and at a poignant spot. Twenty-five years ago, another prominent political figure, a Deputy White House Counsel named Vince Foster, shot himself there."

"Did they find Thornbridge's body?"

"Not yet, but his car washed up on Roosevelt Island."

"Be careful!" Dunn warned. "This could be a ploy. I wouldn't put it past Thornbridge!"

"Not after what he divulged in his suicide note."

"What did it say?"

Fitzgerald demurred. "Geez, Wilbur, I feel your pain."

"Dammit, what did it say?"

"Thornbridge admitted that while working as a CIA agent in Uzbekistan in early 2002, he waterboarded an enemy combatant who turned out to be your father. He told his superiors at headquarters your father confessed to being an al-Qaeda operative, and the reason Thornbridge lied was because he needed bodies at Gitmo. He recanted the lie in his suicide note."

"That's old news," Dunn said. "My father's stepfamily told me all about it."

"Including the part about Thornbridge keeping the lie intact for seventeen years to catapult himself to Vice President?"

"No, I didn't hear that specifically."

"Well, it's true. After 9/11, people were terrified, and Thornbridge took advantage of that. He turned Gitmo into a poster child by claiming its steel bars kept America safe. A central tenet of his poster was a Gitmo inmate he called 'Prisoner X' who he claimed was an enemy combatant U.S. forces had captured at Tora Bora, a man who admitted to having plans to conduct a second attack on America of equally devastating proportions as 9/11. Thornbridge insisted the man's capture and imprisonment at Gitmo foiled the attack."

Dunn had heard the Vice President's repeated references to "Prisoner X," ones he viewed as fear-mongering tactics to bolster his campaign to run for President in the next election. "What are you getting at?" he asked.

"'Prisoner X' was your father."

"No, he wasn't! My father never had plans to attack the U.S.!"

"Of course, not, but Thornbridge portrayed him to be 'Prisoner X.' He revealed that in his suicide note. But when public debate began last year to close Gitmo, Thornbridge knew he had a landmine before him in the form of your father and the lie he'd nurtured."

"A lie which would expose him as a fraud."

"Yup, he knew if Gitmo closed, prisoners would need to be transferred and that, in turn, would generate massive media coverage. Each prisoner's past would be profiled, including your father's, and Thornbridge was adamant on preventing that from happening. Uncovering the lie about 'Prisoner X' would destroy his aspirations to become President as voters would turn against him for jailing an innocent Native American born in the U.S.A."

"So, he shipped my father out of Gitmo early to avoid the press."

"In the dark, yes, without cameras or reporters to document it." Fitzgerald paused. "But then the *New York Times* caught wind of the story."

"How?"

"From the Base attacker's sister, a woman named Irina Mostafa. I believe you know her well."

"Irina went to the *Times*?"

"Yup, she told them she had a story about a Gitmo prisoner which could decide the next election."

"When did she contact the paper?"

"A few days ago, and that's when things began to tank for Thornbridge. A reporter called him to verify that a recently released Gitmo prisoner was the father of someone helping authorities investigate the illnesses at the two bases. But that wasn't the question that did Thornbridge in."

"What did, then?"

"After Craig Braniff learned that Irina Mostafa had approached the *Times* with the story about your father, the Senator declassified the identity of the prisoner who Thornbridge called 'Prisoner X.'"

"Oh, I see where this is going," Dunn said. "The reporter asked Thornbridge to confirm 'Prisoner X' was my father."

"Right, and I'm sure you can imagine the impending story: The Vice President of the United States wrongfully jailed a Native American of U.S. birth after torturing him at a black site following 9/11. Then it turns out the son of that prisoner is a prominent Native American urologist currently employed at Johns Hopkins University who's helping the government investigate the illnesses at the two bases which were attacked." Fitzgerald paused. "I'm not surprised the VP drove his car off a cliff into the Potomac."

21

FROM THE AIR, Dunn searched the arid landscape below for signs of life—anything to take his mind off death. Moments earlier, he'd listened to a phone call Pablo put on speaker in which Yuri described risking further missile strikes to return to the oasis to look for Dunn's father. To his dismay, he met smoldering fires and a wall of boulders that kept him from advancing beyond the water's edge. Certain his stepfather had died, he abandoned what remained of the oasis.

Yet there was more: After freeing his jeep and burying Jacques Bedjaoui, Yuri set out for his home in the Algerian town of Debdeb when he received a call from a friend who'd heard from Bedouin shepherds that a shredded parachute had been found in the desert. Accompanying it was a motor and a single seat into which a dead body was strapped. The features of the corpse matched the description of Ibrahim Mostafa. Upon hearing the news, Dunn noticed Pablo wince before turning away to look out his window. After an interlude of silence following the call, he stared ahead as he conversed for a last time with his deceased brother: "I will never be able to forgive you for what you did, Ibrahim, but you were my brother nonetheless, and for the times we shared growing up, I am grateful for you."

Leaving Pablo to deal with the death of a second family member on the same day, Dunn reached for the binoculars and looked at the Mediterranean port of Gabès approaching from the northeast.

"We will stop there to transfer to the seaplane," Pablo said, his voice quavering. "I left it there on my way to the oasis."

Dunn was touched that Pablo was able to set aside his emotions to address the matter of landing in Gabès, and since he knew the flight to Tunis would be a short one, he reached for the satphone to attend to an issue that demanded immediate attention. After dialing Garrett Fitzgerald, he waited expectantly for his friend to pick up.

"Wilbur, I've been trying to reach you!" Fitzgerald proclaimed. "Why haven't you answered your phone?"

"I wanted some time to myself."

"Why'd you call me now, then?"

"I need your help."

"With what?"

"I need a passport to return to the U.S. Mine's at home, but I'll be in Tunis shortly and can go to the Embassy to pick one up."

Just then a hand delivered an envelope onto Dunn's thigh from across the cockpit.

Dunn turned to Pablo. "What's in there?"

"What's in *where?*" Fitzgerald asked.

"Hang on, Garrett, I was talking to my pilot." Dunn lowered the satphone and raised the envelope. "What's in here, Pablo?"

"Open it. Irina asked me to give it to you."

"Garrett, can I call you back?" Dunn asked. "I need to deal with something."

"Make it fast because you won't need a passport," Fitzgerald replied. "I can arrange for a military transport plane flying from Turkey to the U.S. to stop by Tunis to pick you up, but I need time to make the arrangements."

Dunn pondered the thought aloud: "You say a military airplane can fly me home?"

"Yup, not a problem."

"I'll get back to you shortly," Dunn said. He opened the envelope and found a single sheet with a note penned by hand which he recognized as Irina's writing. After reading it, he folded the sheet, returned it to the envelope, and stared solemnly out the window.

TWO HUNDRED MILES separate the industrial city of Gabès from Tunis, and after changing airplanes and acquiring a new shirt for Dunn, Pablo piloted the seaplane toward the capital. With the flight plan set, he leaned back and looked at Dunn. "Do not do it," he warned.

"Do what?" Dunn asked.

"Take a U.S. military aircraft."

"Why not? It's the easiest route home."

"Life is not always easy. The journey is difficult at times."

"Tell me about it! What do you think I've gone through in the past eleven days?"

"You need time to grieve, and this is where you should do it because your father perished in North Africa."

"Look, I'll deal with my father's death as I see fit. I don't need you to tell me when and where I need to grieve." Dunn grimaced. "I don't even know if I *can* grieve. I knew him for an hour at most."

"You *will* grieve," Pablo replied, "as will I. When great people die, we *all* grieve."

"You're inflating my father's importance."

"Am I? Did he not promote justice?"

"He was caught in the wrong place at the wrong time after 9/11! That's it. He was imprisoned unfairly, but that by itself doesn't equate with promoting justice."

"Your father will serve as a symbol of justice for all," Pablo said. "He survived an unjust imprisonment while many others chose to give up and die. And why did he survive? Because he always held out hope that one day he would again see those he loved, you included. Who can speak to justice more than those who have been imprisoned yet are innocent? Who can utter the call for fairness more earnestly than those who have been tortured?" He looked away before returning glistening eyes to Dunn. "Our father has departed, but his spirit lives on."

SCALLOPING THE NORTHEAST coast of Tunisia, the Gulf of Tunis lies a short distance from the capital, yet while other airplanes made a long arc around the Gulf on final approach to the international airport, Pablo maintained a cruising altitude without altering course.

"Why aren't we descending?" Dunn asked.

"We will land in Tunis if that is your desire, but I must show you something first." He pointed ahead. "That is Bizerte and beyond it the Mediterranean."

Minutes later, to the west, Dunn recognized the cluster of uninhabited islands they'd passed before touching down two days earlier. "That's where you dropped me off before to meet Yuri," he said, pointing to a line of dunes shimmering in late-afternoon sunlight.

Pablo said nothing, riveting his attention to his headset into which he spoke Portuguese.

"Who are you talking to?"

"Just watch the sea."

The sudden change of tone unnerved Dunn, as did the way Pablo peered at the sea. It looked as if he was picking out a spot to end the journey but not in a safe way. Thoughts of a fateful Malaysia Airlines flight from the past crept into Dunn's mind, and he imagined what passengers on the tragic flight might have felt before their captain conducted what was believed to be a suicide mission over the Indian Ocean after leaving Kuala Lumpur with 227 passengers. "What am I supposed to see in the water?" Dunn asked.

"That faint track in the distance. Do you see it, one with a slightly different color than the surrounding water?"

Dunn mirrored Pablo's forward lean. He found it difficult to discern the colors and textures of the water because the sun was low and the swells made for a shifting canopy. "I see something circular," he said, "but that's just a current."

"Currents rarely make circles like that," Pablo replied as he worked the controls to ascend to a higher altitude which brought the track into clearer view.

"It *is* a circle," Dunn confirmed, "but if a current didn't make it, what did?"

"The same thing that made the next one."

Dunn looked beyond the first circle to find a second, more clearly defined one. The sight recalled photos of clearings in Central American forests where pilots discovered lost cities from the past. Eyes widened, he asked, "And what's beyond the second circle?" He pressed the binoculars to his eyes. "It's a trimaran making the circles!" He leaned forward until his belt restrained him. "And I see its name—*Ba'wă!*"

"Yes, the 'circle maker,'" Pablo confirmed. He put the airplane into a descent toward a salmon sea, and as they dropped, the tri grew larger than life, its leviathan yet sleek shape carving brilliant wakes in the water.

From his pocket, Dunn removed the envelope to reread its contents, but the ring of his satphone interrupted him. "Yes, Garrett, what is it?"

"I've arranged for an aircraft to pick you up in Tunis. It's on its way now."

"How soon will it get there?" Dunn asked, his eyes darting from Irina's words to the sea below.

"Real soon, and we can't delay it because time is money. Are you on the ground now?"

"Not yet."

"Where exactly are you?"

"Just north of Tunis over the sea."

"Why did you bypass Tunis? You approached it from the south!"

"I had business to attend to."

"In the Mediterranean?"

"Yes."

"What the hell's going on, Wilbur? I've diverted a large transport aircraft for your benefit!"

"Give me a few minutes. I'll call you back shortly."

"That's what you said a few minutes ago!"

"Look, I promise I'll call you!" Dunn hung up and turned to Pablo. "Is Irina on the tri?"

"Yes."

"Alone?"

"Yes."

"Then get me down! I need to see her!"

"But, the seas are—"

"Get me down!" Dunn implored, his eyes glomming onto her words…

Before there was light, there were heavens, and in heavens a spark; and because you have glowed upon me, and I upon you, we are one in light.

Before there was wind, there were whispers, and in whispers breath; and because you have breathed upon me and I upon you, we are one in wind.

The steep dive Pablo put the seaplane into plunged Dunn' innards towards the floor, yet he kept reading…

Before there were seas, there were rivers, and in rivers tears from the heart; and because you have tasted my tears, and I yours, we are one in seas.

Before there was soul, there was Spirit, and in Spirit awakening; and because you have awakened beside me, and I beside you, we are one in soul.

A sudden banking broke Dunn's concentration, and when he looked out the window he saw the top of a mast streak by. In a blazing instant, the helm flew by, too, but not before he glimpsed a woman commanding the wheel with hair blowing wildly. Twisting in his seat, he watched her duck a shower of spray that exploded from the bow before the stern disappeared. He returned his eyes to the sheet…

Our light, our wind, our seas, and our souls form a circle upon which we traveled together, but circles—like light, wind, seas, and souls—fade with time.

Will you keep a circle with me, or will our circle extinguish forever?

"Get me down!" Dunn cried.

"Be patient!"

Looking ahead, Dunn watched swells race by like marine flanks on their way to battle, some breaking ranks by cresting to send spray into the windshield.

Speeding just above the sea in search of a place to touch down, Pablo cast a wary eye to the side as they overtook the trimaran whose pace had diminished now that all three hulls plied the water. And then it came, a strike against the surface, and like a rock skipping on a lake, the seaplane ultimately exerted its authority.

A rolling turn with the wing almost striking the sea brought the trimaran into view again with its sails luff and hulls dragging, an awkward soiree of objects from different realms—one from sky, another from water—but the words Dunn had read told him the two were destined to meet.

"She's lowering the dinghy to come for you," Pablo announced. "Prepare to exit."

In moments, the same dinghy Dunn rode from Rehoboth Beach to the trimaran approached the seaplane, this time with a skipper whose long brown hair waved freely in the wind. And as before, she swung the dinghy in an arc to bring it to a stop before him.

"Leave!" Pablo ordered. "I need to depart immediately."

Dunn opened his door, swung his legs out, and lowered himself into the dinghy.

"I trust you are resolute," Irina called to him. "Pablo will not return for you."

Dunn engaged her before glancing at the tri. "I know what I want."

Irina's eyes crinkled as she eased the dinghy forward to shut the seaplane's door. A firmer twist of the throttle then sent the vessel forward into open waters where they rounded the seaplane toward the tri. When they reached its stern, Dunn needed no instructions how to board, hopping from dinghy to ladder and then up its rungs.

With the seaplane's motors roaring, Dunn watched it lift into the sky and turn toward the Tunisian coast. From his pocket, he removed the satphone and called Garrett Fitzgerald to announce his decision: No military flight was needed. Instead, he'd circle his way back on his own. How and when that circle would get him to America he couldn't say, but that didn't matter because he knew in his heart the circle he intended to follow would lead him home.

20259873R00165

Made in the USA
Middletown, DE
09 December 2018